GETTING ANSWERS—
THE HARD WAY!

The bored tone of her voice tripped every adrenaline switch I had. Entering the garish suite, I shoved her back to the nearest wall, my left hand curling around her delicious, slender throat. "I'll go with you to Rhea. Now call your thugs off my friends."

Her voice came out as a strained whisper. "I don't know what you're talking about."

I pulled the machine pistol from its armpit holster and held the muzzle an inch in front of her right eye. "You've got three seconds to figure it out. . . ."

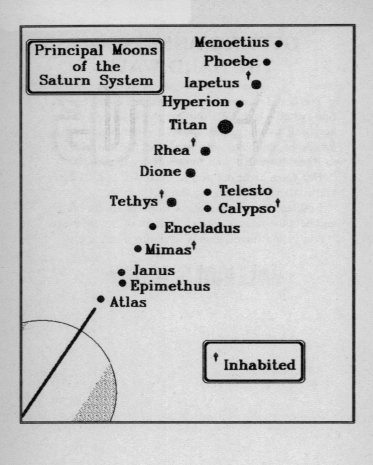

Principal Moons
of the
Saturn System

Menoetius ●
Phoebe ●
Iapetus †●
Hyperion ●
Titan ●
Rhea †●
Dione ●
Telesto ●
Tethys †● Calypso †
Enceladus ●
● Mimas †
Janus ●
● Epimethus
● Atlas

† Inhabited

IAPETUS

WILLIAM S. KIRBY

ACE BOOKS, NEW YORK

This book is an Ace original edition,
and has never been previously published.

IAPETUS

An Ace Book / published by arrangement with
the author

PRINTING HISTORY
Ace edition / April 1993

All rights reserved.
Copyright © 1993 by William S. Kirby.
Cover art by Jean Pierre Targete.
This book may not be reproduced in whole or in part,
by mimeograph or any other means, without permission.
For information address: The Berkley Publishing Group,
200 Madison Avenue, New York, NY 10016.

ISBN: 0-441-35570-6

Ace Books are published by The Berkley Publishing Group,
200 Madison Avenue, New York, New York 10016.
The name "ACE" and the "A" logo
are trademarks belonging to Charter Communications, Inc.

PRINTED IN THE UNITED STATES OF AMERICA

10 9 8 7 6 5 4 3 2 1

For Kathryn,
who told me to quit my other job

For the House of Death is deep down
underneath; the downward journey
to be feared, for once I go there
I know well there is no returning.

—Anacreon of Teos, ca. 570 B.C.

LITTLE JOHNNY FREAK

Little Johnny Freak, cruising down the streets
Softly preaching to everyone he meets.
Run away!
Fly away!
Come away!
Your hearing he buys
Got you tasting lies
Holo-Show for your eyes!

Little Johnny Freak, cruising down the streets
Quietly scanning everyone he meets.
Run away!
Fly away!
Come away!
Know your ev'ry thought
Got you on the spot
Now it's you he has caught!

Little Johnny Freak, cruising down the streets
Wants to vulcanize everyone he meets.
Run away!
Fly away!
Come away!
Your feelings he holds
Emotions he molds
Now it's you he controls!

Little Johnny Freak, cruising down the streets
Puppeteering ev'ry boy and girl he meets.
Run away!
Fly away!
Come away!
Pulling all your strings
Got you walking rings
You're one of his playthings!

Little Johnny Freak, cruising down the streets
Silently killing everyone he meets.
Run away!
Fly away!
Come away!
Gets inside your head
On your mind he's fed
Thinks you're better off dead!

—Aunt Silly Sally's
Third Tiny Book of
Children's Bedtime Verse

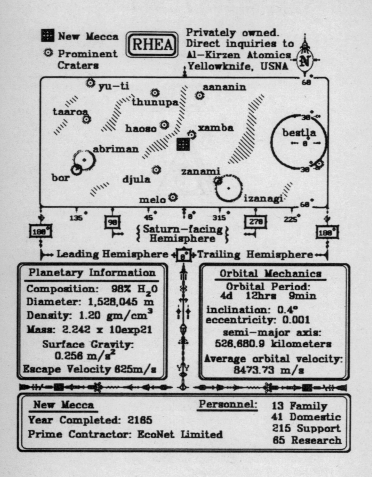

RHEA

New Mecca
Prominent Craters

Privately owned.
Direct inquiries to
Al-Kirzen Atomics
Yellowknife, USNA

N

yu-ti   aananin
thunupa
taaroa
haoso   xamba
abriman   bestla
bor
djula   zanami
melo   izanagi

135° 90° 45° 0° 315° 270° 225°
180° 180°

{Saturn-facing Hemisphere}

Leading Hemisphere 0° Trailing Hemisphere

Planetary Information
Composition: 98% H_2O
Diameter: 1,528,045 m
Density: 1.20 gm/cm^3
Mass: 2.242 x 10exp21
Surface Gravity:
0.256 m/s^2
Escape Velocity 625m/s

Orbital Mechanics
Orbital Period:
4d 12hrs 9min
inclination: 0.4°
eccentricity: 0.001
semi-major axis:
526,680.9 kilometers
Average orbital velocity:
8473.73 m/s

New Mecca
Year Completed: 2165
Prime Contractor: EcoNet Limited

Personnel:
13 Family
41 Domestic
215 Support
65 Research

RHEA

1

The first thing every private investigator learns is that the odds of justice prevailing in any given case are inversely proportional to the amount of credit in the guilty party's bank account. That's why my last client is serving fifty to life for a murder she didn't commit. I can live with that; in this business you lose as many as you win.

It's her husband I'm worried about. I can understand his slicing the district attorney's throat. Hell, that's practically self-defense for someone sitting in the mayor's chair. What disturbs me is his threat to see that I never work again. Two months since his old lady checked into the slammer and not a single client since.

"Look, Jefferson, if nothing's going on, I'm out of here."

"Sure, kid." Jamie's okay. He's on the payroll because a number of doors can be opened with Aryan blue eyes, a regulation mustache, and close-cropped blond hair. Besides, there're leads a bisexual can follow that we antiquated heteros can't even begin to approach. "Don't forget it's your turn to buy esters for the synthahol."

"Shouldn't you cut down on the booze?"

"What are you? My mom?"

"Fine. Don't blame me when your liver ends up in a display case. What flavor do you want?"

"Anything but that cinnamon stuff you favor. Old-fashioned

bourbon would be nice. And grab another liter of ethane base while you're at it.'' He gave me a look like I already had one foot in a body bag and stepped out onto the rusted walkway that services my office module.

Despite the horror stories you've heard, running a business from a module isn't bad. The overhead's next to nothing and when you're located near hundreds of vacant units fallen in disrepair, people naturally assume you must be some kind of genius to still be turning a buck. Nevertheless, as a place to live a metal ellipsoid three meters across by four long would have inspired Dante.

Cradled in its ferroconcrete exoskeleton, the aluminum module responds to temperature changes more rapidly than the surrounding cement. Come winter the office rattles like a loose tooth in its concrete socket, and when the weather turns warm, there's a complimentary acoustical demonstration. The office screams like feedback from God's own amplifier as the building strains to crush the module like a pop can. Multiply that by 300 modules on level fifty-four and again by the ninety levels in Urban Habitat 278 and just try to get a good night's sleep.

The only prerequisites for experiencing this elegance first-hand are a problem with your spouse and fifteen Andy Jacks a day plus expenses. If you don't have the cash, I'll settle for water chits redeemable for 98 percent purity or better. If your pockets are empty, I hear the cops occasionally work for free. There's a police kiosk at the entrance of my level. The nine and one keys work most of the time so you might get lucky. Not that that particular lady spends much time in modular habitats.

The corporate propaganda machines touted modules as the wave of the future. Each unit could be removed and replaced, giving an infinite number of possible environments. They were right about the removal part; most tenants left within a year. A few desperate souls remained, waiting for the replacement phase. In the meantime the environment varied widely but always hovered around the vulgar and hostile end of the spectrum. Not a place you'd want to raise junior, but boarded-over plexiglass and dark corridors provide ample spawning grounds for the kind of misery that keeps me in business.

Or at least they used to. I'd discovered the futility of opposing people who had any real authority during my stint as a lieutenant in the Terra-Luna Corps. Recently, my most consuming pastime has been wondering at the selective amnesia that allowed me to believe I stood a chance against the mayor.

Tired of watching clients not walk through my door, I ordered the synthahol to build another scotch, pulled out the office's trash bin, and sorted through the recyclables. Just another citizen of the United States of North America searching for an exemption come April. Looked like I was going to need it.

The plastic grandfather clock beside my desk read seven-fifteen when the fax kicked in with a final disconnect notice from the Eastern Fusion Board. Thereafter, my outlook on life deteriorated to the point where I was downing shots of Jamie's cinnamon-banana ethane and thinking that after so many of them, they didn't taste too bad. That's probably why things happened the way they did.

She came in and sat down without a word. Her faded blue jeans had been splashed with fluorescent paint and sported enough pockets to hide an arsenal. A skull-and-ax holo-logo from a third-rate splatter band shifted across the front of her blue T-shirt, which had enough holes to start a riot. Over her shoulder she carried a worn leather Vietnam flight jacket with a United States Marine Aggressor Group patch on the back. Typical dress for someone wealthy enough not to worry which European fashion was hot this week.

She certainly had a rich woman's chassis to hang it on. Her legs, stretched out to the side of the chair, were long and sinuous, flaring gently to diminutive hips. Her waist was narrow, her stomach flat. Her breasts were perfectly matched and generous without assuming the colossal size that was becoming de rigueur among the affluent.

Nor had any effort been spared on her face. Full lips, painted cherry red, complemented liquid emerald eyes. Raven black hair framed delicate cheekbones, flowed past a slender neck, and spilled onto her T-shirt. They don't build them like they used to. They do it better.

My first thought was: Complete physical make-overs aren't cheap. Maybe things are looking up.

"Usually, miss, people knock before they come in."

She gave me her eyes another full minute without talking; a hungry feline zeroing in on the most wounded of the city's herd of private detectives. When she finally spoke, her voice was throaty silk trimmed in wet lace. Must have had the vocal cords touched up while she was in for the other enhancements.

"There are two unsavory hoods lurking in the vacant medical module by the elevator. One of them is packing a bone cooker."

No wonder business was dead. Not too many people will walk through a projected dose of high-energy radiation. A bone cooker might do nothing, then again it might dispense lingering death with six or seven different types of cancer. One of the mob's many contributions to the science of human suffering.

Artillery of that caliber implied heavy protection for the thugs carrying it. The minimum sentence for having a bone burner in possession is an all-expenses-paid lifetime vacation on Triton. Sandwiched between liquid nitrogen geysers and third-rate pressure domes, exiles on Neptune's only inhabited moon undergo physical decay with an expected half-life of about seven months.

"Excuse me, miss." I turned to my computer. "Sheen?"

The machine answered with a grating digital reproduction of a two-hundred-year-old movie character. Not many people recognize the cry of the Wicked Witch of the West, but I find the scratchy reproduction useful for keeping clients on edge.

"Yessss . . ."

"Get me the Mayor's Public Relations Office."

"Yessss, my sweeeet."

Two rings, and the telescreen came to life with a burst of static. The man on the other end rubbed his eyes and tried to look attentive. I spoke before he had a chance to wake up.

"There are a couple of stooges parked outside my office with bone burners. Tell your boss that unless they're gone by tomorrow at seven ante meridiem, his prognosis is a severe case of colon cancer." I disconnected before the lackey could work up the outrage to have me traced and arrested.

"You're quite a bold man, Mr. Kayoto."

"Thank you Miss . . . ?"

"Vandimeer, Jessica Vandimeer."

"Well, Miss Vandimeer, didn't your dear old mum tell you it's impolite to enter without knocking?"

"I never knew my dear old mum, and if I had, I'm sure she'd have told me that threatening the mayor is the move of a desperate, if not overly bright, man."

"Your high regard for my intelligence is comforting. What can I do for you?"

She leaned forward and crossed her arms on my desk. Her loose shirt gave me plenty to look at, but what caught my attention was white medical tape wrapped around her left hand. Not a good sign. Things have to get pretty crazy before the prosperous get so much as a scratch. From the width of the tape, her hand must've been broken two or three times. "I need help."

"That's what I'm here for. Would you care for something to drink before we get down to business?"

She must have smelled cinnamon. "No, thank you."

I poured myself another shot. "You know, Miss Vandimeer, I've done my share of traveling yet I can't place your accent. Your vowels come from western Europe, but the way you flatten your syllables puts you somewhere out in the corn belt."

"You miss very little, Mr. Kayoto. The people who raised me were from reunified France, but we lived on Mars Schiaparelli."

"Never had the urge to trust my life to a computer-controlled tin can. What kind of help are you looking for?"

"Mr. Kayoto, I am authorized to pay you a large sum of money to help my employer resolve an important matter."

"Look, doll,"—she flinched at the old-style sexist jargon—"I'm not lifting a finger until you tell me how you got past my two friends with the Hiroshima tanning guns."

"My employer is Abdul Al-Kirzen."

Now, anyone who thinks power is a function of politics belongs on Kiddie Kid Joe with Dolby the Electro-Poodle and Silicon Jane. Al-Kirzen could line his pockets with mayors solely on the interest he earns from energy patents. That he hasn't bothered to tells me who's holding the royal flush and who's bluffing.

"That so? How are things on Rhea these days? Or has Mr. Kirzen gone ahead and bought Saturn, too? I hear the rings are lovely this time of year."

"Mr. Kayoto, I'm not in the mood for trading clever witticisms. Considering your present state, it just wouldn't be much of a challenge." She took a bank card from her pocketbook, read my deposit-only number from the stack of business cards on my desk, and punched in a few numbers.

"Here's a small gift from my employer for considering his problem. I'll be back tomorrow when, with any luck, you'll be sober." She turned and left without another word.

I took my bank card from my wallet and punched up the balance. The screen read 200,135 cr NorthAm, which came to 2,000 Andy Jacksons for each one of the five minutes Miss Jessica Vandimeer had been in my office. I leveled my account with the Fusion Board, adding a moderate bribe to keep my tardiness concealed from the credit bureaus.

The office shook when I pulled the efficiency cot from the wall behind the desk. Probably meant it was snowing again. Tomorrow I'd change my jogging route to pass by a window and see how bad it was. I took off the hammered nickel ring that held my hair in a queue and brushed my teeth with the baking soda I use to keep the fridge from smelling bad.

Lying in bed, my thoughts kept circling over my prospective client and his exquisitely constructed agent. For some reason I found it difficult to remain optimistic about my unexpected windfall. Why all the tension? *The money is on my side. Things are finally looking up.* A soothing cantrip to hold back the vague feeling of apprehension Miss Vandimeer had left in her wake.

2

The computer networks didn't have much on Abdul Al-Kirzen. The powerful have means of hiding their sordid lives from the barbaric masses. What information Sheen dredged up was well over a decade old.

Al-Kirzen made his billions by being lucky enough to hear the swan song of the petrol era before anyone else was listening. By reinvesting profit from oil fields into fusion research, he was able to bathe his corporate physicists in a bottomless pool of funding. They found the key to a controllable fusion reaction a decade before Berkeley. As a result,

Kirzen's corporations hold seventy-three very lucrative patents in atomic energy. Every time you flick on a light, he gets a little richer.

Shortly after his net worth crossed 4 billion Andy Jacks he bought a long-range ion-drive shuttle and set sail for the outer planets. On April 23, 2158, three and a half years after he'd left Earth, Al-Kirzen filed a claim on Rhea. The United Nations first rejected his ownership, but following a series of coded transmissions squirted from Al-Kirzen's ship, a second vote was taken and the claim was accepted by a three-to-one margin. And they say money can't buy friends.

EcoNet Limited began construction on his living quarters on July 10, 2162. An area southwest of Xamba Crater was chosen as the site for New Mecca. According to a retired EcoNet engineer, it was the closest stable area to zero latitude and longitude on Rhea that Al-Kirzen could find. From what little graduate work I completed before joining the military, I remembered several cultures had tried to prove their sacred stomping grounds encompassed the center of the world. You'd think the human race would have long given up such pretenses, but here was Al-Kirzen claiming the same hollow prize for Rhea. This guy was beginning to look like a good character for a psychology textbook.

Still, the view from his kitchen window must be impressive. Saturn's tidal lock on Rhea permanently anchors the gas giant directly above the domes of New Mecca; a pale ball of hydrogen and methane twenty-six times the size of the Moon as seen from Earth. Rhea's small angle of orbital inclination from Saturn's equator, about 0.4 degrees according to Sheen, would mean the rings would always appear edge on; a white streak of ice, reflecting sunlight with laser intensity. In someone else it might inspire humility; Kirzen probably thinks of it as a little sculpture for his backyard.

Construction was far enough along by 2164 for Abdul and Omar, his eldest son and heir apparent, to move in. Since then, kilotons of metal and equipment have made their way to Rhea's orbital docks. No one is sure what he's up to because, of course, few people travel within the Saturn system. Like the old saw goes: Saturn is beautiful but Iapetus will blow your mind.

Cozy in his private citadel, Al-Kirzen adopted the title Amir al-Mu'minin, a phrase my computer translated as, ''commander of the faithful.'' My few Islamic acquaintances preferred the more descriptive "Satan's lure." They took exception to Al-Kirzen's proclamation that the sacred pilgrimage of Hegira was holy in the eyes of God only if it were completed on Rhea. Apparently Islam isn't ready for franchise offices.

Except for more recent articles in the tabloids, suggesting he was involved with some sort of eugenics experimentation, eighteen years had passed without any direct contact with Earth. Not surprisingly, there was no record of a Jessica Vandimeer serving with Al-Kirzen. No doubt she was lying about her name. Don't they always?

The data cores had several megabytes on Rhea itself, none of it promising. The moon is essentially a ball of ice roughly one-ninth the size of Earth. It zips around Saturn once every four and a half days, at an average distance of 526,000 and some odd kilometers. The ambient surface temperature is sixty-eight degrees absolute, thirteen degrees colder than the melting point of oxygen. Not my idea of a relaxing place to build a retirement home.

Having exhausted readily available avenues of research into the doings of Al-Kirzen, I flicked on the news and waited for Miss Vandimeer to show. The anchorman, pectorals bulging through a soak shirt embossed with his sponsor's logo, was cheering the capture of Jane Hamilton. Not yet sixteen, Pretty Jane had slaughtered no less than twenty-three people. A prodigious total, even for a freak.

Her latest victim was a thirteen-year-old pimp, rumored to be her boyfriend. He'd died watching his blood pump out of a hole in his femoral artery. The rusted nail used to puncture his leg was found still clasped tightly in his hand. It looked like suicide. Not that anyone was fooled.

The camera zoomed to a video of Jane taken just after her arrest. She was naked, spread-eagled on some rich toady's freshly cut bluegrass lawn. Her blue eyes were open; pupils fully dilated, staring blankly into space. Several blond braids were matted with blood from a wound on her left temple. A medic wearing a U.N. arm band was feeding her viscous green liquid through an I.V. plugged directly into her carotid artery. Standard procedure for a telepath.

Not that it had worked seven years ago, when an even younger freak pulled a Galil automatic pulse rifle and opened up on Thomas. I struggled with the memory for several minutes before I realized I wasn't alone. Jessica Vandimeer was looking over my shoulder, her face pale as she watched U.N. Security reel Jane Hamilton in.

"Still haven't remembered how to knock, Miss Vandimeer?"

She ignored me, her green eyes glued to the holo stand. "They have no right to treat her like that."

"Yeah, but they caught her. One less to worry about."

"That's not what I meant. Why do they show her like that? She's a human being, not some animal on display."

I looked back at the holovision. The camera was panning across Jane's helpless body, now strapped to a gurney. "Bondage sells, especially when applied to pretty sixteen-year-old girls."

"That's not funny."

The cameraman zoomed to Jane's face. A tear streamed down her dirty cheek. I turned the image off. "I never said it was. Maybe we should step out, get some fresh air." She pulled her coat closer around her shoulders and nodded.

Out on the streets, Neo-Luddites were parading in force, carrying glow-paint placards and yelling obscenities at the autosystems specialists and data-control engineers passing in their alcohol-powered Mercedes. Dressed like the destitute masses from a Dickens tape, the protesters slogged through half a foot of muddy snow to fight a losing battle against machines that didn't get buzzed or ask for raises. I tuned them out and waited in vain for Miss Vandimeer to state her case.

We'd gone about an eighth of the way around the perimeter of the Habitat when I noticed Miss Vandimeer moved with a barely perceptible catch in her hips. The way she ignored it told me the injury was old, perhaps occurring in early childhood.

My curiosity thrives on minor details. Miss Vandimeer's mildly stuttering gait suggested a series of questions that nagged me for the rest of the afternoon. With all the other modifications, why hadn't she had this obvious impediment corrected? Was it because it didn't show up in low-g environments? Did that mean she was telling the truth when she said she came from Rhea? I had to be content with guesses, because Vandimeer wasn't talking. The freak on the holo must have really rocked her.

Clouds had rolled in and the sky had paled to tarnished silver before we completed our circuit around the Habitat. At her suggestion, we took a rickshaw to the FlipSide, an uptown joint on the ninety-eighth level of Commercial Construct 13. The interior of the restaurant was Nul-Humanist lucite, glass, and neon; a revival of a decade-old style paying homage to the triumphant march of progress.

Miss Vandimeer entered a large tip on the maître d's bank card, purchasing us a table overlooking the river. We sipped on carbonated water while 200 meters below, their faces obscured by haze, children mined the muddy banks for mollusks. A couple next to us watched and joked as one child lost her evening's meal to an older boy wielding a meter of steel pipe.

The waiter who took our order had the emaciated look of someone whose cells were trying to build protein out of high-velocity stimulants. I let Miss Vandimeer order for both of us. Nothing on the menu was even slightly familiar.

Under her coat, which she allowed the waiter to remove when he returned with our hors d'oeuvres, Miss Vandimeer wore a full-length silk skirt on top of glossy red heels. The only thing above her waist was a five-centimeter neck band that matched the shoes.

I was less amazed at her immodesty than the fact that her flawless chest bore none of the telltale marks of augmentation. In a room of rigorously engineered perfection, Jessica Vandimeer was unquestionably genuine. I wondered why that should make me nervous.

With some effort, I pulled my thoughts back to the task at hand. "Look, Miss Vandimeer, all this is very impressive, but it isn't gaining you anything. Al-Kirzen isn't getting my help until he gives me something more useful than a pleasant toy to take to bed and play with."

Vandimeer's face went red. Truth always hurts, doesn't it?

"Mr. Kayoto, childish insults will not serve either of us."

"Neither will your lies. Before you slinked into my office this morning, I did some checking around. The only passenger liner arriving from the outer planets during the last five months was the I.S.S. *Star Rider*. Your name wasn't listed. In fact, the lone female from the Saturn colonies was Dr. Elshi Kent from the United Nations' observation post on Tethys. So let's cut the crap about who and what you are." She handled it well, I'll admit that. No gasps or charades at all.

"Very good, Jefferson." Her voice was tauntingly patronizing. I gave her a raised eyebrow and revised my estimate of her intelligence up a few notches. There aren't many women left versed in the subtle technique of verbal manslaughter. "I can see Al-Kirzen's opinion of you is justified. I paid Inter System Shuttles a healthy bribe to keep that information secret. How did you get it?"

"My methods are my own concern." It wasn't the first time Jamie had gotten inside information for me. I'd called him before my morning workout, and he had the goods within two hours. I don't know how he does it. I'm not sure I want to.

The waiter reappeared with two covered dishes and what looked like battery-powered chopsticks. He managed to convey his dislike of my long hair and unshaven face with a quick glance through half-lidded eyes. His voice took on a condescending whine.

"Have you ever eaten Animeat before?"

I had no idea what he was talking about. "No."

He took the covers off the dishes. Dinner looked like a cross between a crab and an octopus. Had its legs been a little longer, I'm sure it could have gotten away. As it was, the best it could do was pull itself ineffectually along the slick china plate with its four sets of claws. I wondered how long it'd be before the same gene-doubling procedure used on dinner yielded a four-armed human.

The waiter motioned to the thing's head. "The best spot is at the top of the neck, where the exoskeleton is thinnest."

He handed Miss Vandimeer one of the sticks, and I watched while she poked her dinner on the back. A tiny spark jumped and the animal died in one silent, convulsive shudder. Doubtless the boys who designed the thing removed its vocal cords to avoid the possibility of any embarrassingly noisy faux pas on the part of the beast while it died.

I duplicated Vandimeer's movement and handed the prods back to the waiter. My client pulled a claw from the animal, and delicately separated the meat from the skeleton. Reminding myself of what I used to think of Great-Grandfather's absurd aversion to scientific advance, I snapped off a claw. The meat was tender and delicious. And all this time I'd thought genetic engineering was useless.

We enjoyed most of dinner in silence before I got back to business. "Now, how about the truth?"

Miss Vandimeer licked the grease off her fingers and tried to sound nonchalant. "I gave it to you already. I'm an employee of Abdul Al-Kirzen. That I work on Tethys and under an assumed name changes nothing.''

Sometimes the best course of action is to let them believe they have you fooled. It's easier to get information from people who think they're superior. "Fine. So what does the great Al-Kirzen want of me?"

"When Al-Kirzen moved his estate to New Mecca, several employees and their families moved with him. About seventeen months ago, the infants of these families started to die. So far, thirty-seven have perished."

"So get yourself a pediatrician."

"We already have. Several of the best medicos in the system have taken up the problem with no results."

"Which brings us back to the original question. What can I do for the great Al-Kirzen?"

"Recently, several people on Rhea have begun to suspect these deaths have more to do with politics than biology. Many believe our enemies are highly placed government officials. I was sent to find someone who was not afraid to face those kinds of odds."

Great. "You mean you're looking for a someone stupid enough to play hardball with the United Nations."

She laughed. "I wouldn't have put it in those words. However, your position and courage against the mayor is getting around the city. When I heard of it . . .''

"You naturally assumed I was the right guy for the job."

"Yes."

Bad idea. On the whole, the U.N. is a decent government. If it has a fault, it's that some of the member states have real Gestapo mentalities. Just ask failed secessionists down in Central America who are trying to scrape a living out of Anthrax-Twelve-infested soil. "Why would the United Nations be after Al-Kirzen?"

"I'll leave that question for my employer."

"Why? Is he coming around for a visit?"

"No, he has no plans to leave Rhea."

This was where I was getting off. After the military had shown me what happens to unprotected humans placed in a vacuum, I'd made it my policy to never again leave Earth. I like having air over my head that won't vanish the first time someone gets careless with the duct work. "Sorry, miss, get someone else. I'm not interested in dying on Rhea."

"We anticipated this problem also. I am authorized to pay you twenty million credits NorthAm—five million Andy Jacksons—for accepting the job, with another ten million AJs at the successful conclusion of the venture."

Fifteen million Andy Jacks. No more spying on cheating wives, no more getting shot at, no more bone cookers outside my door. No more imitation-flavored ethane. All I had to do was be stupid enough to believe I would live long enough to collect. "Sorry, Jessica. No deal."

"You're making a mistake."

"Won't be the first time."

Usually at this point, they start with the begging and crying. Not Miss Vandimeer. She looked like she had expected me to turn her down. "Very well, Mr. Kayoto." She took her bank card and punched in several digits. A nasty suspicion crept through me.

"What exactly are you doing there?"

"I'm canceling the transfer of Al-Kirzen's ten thousand AJs into your account."

"You can't do that, Miss Vandimeer. I considered your case just like you asked. The money is rightfully mine." She ignored my threatening outburst and called for the check.

"I'll be staying at the Carizio for the next thirteen days. If you change your mind before then, my room is suite A. Thank you for a pleasant dinner." She was gone before I had a chance to do anything foolish.

Riding the elevator down to street level, a quick look at my bank card confirmed the worst. My account was down to a half-Jack. Not enough for the steam trolley, much less a rickshaw. The only good news was that my Habitat was only seven kilometers away.

Stepping into the night, I was quickly soaked by greasy rain. Along the streets water vendors hawked their product. Portable neon signs, covered with the grime of melted snow, glowed above plastic and plexiglass stands. "Guaranteed free of all heavy metals . . . You check the mercury levels of our product!"

An old man, gums blackened and hands jittery from systemic poisoning, bartered loudly with a dealer who worked without a United Nations' inspection logo. The man got his price, half of what legitimate stands were asking, and purchased a couple of liters. Speeding a little faster to his inevitable end.

As I left the commercial districts, the property value decreased and the snake-and-scepter signs of the body brokers, each one listing the facilities and schools that would receive your innards after death, became more prevalent. More elite outfits were paying for use of genetic material as well as the major organs. The best prices were going to those who could prove their I.Q. was higher than 140 or that they had power of attorney over someone who tested lower than 90. The wealthy can always use a gene pool of cheap zombie labor.

Reaching the residential Habitat Blocks, I concentrated on generating a sequence of moves that would put me back in business. Top priority had to be the jokers with the bone cookers. Assuming they were on the mayor's payroll, eliminating them should be a matter of forcing action. The first step was placing a call to Sleaze.

Miss Vandimeer's ability to access my bank card's credit withdrawal numbers was another matter. I finally had to admit I didn't know how she'd done it. Back in the office, the single overhead fluorescent light flickering to cold life, I mixed a shot of whiskey and called for help.

"Sheen?"

"Yessss . . . ," answered the digitalized Wicked Witch.

"Ring Holly."

"I'll get her, my pretty."

Holly Mason was another teenage hard-luck case when I found her on the street. She'd already done a few months in a MinPen for hacking and was quickly working up toward the kind of stuff that would sooner or later get her bumped off by one of the multinational corporate hit squads. The white-collar world doesn't care for people snooping in their data nets.

I slapped some sense into her and sent her to school. She was somewhere in Massachusetts completing her Ph.D. in fuzzy logic algorithms.

"She's answered, my sweeeet."

She was a couple of years older than when I had first seen her, but she'd retained the girl-next-door look. Her copper hair was in ponytails, and she still had a dusting of freckles over the bridge of her nose. Holly's always appealed to the hebephile in me.

"Jefferson! What's the old dog up to now?"

"Hello, Holly. I need some information."

"Don't you always? When are you going to move out of that trashy office and get a real job?"

We could go on like this for hours, but after Vandimeer's tricks I wasn't up to it. Holly must have read it in my face. "What do you need?"

"If I wanted to acquire the withdrawal code for another person's bank card, how would I go about it?"

"Assuming you know the name of the mark you want to hit up, all you need to do is try different access codes until you get the right one. Just remember that three wrong numbers in any twenty-four-hour period tags the cops, so you better stick to trying only two codes a day. At that rate it'll take you a little over ten thousand centuries to enter every code. On the other hand, the code might be 000000–0001, and if you're being your usual methodical self, you would get it on the first try."

"Suppose I wanted access by tomorrow."

"Impossible, Jefferson. Can't be done."

"Maybe for us commoners, but what if I were rich? I'm not talking a casual hundred million, I mean real money. Say I had several billion Andy Jacksons backing me, how would I get your access code?"

"Jefferson, it's not a matter of money. Machines don't take bribes. Cash has no meaning to the Interworld Bank Net. To the computers, wealth is nothing but a series of random access data files."

"So what about the people who run the machines? A suitable threat greased with a healthy bribe . . ."

"No way. Can't happen."

Considering her past, it didn't seem possible Holly could still be this green about the real power of money. "Say I find some bank official who's down on his luck . . ."

"Kayoto, listen for a sec, okay? This is my area of expertise, remember? The IBN machines possess self-determinate algorithms. They constantly change their own programs, including their own master access codes."

"Try it again, this time in English."

"The first IBN machine was put on-line by Euro-Comm of France. Its master access code, including the numbers that would open everyone's account to prying fingers like yours, has been published numerous times—000714-1789 in case you're curious."

"No doubt in commemoration of the storming of the Bastille. I'm surprised several people didn't guess it in advance."

"You can impress me with your knowledge of history some other time, Jefferson. For now, shut up and listen. The code wasn't meant to fool anyone. You can log on the Paris network and try it if you want to, but I guarantee it won't get you anywhere. A micro-second after the machine went on-line, the code was changed by the computer itself. I don't care how many people you bribe, not a single one of them can get you into the data cores."

"Fine, so I get hold of a couple of top-flight hackers and break in."

She shook her head like a teacher confronted with an unusually slow student. "Look, the most conservative estimate is that every IBN program changes its own master access code twenty thousand times every nanosecond. You think any driver can stay on top of that? The system is foolproof."

"So foolproof a woman came in her yesterday and punched up my code." I hadn't meant to tell her my problems. Holly's the type to call in the riot squad at the sound of a single gunshot.

"Nothing mysterious there. You've been fingered. Some of my friends on the street made a living doing the same thing. I know a fixdigit who can tell you your bank code just by watching your fingers move when you enter your personal access numbers."

I knew about such people. I'd even employed a fixdigit on occasion to collect fees from reluctant clients. I knew their tricks, and how to outwit them. I never enter my code in plain sight and I've trained my fingers to brush certain keys without punching them.

"I don't think she could have done it that way."

Holly pulled up her hands in frustration and shrugged. "Well, then she read your mind."

"Very funny." It was the wrong tone to take. Holly leaned toward her screen.

"What's all this about anyway? Are you in trouble, Jefferson? You need some money? Is the Fusion Board going to disconnect you again?"

"No, Holly, I'm fine, just a little baffled, is all."

"I'll come over if you need me."

"I know you would, but it's nothing. Really." I cut her off before she could tell me she was buying a ticket on the next airship out. I hadn't been off the screen for more than two minutes when another call came in.

The mayor's bald head reflected light like a low-watt sodium bulb. He caught my eye, took a few hits from his cigar, and let me sweat it out in silence. I don't know how he expected me to react, but I leaned back in my chair and gave him a yawn. He wasn't too impressed.

"Kayoto, I'm only going to say this once, so pay attention. Your message came across my desk this morning. I don't know what you're talking about. I don't have anyone watching you. Small-timers don't rate that kind of service.

"You can keep your delusions of grandeur if you want, but if you threaten me again, I'll have you shot. Is that clear?" He made a rumbling sound that may have been a laugh. "Oh, and give my regards to my wife."

I heard a young girl's giggle, and the circuit went dead.

3

Jamie didn't think much of my clean-up-the-neighborhood campaign. He squinted his blue eyes at me and tugged at the end of his mustache.

"Why do you always spring these peculiar mental aberrations on me the first thing in the morning?"

"So we can get through your objections before midnight."

"Jefferson, have you looked at a news fax lately? The police shoveled five hundred dead cats out of City Hall this morning and unless the mayor rescinds the Urban Hunting Season, the animal nuts have promised to infest every stray in town with some new strain of rabies. You have any idea how many people will die from food poisoning alone? Don't you think the mayor has more important things on his schedule than calling you up just to feed you a line?"

The fact that he was making sense wasn't helping my mood at all. "You got a better candidate? We're talking about a good deal of political muscle, and Mr. Mayor is the most logical suspect."

"Yeah? I can think of ten or twelve wealthy people who're pissed off enough to do you in. Besides, even if it is the mayor, what makes you sure you won't get fried anyway?"

"Because the one thing the mayor doesn't want is publicity. The joy boys out there are for show. The mayor knows if I'm burned, the first thing I'll do is go to the press. After the business with his wife, it'd pull him down and he knows it."

"You mean you hope he knows it."

"It's an acceptable risk. Anyway, unless we take them out, we might as well close shop. We go with it; tomorrow at ten."

"You're a real stubborn bastard, you know that?"

"Yeah, but my other sterling qualities make up for it."

He shook his head. "I've got to dig up some stuff. See you tomorrow."

I had Sheen place a call to the city's reigning champion of yellow journalism. An alluring fifteen-year-old dressed in glistening body oil appeared on the screen. She'd had the *Inter Nos* Fax emblem tattooed on her left breast. Sleaze once told me her office air conditioner was always on high. Keeps her nipples at attention for prospective advertisers. She's the kind of kid corporations recruit right out of middle school.

"*Inter Nos.* I'm Tracy, how may I help you?"

"Give me Ivan Sorenson."

"One moment, please." The screen went blank for a couple of seconds before Ivan's hawk face came on. He smiled when he saw me, flashing a mouth full of clear urethane teeth. The results of too many candid questions and not enough credit to buy bio-implants.

"Well, what do you know? Six weeks since the election, and Jefferson Kayoto is still alive. If I were a betting man, I'd've laid odds against you."

"Thanks, Sleaze. Nothing like reassuring words from friends."

"That's what I'm here for. What do you want?"

"Business is down a bit. How about joining me for a drink this evening?" I ran a hand over my closely trimmed beard. An old signal warning him our conversation was probably being monitored.

He gave a long sigh. I'd made use of his services before, a

couple of times landing him in the emergency ward. Not that that ever stops him. Like all good journalists, Ivan's curiosity is greater than his desire to keep breathing.

"I'll be done here at eight. O'Henry's at eight-thirty?" He blinked twice.

"Sounds good. I'll even pick up the first round."

I walked into O'Henry's at six-thirty. Ivan was already there, a Tom Collins cradled in his bony hands. We took a seat in the noisiest part of the bar, directly in front of the wide-area holotank. For a time we watched the game with the rest of the crowd. I was fidgety. Even with three-dimensional projection, football is monotonous. Thank God spring training was only five months away.

Finally he turned to me. "What's up?"

"Someone's leaning on me. It's putting a definite cramp in my business."

He gave me a long sigh. "Who?"

"It's got to be the mayor. He's got a couple of thugs armed with bone cookers watching my place."

"Wonderful. You're going to get me killed, you know that?" He finished off his drink with one swallow. "What do you have in mind?"

I told him. He looked at me and rolled his eyes. "Shit. You think this up by yourself or did you get divine guidance from dial-a-prayer?"

The last thing I needed was a bloody amateur picking holes in my plan. "There's a vacant tattoo module three units down and across the walkway from my office. The door should be easy to jimmy. You can get your shots from there."

"Our readers will love it. 'Private Detective Finds New Way to Die.'"

"You in or not?"

"Yeah, you only live once, right?" He stood up and grabbed his coat. "Jefferson? I've seen people who've been hit with bone cookers; arms and feet swollen to twice their normal size, bones turned to toothpicks. It's a very painful way to check out. You better be right on this one."

4

Jamie hobbled down the dim corridor dressed in mud-colored U.N.-issue pauper's pants. His hair was gray and he used a dented aluminum cane to offset a badly overplayed limp. Two figures materialized from an abandoned module between my office and the lift, intercepting him about ten meters from my door. Their backs were to me, exactly as planned. Jamie kept them occupied until I was right behind them.

"Take off, old man." His part finished, I wanted him out of sight before the thugs saw through his disguise. He gave me a warning look and tottered away.

Of Jamie's two assailants, the least menacing was a heavily built young man wearing mirrored Lennon specs and a black trench coat. If the blank look on his face was any indication, he was hired muscle; a neighborhood bully just trying to make a buck.

His partner played the game in another league. Diminutive in stature, her face had aquiline features accented by a mane of flowing red hair cut in a mohawk. A hairline scar ran down her left cheek. She wore cycle leathers and her black hip boots were glossy with polish. And when she moved, which was rarely, she moved with the fluid grace of a trained fighter. If there was any doubt as to her professional status, one attempt to meet her gaze was enough to erase it.

The irises and whites of her eyes had been dyed jet black. The effect on her handsome face was unsettling even before you realized the coloring made it impossible to tell which way she was looking. To the uninitiated, it might seem a cheap scare tactic; a pair of shaded glasses would obviously supply the same concealment. But glasses are easily broken in a fight, and if you don't think you need to know where your opponent is looking, then you're making the kind of mistake that explains why so few novices in the hand-to-hand-combat business make it past their first fight.

Because I recognized her for an accomplished fighter, I paid my respect by addressing her rather than her hulking sidekick. "Well, girls and boys, I'm flattered. I take it as a real token of your friendship to stand out here all day and screen my clients. However, a recent downturn in business has rendered your services unnecessary. I'll be happy to give you both good recommendations for your work, but in the meantime, why don't you pack up your toys and shove off before you get hurt."

The woman flashed me a perfect smile and nodded to her accomplice. So, my first impression had been correct. She was in charge. With any luck she was as professional as she looked; everything depended on her controlling her emotions. Not necessarily the case for her boyfriend. As he turned to slink back to his hiding place, I sidestepped in front of him and jabbed my right knee in his crotch. He doubled over, retching on the pitted steel of the walkway.

I had only a split second to realize my mistake. The woman moved with feral quickness. Her left hand flicked out and caught me on the base of my skull.

Bright sparks jumped around in my head. My vision cleared in time to see the man peel himself off the walkway and assume a cautious crouch. This wasn't according to plan at all. In a pinch I could handle him. She'd just pound the shit out of me.

"Stop." Her voice was one used to giving orders.

"Why? We don't have to let this punk push us around."

"Think again." I licked my fingers and ran them down his shades. He didn't take it too well. The bone cooker was out and pointed square at my chest. His finger wrapped around the trigger and I was definitely having second thoughts.

Fortunately onyx eyes was keeping her perspective. "Put that away, you idiot. You want everyone in the city to see it?" He snarled and whisked the weapon back under his coat.

"Next time you're that stupid," he said, "you're dead."

Never let someone else get the last word. "Yeah? I hear the geysers on Triton are really romantic. You two should have a blast when you get there." I deliberately turned my back and walked to my office. It took everything I had not to run.

Sleaze Sorenson is nothing if not quick. When my fax spit out the evening addition of *Inter Nos,* the front page was covered with color photographs of me confronting my erstwhile guardians. In the lower left corner a black-and-white inset caught the mayor's hand indiscreetly goosing a young woman. The headline read, "Mayor Fiddles with Teenager While Citizens Burn." *Inter Nos* didn't think much of the mayor. I wasn't too hot on him myself.

In every way, it seemed a satisfactory operation. The police surfaced within the hour to cuff my watchdogs and the judicial system, moving with uncharacteristic speed, held a perfunctory trial three days later. In a courthouse packed to the rafters with media mongrels, a three-man jury handed in a guilty verdict to a judicial computer who impartially handed out two passes on the next shuttle bound for the Neptune System. I patted myself on the back and celebrated with a glass of synthetic beer.

But after a week passed without a solitary client, I was forced to admit I'd missed something. Several times I was almost desperate, if not hungry, enough to see Miss Vandimeer. Somehow, though, Jamie seemed to come up with the money to keep the power coming and the fridge stocked. I was certain if we could hold out a little longer, the mayor would give it up.

It was early Tuesday morning, nine days after the trial, when I got the call from the McDonald Hospital Intensive Care Sector. Jamie had been brought in by an unidentified woman. Both his arms had been cracked across the radius and ulna. His left leg was broken once across the femur and twice on the tibia. Three ribs had been snapped inward, stopping millimeters short of puncturing his lungs.

5

"Well, well, Kayoto, what are you into now? Screwing your clients' daughters again?" The cop had been waiting for me at the hospital door, his riot gear piled on the floor beside him.

"Shove it, Donaldson."

"Jamie's beat up pretty bad. He had a note written on his

back addressed to you. It was scribbled in his own blood. Wanna hear it?''

Donaldson's okay for a cop, but he has the same problem all cops have. Too smug. I grabbed him by the collar and pushed him against the wall. Green tiles came unglued and shattered on the floor. ''Cool it, Kayoto. You want to spend the night downtown?''

Much as I felt like expressing myself more clearly, I couldn't help Jamie by getting locked up. I set Donaldson down, mockingly straightening his collar. He took a pad from his belt and cleared his throat theatrically.

'' 'If Jefferson Kayoto is still in business next week, his friends will pay with their lives.' I'm going to ask you again; what are you into?''

I've made one or two enemies, but none had ever been gutless enough to strike back at my associates. Even the mayor has more class than that. I went with the truth, though I hardly expected Donaldson to start trusting me now. ''Nothing. Business has been dead lately.''

''Don't feed me that shit. I can't turn on the news without hearing some semi-literate anchorwoman drool your name. Half the city thinks you're some kind of fucking hero for being stupid enough to stand in front of a bone cooker.''

''You know something, Donaldson? Working on the street has done nothing for your language.''

''Don't try and be cute, Kayoto. You don't have the looks for it. Why do you suddenly rate the goon squad stomping outside your door? Why did Jamie take the fall for your brainless heroics?''

''You think if I knew, I'd be standing here yapping to you?''

Donaldson gave me a long look and started suiting up his urethane body armor. ''You can't win this one, Kayoto. We'll do our best with Jamie but you might as well know that if you get caulked now, we've been ordered to botch the investigation. I don't know who's behind it, but you better shape up or you're going to lose it.''

The surgeon who'd put Jamie back together wasn't much help, either. I sat on a faded leather chair while she sipped cold coffee from a Styrofoam cup and went through the everything's-going-to-be-okay routine.

''I've seen hundreds of beatings, but nothing like this. It's a work of art.''

I may be overly cynical, but it sounded to me like she was jealous. "What do you mean?"

"Precision on this level indicates a professional black market surgeon was employed. The bones were broken with extreme care; every fracture clean and simple. He'll be up and walking within a week. A couple of months from now, you won't even be able to tell anything was wrong."

"What about the blood on his back?"

"Taken by syringe from his arm. It must have been about as painful as making a donation to the Red Cross. Damnedest thing I ever saw."

"Can I talk to him?"

She consulted a minicomputer on her wrist and nodded. "You've got five minutes. He's doped up, so don't expect much."

Jamie was flat on his back, his arms and left leg in traction. His chest was in a cast and he had to work to breathe. The doctor started the reassurance flowing again.

"He'll be out of traction before you know it. In the meantime, we'll keep him so juiced on endomorphines and joy buzzers he'll think he's on vacation."

"Got that right," Jamie whispered from the bed. "Don't feel a thing." His eyes were glazed over and his pupils were contracted to pinpricks despite the dim fluorescent lighting.

"Jamie, who did this to you?"

He shook his head, careful not to dislodge the oxygen tubes taped below his nose. "One moment I'm playing a Sherlock Holmes mystery in my virtual image bubble, and the next thing I know, I wake up here with the doctor telling me I'm going to be okay. I didn't even know what she was talking about until I saw the plaster hanging on my arms."

"Someone did a pretty thorough job on you. You must remember something. Broken arms aren't the sort of thing you sleep through."

"Jefferson, there was nothing. No pain, no sensation at all. I just woke up like this."

The surgeon gave me the same warning look doctors must practice in the mirrors at med school, and I said a quick good-bye. Jamie fell asleep before I was out the door.

"Who brought him in?"

"A young woman. Blond hair, brown eyes, about a hundred eighty centimeters tall. She refused to leave a name."

Probably one of the mayor's many female acquaintances, but there was no way to track her. The eye color could have been contact lenses and the hair was probably dyed.

"Why wasn't she held for questioning?"

The doctor sighed. "Look, in this city it's a victory when they decide to scrape the dying off the pavement. The last thing we're going to do is discourage what small measure of altruism remains by grilling everyone who brings in a warm body. Our policy is pretty much 'no questions asked.'"

Leaving the hospital with almost as little information as I'd arrived with did nothing for my sour mood. Walking back to my office, an overweight wino stumbled into me and my gut reaction nearly cost him his right arm. Stunned by my reflexive anger against a defenseless drunk, I began to appreciate the psychological expertise of Jamie's attackers. With Jamie's memory wiped clean, there was little chance of finding his assailant. For all I knew, the old boozer was the culprit. Behind a skillful charade of alcoholic torpor, he might be sizing me up for the next round of bone breaking. How do you defend yourself against an enemy who has left no traces?

Whoever was after me, they wanted me off balance; jumping at every stranger I passed, not knowing when the ax would fall. If my reaction to the wino was any indication, they were doing a bang-up job. Unless I calmed down, I might as well stay locked in my office, my back against the nearest wall. Paranoia is a wonderful tool for keeping people on a leash.

6

There's a popular myth that among criminals, there exists a code of honor. Rule one in this unwritten canon is supposedly: "Thou shalt not squeal on thy comrades." If you append that with: ". . . unless you can make a quick buck doing it," you'll come a lot closer to reality.

Making a quick buck is Lube's specialty. A handsome young

street urchin, Lube usually works his scam on uptown restaurant crowds. When he showed up at my place, a day after Jamie was put through the works, Lube was dressed in his favorite valet's vest. The gold name tag on his chest was currently engraved with the name Johnathon Smyth. For some help in finding a parking place, and a solid tip, respectable-looking Mr. Smyth would have your Porsche stolen and on the auction block before you finished your aperitif.

The two of us shared a symbiotic relationship. He ripped people off and his marks paid me to get their property back. As long as he was honest about who he fenced the car to, my calls to him were strictly business. Since I never turned him in, he was willing to do me the occasional favor of squealing.

"What's the ruff, Gov?" Lube's trademark in the underground was a pathetic imitation of low-brow nineteenth-century English.

"Someone took Jamie for a workout. I want to find out who."

"Flash or Footpad?"

"Professional. A highly skilled medic."

"Cor, can't be more'n three score of 'em, and they all have larks for friends."

"Good. See if any of them are talking."

The operation took most of a day. Between Sleaze, who gave me access to valuable information from *Inter Nos* back files, and Lube's snooping, I was able to track Jamie's malpracticing surgeon to an abandoned amusement park in the Warehouse District. According to the latest rumors, Dr. Ansil ran his services out of Professor Mordred's House of Pain.

Once we located the old horror house's battered wood sign, Lube beat a quick retreat. "Glocky, you are, wanting to lurk in there. Cut you up and sell you to the brokers, he will."

The first sign of occupation was in the Chamber of Vampires. A battered mannequin with chipped fangs leered at me, his coat of dust and spiderwebs not quite concealing an optic pickup in his knee. Somewhere above, servomotors whined every time I moved. Most likely a combat laser wired to the camera.

The doctor's assistant, a disheveled kid missing her left arm from the elbow down, materialized from the shadows and put the business end of a .38 against the zipper of my blue jeans. Her boss, whom I only saw as a dark silhouette, looked me over and took a hit from something rolled in bright red paper. "What do you want, and make it quick. I got a fetus just dying to go to the brokers."

"You did a scare job a couple of days ago on a Caucasian male. Blond hair, blue eyes, mustache."

"You got nothing on me. I do a little plastic work, and maybe a toddler extraction now and then. Nothing else."

"I'm not a cop. The name's Jefferson Kayoto."

"Yeah? I thought you looked familiar. Step into the light." Her helper jabbed me in the groin with the barrel of the gun and I stumbled into a pool of dusty sunlight. Overhead, rusted gears swiveled to follow me. "I know you. Word is, the mayor wants you grilled."

"Just tell me about the guy you did."

The figure shrugged. "Handsome kid. Squealed like a stuck pig. No guts."

"He told me he didn't remember any of it."

"So he's lying. Trying to save face."

Had it been anyone but Jamie, I might have believed it. "You do any brain work?"

"No, strictly ribs and limbs."

Which meant Jamie's memory had been fiddled after the operation and Dr. Ansil, the best lead I had, just turned into a dead end. "What about the girl who brought him in?"

"Dizzy blond. Brown contacts, pink glove on her left hand. Didn't speak much. You after her?"

"Yeah. Know where she went?"

"She took him to a hospital, if you can believe it."

"Five Andy Jacks if you can tell me where she is."

"She didn't say and I didn't ask. Now split. I got a special delivery to make."

Holly called a day later. Her hair was tangled and her face was pale. "Jefferson, someone left a message on my screen." She punched it up.

YOU ARE GOING TO DIE UNLESS KAYOTO IS OUT OF BUSINESS WITHIN THREE DAYS.

"That's not all." Her voice was shaking. I saw rings under her eyes and realized she had been crying. "When I came home from class yesterday, there was blood all over my bathroom walls. I called the police. They did a full analytic scan."

From the nervous apprehension in her eyes, I knew what she

was going to say. "It was my blood, Jefferson, mine. I don't even know where it came from. Someone took it, and I didn't even know it."

Why? Why do this to someone not even living in the city? What did the mayor hope to gain? Unless . . .

Within a few seconds, every theory I'd made about who had ordered the attacks against my friends fell apart. Mr. Mayor wasn't behind any of it. Not the bone cookers, not Jamie's flawlessly broken body, not this. I knew who was. Venus with a pink glove on her broken left hand and brown contacts covering green eyes. So much for the money being on my side.

"Holly, listen to me." She sat staring at the screen, her eyes unfocused. "Holly!" I was close to yelling. "Look at me." I waited until she was seeing me. "I know who left the message. I'll take care of it. Okay? Do you understand?"

"Jefferson? What's going on?"

"Everything's under control. No one's coming after you."

"Do you need help?" She tried, unsuccessfully, to level the jitters out of her voice. Damn the woman who had ordered this.

"No. Stay away."

"I heard about Jamie."

"Then you know how important it is to keep clear." And knowing what I had to do, I had to tell her at least part of the truth. "Holly? I'm going to be away for a while."

"Where're you going?"

"Off planet."

Holly knew enough of my past in the Terra-Luna Corps to know I'd never voluntarily leave Earth again. Not after the massacre on Humboldt Station. "Is it that bad?"

"It's not what you think. I'm getting paid handsomely. I promise everything will be all right."

7

Packing didn't take long. No matter how much time I spend in one place, I never accumulate much of anything. I hid my old-style machine pistol, a nine-millimeter Stoeger Luger, under my full-length duster and grabbed my duffel. Just before leaving, I used the key to scratch my name from the office's circular plexiglass window.

On my way to the Carizio I stopped by the hospital. As the doctor had predicted, Jamie was ambulatory and going through painful sessions in the physical therapy wing. Yet despite his appearance of general health, he seemed agitated and easily distracted. His therapist passed it off as something called Anderson's syndrome and told me not to worry.

Although I was far from certain Jamie understood my hasty explanations, I gave him a censored account of my plans and left him the keys to the office. Maybe he could get some money selling it. After a short stop at the bank I was on my way again.

The Carizio won its fifteen minutes of fame by being the first skyscraper to rise a vertical mile above its foundation. That it was also a featureless bundle of plexiglass and ferroconcrete tubes didn't seem to bother the millions of people who flocked there each year.

Suite A was the top floor. The price for staying there one night, so the booklet handed out at the hotel's door claimed, was 3,000 Andy Jacks. Impossible for the mayor to hide such an expense. If I'd been thinking a week ago, I'd have saved Jamie and Holly a lot of trouble.

The express elevator, finished in hammered silver and encrusted with semiprecious stones, took eight minutes to reach the top floor. I sat beside a group of Brazilian tourists and tried to keep my patience. When the doors opened, the

SouthAms flocked to the observation windows. An information kiosk directed me to a corridor behind the elevator.

A blond muscle man dressed as an eighteenth-century French page waited for me at the end of the hall. He flexed an armful of steroids and mumbled my name to a wall intercom. I couldn't hear the answer, but he turned to me and grunted. "Miss Vandimeer is expecting you, Mr. Kayoto." He led me into the waiting room and went back to his vigil. The reinforced door on the far side of the room clicked open, Vandimeer's voice coming from within.

"Do come in, Jefferson."

The bored tone of her voice tripped every adrenaline switch I had. Entering the garish suite, I shoved her back to the nearest wall, my left hand curling around her delicious, slender throat. "I'll go with you to Rhea. Now call your thugs off my friends."

Her voice came out as a strained whisper. "I don't know what you're talking about."

I pulled the machine pistol from its armpit holster and held the muzzle an inch in front of her right eye. "You've got three seconds to figure it out, and you're staring at the bonus prize awarded to contestants supplying wrong answers."

"Don't be absurd. You fire that Wild West relic and hotel security will be in here before you can wipe the blood off your hands." Apparently she didn't understand the significance of the flared Browning silencer on the gun's barrel. I moved the Luger a few centimeters from her head and buried half the magazine into the wall beside her. The only sound was a dull thud; the hot acrid smell of spent powder filled the suite. I recentered the gun on her forehead.

"I've got nothing to lose, and you don't have long to live. I've killed prettier women than you."

They say women have special intuition about men. Miss Vandimeer must have put it on-line because her eyes opened wide. "Okay, I'll tell them you've agreed to help us."

"Very good." I released my grip, allowing her to massage her throat. "Where's my five mil?"

"It has already been credited to your account." I pulled my card, for the first time in my life seeing a nine-digit balance. According to the chronology listed beside the credit report, the amount had been deposited the second I walked into the Carizio. Evidently Miss Vandimeer had a stoolie watching for me at the door. I never liked being the focus of such efficiency; it all too often turns out to be remorseless.

"Jefferson, I'm sorry about Jamie. What happened wasn't my idea."

"Yeah, sure. How did you get my bank account access code?"

"I hired a professional by radio while I was still on the *Star Rider*. Your code was waiting for me when I landed. I don't know who got it or how they did it. Part of the deal was we would never meet. When I received the information I was instructed to make a payment into a deposit-only account. The account was registered to a secondhand software dealer on the riverfront. That's all I know."

Standard procedure for employment of a fixdigit. And exactly the sort of answer given by someone who'd read about it but never gone through it.

"What was the name of the software dealer?"

"Low Risk Disk."

A year ago, it would have been a good answer—Low Risk Disk had a shady reputation. But they'd been busted last spring for fencing African military software—computer-aided design for metal-eating bacteria, if I remembered correctly. These days, you can bet when a salesman at Low Risk so much as took a piss, the United Nations was in the sewers making sure he wasn't passing anything illegal.

"Miss Vandimeer, let me congratulate you for a perfect score. Two lies in two answers." She did a good job of acting outraged, carrying the part so far as to even attempt slapping me. I caught her wrist and pushed her arm away. She tripped back into an overstuffed couch and I fenced her in with my arms. "I don't have the patience for this. Just tell me when we're leaving."

"The luxury ship I.S.S. *Far Hand,* bound for the Saturn System, disembarks from Elf Hive in one hundred eight hours. Tickets have already been purchased in our names. We're to catch a private aerorocket piggybacking a Boeing Stratomaster tomorrow at eight."

Pleasure cruises to the Saturn System are the province of wealthy "adventurers" who want tell their peers they've seen the colony on Iapetus firsthand. It's this decade's answer to last century's chemical dump sleep-ins: substitute Iapetus's population of freaks for the leaking barrels of organo-metallics, take whatever drugs make you feel invulnerable, and then see how close you can get before Father Death takes you home.

Since the rest of us aren't that bored with life, service to Saturn is rare; it'd be months before another ship headed out. This meant Miss Vandimeer had only a limited amount of time to persuade me to take her case. Since I didn't swallow the money she'd been fishing with, she tried the more forceful hook of molesting Jamie and Holly. Looks like she caught herself a real sucker.

"Wake me up when it's time to go."

I took her room and locked the door. After what she'd put me through the last two weeks, I figured I needed the bed more than she did. She surprised me by not pounding on the door or calling up room service and having me tossed out.

Not that I slept anyway. The top floor of the Carizio swayed in harmony with the immense forces even the smallest of breezes exerted on her mile-high flanks. No doubt the rich who lounged in the upper floors found the rocking motion pleasant. As I lay on the overly soft king-size bed, all I could think about was the empty space below my window.

The hotel's information booklet, the only reading material I had, increased my discomfort by pointing out that several floors of the hotel were devoted solely to hydraulic machinery required to keep the structure in dynamic equilibrium with Mother Nature. A foolish delusion since, in the long run, Nature would surely have her way.

8

The airport was, like all airports, blandly utilitarian and shrouded in sweaty desperation. I ate a stale doughnut while Miss Vandimeer checked in my duffel and her thirteen suit-cases at the United desk.

Riding the beltways and marching through the concourses, she escorted me like a politician screening her richest lobbyist.

When I had to use the head, she steered me to a unisex room, thoughtlessly standing at my shoulder while I went about my business. I felt only slightly mollified when we started for the door and she ran head on into a computer jockey. His briefcase popped and optical storage disks scattered across stained floor tiles. He shot Vandimeer a murderous look and for one cheerful second I thought he was going to give her a riot act. But he quickly composed himself, becoming almost apologetic.

Did he look familiar? A past client? Or had I seen him at Jamie's place? Miss Vandimeer hurriedly helped him pick up and sprinted me out of the rest room before I could be sure. She fidgeted all the way across the terminal.

"Too much caffeine this morning?"

She ignored me and hurried through security.

I slipped a couple hundred AJs of Al-Kirzen's dough into the chief of customs' account. He didn't even blink when I walked through the scanner with my machine pistol. A play of his hands across his security keyboard cut the alarms before they sounded.

Our parent flight was a Boeing 7070 Stratomaster to Bangkok. On the other side of a cracked concourse window, a United flight crew hoisted our aerorocket, the *Daedalus,* to the back of the seventy-seventy. Al-Kirzen's circle-within-triangles logo, a stylized oasis among arid dunes, was etched into its flat black ceramic heat shield.

It took the Stratomaster fifteen minutes to reach its cruising altitude of 23,000 meters. The lushly padded chairs in first class shivered when rocket motors took over from oxygen-starved jet engines. A few minutes later, a prim stewardess told us it was time to board our piggybacked aerorocket. Miss Vandimeer and I were the only two to climb through the connecting sleeve of air locks.

Our launch window opened seconds after the Stratomaster reached her apogee. The *Daedalus* boosted off the jet's back and fired its lox-hydrogen engines. After separation was complete, the pilot stepped from the command capsule to tell us we would be docking at Lagrange Five in three hours.

In the tepid, recycled oxygen of *Daedalus* I unaccountably found myself reliving a childhood adventure. Fresh out of a state-run elementary school, Thomas and I had hustled for weeks to save enough money to buy tickets for a day of swimming in the Atlantic. Each of us wearing a set of used

med-lab goggles, scrounged from a hospital trash bin, we
scoured the shallows for imagined riches.

Lured to the bottom of a deep tidal pool by a rusted set of
bed springs, my leg had become entangled. I could feel the top
of my head break the surface, but my mouth and nose were at
least seven centimeters underwater. When Thomas couldn't get
me free after a minute of frenzied pulling, he dived for the
bottom and came up with half a meter of twisted copper tubing.
It took him fifteen minutes to free my leg, while I breathed
stale air through the small tube. Although I knew my brother
was close to panic, I felt strangely calm. Even when waves
occasionally sent brine down my breathing tube and after my
mouth had been filled with blood from the tube's rough edges,
the only thought that occupied my oxygen-starved brain was:
What a stupid way to die.

"Mr. Kayoto?" The pilot's voice had dropped in pitch after
eyeing Vandimeer's physique.

"What?"

"I said, would you like to come up to the cockpit for a look
at Earth?"

"No, I'm fine, thank you."

"Miss Vandimeer?"

"I'd love to."

After chaperoning me all morning, Vandimeer's willingness
to allow me ten minutes of privacy seemed peculiar. There had
to be a reason she felt it safe to let down her guard now. Had
some threat failed to materialize at the airport?

With what little I knew about Jessica it was impossible to
decipher her motives, but it was curious how easy it was to
follow her emotional swing from anxiety to relative calm.
Professionals are never so transparent. So why would a man of
Al-Kirzen's means hire a novice?

Whatever Jessica's concerns, once back from sightseeing
she remained relaxed while deftly maneuvering around the
pilot's clumsy advances. I was relieved when he eventually
realized he was striking out and returned to the cockpit. It was
anyone's guess how many red lights were flashing on his
control readouts while he was trying to score with my charming
companion.

The three hours to Elf Hive passed in tedious slow motion.
Vandimeer fell asleep, from which I derived the satisfying
conclusion she hadn't slept last night, either, but I was wound

too tight. After what seemed like several days, I was able to put
aside my discomfort by tuning the holoscreen onto an Argen-
tinian documentary on Paris sex shows. Sad to report I reached
Elf Hive without learning anything new. Must be getting old.

The space station at Lagrange Five would have been a dis-
appointment to twentieth-century romantics. Instead of gleaming
labs populated by well-groomed professionals dressed in im-
maculately clean smocks, there was the nine-to-five grind and
a society where the word *astronaut* was an insult denoting
someone with too much education and too few skills. In place
of an elegant pinwheel, there were megatons of lunar regolith,
lifted by the Tranquility Rail Cannon, alloyed with lead, then
plastered to titanium girders. In the harsh sunlight it looked like
a chiaroscuro study by Picasso. It wasn't pretty, but it kept
lethal solar radiation away from the fragile life within.

If the environment outside Elf Hive was hell for mortals, it
was utopia for their machines. Vacuum distillation towers
hundreds of meters tall drifted beside the station, a grove of
metallic trees glowing red with the flashing of a thousand
warning lights. Closer to Elf Hive's bulk, automated assembly
matrixes extruded skeletal framework for the next layer of
habitation. From every side of the station, thin foil fingers of
multiband-gap solar-conversion cells struggled to quench Elf
Hive's insatiable thirst for energy. The station itself bristled
with sensors and work modules. It was a lot bigger than I
remembered.

We boarded Elf Hive from the commercial hangars in
SecDyn Quarter. A medical team wearing Imperial Russian
burgundy and gold whisked us away to a nearby medical bay,
ordered us to strip, and gave us both complete physicals. I
found myself averting my eyes from Jessica's prone form as
she submitted to the doctors' proddings, concentrating instead
on two computer screens filling with information as the medics
continued with their poking.

"Right arm up, please, Mr. Kayoto."

I absentmindedly followed instructions, belatedly remembering a Terra-Luna Corps medic who used to give the same
order, and received a painful injection in the sensitive tissue
under my arm. I looked down to see a male nurse dabbing
alcohol at an angry red welt. In a bored monotone he recited the
same litany the corps medic had given me.

"Diphosphonates and a calcium booster, set on diurnal time

release. Keeps your bones from turning to jelly. If your stay here is extended to over two weeks you will report here for another.''

''I'll be sure to conclude my business before then.''

He dutifully ignored my sarcasm and pulled a bulky pair of bubble pants from a nearby storage locker.

''This is your first time in a low-gravity environment, Mr. Kayoto?''

''No, this is my last.''

''Your profile shows you may have problems with systemic circulation, particularly in your lower body. If your legs tingle as from sleep or appear pallid, you must wear a Chibis suit until circulation returns to normal. This will encourage blood flow by systematically increasing and reducing pressure over the affected area.''

I hadn't been in bubble pants for years and wasn't looking forward to reacquainting myself with them. They might be reasonably good for the circulation, but they're unsurpassed in fostering blisters and skin rashes.

After allowing us a few minutes to dress, the medics issued us a pair of low-g sandals and gave a short lesson in how to walk so that the velcro soles maintained contact with the station's thick carpet. The motion required was awkward, and despite the training I received in the military, my leg muscles were accustomed to the smooth inverse square of gravity rather than the on-off friction of velcro. Jessica was much better at it, although her persistent limp appeared even more pronounced in the low gravity.

Reservations had already been made in Miss Vandimeer's name at the Hotel Saint Matthew. The hotel's platinum-colored taxi, a battery-powered golf cart with thick brush treads, was waiting to take us across the station to the hotel sector.

''Ever been to Hotel Saint Matthew before?'' The cabby had his hair greased back in a Reagan and smiled too easily. A gory tattoo on his shoulder, displaying a large-busted female chained to a cross, declared his affiliation with God's True Church. Fluorescent lettering underneath proclaimed the apocalypse was near at hand. I wasn't holding my breath.

''Haven't had the pleasure.''

He deliberately ignored, or more likely missed, the derision in my voice. ''You'll love it. Best place in the system to relax and enjoy yourself. If you'll take my advice, spend some time at Orpheus Window; it's an exclusive on L5, you know, and don't miss Proteus, located in the main lobby.'' He continued with the hard sell as we crossed SecDyn and entered the hotel quarter, SecTree. I tuned him out, ogling the scenery like a boy from a jerkwater farm commune.

In spite of my short tour of duty on Elf Hive I'd never been to any of the civilian sectors. The corps didn't want the people's romantic image of their fighting men and women blemished by marauding alcoholics in wrinkled uniforms. Compared to the stark military barracks of Elf Hive, located in an isolated corner of SecChetyre, the commercial quarters were dazzling.

Exotic was the only word to describe the people. Residents who had four or five generations of Elf Hivers behind them were pale white. Like fish trapped in a subterranean river, the colonists were losing their coloration. There wasn't much need for melanin in a place where direct sunlight would result in a lethal tan.

More eerie was the height and weight differential. The shortest of them had a good eight centimeters on me, while the heaviest massed a scant sixty kilos. Many had reinforced the elfin image by having their earlobes removed. Looking at their ethereal forms, I wondered how many generations would pass before fertile mating between Earth and Elf Hive was no longer possible.

We traveled through narrow side corridors, avoiding the congestion at the Core. On either side, motels, casinos, and seduction palaces assaulted us with bright neon and animated liquid crystal displays. At the gates of Disney's Universe a soapbox savior preached at a disinterested crowd. The taxi driver slowed down, ensuring we had time to absorb the message of God.

''. . . after the Great Flood the people said, 'Come, let us build ourselves a city and a tower with its top in the sky.' God Almighty leveled the Tower of Babel in his righteous wrath, but the cities of Babylon have risen again and built a new tower. L5 is the E-sag-ila of our day and doubt not that God will . . .'' We crept around the corner of the complex and the rest of the sermon was lost.

Outside the Hotel Saint Matthew the preacher's cataclysmic prophecy was trying to come true. An environmentalist handed out pamphlets cataloging the effects Elf Hive's neo-plastics and abundant transition metals had on Mother Earth's genetic baseline. Hardly a new issue; I can still remember the outcry after the dolphins followed the dodo and the elephants down extinction road.

According to the booklet shoved in my hand, the Gaia nuts were two General Assembly chairs away from having enough muscle to shut down trade with the Lagrange Stations. If eco-advocates got their majority in the United Nations, they would certainly proclaim Earth's massive consumer market to be forbidden fruit. Then the zero-g manufacturers would be the species facing mass extinction. In the meantime Elf Hive lived its twilight days in more than oriental splendor.

The lobby of Hotel Saint Matthew was fifty meters square by twenty high. More than anything else I saw at the hotel, it impressed me with the immense wealth of the place. In an environment where air and volume are the most precious resources, this kind of opulence must have run millions of AJs a year.

From sixteen onyx pedestals scattered about the room, marble gargoyles stared at the centerpiece of the lobby. Proteus floated a meter off the floor; a freshwater aquarium in the shape of a sphere six meters across. Between the water and surrounding air, there was nothing except surface tension and the gods of micro-gravitational physics.

Fish darted around within the water, their swim bladders orienting them away from the slightly higher pressure at the center of the sphere. Inch-long Madagascar rainbows swam along the crest of the aquarium, their colors brilliantly reflected by the sphere's internal lighting system.

A porous metallic globe a meter in diameter squatted in the center of the aquarium. An engraved plaque below Proteus explained that within the smaller orb, biological filters and low-pressure aerators kept the water from going stagnant. To prevent corrosion the ball was made of platinum, purchased from K.A.M. to the tune of 86 million Andy Jacks.

From Proteus's silvery heart, a narrow column rose to the ceiling, where two giant concave hemispheres loomed on either side. Fresh water flowed through the column, sucked down by the orb to replace water lost through evaporation.

"It's wonderful!" Miss Vandimeer's face was radiant.

"Thomas would have loved it."

She looked at me. "Your twin brother."

It wasn't the first time she'd surprised me with personal

information. But then, with Al-Kirzen's money behind her, there wasn't much I could hide.

"When we were growing up, he was always building model rockets and reading secondhand science fiction. He often talked about traveling to Mars or the Galileo colonies around Jupiter." I felt a dark mood coming on, the way it usually did when I recalled one of Thomas's unfulfilled dreams.

My sullen reflections were interrupted by a metallic grating sound over head. I looked up so quickly the reflex almost tore my slippers from the carpet. The two hemispheres were descending from their perches, closing in over Proteus.

Jessica was looking up as well. "What's happening?"

I nodded toward the plaque. "According to this, internal currents would eventually scatter Proteus's thirty-seven metric tons of water if it were not periodically remolded."

We watched until the aquarium was completely enclosed, then flagged down a ruby-uniformed bellhop to show us to our rooms. Miss Vandimeer barely glanced at her lavish suite before racing out on some private errand. In her rush she forgot to tip the bellhop; a major violation of high-society etiquette, excusable only by pleading guilty to some form of anxiety.

My subconscious must have been working on Vandimeer's mood swings because I now intuitively knew the cause. The sole communication set on the *Daedalus* was reserved for the pilot. Only a certified emergency call could reach a passenger. But here, as well as back at the airport, I would be fairly easy to contact. Why would that make Vandimeer nervous?

Tracking down Jamie took a good half hour. He had been discharged from the hospital and no one answered at his home number. I buzzed several of his favorite hangouts before it occured to me to try the office. He answered on the first ring.

"Jefferson! Thank God! I've been trying to get you all day."

"What's up?"

"I . . ." A lopsided smile ran across his face. "I don't know, really, but it's terribly important." He giggled and swiveled around on the desk chair.

"Jamie? Are you drunk?"

A series of expressions contorted his face as he struggled to compose himself. For a second I swore I saw a look of utter fear twist his features. Then he was giggling again. He picked up a marker and wrote something on a sheet of paper.

"I remember what was so important. I've got it right here."

"Show me, Jamie. Hold up the paper so I can see it."

"Nope. It's a secret." He pounded his hand down on the desk and leaned back, laughing like a madman.

"Jamie! Unless I see what's on that paper, I'm going to wring your neck when I get back."

"Can't you take a joke? You always were sour. Lighten up for a while." He picked up the paper and pressed it against the video pickup. The screen went dark.

"Jamie, pull it back a little. I can't see anything."

"That's your problem, isn't it?" He pulled the paper away and ripped it apart. But not before I saw it. A large eye encircled by concentric rings. Underneath was a series of alphanumerics: UN9976. It didn't mean anything to me.

He shook with another fit of laughter. "The secret of the universe is enclosed in Jessica Vandimeer's dress. Good-bye, Jefferson."

"No! Jamie, wait!"

He glanced up at the screen in surprise. "Hey, Kayoto. How are you doing? Where you at? I've been waiting for you all day."

"Jamie. Listen to me very carefully. Take the marker and write these numbers down." He grabbed the marker and saluted.

"Yes, sir!"

"Four four nine seven eight three—three four three four." He wrote the numbers on the desk, ignoring the paper beside him. "Good. That's the new withdrawal code for my bank account. There's plenty of cash. If you find out anything about Vandimeer, call me. You can reach me here until the I.S.S. *Far Hand* leaves port."

"I already found out everything I need to know. I told you. It's not my fault you're too busy to listen."

"What? What did you find out about her?"

"A friend of mine hid it in her dress. I asked him why and he said he did it because he felt like it. I told him I didn't think that was very funny. But you know something? It is funny. It's hysterical." He giggled for a second, and then his face went serious. "She'll kill you. She has to now. I know her secret." His voice was emotionless. Sweat was standing out on his forehead, his fingers rubbed at his temples. "I can't do it, Jefferson. I'm sorry. Good-bye." He reached for the com switch and broke the connection.

9

Like a city from the Dark Ages, Elf Hive is divided into quarters, which in turn are clustered around a central keep. Elf Hive's stronghold is the Core. As with earlier citadels, its main function is social, but in times of danger it also represents sanctuary. Theoretically, if any peripheral section of Elf was punctured, safety was guaranteed behind the bulkheads of the Core. Isn't that what they said about the notorious ocean ship, R.M.S. *Titanic*?

The Hotel Saint Matthew was in the outer ring of SecTree. I left the hotel determined to extract from Miss Vandimeer an explanation for Jamie's drugged condition.

I angled in toward the Core, stopping at the first police kiosk I saw. There was a chance my employer's wealth and a little fast talking on my part could save me a lot of footwork. It was a long shot, but the potential payoff made the slim odds worth betting on. I punched the red emergency button on the kiosk. No point in doing things halfway. "I would like to report a missing person."

The cop on the screen didn't even bother to look up. "Name and age of missing?"

"Jessica Vandimeer, about twenty-three."

"Time since last seen."

"A couple of hours."

Now the man looked. "What is this, you trying to be funny? Maybe she ran into an old friend."

"I think she's in trouble," I lied.

"Half the people up here are in trouble, what do you want me to do about it?"

I read the name on his badge. "Let me rephrase my request, Officer Valdez. My employer, Abdul Al-Kirzen, doesn't want

41

anything to happen to Miss Vandimeer. If something does happen to her, then I will make certain Mr. Al-Kirzen hears about the uncooperativeness of the Elf Hive police force.''

"Hold on, buddy. Let's not go jumping to conclusions. Give me a minute to check on her.'' The officer spoke to his computer and consulted a couple of read-outs outside my field of vision. "Nothing on emergency . . . L5 General is clear . . . nothing on the beat screens . . . passenger shuttles report no tickets under that name purchased in the last five hours.'' He game me an apologetic shrug. "I'm afraid there's not a lot I can do. Al-Kirzen's wishes or not, we can't mobilize the force for someone two hours overdue. If she's still missing in twenty-four, I can get authority for a full-scale op. Try back then.'' The screen went dead.

So much for the easy way out. Looked like I would have to dig her up by myself.

I continued inward, passing through the Plaza at Elf Hive. A series of boutiques and shops catering to the tycoons who could afford a night at one of SecTree's exclusive hotels, the Plaza was a reproduction of Mediterranean open markets. I was able to search the area quickly, but Miss Double Cross wasn't in sight.

The main level of the Core buzzed with commerce. People of all social strata, from the minimum-wage workers of SecChetyre to corporate CEOs dressed in silk and satin, carried out transactions of varying legality. I checked every dingy bar, narrow walkway, and skin theater without coming across any hint of my client.

Adjacent and counterclockwise from the hotel sector, Sec-Dyn held the hangars, warehouses, and ship-repair modules. The hangars, though huge, offered no concealment. I covered them in less than an hour and moved on to the drydocks.

Only one ship was in for repairs, an L.D.C. Boothill Express with an Ethiopian flag stenciled on the side. Technicians in full radiation suits worked around the ship's fusion reactor while a shielded pump drained mercury from the ionization chamber. Unless Jessica was suicidal, she was somewhere else.

Anemic rats, escapees from corporate bio-science labs, ran along the dusty corridors of the warehouse sector. Among their ranks were several with two tails, along with at least one who had no eyes. I wondered what advance in genetics he represented.

Checking every hallway as I moved through SecDyn, I tried each door. All were electronically sealed. Without access codes, Miss Vandimeer couldn't have gained entrance to any of them.

Micro-resolution holograms played corporate propaganda across the halls of SecDva. The ice blue demon of the Kobold Asteroid Mining Consortium held court with the augmented angel of Chin Genetics and the lemon yellow griffin of Annex Chemicals. Further down the passageway, Kamerlingh Onnes Limited played magnetic tricks with their newest line of superconducting ceramics.

If Vandimeer had inside connections with any of the thirty-two companies of Elf Hive's manufacturing district, I'd never ferret her out. The bigger fry flew their own ships and for all I knew, Traitor Jessica was headed for Luna or Ceres on a K.A.M. Consortium shuttle. If she was on the run my only chance of tracking her depended on her not having access to corporate shuttles.

Other than L5 General Hospital, SecChetyre was restricted access. There were three entrance corridors that, according to the locals, only ran one way. And once you were in, the only way out was the "polymer dress," a euphemism referring to the plastic used in body bags.

The majority of SecChetyre's volume was taken up by sleeping units for Elf Hive's working class and barracks for the Terra-Luna Corps. I'd been stationed there for a few weeks right after completing basic training. God Almighty, what a time that was.

Standard workers' contracts for Elf Hive ran twenty years. If you broke contract you forfeited every half-Jack you made, but if you made it through "the Long Score," congratulations, you're a multi-millionaire. Of course, too many people collecting the Long Score would eat into corporate profit margins. To ensure against this, the companies lined the corridors of SecChetyre with every form of entertainment their workers, and incidentally the enlisted men and women of the Terra-Luna Corps, could desire. These shops, all company owned and operated, siphoned the workers' paychecks back into corporate tills.

It must have been a red-letter day in the annals of corporate history when some psychologist pointed out that by making these shops as degenerate and depraved as possible, they could render additional protection against employees making the Long Score. Take an average group of people, put them in a confined environment, provide for every sexual fetish, offer every mind-altering drug, and see how many of them survive twenty years.

Fortunately, the good old boys in the companies provided an easy way out. When the domination stages, midnight flashbacks, and sado-whores got to be too much, you could get into an exterior service and repair capsule, called Exrecs by the locals, and blow the hatches. This is called "airing it out."

When someone cashed it in by airing it out, the Terra-Luna Corps was called in to retrieve the valuable Exrec and shepherd it back to an interior repair bay. I performed this operation so many times, I could even "shell" what was left of the body out of the capsule before bringing the mess inside. I became an expert at working the military's mechanical waldo systems. That's why I was chosen to air out Humboldt Station on Luna by blowing their hatches from the outside. For my efforts, the big brass awarded me the Crimson Star, and told me to forget about the seventy-three children who had been inside the dome.

During my time on Elf Hive, I made a number of acquaintances within SecChetyre, many of whom owed me favors. If Mink were still tending bar at Resolution Entrance, SecChetyre's sole link to the Core, she'd probably let me in long enough to look for my corrupt client. But of all the hiding holes on Elf Hive, SecChetyre seemed the longest shot for finding Vandimeer. People of Vandimeer's refined tastes tend to find its pleasures a little hard to swallow.

Having drawn a blank, I decided for one last shot at pressuring the police. This time I went to Elf Hive Security in person, knowing that if Jessica had put even a fraction of Al-Kirzen's money to use the local cops would never find her.

Contrary to all my expectations, it took them all of fifteen seconds to track her down. She was in the intensive care unit of L5 General, her condition listed as critical but stable. I was so stunned I barely noted the worried look Officer Valdez gave me as I left.

10

The duty nurse, dressed in a white halter top with long sleeves, was attractive even though her willowy height made her appear anemic. Why is it you always have to be rude to the better prospects? "What room is Jessica Vandimeer in?"

"Are you a member of her family? I'll need to see some form of I.D. before I release any room numbers. What did you say your name was?"

"Never mind." I swung her computer terminal around and typed in Jessica's name. Room 12, main level. I like computers, they try so hard to be cooperative. Too bad the same can't be said for pretty nurses.

"Sir! You can't do that! Stop!"

I ran to the room, but either by bad luck or shortcut, a balding medic wearing old-fashioned bifocals beat me to it. He carried a low-voltage riot prod. Not that he looked like the type who had the guts to use it.

Sizing up his fifty-five kilos, I took a confident step forward, my hands reaching up to disarm him. With a flick of his wrist, he lashed out with the prod and brushed my left leg. I didn't feel anything, but when I tried another step forward my foot remained glued to the velcro, my numbed leg muscles unable to pull it free.

The medic huffed himself up and waved the prod in my face. "I don't know who you are but this is a hospital. We don't tolerate uninvited people running loose in the halls. The effect of the stunning prod will wear off in a moment. When it does, you will turn around and leave. Do I make myself clear?"

Doctors think of their patents as prized possessions. I knew that, I just hadn't been thinking clearly. "I'm sorry, Doctor. I'm worried about Jessica."

"Fine, go back to the front desk and follow procedure." He spoke into a wall com. "I've got him under control, Miss Sandra. Tell the others to return to their duties." He turned back to me. "Your leg should be waking up."

I felt the nerves tingle. "Yeah, it is." I tested the leg to make sure it was strong enough to pull free from the velcro.

"And now you're going to let me in that room." I gripped the end of the prod with my left hand, closing my fingers as hard as possible. My whole arm went numb, but he had to loosen the prod from my hand before he could use it more effectively. I pivoted on my left foot, nearly losing my balance as the velcro slipper tugged at the carpet, and grabbed the handle of the prod with my good hand. He had time to inhale for a yell before I dragged the prod across his chest.

Every muscle in his body spasmed with such force he lost contact with the floor. I hastily grabbed his ankle and anchored him back to the carpet. At first I feared he was seriously injured, but his pulse was strong and even. Trust a medic to carry a non-lethal weapon. I left him sitting in the hallway and opened the door he'd been guarding.

Miss Vandimeer was under a full support system. The only sound in the room was the whisper of machines forcing air to and from her lungs. The beautiful eyes were closed, her face was white. A plastic tube carrying saline and glucose pierced her right arm. Wires snaked from under the white cotton sheet covering her, filling watchful computers with rates and pressures. I stood over her for several minutes, unaccountably finding myself remembering Jane Hamilton's similarly prone form.

"She was almost dead when we got her here." The doctor was leaning against the doorway. His voice was shaky and he looked pale, but he appeared otherwise unhurt. "She collapsed in a lift tube. No one saw it happen. At first we thought it was an epileptic seizure, but the brain activity was totally wrong. Another few seconds and we would have lost her."

"When did it happen?"

"About five o'clock Greenwich Mean."

Roughly the same time I finished the strange call to Jamie. "Where?"

"The executive lift in the Hotel Saint Matthew. We haven't ruled out the possibility of neural toxin. You here to finish the job?"

Good question. Jamie had shown all the symptoms of someone wired on a broad-spectrum hallucinogen. I knew him well enough to know he'd never take that sort of trip voluntarily. Since Al-Kirzen seemed determined to destroy my friends whatever I did, the least I could do was pay him back by removing one of his field agents.

But as my hand unconsciously moved to the Luger, my eyes were drawn to the cardiac monitor, tracing out Jessica's heartbeat in an oscillating wave. Life distilled to mathematical formula. If I pulled the gun and put a bullet in her brain, the only indication would be the wave settling to a line. The machines would continue forcing air into her lungs and pumping sugar into her blood. Juxtaposed against Vandimeer's human beauty, the thought of cold machines mimicking her life revolted me. I let the pistol drop back into its holster. "No, I'm not here to kill her."

The doctor moved to stand beside me. He brushed a lock of raven hair from her forehead. "She's very beautiful."

I handed the prod back to him. "The dangerous ones always are."

Returning Earthside was technically a breach of contract but I had more than sufficient cause. Retracing my steps to SecDyn, I picked a shuttle carrier at random. The man behind the desk took a long look at my disheveled appearance and kept one hand out of sight. Right where the police call button would be.

"I need passage on your first shuttle to Earth. Final destination isn't important." It sounded suspicious even to my ears.

"That would be Pan Am shuttle four twenty-three, direct to Saint Petersburg."

"I'll take it." Flights connecting Imperial Russia with the United States of NorthAm left hourly.

"Thirty-two thousand cr NorthAm, please. The deposit-only account number for your purchase is 113355-7799."

I took out my card and entered the amount on my new account. The insufficient funds light came on. I called for the balance. Zero; someone had drained the account. My old number yielded similar results. Without a half-Jack of credit, I was trapped on Elf Hive. I hoped Vandimeer lived long enough to regret it.

"Is there a problem?" The ticket agent wore an oily smile. He must have seen my expression.

"I appear to be broke."

"What a shame. If you want to report credit theft, there is a police kiosk down the hall to your left."

"Yeah." I didn't even feel up to wiping the condescending grin off his face.

When I got back to the Saint Matthew, where, courtesy of Vandimeer's open account, I could at least get dinner, another surprise waited for me on my suite's dining room table. A steak knife had been thrust deep into the mahogany, pinning a note to the scarred wood.

THE LORD YOUR GOD EXECUTES JUSTICE FOR THE ORPHAN AND THE WIDOW, AND BEFRIENDS THE ALIEN, FEEDING AND CLOTHING HER. SO YOU TOO MUST BEFRIEND THE ALIEN.

It read like the Old Testament, something out of the Pentateuch, perhaps. The second reference to the Bible in one day was too much to be coincidence. Someone had been watching earlier when our taxi had passed the preacher. The same person could break into my room at will. This was his way of letting me know I was under scrutiny by people way out of my league.

The cause of this unwanted attention wasn't hard to find. The female pronoun in the passage stuck out like a sore thumb, an obvious substitution with Miss Vandimeer as the object. I had a nagging feeling there were other, hidden warnings within the text, but I was too tired to play cryptographer.

11

A message tagged "urgent" was waiting on-screen the following morning. Miss Vandimeer was conscious and wanted to talk as soon as possible. All things considered, breakfast seemed more important. I ordered real eggs and charged them to Vandimeer's open account. The amount, sizable as it seemed to me, probably wouldn't even register on Al-Kirzen's books.

I also took the chance to do a thorough job of searching Miss Vandimeer's luggage; all thirteen suitcases. There were a number of things of interest, but only one was important. A scrap of paper torn on three sides. The only words left were, "not Rhea. Kill her." I put it in my pocket and headed for L5 General.

Walking through the Core, I considered what few alternatives were left. It took a depressingly short time. Without credit, getting home was impossible. Worse yet, there was no way Jamie and I could reach one another. Even assuming he was safe, which didn't seem likely, he didn't have the thousands of AJs it would take to contact me up here. My relatively short conversation with him had set me back 1,200 Andy Jacks. That had been back in the good old days, when I'd been rich.

When had the Jacks disappeared from my account? It had been there when I was talking to Jamie, otherwise the circuit would have automatically cut off as soon as my balance reached zero. Sometime between the screen conversation and my attempt to get off the station someone had infiltrated my account. The bad news was, prime suspect looks to have been incapacitated and on her way to L5 General at the time of the heist.

My second visit to the hospital was very different from the first. The male nurse at the admission desk had my name on his computer, and was only too eager to point the way to Vandimeer's room. The doctor I'd encountered the previous night was still attending the machines encircling Miss Vandimeer.

"Leave us." Her voice was a scratchy whisper.

He looked at me suspiciously. "Are you sure that's wise, Miss Vandimeer?"

"Your concern for my well-being is commendable, Doctor, but I will speak with this man in private." The medic appeared ready to argue further, but he abruptly turned and left, closing the door softly behind him.

"He said you came here last night. He thought you wanted to kill me." She looked better this morning; some color was returning to her face.

"The idea occurred to me." I couldn't see any reason to lie.

"Why didn't you?" Despite her helpless state, there was no

apprehension in her voice. She watched me carefully while I considered my answer.

"Couldn't see the advantage of it. Today, though, I think I might."

"Can I at least know the reason?" If she felt any fear, she hid it well.

"Why are your goons feeding Jamie hallucinogens? The deal was I follow orders, he's left out of it."

"Jefferson, I swear to you, I don't know anything about it."

"Just like you don't know anything about my bank accounts being drained?"

"No, you're right, I lied about that. But I couldn't stop it from happening. I told them it would only make things worse."

"Told who?"

"Al-Kirzen has agents on Tycho Luna who have cracked IBN's access code."

"I was told that's impossible. You'll have to do better."

"They did it with a Cray AI. It stays in IBN's data cores by upgrading its own programming to match IBN's changing access codes."

I didn't know enough about computers to assess whether or not Vandimeer's explanation was feasible, but after my conversation with Holly I doubted it. Not that confronting Jessica with my skepticism would do me any good. On the other hand, she'd just provided me with a ticket home. "So you can take money out of any account you wish?"

"Yes. My employer finds it a useful tool to bargain with."

"In other words, I'll never get any money out of this."

"I don't know what Al-Kirzen will do."

I did, but it was hardly the end of the world. I'd been screwed before. "Well, I damn well know what I'm going to do. The deal's off, Miss Vandimeer. Reimburse me for my time, and I'll be going back to Earth."

"You can't do that!"

"Wrong again. I've been in your employ for the last day and a half without any pay. Any judge who sees the evidence will award me enough money to get home. If Al-Kirzen wants to mess with that, it's his own funeral. I don't know if you're up on recent history, but ever since the Carte Blanche Purge, the U.N. Justice Department doesn't peddle to rich snobs."

"No, Kayoto, you don't understand. Your comrades on

Earth will be killed. Al-Kirzen's men will ice them before you can give them warning."

I grabbed her by the shoulders and shook her roughly across the bed. "I don't see how either my friends or I have much to lose. What have they done to Jamie? Tell me!"

She was crying now, an old ploy that doesn't work on me. "I don't know, Kayoto, I really don't. But at least he's alive. He won't be if you go back."

She was right. I don't have the resources to protect anyone against Al-Kirzen. If Jamie was going to have any chance at all, I was going to have to be a good boy. I released Miss Vandimeer, wondering why the increased tempo on her heart monitor hadn't brought the medic back in.

"The doc thought you might have been poisoned. Any idea who could have done it?"

"No, I don't remember anything. I was coming back to the hotel and the next thing I knew, I was here." The same experience Jamie had. But why had the technique been applied to Vandimeer? Wheels spinning within wheels, most of them behind my back. As soon as possible I'd have to squeeze the facts out of pretty Jessica.

She reached up and clasped my arm. "I'm sorry it's turning out like this."

I shrugged away from her touch. "So am I, but your excuses don't cut it. The last thing I need is fabricated sympathy."

She looked away, but composed herself quickly. "Our plans haven't changed. We leave for Saturn in three days. Now go, I'm tired."

I spotted him the next day, trailing me through the Plaza. He was a professional, but the closed environment of Elf Hive made spying difficult. Standing under the green-and-white striped eaves of a fruit vendor, he was a tall, bland-looking man, the type of person you'd pass a hundred times a day without noticing.

I gambled on one close pass. He was as average as he first appeared in all respects except one; his voice, which I overheard as he bargained with the vendor, was electronically synthesized. I'd never heard a chip voice and would never forget the flat and emotionless tone of this one. I risked several more covert glances from a distance, but my observations didn't tell me anything about who he was or who he worked for.

I spent the remainder of the afternoon—a subjective and depressingly artificial time of day on Elf Hive—at the Hotel Saint Matthew's space window, Orpheus. Despite the pretentious name, it had very little to recommend it. Orpheus was an eight-meter oval of plexiglass encased in a mesh of titanium wire, while the Window Lounge was a claustrophobic chamber buffered from the hotel by pressure bulkheads and quick-seal airlocks.

Even with the elaborate safety precautions, the port had shattered twice in its short history. Three people had been sucked outward and shredded against the titanium web when a derelict satellite collided with the window. Another seven had gone the same way when a South Carolina Confederate Separatist duplicated the incident with an Exrec.

I stood with my nose an inch away from the port and watched the continents spin through the terminator into dawn. It was the first time in my life I'd ever felt homesick.

12

I slid a pair of Coke bottle glasses on and stepped to the front desk of the Croesus. Since breakfast, I'd visited fourteen of Elf Hive's twenty-one hotels with nothing to show for it.

"Excuse me," I whined at the clerk, "my name is Hanover Wilson. I'm the personal assistant to Dr. Elshi Kent, a noted planetologist who passed through L5 four weeks ago. She recently discovered some documents were missing, and has reason to believe she lost them on the station."

"And you think the papers might be here?"

I tried to look embarrassed. "I'm afraid Elshi is the absentminded scientist who defined the stereotype. She doesn't remember the name of the hotel she stayed in. Would you be so kind as to check?"

"Of course." He entered a few lines on his computer. "Ah yes, you're in luck. Dr. Kent was with us on the ninth and tenth of last month. I'm not aware of anything found in her room, but let me ring the maid who works that wing so we can be sure.''

A grossly overweight woman wearing liters of makeup answered the clerk's page. From what I understood of Elf Hive's sexual mores she, being a scarce commodity because of her massive dimensions, would be in great demand. Maybe that's why her voice was pitched in bedroom tones. ''I remember Miss Kent, but her room was empty when she left.''

''Do you have any idea where she spent her time on the station?''

The woman gave me a suspicious look. ''I don't think she left her room at all. There's not much to do on Elf Hive for a ninety-year-old woman bound to a wheelchair from multiple sclerosis.''

So. Discounting the possibility that Jessica was a consummate actress, she had lied about passing through Elf Hive under the name of Elshi Kent. Was it too much to ask for clients to be truthful about false names? I beat a quick exit before the maid could start with the embarrassing questions.

With nothing worthwhile waiting in my room, I took Metal Voice, who'd accompanied me through the morning's venture, for a tour of Elf Hive. In the dense press of the Core, I tried several rudimentary ditching ruses to no effect. Whoever Metal Voice worked for, he was good.

I took revenge on him by dragging him into a holographic reenactment of last century's *Queen of Night* debacle. I snoozed for the first two hours, while the *Queen* crept out to Jupiter and started her voyage home. The Dolby reproduction of Capt. Indigo Caruthers blowing the *Queen*'s hatches startled me into wakefulness. His six-man crew had time for one gestalt shriek of horror before the end.

The director panned through the lifeless ship, finishing his work in the captain's cabin. The camera zoomed to a tight focus on the now-famous Amazon River documentary playing an endless loop to the dead ship. From my days in school, I remembered the psychologists of the time blamed Caruthers's madness on ''unsuccessful adaptation syndrome,'' as if ''cabin crazy'' were too conventional.

I left the holotheater depressed with the knowledge that the *Far Hand* would have to travel almost twice the distance of the *Queen of Night*. My tail followed me back to the Hotel Saint Matthew, absentmindedly munching on a bag of popcorn.

As I stripped for bed that night, a crumpled piece of paper fell from my jeans. I unfolded it and held it under the room's reading light. "Holovision. 12:30 am Greenwich Mean. Channel 56." The note could have been put in my pocket anytime during the day. It was the kind of stunt to impress upon people how little freedom they had. A cheap but highly effective ploy.

Channel 56 was twenty-four-hour news. It catered to the kind of sensationalism that had made Sleaze's employers wealthy. Half an hour after midnight, they broadcast an attempted escape from a U.N. MaxSec. The prison's cameras replayed the blown escape in slow motion while the newswoman's liquid voice took delight in the details.

"Amber Whitehorse, former employee of Al-Kirzen Atomics, United States of NorthAm Yellowknife division, was lasered down earlier this evening while trying to escape from the United Nations' U.S.N.A. Eastern Seaboard holding facility. Miss Whitehorse was scheduled for deportation to Triton after being convicted of possession of a DeSole Anti-Personnel Radiation Sling, more familiarly known as a 'bone cooker.' Amber Whitehorse was the five thousand seven hundred twenty-fourth prisoner to die in U.N. holding facilities this year." The holo flashed to a close-up of Whitehorse's face, and even without her black-on-black eyes, I'd recognized her immediately as the woman I had confronted outside my office.

Replayed from a different angle, the MaxSec's security cameras tracked Whitehorse as she sprinted across a muddy courtyard and sprang up a section of razor fence. She was a good ten meters off the ground, her hands already trailing ribbons of flesh, when the automatic perimeter system kicked in. A hydrogen fluoride combat laser caught her in the crotch and stroked up to her head. There wasn't much left on the fence when the laser shut down.

As I watched the scene, replayed several more times in slow motion, certain details caught my attention. First, the woman I'd parried with outside my office had been cool and intelligent; hardly the type to make the fatal mistake of trying to outsmart lasers mounted with motion sensors. Second, the woman climbing the fence had leaped from the ground off her right foot, and she reached higher up with her right hand. I still had an ugly bruise on the right side of my neck to show that the woman who had attacked me had been a southpaw.

Notwithstanding the gruesome evidence of the camera, my

guess was that Miss Whitehorse was still among the living. The woman on the fence was one of Abdul's less useful pawns made over to look the part. For a man of Al-Kirzen's influence, switching the two women would have been a simple matter of thinly veiled threats greased with an easy flow of money.

Still, Abdul's effort to save Whitehorse indicated she was an integral part of his organization. Not that her name would appear on any payroll spreadsheet. She was one of the hidden elite; a corporate counteragent or assassin.

I wasn't sure about Mr. Metal Voice, or why he was following me around like a lost puppy, but Whitehorse's presence clearly indicated the kind of people I was playing with. I wondered if they'd finished off Jamie.

Miss Vandimeer was discharged from L5 General eight hours before the *Far Hand* was due to disembark. She was pale and her movements were shaky. It was hard to keep hating someone in such obvious misery, but I remembered how Holly had been dealt with and managed it.

13

A lackey from the hotel fetched our luggage and we rode another platinum taxi to SecDyn and the Intra-System Ships' passenger docks. I sat beside Vandimeer, my thoughts leaden with the realization that even if I found who was killing the children on Rhea, the billion kilometers that separated Earth and Saturn meant well over a year would pass before I could return to the Terra-Luna System.

With fatalistic acceptance I walked down the royal purple carpet that led to the *Far Hand*'s five-meter-tall exterior hatches. A man decked out as a nineteenth-century African explorer ran a computer check on my passport and first-class ticket, twirled his handlebar mustache, and waved me aboard the ship. My prison for the next seven months.

Passing through the exterior airlocks, I followed Jessica

along a somber gray passage that pierced the ship's ten-meter-thick outer hull. We stepped through the interior airlocks into a dazzling hallway of polished bronze. Oversized rivet heads rippled along the seams of the metal plating, each one buffed to scintillate in the red neon lighting. Eight meters into this hallway two corridors branched off, curving around the cylindrical ship to meet on the other side. A placard identified them as access ways to rooms 1-B1 through 1-B8.

Jessica continued on straight until the corridor opened into a large circular arena, forty meters in diameter. Like the hallway we had come from, the room was plated in bronze. Off to the left, a large neon sign depicted a muscle-bound giant straining to push a boulder, half again his size, up an impossible incline. A glowing sign marked him as Sisyphus, and the bronze arena he presided over as level one: Exercise Chamber.

Along the arena's gleaming circular wall were four doors, spaced ninety degrees apart, leading to suites 1-A1 through 1-A4. Between the suites, four corridors, one of which we were standing in, led back to rooms in the B ring.

Jessica stepped into Sisyphus with a grimace. Every passenger was required to spend at least half an hour a day here, working up a sweat under the watchful eye of the *Far Hand*'s medical staff. A necessary evil to prevent muscle and bone atrophy during prolonged periods of low gravity.

Scattered about the room were chrome friction-controlled weight machines and gilded magnetic induction exercycles. Along with the more traditional equipment there were ten workout tables, their electrodes dangling in zero-g like coiled vipers. Offerings made to appease the malevolent gods of weightlessness.

"The one arena on every luxury cruiser you never see in the brochures." Jessica pointed to one of the tables. "You ever tried one of these?"

I shook my head.

"Don't." She didn't elaborate.

We wove around the equipment to the elevator tube, a thick metal column in the middle of the room. The tube shot through the ceiling of Sisyphus; an alloy spinal cord running the length of the *Far Hand*. We stepped in and Miss Vandimeer told the attendant to take us to level seven.

On the way up I noted that a code was required to take the elevator to the three second-class levels located below level one. No doubt the scientists, administrators, engineers, and miners—the unfortunates who would be taking positions on one of the Outer System moons—found it equally hard to reach the first-class levels. Their living arrangements must have been appalling to warrant such strict separation from those of us moving through the opulence of first class.

The doors opened on the *Far Hand*'s main ballroom, the Morpheus. The circular room was finished in a reflective metallic surface tinted cobalt blue. Dotted along the walls and ceiling were silver constellations and comets. The floor was 5,000 square meters of black lucite, slick and so polished we could see our reflections walking below us.

Directly across from us, a neon image of the god of dreams presided over a digital clock with glowing azure numbers. The display counted off the seven hours remaining until departure from Elf Hive. Jessica walked to door 7-A3, pulled an old-fashioned metal key from her coat pocket, and let us into our suite.

The decor was cherry wood accented with fine Italian marble. Incandescent wall globes, spaced between reproductions of pre-atomic art, glowed with warm light. A partition running radially from the door to the back wall split the suite in two. A mahogany door fitted with dead bolts on both sides provided access between the rooms. With a wave of her hand, Miss Vandimeer indicated the starboard rooms were mine.

"I chose this divided suite as being the best suited for our travels. Now, if you'll excuse me, I want to get settled in." She went through the door and pulled the dead bolt.

My section of the suite was easily three times the size of my office. Along the port wall, a full-sized bar stocked with the genuine article sat under a reproduction of an Edvard Munch engraving. The outer curved wall was taken up by a king-size bed, a bathroom, and a small kitchen. My duffel had been left on the bed. Apparently the porters hadn't known what to do with it.

I mixed up an approximation of an old-fashioned in a plastic bulb and sat down in front of the room's meter-square holotank. I flipped through 340 channels of junk before coming across images picked up by the *Far Hand*'s exterior optical array. Using the holo's input keyboard, I centered the display on Earth. Somewhere under the rack of clouds curling up the Atlantic coastline was home.

Six and a half hours later a tiny jolt announced the *Far Hand* had reversed her magnetic field and cleared Elf Hive's alnico docking grapples. The room's red "secure" light flashed on and I dug my fingers into the thick carpet. A quick series of sharp velocity changes pulled me in several different directions as eight bulky Insys tugs muscled the *Far Hand*'s 485,000 metric tons of mass into its trajectory window.

Our insertion complete, a battery of red HeNe lasers shot out from Elf Hive and stroked the surface of the *Far Hand*. They played randomly across the ship for a minute before synchronizing and shooting off toward the ashen yellow point of Saturn. Send-off complete, the *Far Hand*'s mass converters rumbled to life. Two hundred meters below me, streams of ionized particles flowed from the ship's seven rhenium thrust chambers.

From a dead stop, the *Far Hand* reached its cruising acceleration of .01695 meters per second squared in less than a minute. The ever-increasing velocity pushed me against the suite's floor, giving me slightly under .002 my natural weight. Enough gravity so with the greatest of care it was possible to drink from a glass, but not enough to rid the toilets of their damn suction fans.

I locked the door to Miss Vandimeer's rooms and called up the aft camera's panorama of Earth. Baja Island spun into view, guarding the southern end of the verdant algae farms of Needles Bay. Sunlight touched the Pacific and the ocean answered in luminous shades of deep blue. Hypnotized by the dark hues of the water and the almost fluorescent tints of the atmosphere, I fixed another drink and watched the planet spin below me.

Clouds hanging over the scattered archipelagoes of Indonesia were peeking over the eastern edge of the planet when I heard Miss Vandimeer knock several times on the door that separated our rooms. I ignored her and drank myself into oblivion.

I awoke sometime later with saliva flooding my mouth and my stomach heaving in the weak gravity. I rushed to the bathroom, several times flying off the floor when my inexperienced muscles pushed too hard. The sickness relented only when my stomach was empty. Pulling myself to my feet, I passed a mirror full of tangled hair and swollen eyes.

The holo was still focused on Earth. A data window at the bottom of the display placed the ship's outward velocity relative to the sun at a meager 518.67 meters per second. We had traveled just under 8,000 kilometers in eight and a half hours. A digital readout counted down the hours left in the voyage: 5,103. Shit.

Staring blankly at the readouts, I became aware of a hushed whisper from Miss Vandimeer's room. I pulled the dead bolt on my side and opened the door.

Jessica was sitting up in bed, her arms wrapped around her knees. A static charge had built on her hair, causing it to swirl out on the weak gravity. Green eyes looked at me from behind a mane of silky black strands. A ghost of a smile touched her lips.

"Didn't your dear old mum tell you never to enter a room without knocking?" I saw that she had been crying; the sound that had drawn me into her room.

"You want to talk about it?" It was a dirty trick. Wait until your client gets emotional, then pump her for information.

"No." She brushed the hair from in front of her face. Tiny sparks jumped as her fingers grounded the electrical charge. She tried another smile. "You look terrible."

"Thanks. You wouldn't have a mint, would you?"

"I'll get one." She uncurled with feline grace and walked across the room. I noticed for the first time she was naked, her lithe profile enticing in the dusky light. Unaccountably, I found myself blushing. I hadn't gone jittery at the sight of a woman since my fifteenth birthday.

She handed me a white lozenge and then, amazingly, she was against me, her fingers tightly entwined in the front of my shirt. "I hate it out here."

I put my arms around her shoulders and turned up the charm. With a little luck, I'd finally get some answers.

"You can always go back to Earth when this is over."

"No. I can never go back." Her voice was warm and wet on my chest.

"Don't be silly, you can do anything you want."

She was quiet, fighting a sudden onset of shivers. After a period that might have been hours, she whispered, "He's crazy, I know he is. He'll kill me when he discovers I love another man."

So many things I could have said to that. Comforting words another man would have spoken were lost in a moment.

"Who? Al-Kirzen? What do you mean?"

She looked up with a start and pushed herself away. Watch how skillfully she composes herself. See how swiftly the wall grows back around her. "Thank you, I'm much better now. Please leave." So much for Kayoto charm. I walked back to my room, shutting the door softly behind me.

Mother Earth still floated in the holotank, the image seeming to grow smaller with each passing second. The data window showed our distance at 18,500 kilometers and our velocity at 793.26 meters per second. I fell asleep on the floor, my knees tucked up to my chest in the fetal crouch of low-g sleep.

14

The LCD clock read 11:45 A.M. Greenwich Mean. The *Far Hand*'s aft camera had switched over to a view of the sun. Old Sol looked a little green through the camera's tungsten filters. A group of spots, cancerous lesions on an aging star, darkened the Southern Hemisphere.

Groaning with stiff muscles, I stepped into the shower chamber and turned the hot water on full. I had three minutes of scalding bliss before the red water usage light blinked on. I ignored it and thirty seconds later the water shut off of its own accord.

I entered my breakfast from a computer menu and a handsome young boy brought it to me on a gold tray. He looked tired and haunted. I'd heard the serving crew was under orders to obey every whim of the passengers. I wondered how he'd passed the night.

I was still sipping on a mug of hot tea when a timid knock sounded on the outer door. I didn't bother getting up. "Come in."

A girl, her red hair pulled back in a businesslike ponytail, stepped in. A triangular yellow medical patch had been sewn on the right breast pocket of her uniform. "It's time for your workout, Mr. Kayoto. If you'll follow me down to Sisyphus?"

Just what I needed after last night; a strenuous workout.
"And if I don't choose to exercise today?"

She put on a grin. "Then I'll call a couple of big burly
orderlies and have them drag you down. It would be a lot easier
if you came with me. It's really not that bad."

The exercise arena was filled with sweating and swearing
people. Waiting lines had formed behind each of the workout
tables. A woman was strapped down on the one closest to me,
electrode patches pasted across her naked body. She grimaced
as a small current alternately juiced opposing sets of muscle,
flopping her around the table like a high school biology
experiment. Her eyes screwed tightly shut as the machine took
control of her body. Even without Miss Vandimeer's advice, I
would have avoided the tables at all costs.

I opted for a bike fitted with a magnetic resistance flywheel.
The medic wrapped a blood pressure cuff on my arm and a hold
belt around my waist. "We'll begin with minimum resistance."

I started pedaling, finding it surprisingly easy. But as the
young girl measured my pulse, she added current to the flywheel. The induced magnetic field of the wheel fought with
fixed ceramic magnets arranged around the rim. Soon I was
covered with sweat as she gauged my performance and forced
me to work at my maximum potential.

"Your records indicate you had to take calcium boosters on
Elf Hive. While we do have a weak gravitational field aboard
the *Far Hand,* enough so that I don't think we need to worry
about a Chibis suit, you will have to continue with the calcium
treatment."

"Back in the old days, they used to kill bearers of bad
news."

I was rewarded with a brazen smile. "I know the shots are
painful, but for people of your genetic makeup bone atrophy
follows an exponential curve."

"Meaning I'm outmoded?"

"Not in my book."

Unconsciously responding to her flattery, I pedaled harder,
only belatedly realizing how smoothly she had manipulated
me. I gave her a sour stare. "How many years of psychology
did you take to get this job?"

"None. I was being sincere."

I took in her figure and estimated her age at sixteen, maybe younger. "Aren't you a little young to be making passes?"

This brought forth a giggle that pushed her age back several months. "You are new at planetary travel, aren't you?"

"What's that have to do with it?"

"Ever heard of UAS?"

"Unsuccessful adaptation syndrome."

"That's it. After the *Queen of Night* came back with a crew of corpses, the mind gurus spent several years studying human reactions in closed societies. Went to Java and Brazil to study native cultures. They discovered loose sexual mores were one of the keys to beating UAS. Things can't get much looser than on the *Far Hand*."

Amazing what the human mind is capable of rationalizing. The last sexual revolution goes stale, so we build a new one, this time in the name of science, for the sake of mental health. As long as it serves to hide real motives and gloss over everyone's least wholesome perversions, it works. It occurred to me that this loose code of conduct had more to do with the *Far Hand*'s success, at least as far as first-class was concerned, than any real interest in touring the Outer System.

"Come on, Jefferson, you're slacking off."

"What's your name?"

"Sandra, and in answer to your next question: yes, I have to do this every day, too, so I know exactly what it's like."

"Serves you right. Have you dragged my cabin mate down here yet?"

"You mean Miss Vandimeer? She was here at seven. She did her half hour before I was on duty."

"Figures." I sucked in a few gulps of air before continuing. "Any idea where she is now?"

"Sorry. I can have her paged if you need to see her."

"No, that won't be necessary." Why should I care anyway?

Sandra put me through another ten minutes of upper-body exercises before letting me go. I was given two minutes in the communal showers, then herded to a dressing room. Sandra was waiting with fresh clothes. I dressed, trying to ignore her appraising look. I took my time going back to my room, trying to convince myself I was sightseeing and not looking for anybody.

The level directly above Sisyphus housed, in addition to its four suites and eight rooms, the ship's botanical gardens, called

Elysium Fields. This arena was a riot of colorful flowers and lush, green leaves. The walls, plant holders, and benches were intricately designed wrought iron. Cobblestone walkways meandered around Elysium's flora, dividing the area into six small ecosystems. As the *Far Hand*'s voyage lingered on, I found myself drawn to this level and its small slice of Earth.

Level three held the *Far Hand*'s secondary ballroom, the Bellerophon. By chance it was completely empty when I passed through, its copper walls sterile and cold.

Directly above was Tantalus, the ship's cafeteria and dining hall. I stopped for a sandwich and a glass of ice water. Three tables away, my shadow with the digital throat ate caviar and sipped at some chocolate-colored drink. He caught my eye and smiled.

Mnemosyne, the ship's library, was on level five. Neglected books sat next to idle microfiche readers and holographic databases. A man old enough to be my grandfather snoozed in an overstuffed chair, the latest issue of *Aphrodite* folded over his ample stomach. Reliving the conquests of youth.

In contrast, the next level, Icarus, was the most popular area on the ship. Here people donned mechanical wings of delicate aluminum feathers glossed in candy colors, and took to the skies. Jessica was there, swooping gracefully around less capable fliers, her arms easily working the wings' controlling surfaces. She flapped in my direction, swooping down until her stomach was only centimeters off the floor. When she was so close it seemed she must hit me, she pulled the wings forward, cupping them against the air. I saw muscles tighten above her pink sports bra as the wings grabbed hold and her speed dropped. She was a quarter meter away when the wings brought her upright in a stall and set her gently on the floor. Her face was flush with exertion and excitement.

"Good afternoon! You look much better today."

"The wonders of modern science and a half hour under the none too gentle hands down on the exercise arena."

She flashed her easy smile. "Look, Kayoto . . . Jefferson. I'm sorry about last night. I don't know what I was thinking."

"My fault as much as yours. Why don't you take me to dinner tonight and we'll talk about it?"

"From any other man, I consider that a come-on. From you, it sounds like an invitation to a cross-examination. You never give up, do you?"

"Sorry. Blame it on instinct."

"I'll forgive you only if you're the one who gets dinner. If you can act the proper old-fashioned gentleman, you'll probably have more luck weaseling information out of me."

"Deal. Meet me at our suite at seven-thirty?"

She nodded, pulled her cinnabar wings down with a snap, and shot straight up. With a final smile at me, she turned and looped around the arena.

I continued on my tour, more out of stubbornness than any real desire. Skipping level seven, I went up to Minos, a huge maze that filled level eight's entire arena. The labyrinth was built with movable plexiglass panels that slid on a webwork of cadmium yellow rails. Every day, the paths winding around the three-dimensional maze shifted and changed. New passages opened up, while other routes became dead ends. For an extra ten Andy Jacks you could purchase a ball of twine and solve the maze in the classical manner.

Somewhere in the twisting pathways, a holographic minotaur caught sight of a group of passengers and roared with hungry delight. I looked through the translucent panels and saw a potbellied man chugging away from the bull-headed illusion. Anyone "caught" by the monster would be pulled from the maze by one of the numerous attendants and forced to start over. I waited for the inevitable end before moving on, an anticlimactic moment when the man ran out of energy and stood panting while the minotaur closed in.

The next level held Aesculapius. The walls were titanium white, hiding speakers overflowing with soft Muzak. The twelve cabins on level nine were reserved for blue-hairs and others needing constant medical attention.

Beyond the medical deck, access was restricted to the crew. It was the only place on the *Far Hand* they could escape the wanton appetites of the passengers.

15

The serving crew put the finishing touches on the six-course meal spread out on my table. With a final flourish, the head waiter set a bottle of champagne in an ice bucket and quietly left. I pulled out a chair for Miss Vandimeer and motioned for her to take a seat.

"I thought you were going to take me out."

I slid her chair to the table. "Considering all we have to discuss, I decided privacy was more appropriate." I took the covers off several plates. "To be honest, though, I've never faced a dinner like this. I have no idea what comes first."

Vandimeer laughed. "Some kind of host you are. Here, start with this." She handed me a plate of reddish soup and I got a good look at an angry bruise on the back of her right hand.

"How is your hand doing? As I recall, it was in a full cast the night you first came to see me."

She rubbed at the bruise with her other hand, a motion more to conceal than comfort. "Much better."

I took a slurp of soup, careful to note which spoon Jessica was using. It was smooth and delicious. "You know, of course, I'm hardly going to let it rest at that."

"I suppose not, but I'm afraid you'll be disappointed. Coming from a moon with comparatively little mass, I was not prepared for Earth's gravity. I tripped while stepping from the *Star Rider*'s surface shuttle and found my reflexes sadly inadequate for the speed at which your planet pulled me down."

A likely enough occurrence, except that I knew Jessica hadn't been on the *Star Rider*—an aged scientist named Elshi Kent had been the only female from the Saturn System—and that the next flight carrying a female passenger from the Saturn

System had been the *Manx*. It had reached the Terra-Luna System thirteen months before the *Rider*. Long enough for broken bones to be out of a cast.

"And here I was suspecting something sinister. What comes after the soup?" She uncovered a dish of meat that had a slight fishy flavor.

"If you're going to ruin dinner by being inquisitive rather than romantic, it's only fair that I get to ask a few questions."

I wiped greasy fingers on my jeans before remembering the linen napkin folded over my other leg. "Ask away."

"Where did you run across Jamie?"

"I found him in the city's sewers three days after he'd escaped from a U.N. orphanage. His parents had been strangled by his older sister, a telepath whose career was ended by a U.N. police sergeant who emptied an Uzi into her head. Most people in the orphanage didn't care to associate with a boy who had the ill fortune to be related to a freak. Jamie was seven years old when the orphanage's master locked him in a closet. Fortunately the back wall was rotted and he was able to kick his way out."

"Considering how balanced he appears to be, I never would have guessed. Of course, your story leads one to wonder what exactly it was you were doing down in the sewer at the time."

"Too bad you've already asked your question. What should I eat next?"

"The fruit salad, but not before you take a drink to clear the palate. Was that your question, or did you have something deeper in mind?"

I went to the computer console and ordered the machine to pull up the passenger list. After some fiddling around, I got a picture of Metal Voice. The computer identified him as Frederick Guring. "You know this guy?"

"Except for the fact he followed us up from Earth, I have no idea who he is. He certainly doesn't work for Al-Kirzen."

"Fair enough." I took it on faith she was lying.

"The main course is next, use the dinner fork." I waited to see which fork she meant before digging into a gamey-tasting bird covered with gelatinous sauce. We ate in silence for several minutes before she spoke again.

"What are the chances of us getting romantically involved before we reach Saturn?"

Jessica was smiling, her green eyes studying me. I cleared

my throat to cover the sudden suspicion that she knew exactly where my thoughts were leading. "I don't know. Too many variables."

"A typically calculated answer, I should have expected it. Don't you ever loosen up?"

"Not when I feel my life is on the line, no."

"Just curious." She licked her fingers and uncovered a dish of chocolate pastries. Finally, something recognizable. I took a couple and leaned back.

"An understandable trait. You know, I was so curious back on Elf Hive that I went through your baggage." Now, why had I said that? People are rightfully protective of their personal property, and antagonized women are rarely helpful.

"Really? Did you find anything interesting, or were you just sniffing panties?"

She was good, but I could play this game too. "No, I wasn't after your underwear. I employ several thirteen-year-old girls who mail their used garments to me."

"Charming. I realize your metabolism isn't used to Greenwich Mean but the evening is wearing on, and I'm feeling tired. Could we carry on this wonderful conversation in the morning?" Her voice had gone cold, a sure sign I was onto something.

"I wanted to ask about a scrap of paper I found in one of your dress pockets. It must have been caught in the fabric and stuck there when you threw the rest away. Would you like to hear what it says?"

"Do I have a choice?"

"Jamie thought it was pretty important. He managed to let me know you were hiding something in your clothing. A pretty amazing feat, considering the pharmaceuticals your thugs have been force-feeding him, don't you think?"

"Mr. Kayoto, we've been over this ground before."

Why did she always bring out the worst of me? "No we haven't! Not nearly enough! I haven't forgotten what Al-Kirzen has done." So much for pleasant after-dinner conversation.

"The message, Mr. Kayoto? The one you're so anxious to acquaint me with?"

My anger doesn't usually include a short fuse, but Miss Vandimeer was good at lighting it off. I took another chocolate from the pastry dish and worked my temper under control.

"Considering our relationship so far, you take a lot of chances."

"Not at all. You're not the type to slap women around."

"You might be surprised. The paper in your dress pocket read, 'not Rhea. Kill her.' Any idea what it means?"

"Yes. The woman who was watching your office was a merc hired by Al-Kirzen. Her name is Amber Whitehorse. Apparently she has since become disenchanted with the arrangements. She recently turned on us and has become somewhat of an embarrassment. The full message told me Miss Whitehorse was no longer taking orders from Al-Kirzen's people on Rhea and I was to kill her before she caused my employer any more problems."

"I don't see you as a hired gun."

"You might be surprised."

"Is there any possibility she's behind New Mecca's escalating infant mortality rate?"

"No."

"You sound very sure of that."

"My employer checked her out very carefully. I was told she was clean."

"And yet you were sent to kill her. You will excuse me for saying so, but that sounds very odd. Were you successful?"

"She was being held in a MaxSec. I led her to believe that Al-Kirzen had bribed the warden to power down the perimeter defenses. She attempted to escape with predictable results."

After that fine piece of prevarication, there wasn't much to say. We finished dinner with a tiny bowl of salad, a poor dessert for someone used to finishing his meals with sucrose. Jessica excused herself as soon as she was finished, but as she opened the door back to her rooms she turned to me. "Jefferson, I have one more question."

"Shoot."

"How much of what I told you do you believe?"

"None of it, actually."

"I'm glad. I'd hate to think I'd dined with an idiot. I do have one sincere thing to say, if you're interested in hearing it."

"Couldn't hurt."

"There will come a time when you will suspect me of carrying out the most heinous of crimes against you. I want you to know that whatever happens, I never forced anything on you. What happens between us, if anything, will be natural."

"I don't understand."

"You will." And she was out the door. I was left with chilled champagne, a lot of questions, and a hollow feeling for what the night might have been.

16

If, during the following weeks, I was out of place on the *Far Hand,* Miss Vandimeer was right at home. She wined and dined with the best of them. Every other night, she'd slip into a new dress from Paris or Havana and parade around Morpheus and Bellerophon. Since my room had a window looking out on Morpheus, I saw her several times gliding across the ballroom floor. It didn't seem to bother her in the slightest that most of the men hanging on her elbow were twice her age.

For the first month and a half of the voyage we barely spoke to one another. She seemed to have withdrawn from me after our dinner, and several times I could have sworn she took great pains to avoid me. And if the male voices I heard coming from her room were any indication, she had other things on her mind than talking about the deaths of several children.

I took my cue from her and tried to forget about the case. Luckily, my rooms had several distractions, including a Holographic Virtual Reality Bubble. I had never been in Jamie's HVRB, but on the *Far Hand* it was one of the few escapes I had. I spent countless hours in an old-model F-15C Eagle shooting down French-built Mirages over the white beaches and deep blue waters of the Mediterranean.

The machine's library also contained a number of pornographic templates. I tried it once, stopping suddenly when I realized I'd programed my partner as a physical duplicate of Jessica Vandimeer, right down to her limp.

The rest of my time was taken up on Elysium, examining the bizarre effects of microgravity on the plants, or at the library, eyes buried in microfilm. When I wasn't working through

Panning's *Complete Mark Twain* or issues 1 through 500 of *The Amazing Spider-Man,* I studied, with the *Far Hand*'s close pass to Iapetus in mind, the four divisions of telepathic control: memory access and retrieval, sensory stimuli and deprivation, muscular/motor control, and forced emotional response. In other words, the infamous "Freak's Quartet" of scanning, preaching, puppeteering, and vulcanizing. About the only new information I came across, in my admittedly light reading, was an explanation of how the word *vulcanizing* came to be associated with control of another person's emotions. Just another word handed down from the television generation.

Nowhere did I find any reasonable theory for the telepaths' homicidal drive. The few guesses I came across belonged in *Mein Kampf.* A surprising number of so-called experts wanted to solve the problem by sterilizing anyone even remotely related to a telepath. Not that anyone has come up with a better idea.

From what I read, the current method for nailing freaks had all the sophistication of a crap shoot. After several police departments were literally exterminated by telepaths, the United Nations hit on a technique they called "mass induced sensory overload." Throw enough people at a telepath and sooner or later there are too many factors for the freak to control. She either forgot to keep officer X from drawing his automatic, or went into a seizure when the effort of puppeteering every attacker overloaded her brain.

Thomas, alone when he faced his attacker, didn't stand a chance. I was told by the broker who handled my brother's remains that Thomas had been smiling when died. Whether the freak had puppeted the smile, controlling the nerves and muscles in Thomas's face, or had merely implanted an overwhelming feeling of joy, there was no way of knowing.

It was conceit to think I could have done anything had I been at his side; I'd have been just another toy for the freak to play with. That didn't stop the guilt. The one time in his life he needed help, and I was in the basement of the university library cramming for my final exam in History 817.

While the *Far Hand*'s diversions temporarily distracted me from work, I inevitably felt the need to do something constructive. When, seven weeks into the trip, Jessica still wasn't talking to me, I began to get restless. It finally reached the point where I got fidgety enough to corner Metal Voice.

I found him in the Star Farer's Lounge, a trite bar located in the ring of boutiques encircling Bellerophon. The three holo-tanks around the perimeter of the Star Farer were filled with images of Mars; we'd passed the aphelion point in the red planet's orbit a week ago. According to the copper-colored data kiosk behind the bar, the Far Hand, still accelerating at .0017 of a g, was now moving at a respectable 74,500 meters per second. 3,879 hours to Saturn.

Metal Voice was sitting at a corner table, nursing a glass filled with some blue concoction and looking as bored as I was. I grabbed a beer and a chair and joined him. He didn't seem surprised to see me.

"Have a seat, Mr. Kayoto. I was just thinking about you."

"Flattered I'm sure, Mr. Guring, but you're not my type."

"Actually, I was thinking about how you handled your last case. First-rate work. Not many people would have seen past the frame the mayor put around his wife. How did you figure it out?"

If you want to put a stranger off balance, walk up to him and start telling him his personal history. I rolled with it.

"The conviction rested on the mayor's somewhat lurid account of a green laser blade that supposedly relieved the district attorney of his head."

Metal Voice took a pull at his drink. There was something swimming on the bottom of the glass. "It was at a social function, was it not? The mayor's wife had been in charge of programming and tuning the variable dye lasers used on the dance floor."

"And the natural assumption was that if one of the lasers killed the D.A. then the programmer was behind it."

"A reasonable hypothesis. Why did you find it objectiona-ble? From what I understand, she had the ability to jack a laser up to killing potential. And as for motive, there can be little doubt that the district attorney was her former lover." He finished whatever he was having with a gulp, and I caught a glimpse of a modified pectoral fin going down the hatch.

"Whoever had set up the machine covered his tracks by arranging for the weapon to overheat and melt to slag after its job was done. An undereducated bellhop was the first person to reach the laser. All he could tell me was that there was water condensation on the walls."

"I fail to see the significance."

"Of readily available lasing systems, there are several with sufficient power to melt bone, but only one is water cooled."

"Q switched Berkeley YAG pulse laser."

Anyone who knows weapons that well can't be in a respectable line of work. I studied him more closely in the soft light. Clean shaven, blue eyes (probably implants, which implied a good deal of money), brown hair, and bulging biceps overflowing a short-sleeve leisure shirt. It was hard to tell in the ruddy light, but his arms looked free of steroid-induced acne. If he'd created the muscles through nothing but old-fashioned weight lifting, it indicated a certain strength of willpower.

Under the circumstances, I had no lever to pry answers from him. And even assuming he played the game on both sides of the bed, I doubted Jamie's considerable charisma would've had any effect. The best I could do was keep talking and hope for answers.

"Correct. However, yttrium aluminum garnet lasers emit radiation in the near infrared, invisible to the eye. So much for the mayor's brilliant green beam."

"Of course. Astute observation." His laugh was a flat, metallic whine: glass across a chalkboard. "How did it come to pass that a reasonably intelligent man like you got caught up with Jessica Vandimeer?"

"She didn't leave me with a whole lot of options. How did a snoop like you end up on her tail?"

He reached into his breast pocket, pulled out a pastel blue ID card, and snapped it on the table in front of me. Hans Reinhart, a full-bird colonel in the United Nations Security Force. Great. "What does the big brass want with my client?"

"Don't play the fool, Kayoto, she's the most dangerous person on this ship. She makes you and me look like rank amateurs. You think just because you're strong enough to stay out of her pants, she's not going to find some other way to turn you into a puppet?"

I gave him a condescending smirk. "Find the life of a peeping Tom exciting? Bugging rooms is illegal. Or is the mighty U.N. above the law? I bet the press would love to know how you do it."

He laughed at my crude attempt at spook psychology. "You don't get it, do you? You have no idea the kind of shit you're in. Your chances of making it back to Earth outside of a body bag are about one in a million. You should have let her goons burn the fag and told her to get lost."

Had the Star Farer been well lit, I'd have spent the night in the ship's brig. As it was, I hoped his jaw hurt half as much as my fist. "I don't like you, Mr. Reinhart, and I don't like you snooping around my life. Do yourself a favor and spend the rest of the trip peeking under old ladies' skirts instead of into my client's room."

He wiped the blood off his chin with the back of his hand. "I'm not the enemy, Kayoto. Why don't you check the data on accidental deaths occurring on flights from Terra-Luna to Saturn? I think you'll find it instructive. When the knife slides between your ribs, her hand will be on the hilt, not mine."

"Your concern is touching. If you'll excuse me, I'm going to do a little house cleaning."

Jessica was out when I reached our suite, but the door between our rooms was unlocked. I found eleven bugs in her cabin; four with audio only, seven with full video capabilities. Then there was the thing hidden behind the couch; a glossy black cube seven centimeters to the side. My pocket diagnostics told me its only function was to project a finely tuned electrostatic field.

The bugs and the black box were cleverly hidden, but after digging them out it was hard to see why Reinhart considered Jessica a professional. Anyone who lets their privacy be so compromised hasn't been playing the game long.

I was seated at Jessica's dining room table attempting to dissect the odd electrostatic device when she came in from her outside door with an old man on her arm. She gave me a questioning look.

"Your room has several interesting extras not advertised in the sales brochure."

She glanced at the micro-electronics scattered around the table and disentangled herself from the codger. "Thank you, Mr. Keefer, for a most excellent evening. I find, however, that I must take a rain check on tonight's activities. Perhaps some other time?"

The man at her side shot me a venomous glare and excused himself. I went back to working on the black box's miniscrews.

"Isn't he a bit old?"

"Jealousy? From the great Sherlock Holmes? I never would have guessed. And watch the old man bit, he's only five years older than you.'' She walked over and stood behind my shoulder. ''Would you care to explain what all this is?''

''Surveillance electronics.''

''Say 'bugs.' I can take it. Who're you going to listen in on?''

It wasn't like her to be this slow. ''Actually, I pried them all from your walls. The one hidden in the shower head was most ingenious. Someone's keeping very close watch on you.''

You never know what's going to get to them. Threaten her with a knife and she barely notices; tell her someone's watching her in the shower and she falls to pieces. The color drained from her face and her eyes went wide. ''That's impossible.''

Having been exposed to her immodesty, I didn't for a second believe she was upset about being caught buck naked. ''Afraid not, sweetheart. I found ten of the little buggers; probably missed ten more.''

She shook her head and sat slowly in the chair next to me. For the first time since I had met her, some of her towering confidence was gone. What was happening in here that she wanted to keep concealed? And if it was so all-fired secret, why did she always leave our adjoining door unlocked? Curiouser and curiouser.

''I'd have known if I were being watched. Is this a joke?'' There was an imploring edge in her voice.

''No. I don't pull pranks on clients, even ones I've been forced to take.''

''It can't be.''

''It is. You going to tell me why you're upset about it?''

''I'd rather not.''

''Figured as much. You know, this whole thing would be easier if you'd just tell me what the hell's going on.'' I turned the screw I was working on a half rotation.

''You wouldn't like it.''

I worked the screw another quarter turn and felt it snap. Probably a built-in fail-safe. Opening the cube now would be impossible without better tools. Frustrated, I tossed it aside. ''I'd like it more than your current repertoire of half-truths.'' She smiled a little at that, but it vanished too quickly.

''I'm sorry, Jefferson. This isn't turning out too well, is it?''

When a reluctant client starts getting apologetic, it's time to get answers. ''Jamie was trying to warn me about you, wasn't he? He knew your instructions were to see I never got back to Earth."

She looked away. "It's more complex than that."

So. "How you going to do it? Poison? A bullet in my brain? How about something exotic like explosive decompression? You can puncture my suit while we're out strolling among the glaciers of Rhea."

"Stop it!"

"You know, you don't seem up to killing. Maybe if I helped, it's be easier. Want me to go fetch my gun?" I kept my voice light and bantering. There was always the chance her anger was a snow job.

She grabbed a handful of solid state microboards from the table and threw them at me. "Get out. Leave me alone."

I stood, holding her chin between clinched fingers, forcing her eyes to mine. "I'm very hard to kill, Jessica. When I'm finished with whatever Al-Kirzen wants me for, keep out of my way. Maybe we'll both get out of this with our skins."

17

Jessica came into my room later that night. She was wearing a silk robe; the play of fabric across her body was somehow more alluring than nudity would have been. She stood several meters away until I had a chance to awaken fully. She held a handful of bugs.

"You missed these."

I rubbed the sleep from my eyes. "Forgetting for the moment how you suddenly became such a countersurveillance expert, since I have the feeling you won't tell me anyway, go ahead and put them on the table. I'll look them over in the morning. They might be of use."

She set the electronics down. "I didn't wake you because of these." She gestured at the bugs. "I came to ask you a question."

I was about to make some flip remark about waiting until morning, but something in Jessica's manner made me pause. From the hushed tone of her voice and the way her gaze drifted around the room, it seemed to me she was under a great deal of emotional distress. I propped myself up higher on my pillows. "What is it?"

"You know the note in my dress pocket was a warning from Jamie. Why haven't you used the machine pistol? I've studied your past closely. You've killed women before, the last only three weeks before I came to you."

The unpleasant memory resurfaced from the depths I was trying to bury it in. "Amy Austin. Captain Donaldson kept yelling in my ear to fire. We were lucky the thrust of the bullets carried her away from the fulminate." I realized I was babbling, but I couldn't seem to stop. "I still can see the look on her face; the absolute shock when the hollow-points hit her in the chest. Watching the man she'd slept with the night before pull the trigger."

"I know." Jessica walked across the room and sat by the head of the bed. "You haven't answered my question."

"If Al-Kirzen thinks you're going to kill me, then I know where the threat is. If you disappear before you get your shot, I won't know where the bullet's going to come from. It's safer to keep you alive." Pure bullshit, of course. The most dangerous assassin is the one you can't bring yourself to kill. Jessica knew that as well as I did. Her fingers traced the scar tissue over my ribs.

"This is where Louis Mondragon slashed you after you told him you had the evidence to put his daughter behind bars for murdering his wife. You should have called the cops instead of going in alone."

"You've done your homework." I pulled her up beside me on the bed. She put her hands on my chest and swung her right leg over to straddle me.

"What's it like growing up on Earth?"

"My experience with it wasn't so great." I rubbed her shoulder blades and worked my fingers down her spine to the small of her back. After several repetitions, the tight muscles in her back loosened. She arched forward in response, her eyes lidded with contentment.

"When you're raised on a colony, everything exists in stasis. You know everyone, you know in advance how they'll react to any given situation. You know the temperature tomorrow is going to be the same as it's been for the last decade. You know if your room had a window, everything outside would look the same a century from now as it has for the last millennia. I always dreamed Earth would be different—less stagnant.''

"You'd have been disappointed. Weather is more of a hassle than anything else, and people are pretty much the same wherever you go.''

"No, you're wrong.''

And she was kissing me, her lips brushing mine. A hundred unanswered questions scattered and were forgotten. Sensations flowed into my awareness, each one new and startling.

I felt the spark of her pulse racing in her wrists, her warm throat alkaline under my mouth. Satin black hair left a trace of musk as it played in the low gravity. Her breath whispered in my ear—quickening with the insistent rhythm of her hips over mine. Slick wetness touched my legs. And when the universe tumbled away in orgasm, it seemed to me I heard her laugh; an exhilarating sound of pure elation. Yet the silence was unbroken.

18

He was waiting for me a few days later when I came into my cabin alone. Hiding behind the door, metal voice box and all, Reinhart shattered my kneecap with a steel-toed boot before I even knew he was there.

He stood over me, making sure I was clear-headed enough to hear what he was saying. "Well, well. She finally got her hooks in you. She looked at you with those big green eyes, and you just fell in.''

I was flat on the floor; blood pumping from my knee where a piece of bone had punctured the skin. I've heard people claim after a serious injury they feel more shock than pain. I guess I'm not that lucky. My whole body convulsed back and forth in harmony to the agony shooting up my leg. I wanted to yell at him, but all I had energy for was a whisper between clinched teeth. "You bastard. What do you want?"

"I want to kill you. My orders are to give you a choice. Either cooperate with us, or you're finished. You have one week, spent in the hospital bay no doubt, to consider it."

He didn't even bother to tell me what he was talking about. He stepped down on my crushed knee. I felt bone grate over bone, and then thick blackness.

I awoke in the sterile white rooms of Aesculapius. It must have been shortly after passing out because my leg was still a mess. People were talking about blood loss and bone shards. Someone stuck a tube in my arm and filled me with sleep. The last thing I saw before consciousness fled was Reinhart opening a door that led into a painfully bright room. A row of bodies were lined up on tables. As my mind faded under the drugs, I thought, what a silly way to travel to Saturn.

Jessica was there when I awoke the second time. She hovered nervously over my bed. I reached up and took hold of her wrist. "How long have I been under?"

"About seven hours. They had to rebuild your entire left knee; the patella was fragmented. It's going to be about a week before you can get up but the doc says you'll be okay."

I'd be a lot better as soon as Reinhart was in the brig. "Get me the chief medic."

Dr. Amanda Gahining's skin was as black as night and she carried herself with calm grace. She reminded me of my ex-wife. "How're you feeling?"

"I've been better. I need to talk to one of the ship's officers about what happened."

"I'm sorry, Mr. Kayoto, but a minor flying accident on Icarus isn't likely to interest them too much."

"What do you mean?"

"The man who brought you in, a gentleman named Guring, gave a graphic account of the horrible accident you had while trying an Immelmann. Really, Mr. Kayoto, you should stick to beginners' maneuvers until you've had a little more practice."

"Doctor, if you check my rooms, or my luggage manifest, you'll see nothing that has anything even remotely to do with flying. I've never done it in my life."

"That's true," Jessica said, "Jefferson has always thought of flying as a silly sport." How did she know that? Her endless reservoir of knowledge about my private life was beginning to play on my nerves.

"Then maybe you can tell me why you rented a pair of wings yesterday morning? Your purchase was recorded on the ship's computer."

"Cut the crap, Doctor. Look at my knee, for God's sake. Have you ever seen a flying accident do that to bone? That's not a break, it was shattered."

Gahining cleared her throat. "Mr. Guring carries a U.N. security card. He gave a very thorough demonstration of his ability to erase my university degree from the United Nations Medical Association network. He made it quite clear that if I made any waves on your account, I'd have to find another profession. I'm too old to go through med school again. I'm sorry, Mr. Kayoto, but my report will state you crashed in the flying arena, nothing more."

I should have known. Doctors can be blackmailed just like everyone else. "So much for trusting your friendly shipboard doctor."

"Don't knock it. I saved your life."

"I'm sure you did. Heaven only knows gangrene had probably already set in. I thought for sure you'd have to amputate."

"I'm not talking about your knee. I'm talking about this." She held a plastic petri dish in front of my face. Inside were three tiny spheres; so small I had to squint to see them.

"I dug these out of your carotid artery, underneath that colorful bruise decorating your neck. You're lucky I did a full scan."

"What are they?"

"Synthetic polyacetylene derivative encased in slow-dissolving protein. Once the case disintegrates, death by respiratory paralysis follows within five minutes. It's really quite an elegant weapon. From the thickness of the protein shell, I'd say you had about a week left."

Wonderful. I had so many people after me, they were getting in each other's way. The arterial grenade was no doubt a parting gift from Amber Whitehorse, implanted by microneedle when she used my neck for a karate demonstration.

Gahining dumped the lethal spheres into a trash tube and pushed the Empty button. The tube closed and there was a rushing sound as a vent to the fusion engines opened. Case closed for Dr. Gahining.

"In the future I recommend staying clear of U.N. security." Having reached the erroneous conclusion the grenades had been placed by Reinhart, she wanted nothing to do with them. "I'll leave you two alone. If you need anything just ring the nurse."

Jessica pulled up a chair. "Amber Whitehorse."

"Had to be. She was the one who left the bruise."

"Now you know why I had orders to kill her."

"Some assassin you are. She wasn't the one killed during the MaxSec escape and you know it."

Jessica shrugged. "Probably not, but she isn't on the *Far Hand* or we'd have seen her by now. Your knee breaker is a more serious problem. Do you know who did it?"

Why the change in topic? What did Jessica know about Whitehorse? "It was Guring. His real name is Hans Reinhart and he's a United Nations security officer. I'm going to have to do something about him."

"What's his game?"

"I don't know, he mentioned you most prominently but he didn't say much beyond that. You going to tell me why U.N. bigwigs are so eager to get their hands on you?"

"It doesn't make sense." She had that hunted look again. "I've got to check something out, Jefferson. I'll be back as soon as possible." She gave me a quick kiss on the cheek and was gone.

Whatever she was after took longer than she expected. Visiting hours ended with no trace of her. People like Reinhart, however, have ways of getting past locked doors. He stepped into my room just after midnight.

"I see you're doing better, Kayoto. Must have been a nasty fall you took. Good thing I was there to save you, but I understand that is what friends are for."

I understood Reinhart well enough by now to know he belonged to that small subset of humanity who got high inflicting pain on others. Talking with his species of *Homo sapiens* is useless; anything you say is an excuse to break things. I stabbed at the nurse call button.

"I'm afraid the duty nurse has fallen asleep at his post, Jefferson, but I'll be happy to get anything you want."

"Good. Why don't you get the hell out of my sight?"

"Such an attitude. It could be dangerous—even terminal—to someone in your position."

"What do you want? Or did you just stop by to work on the other knee? I'm sure someone of your obvious talent could find a myriad of ways to amuse himself on a bedridden patient."

He smiled. "Actually, what I want from you is everything you know about Jessica Vandimeer—besides the fact that she's a good fuck."

"Envy? From a U.N. torturer? I'd've thought they'd bred base emotions out of their commanding officers."

"Not at all. You can be sure when I'm done with you, she'll get hers. Now, you're going to tell me everything."

"Why don't you just bug her room again. I promise we'll screw with the light on if it helps you make it through the night." I was chattering like a fourteen-year-old on a first date. I tend to do that when I'm scared.

"I'm afraid she's taken steps to make that impossible. However, you'll be happy to know I have other means of information gathering at my disposal." His hand moved so quickly that even had I been mobile, I doubt I could have dodged it. I felt a pressure injector push briefly at my shoulder. "No need to worry, Jefferson, it's only a mild Barbie tempered with sodium pentothal. Sleep tight." The world roared in my ears, and the room blurred and went black.

19

My mouth tasted like rusted steel wool. I could barely feel it past the headache kicking behind my temples. My newest forte: waking up in pain.

"Aren't we popular with the government?" I recognized Gahining's voice. I tried to open my eyes; felt my pupils shrink from the light and decided against it. "You're lucky he knew what he was doing. If this morning's urine sample is even half-right, you had one hell of a party last night. Let me guess, Reinhart stopped to visit.''

''So you know his real name. Give the doctor a gold star. What did he pump into me?''

''You don't remember anything?'' She asked it in an offhand matter, but intuition told me she was apprehensive. I forced my eyes open.

''No.'' Neither had Jamie or Holly. Or Miss Vandimeer. Was he the man behind the attacks?

''Not too surprising, considering what we found. If the dosage would have been a few milligrams higher, we'd be having us a funeral with you as the guest of honor.'' Gahining definitely looked relieved at something more than my continued breathing. I wondered what guilty secrets she had locked away.

''What did he do?''

''Knocked out our security and night shift with chloroform in the air ducts. Crude but effective. After making his way in here, he dumped a generous quantity of moderately lethal barbiturates into your shoulder. If you had any secrets, it's a fair guess you babbled them under hypnosis.''

It would have been less trouble if he'd've just asked. I didn't have anything to hide. He was welcome to what little I knew about Jessica Vandimeer. ''When can I get out of here?''

''You have six days to go, but don't worry about friend Reinhart. This morning he offered me an outrageous payoff to keep his nocturnal activities under wraps. Fortunately, my office recorder was on. I sent him a holotape of his attempted bribe and told him if I saw him in the hospital again, I was going to release the tape to the press via radio.''

''Gutsy move, Doctor. He can cause you a lot of grief.''

''He probably will no matter what I do now anyway. After what he did to my staff last night, I might as well drag him down with me.''

Fine with me, except Reinhart wasn't the type to bother with bribes. He had more of a big-stick mentality.

Jessica came in as soon as visiting hours permitted. I didn't see any purpose in telling her about last night's drug sampling; for some reason it didn't seem important. She pulled up a chair to the head of my bed. She hadn't spoken four words when I knew we were going to have one of those maddening conversations. "It wasn't Reinhart who broke your leg. I checked him out. He couldn't have done it."

I gave her a raised eyebrow. "What do you mean, 'checked him out'?"

"It's not important, but I know he couldn't have done it."

"Jessica, that's absurd. I clearly remember his smiling face."

"Then it was someone else made up to resemble him. I tell you he couldn't have done it." She sounded very sure of herself. What information did she have that I wasn't aware of?

"How do you know?"

"I just do."

"That's a remarkably uninformative answer."

"You'll have to trust me." And I was supposed to be satisfied with that.

Against all my expectations, Reinhart didn't make a cameo that night. Nor at any other time during the rest of my stay in Aesculapius. I guess I should have been relieved, but I was too busy thinking up diabolic reasons for his absence.

I spent the remainder of my convalescence, at least when Jessica wasn't at my side, reading up on Saturn and her moons. As my client was reluctant to talk about her case, the least I could do was dig up some background information. For six days I pretended I was back in school, cramming for a final in Astronomy 101.

Saturn's pastel clouds and hurricane winds, forever beyond the petty schemes of man, didn't merit much examination. The only detail about the planet I kept in mind was its size. Saturn's mass in kilograms knocked out twenty-seven digits before reaching the decimal point; a mass roughly a thousand times that of Earth. If I ended up on Rhea, situated a good distance down Saturn's gravity well, I'd better make sure someone had the desire and money to come fetch me. Right now, the odds didn't seem so good.

The outermost inhabited satellite in the Saturn System, Iapetus, was colonized in 2087 by United Nations mandate. Inhabitation began shortly after the U.N. Assembly of Human Improvement unanimously passed Resolution 9976, which exiled all telepaths to the moon. Strict directives regulated contact with the colony. The last thing Terra-Luna and the other settlements needed was a bunch of psychopathic killers let out of their cage. They're hard enough to catch singly; en masse they'd exterminate us within a year.

The current population of the Iapetus colony was estimated at eight hundred. U.N. records indicated that three or four people were still sent to Iapetus every five years. According to official reports, the number was steadily decreasing. Considering the natural advantages inherent in telepathic ability, it seemed likely the United Nations was laundering the figures.

The U.N. science station on Tethys, dubbed Christaan Huygens, was less exotic. The outpost had been set up to study Saturn and her rings. Billions of credits poured into the moon, for which the rest of taxpaying humanity received a string of obscure scientific documents. Since Tethys was the only port of call during the *Far Hand*'s layover in the Saturn System, I'd get a chance to marvel at the newest scientific breakthrough of the millennia firsthand before blasting off to New Mecca. The computer also displayed a solitary man-made structure on Calypso, which hung in one Tethys's Lagrangian Points, but gave no information as to what it was.

The innermost permanently inhabited moon was Al-Kirzen's. The ship's computer net had even less on Rhea than I had been able to find back on Earth.

The remaining moons were of lesser consequence. Titan and its meter-deep Dionysus Sea were novel enough, but so far no one had any luck turning all that ethane into anything useful. Apparently the boys in the planetary sciences haven't heard about straws yet.

Kobold's automated ice mine and rail cannon on Mimas appeared as an eight-sided crater with concentrically smaller octagons terraced down toward the core of the tiny satellite. The moon looked to have about three years of life remaining before being swallowed by mankind's insatiable appetite for water. Its rapidly decreasing mass was no longer enough to shepherd matter away from the Cassini Division, and the most famous section of empty space in the solar system was slowly being filled.

I finished my survey one sleepless night, watching computer animation trace out the orbits of moonlets Janus and Epimethus. The two danced around Saturn, trading orbits every four years in an offhand way that seemed to ensure collision. I ran the computer simulation ahead several hundred million years without the moons so much as giving each other a brushing kiss.

Gahining released me on December 11, one day after she promised. I had been out less than a week when I noticed a conspicuous change in Reinhart's and Jessica's behavior. While the United Nations' hood no longer appeared interested in me, Jessica now went to great lengths to assume his vigil. It was unclear if she thought I could protect her or vice versa.

It was only 3,564 hours until we reached the Saturn System.

20

On December 17, in keeping with the *Far Hand*'s destination, the passengers began the three-day celebration of Saturnalia. Despite the five orgies and plentiful chemical hors d'oeuvres, enough of Christmas and Hanukkah and Mawlid al-nabi had been incorporated into the ancient Roman holiday to keep the traditionalist placated. The builders of the *Far Hand* understood their ship was too small and fragile for a religious war.

It was a measure of Jessica's influence over me that I agreed to take some part in the festivities. She cajoled and prodded until, with ill grace, I capitulated and agreed to sign on as her teammate in the Golden Fleece Scavenger Hunt. The event was scheduled for the nineteenth on Minos, the prize being twenty grams of organically grown cocaine.

Of the majority of other sports offered during Saturnalia, I remained a stubborn non-participant. This included withdrawing my name, which Jessica had so freely offered, from the Gods and Goddesses Ball scheduled for the eighteenth. Contestants were to show up nude, their hair and makeup supposedly suggesting a deity of the past. From what I had seen of the ship's passengers, there were too few people who fit the basic requirements. Besides, it was held down on level three, and I hadn't gotten over my first impression of Bellerophon's cold copper walls.

Of greater interest was Earth I.C., which occurred on the same day. The ship's kiosks displayed, in the most elementary of graphics, how Earth was presently in inferior conjunction with respect to Saturn. This minor astronomical happening was marked with guided tours of the *Far Hand* called, not too imaginatively, Odysseys. Sandra, Princess of Morning Exercises and Torture, was listed as one of the tour guides. I entered Jessica's and my name under hers.

The tour began on level one and worked upward, past level nine, into the crew quarters and the ship's bridge. It took an hour to reach Aesculapius, the only reason I had signed on in the first place. I wanted to know more about the roomful of sleeping people I'd seen just after Reinhart had broken my leg. We were on the verge of leaving before I realized Sandra had shown us everything she was going to.

"Excuse me, but the medical section seems smaller than the arenas on the lower levels. Is it just me, or is the ship's treasury hidden behind one of the walls?" *Or are you hiding a room of unconscious people on steel gurneys?*

Sandra seemed perplexed by the question. "I don't know, Mr. Kayoto. To tell the truth, I've never noticed it before. I'm sure Chief Medic Gahining could tell us. Should I ring her up?"

Absolutely not. The last thing I needed was to arouse suspicion. "No, don't bother. What's a ship without a little mystery?" Everyone chuckled a bit and, hopefully, forgot about it.

The rest of the tour was disappointing. The crew's quarters were nearly vacant and the one member we saw, a blond woman I only briefly glimpsed, hurried away from us. The bridge was nothing more than a bank of computer terminals serviced by men and women wearing headphones and mikes. For a supposedly romantic occupation, piloting a starship looked about as exciting as typing data entry.

I avoided the rest of Saturnalia's vacuous partying, hiding in my room until the scavenger hunt forced me out. Jessica and I were herded up to Minos with forty other couples. We were given a list of treasures hidden within the maze. The first couple to find all twenty items and return to the staging area won. Three holographic Minotaurs had been set loose. Anyone caught suffered the penalty of losing all accumulated treasure.

Unlike the majority of the couples, Jessica and I split up. She pointed out that we'd cover more ground working separately, and have a better chance of winning.

"Jessica, I hate to shatter your plans, but I couldn't care less if we win. Cocaine is for juvies."

"I know, I'm too old fashioned to enjoy it, either. That doesn't keep me from wanting to cream all these rich snobs in a contest."

"Excuse me for reminding you, but you work for the richest snob of them all."

"So you're going to rob me of what little satisfaction winning would give me?"

I laughed. "You have a point. I promise to be a good boy and do my best."

After finding the first treasure on my half of the list, the key to the Library at Alexandria, I found I was enjoying the hunt despite myself. Threading through the transparent corridors was an exhilarating mental challenge, and it was with more than a little satisfaction I discovered I was doing better alone than most couples were.

I was picking up my last treasure when I saw her. Her long hair was now blond and her nose had been given a Roman profile, but the most obvious change was in her eyes. Whatever dye she'd been using back on Earth, she'd allowed it leach out, revealing deep yellow irises. Through a single sheet of plexiglass, Amber Whitehorse looked at me and grinned.

She wore a crew member's uniform with a name tag that said Fiona Williams. She brought up her left hand in a salute. Poking from its outer edge, the steel gleam of a microneedle reflected in the neon light of the maze. I was certain that whatever it contained, it'd work faster than the protein buffered cicutoxin she'd wielded back on Earth.

For the moment I was safe, but I didn't think much of my chances. She probably knew Minos by heart, whereas sooner or later I would walk into a very dead end. She gave me a full minute to realize my predicament, then was off, moving down a level and to her right.

I dropped my accumulated wealth of imitation gold bars, diamond crowns, and silver rings. Winning the contest would be poor consolation for dying at the finish line. I used the yellow hand rails to move up and to my right; the opposite direction Amber had gone. As I pulled myself along, I couldn't help but feel she knew I would choose this route.

Picking corridors almost at random, I raced along as quickly as my arms could pull me. Far too often I came against cul-de-sacs of plexiglass and had to turn around. About the seventh time this happened, Amber was waiting for me on the other side of the clear panels. She held my bundle of treasure and shook her head.

After a half hour of playing hide-and-seek, the maze faded into a nightmare of twisting plexiglass and burning arm muscles. No matter where I went, or how hard I pulled, she was always close. One minute she was a shadowy figure barely seen through several sections of scratched plexiglass, the next she was one panel away.

I saw Jessica once, but I couldn't get her attention through the sound-absorbing walls. It was almost a relief when, turning a corner looking behind rather than ahead, I ran straight into Amber's arms.

"Time's up, Kayoto."

I backed away from her embrace, keeping an eye on the hand with the needle.

I had no illusions about being able to beat her in a fight. I can hold my own in a street brawl, but against a trained assassin with a poison needle, my chances were nonexistent. The only advantage I had was greater strength—not much of an edge in the cramped, low-gravity environment of Minos. I filibustered for time and hoped for inspiration.

"So tell me, what does the well-equipped assassin pack these days? Hemlock?"

From my all-too-close vantage point, she looked like a health store model. Toned muscle on a cheetah frame. Only the scar on her cheek marred her otherwise perfect features. I grabbed the hand rails and waited for her to move.

"Nothing so passé. Ever hear of Dugan's serum? It acts like a cross between HIV and malaria with the added advantage of being more communicable than either. Not deadly, but enough to keep you delirious and in quarantine until you get back to Earth."

"Imagine my relief."

Having exhausted my ready supply of witty remarks, I went with a kick aimed at her right breast. Fighting fair is for people who like hospitals. She blocked it easily, but in using both hands, she lost contact with the maze. Unable to hold on to my foot, she tumbled back in the weak gravity.

I got a good lead on her, but it wouldn't last. My arm muscles felt like wet spaghetti while Amber, about thirty seconds behind and closing, showed no sign of tiring. If this turned into an endurance contest, I'd come out the loser. I could stay ahead of her for five minutes if I got lucky and didn't run into a closed passage.

Between adrenaline and stupidity, I almost missed the one thing that could save me. A ghostly minotaur lumbered down a side corridor, chasing a squealing couple of treasure hunters. I was past the junction before my eyes registered the scene, and had to turn back. For a brief second, I was pulling straight at Amber.

Then I was behind the holographic monster, actually shooting through his body before the alarms went off. Officially, I had just been eaten by the same monster knocked off by Theseus in ancient Crete. Infinitely preferable to being poisoned by a modern Amazon.

I managed to keep my distance until Minos's human attendants caught up with me and ushered me to the staging area. As I'd hoped, Amber didn't risk striking in the presence of other crew members. She must have realized the game was lost because she was gone the second the alarms sounded.

There was another disturbing, although less lethal, surprise waiting for me at the beginning of the maze. Jessica Vandimeer was smiling from the center of a large group of contestants. Grand prize in the Golden Fleece Scavenger Hunt. Working alone, collecting treasure from my side of the list, which she had seen only briefly, Jessica had broken the ship's record for the treasure hunt by twenty-six minutes.

If I hadn't been so conditioned against the impossibility of what I was seeing, I would have known Jessica for what she was the instant I saw her standing there accepting first prize in a contest she couldn't possibly have won. Among the cheers and smiling faces, I felt for the first time the weight of Reinhart's mysterious warning. As Jessica stood on the winner's platform, there were sinister undertones coloring her smile. There was nothing I could put my finger on, except for an uneasy feeling she was somehow contemptuous of those who crowded around her.

She saw me and pulled me to her side.

"My partner and I thank the crew of the *Far Hand* for this marvelous grand prize. However, in keeping with the spirit of

Saturnalia, we'd like to give as well as receive." She took the pouch of coke and tossed it into the crowed. A couple of hand-holding teenage girls ended up with the prize, and were off to celebrate in private.

As artificial night came to the *Far Hand*, I faked a headache and talked Jessica into staying out and enjoying the round-the-clock celebration. I needed the time alone to sort through recent events, especially my growing feelings toward the woman who had lied to me from the moment she entered my office. I settled in a reclining chair with a snifter of brandy, closed my eyes, and sifted through everything I knew about her, trying to build a plausible story to account for her actions.

It all starts when Jessica Vandimeer comes to Earth about eighteen months ago. Her objective is to find someone to solve the mystery of why children are dying on Rhea. She tries doctors first, but they provide no answer. Why? Because they never make it to the Saturn System. Reinhart had said as much when he told me to check the records for fatalities.

I turned to my computer terminal and pulled up data on all the deaths registered in the last two years taking place on ships headed out to the gas giants. The machine spat out a total of 366, of which 360 resulted from the terrorist attack on the *Stellar Knight* while she was in orbit around Ganymede. Of the other six, four had been medical doctors. All the deaths had been results of bizarre accidents. No charges were pressed.

Four dead medics on four different ships headed to Saturn. Four medics sent by Jessica to find out why children were dying on Rhea. Amber Whitehorse, listed under the name of Fiona Williams, had been on all four flights.

The deeper I looked, the more I wished I was back on Earth. All the doctors had died on Insys Shuttle flights, a corporation owned by one of Abdul Al-Kirzen's subsidiaries. He had placed Amber on those flights and the medics had died on his orders. And now she was after me.

Why would Al-Kirzen kill medics who were trying to help his colony? It didn't make sense, unless the doctors had a different destination. I pulled up all the news files for the last two years on Tethys. For three hours I searched for evidence of a medical emergency. Nothing.

That left Iapetus. Impossible as it sounded, I was sure I'd hit on the answer. It fit too well with what few facts I had to be coincidence.

I already knew the note in Jessica's dress pocket was from Jamie, not Al-Kirzen. My partner must have discovered she was trying to help the telepaths. Perhaps he saw something the night he was maimed by the black market surgeon. Or did Jessica, almost certainly the woman who took him to the hospital, accidentally give something away? Whatever tipped him off, he tried to warn me Jessica was in the employ of Iapetus and not Rhea. Somehow, Vandimeer intercepted his message.

But why the elaborate hoax with the assumed name? Because Jessica didn't want me to know just how long she'd been looking for help. She was afraid if she told me the others had been killed, I would've turned her down despite the pressure she was putting on me. Idiot that I am, I tossed out Dr. Elshi Kent's name for her to appropriate.

Al-Kirzen's motives were becoming comprehensible as well. The last thing he wanted was a thriving colony of freaks for next-door neighbors. He gave Amber Whitehorse orders to stop any assistance from reaching the colony. Far from being employed by Al-Kirzen, Jessica was working against him.

Who was she? I checked police records from the U.N., the F.B.I., and the Outer-Systems Marshals. Assuming Jessica Vandimeer was her real name, she had no record. I removed all constraints from the computer's search program, and told it to find any record of my client. After chugging for an hour and a half, the machine came up with one reference to the name Jessica Vandimeer.

Eighteen years ago in the Mars System, a girl, then five years old, ran away from her father, the noted zero-g mogul Jon Pierre Vandimeer. She was picked up in a Salvation Army shelter in the Valles Marineris Dome and returned home to Phobos Station. At the time there had been some suspicion of child molestation, but the elder Vandimeer's money was enough to hush the matter up.

Since then, there was nothing on the girl and very little on Jon Pierre. His wealth was insignificant compared to Al-Kirzen's, but large enough to keep him out of print. All I could find was the persistent rumor that although he'd actually committed suicide several years ago, his corporations concealed his death in order to keep his wealth solvent.

I pulled up one fuzzy holograph of little Jessica Vandimeer. She was sitting, face stained with dirt and tears, on a torn-up couch in a safe house. It was my client, her green eyes opened wide with fear.

I was getting closer to the truth, but answers to several questions remained obscure. Why had Amber been cutting off my business back on Earth? She seemed to have been working with Miss Vandimeer in that respect. Why hadn't Al-Kirzen simply killed Jessica rather than assassinating the four doctors? The only explanation I could come up with was that Al-Kirzen needed something from her. And why had Jessica ever claimed to work for Al-Kirzen in the first place? If my reasoning was anywhere near correct, they weren't even on the same side of whatever it was I was caught up in.

I needed more information. Since Jessica didn't care to give me any, that left Reinhart or Whitehorse. All things considered, I didn't think they were likely to come over for dinner and have a pleasant chat about why they wanted to kill me. Maybe Reinhart's bugs could be put to use.

The wall clock read 3:24 when I gave it up. I crawled into bed without sorting through my relationship with Miss Vandimeer. I was afraid I might come up with some sensible reason for not sleeping with her again. There'd be time to distance myself from her after the *Far Hand* finally reached Saturn.

21

Putting together a receiver for Reinhart's bugs was just this side of impossible. The broadcast frequency had to be altered, so Reinhart wouldn't pick up any conversations I was listening in on, then the other bugs had to be cannibalized to build a receiver for the new frequency. It was meticulous and draining work. I could stand about two hours of it a day before my temper went.

On December 31, after admonishing me for spending too much time slouched over my table playing with electronics, Jessica presented me with a black tuxedo and tickets to the

New Year's Ball. As it was to be held on Morpheus, just outside our door, the least I could do was yield with style.

"Of course I'll go, but I've got to take care of a few minor details first."

By the exasperated look she gave me, I could tell my sense of style was a little rusty. "Can't you forget business for even a few hours?"

"This is too important. I'll be back in plenty of time for the dance."

I found what I was looking for in K.A.M.'s retail boutique on deck three. Black urilite diamonds. Found only in the heart of achondritic asteroids, they shimmered with midnight allure. I chose a necklace of fifty one-karat stones, telling the cashier to charge it to Vandimeer's account. I was now fairly certain she wasn't on Al-Kirzen's payroll—a conclusion I'd so far kept to myself—but as Jon Pierre's daughter she could afford it.

If the necklace looked good in its display case, it dazzled around Jessica's throat. "You're supposed to say, 'Ahh, you shouldn't have.'"

She admired the diamonds in her bedroom's vanity mirror. "But you didn't. My account registered a substantial debit earlier this afternoon."

I couldn't resist the chance to fish for answers. "You mean Al-Kirzen's account."

She turned to me and laughed. "Please, Mr. Jefferson Kayoto, don't pretend to believe every subterfuge I feed you. I know you too well."

"And I know you too well to expect an answer to who's backing you, and how you managed those tricks with my bank account back on Elf Hive."

"Then you also know baiting me with reverse psychology won't work, either. I'll make you a deal, though. If you can guess how I drained every half-Jack from your account, I'll tell you the rest."

"Fair enough."

"Jefferson?"

Preoccupied with her mastery of plundering, I grunted in response.

"It's the most wonderful gift anyone has ever given me."

Nothing more dangerous than a beautiful woman going emotional. You see it once, and you start thinking you might really mean something to them. "I'm glad you like it." I made a show of looking at the clock. "We'd better get dressed, the ball started half an hour ago."

She pulled a garter from the pile of clothes at the foot of the bed and snapped me. "Sentimentality is definitely not one of your strong points."

I trimmed my beard to a shadow, and put my ponytail in a band of hammered silver Jamie had given me. He bought it after the one and only time he'd made a pass and I turned him down. Damn me if I knew where he got the money for it, but I couldn't argue against the man's sense of taste.

Jessica wore a full-length scarlet dress that left her back and shoulders bare. Arm in arm, we stepped out our door into the flashing holograms and rainbow lasers of Morpheus. A heavily synthesized Strauss waltz, flowing over a reggae beat, carried couples around the floor. Above the elevator doors, a billboard-size neon display flashed a one followed in rapid succession by five zeros. Celebrating the *Far Hand*'s velocity reaching 100,000 meters per second.

Dancing in low gravity is an art requiring gentle touch. Any type of energetic movement sent the dancer bouncing off the floor. The only motion possible for all but the most talented was slow skating across the slick lucite. I was fairly good at it; Jessica, wearing heels, made it look easy. At midnight, we left the ballroom for the privacy of our suite. What little immunity I had against her vanished in her beguiling embrace.

22

It was mid-January before I was ready to try my bugging skills. Of course on the *Far Hand,* it might as well have been June. Strange that after all these years of loathing sub-zero winter weather, I should find myself missing it.

The ship was gearing up for its second round of partying, tritely designated as Bacchanalia, when I approached Sandra down on Sisyphus. If I was looking for something less monotonously warm than the *Far Hand,* Sandra's cool reception fit the bill.

"I notice you're spending a lot of time with Miss Vandimeer."

"You notice too much."

"She's very pretty, isn't she."

"Yes." I could see where this was leading, and tried to head it off. "Sandra, I need you to do me a favor. Do you know everyone on the crew?"

"There're only thirty-five of us."

"How about Fiona? Twenty-six with yellow-brown eyes, strawberry blond hair, and an athletic build."

"You mean Miss Whips and Chains? Yeah, I know her."

"What can you tell me about her?"

"She was a late addition to the crew. I don't know what she does, if anything. We got orders from way up that she was to be left alone. I, for one, am happy to do so. Believe me, if you're thinking of leaving Miss Vandimeer for her, you could do better. I know a young woman who works in the exercise room . . ."

I overlooked her advances and handed her my masterpiece of jury rigging. "Can you put this in her room?"

"I'd rather not. She's got this thing about girls. If she caught me snooping around, she might get the wrong idea. The last thing I need is to give your fellow passengers ideas by showing up with rope burns on my wrists and ankles. Some of your traveling companions have rather deformed fantasies."

I tried my earnest-imploring voice. "Come on, Sandra. It's really important to me."

"You're an unscrupulous bastard, you know that?"

"So I've been told. All the more reason you should be happy I'm messing up Jessica's life instead of yours."

"Well, I'm not. I would have settled for either of you, now I'm stuck with the near-deads on level nine." She sighed and gave me a tired smile. "Give it here. I'll see what I can do."

Two days later Sandra put me through a workout twice as hard as anything I'd gone through before, then told me she'd placed the bug under a chair in Amber's room.

The performance of the microphone was disappointingly inferior. Despite hours spent fiddling with the frequency modulation, reception remained weak and intermittent. I rigged the pickup in my room to tape input in twelve-hour loops.

Fifteen minutes of fast-forwarding through the recordings was usually all I needed to determine if I had anything important.

It quickly became obvious that friend Amber had a voracious sexual appetite. Every other night, groans and squeals filled my ears. She seemed to prefer her men in couples and her women gagged and helpless. Entertaining no doubt, but hardly helpful. After several days, I was beginning to think I was out of luck.

Bacchanalia kicked off on January 28 with a wine social on Tantalus. I've always held that wine is for people who can't handle the real thing; a conviction strengthened by the *Far Hand*'s overly sweet vintages. Jessica, showing herself to be a complete novice, thought they were delicious.

The Venus-Adonis contest was held later that night on Bellerophon. Jessica wanted me to enter, but backed off when I pointed out all male contestants had to have shaved chests and hair cut above the collar. Jessica finished second in the Venus contest, behind a woman with a bust measurement enhanced to at least forty centimeters.

The Adonis contest was won by Reinhart, his muscular frame tanned and oiled. Standing on the winner's podium, he looked me in the eye and smiled. The crowd broke into applause.

23

The highlight of Bacchanalia was the Pyramus-Thisbe Orgy, held among the plants of Elysium. Jessica paid extra and got us in as spectators only. Most of the performances struck me as energetic but clumsy. The exception was a middle-aged three-some who moved like professionals. I pointed out their acrobatics to Jessica. She gave me a smirk as one of the ladies twisted to better accommodate her partners.

"If you want to try that, warn me half an hour in advance so I can start stretching out."

"I'll make you a deal. I'll never ask you to do that, if you never ask to do what they're doing." I pointed to a couple rolling around in the rose bushes. Their flanks were covered with blood from the thorns.

Despite all the stimulus, or perhaps because of it, we spent the remainder of the night in our suite conversing over a backgammon board. I counted off my last two pips and took a sip of akvavit.

"The doubling cube is on eight, against six pieces on the board, equals another forty-eight Andy Jacks, bringing the total to seven hundred eighty-four AJs in my favor. Had enough for one night, or do you want another game?"

"Set it up again. Your luck is bound to run out sooner or later. No one's that good."

Luck had nothing to do with it but on the backgammon board I usually had to let my opponents take what comfort they could. I placed the pieces and rolled a five. Jessica came up with a six and moved her back pip through a Lover's Leap.

"What was that about luck?" She stuck her tongue out and smiled. One of the few times she ever showed her young age. We played in silence for a while, my skill slowly overtaking her remarkable ability to throw doubles. We finished with another twenty-four points in my favor.

She set up the pieces again. "The amazing thing is, I still don't know how you do it."

"Intense concentration."

"I see. In order to win I should disrupt your thoughts?"

"You never know, it might work."

"Okay, ask me a question; anything relevant to the mysterious case you find yourself involved in."

We played a few rolls. "Tell me about your father."

She looked up sharply, her features hardened in anger. I backpedaled quickly. "I'm sorry, that was uncalled for. Let me try again."

She rolled and moved a piece to cover my six spot. "No, it's all right. I should have realized you'd have traced me by now. I thought about using a different name, but you'd have seen through that even faster. Why do you want to know about Jon Pierre?"

"It's you I want to know about. Your home life seemed a good place to start." I felt like a snake when she accepted the ruse as a compliment.

"Dad was . . . sick. I don't know what other word to use.

I'm sure he'd been a kind man once, but the struggle to the top warped his judgment. It got to the point where he felt he had to control everything, including his wife and daughter. Mom filed for divorce, but didn't have the clout to save me. Jon took it out on the only person he could. It wasn't pleasant.'' I saw goose bumps rise on her arms.

"The fax says he's dead."

"I wouldn't be surprised. He was going under when I left him eighteen years ago. I went to a boarding school as soon as I was old enough."

"You're in control now, aren't you? You run his corporations under his name. That's where you came up with all the cash for this."

"Yes."

"Why are you helping the telepaths on Iapetus?"

Bull's-eye. Her reaction was like a woman physically struck. Her voice quivered. "That's the silliest—"

"Jessica, please, give me some credit."

She inhaled deeply. "Their children are dying. I picked up their plea for help on one of Dad's deep-space receivers. I recruited four doctors to travel to the Saturn System to help."

"For what purpose? Travel to Iapetus is restricted and no one gets off the moon alive."

"I was going to set the medics up on Calypso. The research station on Tethys has a base there and I have enough connections with the staff to get access. From Calypso, the doctors were to receive bodies from Iapetus. Hopefully, autopsies would give Iapetus some clue as to why the children were dying."

"And since the children were dead before hitting the security on Merlin's Ladder, the United Nations wouldn't know anybody was lifting from Iapetus. You must have arranged a shuttle to ferry the bodies from the colony to Calypso."

"Yes, except it all went wrong."

"The doctors were murdered before they could reach the Saturn System."

"Yes."

"Everything you said about working for Al-Kirzen was a lie. You used the name because you were suspicious he was behind the murders, and you wanted me to dig around his turf."

She nodded. "He's one of the few people in the system who

has the money to place assassins on deep space shuttles, and his location on Rhea gave him motive.''

I leaned back to consider it. Close, but not quite the truth. Jessica stood and headed for her rooms.

''Where are you going?''

''After what happened to Thomas, I don't blame you for not wanting to see me anymore.''

''Jessica, wait a minute. I'm a little sore about being used as target practice for Al-Kirzen's hit squads, but I hardly see how you could've gone about it any other way. Had you mentioned telepaths back on Earth, you'd never have gotten me to come this far. I admire your resourcefulness.''

Her look of relief was unmistakable. I wondered if she could read me that easily.

24

One week later, having reached the midpoint of its voyage, the *Far Hand* shut down its engines. Coasting at 155,967 meters per second, she fired her aft starboard and forward port steering rockets. For eighty minutes we were weightless as the ship flipped nose over blasters.

At the end of the maneuver, the main engines fired again, this time decreasing our velocity rather than adding to it. If all went well, we'd come to a complete stop in another 2,556 hours. After the games we'd played during the zero-g period, Jessica and I slept the first eight hours of it.

Toward the end of February, the ship's bio-engineer goaded the annuals of Elysium into blooming. Jessica and I spent several hours a day among the orchids and ivy, quietly discussing trivial matters.

After my marriage went sour I never figured to get close to another woman. When Thomas died, Jamie claimed I retreated even further. Somehow understanding my reluctance, Jessica never pressed for a commitment, even something as short term as a monthly contract. If anything, it seemed to me she worked hard to keep a certain distance between us.

I was astonished by how comfortable her continued presence felt. For a time, I was able to forget about the troubles I'd left behind on Earth. Yet every so often, she exhibited an odd aura of aversion for other passengers, and I found myself strangely tense in her company.

The *Far Hand*'s penultimate party, Auroria, started on March 21 with the Assassin's Ball. Everyone attending was given the names of six others at the dance, the objective being to "kill" these people with a squirt gun loaded with carmine dye. I'd seen too much of the real thing to have fun playing around with the idea. Jessica signed on as a "coupled solo"—a designation for single dancers who had partners off the dance floor. I wasn't surprised when she won.

I occupied the evening losing to the computer at chess and listening to the bug in Amber Whitehorse's room. For a change, she was spending the night celibate. When I heard her door buzzer ring, I put the computer on pause and turned up the volume. An angry baritone voice surfaced out of the ever-present ocean of static.

". . . went crazy . . . whole dome blew, forty-five people dead . . . Kirzen killed seven more . . . ver seen him so . . ."

Amber's voice was a calm counterpoint to the man's angry rumblings. ". . . not surprised. Elle always struck me as . . . Jessica was a better . . . but Omar wanted to screw . . ."

". . . bout the guy she's . . ."

". . . had two chances . . . knows I want him . . . ame's Jefferson Kayo . . . n't think he understands what Jessica . . . obvious she loves . . ."

". . . ake action?"

". . . until we reach Tethys . . . accident."

". . . Reinhart?"

". . . idiot . . . stands less than Kayoto . . . pleasure to kill . . ."

". . . n't like any of . . ."

". . . not paid to . . . keep Jessica safe . . . perfect genetic . . ."

". . . ucking crazier than . . ."

". . . know, but he pays . . ."

The conversation ended and I heard a door slam.

Two days later, the bug picked up Amber's voice again. The clarity of reception meant she was within centimeters of the device when she spoke.

"Third time's a charm, Kayoto. Only fourteen hundred sixty-four hours until we reach port at Tethys. See you then."

There was a loud crunch, and the bug went dead. I couldn't bring myself to ask Sandra to plant another.

Auroria ended with a ship-wide poker playoff. Contestants, playing on tables set up in the library, anted a thousand Andy Jacks in four-handed tables of dealer's choice. It was the one contest Jessica didn't have to talk me into entering. I'm better at cards than I am at backgammon.

The first few rounds were easy to the point of being tedious. I had built up a stash of just over ten thousand Andy Jacks by the semifinals, where I hooked up with Jessica and a couple of unknowns from deck three. If anything, Jessica had done better than I had. She had fifteen thousand on her poker chip's readout. It took her all of thirty minutes to lose the whole thing to me. How could she have played well enough to get this far, then do so poorly in the semifinals?

The final round was anticlimatic. I had so much more money than the other three players, I was able to bluff my way to victory in just under fifteen minutes. My take was 120,000 AJs. I cut out of the celebration early, snuck away from Jessica, and grabbed hold of one of the ship's page girls.

"I want to use this credit to send a message back to Earth."

She looked at the amount. "At this distance, sir, this amount won't get you much. We're several hundred kilometers past the orbit of Jupiter."

"Will it get me four letters?"

"Easily, but what—"

"Just send this: R U O K." I gave her the number of my office telescreen. "How much does that leave me with?"

She punched a line of numbers into the miniprocessor she had on her watch. "Sixty-eight thousand."

"Tag the end of the message with a funds available for return and send it off pronto."

Jamie must have been checking in regularly, because there was a message waiting on my computer when Jessica and I got back from dinner that evening.

O K DONT GO

Jessica read it over my shoulder. "What's that all about?"

"I used the poker money to get a message to Jamie. He understood my message and got one back. At least your people aren't drugging him anymore."

"I never had any people on Earth." I delivered my raised eyebrow. "Don't give me that, Jefferson. I'm not lying about this and you know it."

"All right, I believe you"—I didn't—"the important thing is, everything seems normal back home." I reached to turn the machine off.

"Wait a second, you've got another message coming in."

I turned to the screen and watched it come up letter by letter. I was receiving it at the same time it was being entered. A tiny spaceship icon in the upper left corner told me it was coming from inside the crew's quarters.

> AL-KIRZEN PROFFERS A DEAL. YOU RETURN TO EARTH ON THE FAR HAND, AND YOU WILL FIND BUSINESS AS USUAL. IF YOU DISEMBARK ANYWHERE IN THE SATURN SYSTEM, YOU WILL BE TERMINATED. IF YOU INJURE JESSICA VANDIMEER IN ANY WAY, YOU WILL BE TERMINATED. IF YOU IMPREGNATE JESSICA VANDIMEER, YOU WILL BOTH BE TERMINATED. REPLY WITHIN 48 HOURS.
>
>   A.W.

I looked at Jessica, but it was clear the message meant as little to her as it did to me. "Looks like you have a guardian angel on board."

"Some guardian. I hope you've been keeping up on your birth control."

I nodded. "Take it on the first day of every quarter. How about you? Feeling motherly?"

"No, I'm regular as clockwork and haven't missed a period yet."

"Good, I was worried about all the guys you showed around your cabin during the first several week on board. I'd hate to be sent to hell for someone else's sins."

She broke out laughing and I had to wait patiently until she got her breath back. "The inside of my cabin was all any of them ever saw. I was trying to make you jealous and you wouldn't play along."

"My fault entirely," I said wryly. "Any idea why Kirzen

wants you in one piece and without any internal passengers along for the ride?''

''No. Have you found out anything?''

''Possibly. Did you have a partner named Elle helping you?''

''How did you find out about her?''

''I think she's dead.''

The color drained from Jessica's face. ''What happened? How much do you know?''

I motioned toward a couple of chairs, but Jessica was so stunned she slumped to the floor. I sat lotus, facing her with my hands on her shoulders.

''I'm sorry. If you would tell me everything, I'd stop throwing curve balls. I'm in the dark as much as you.''

''When did she die?'' Her voice was husky with emotion.

''I don't know the exact date but it was within the last week. She died on Rhea.''

''Impossible. She was on Luna, looking for help just as I was down on Earth. She'd never have gone to Rhea.''

''Neither would you, but look at the interest Al-Kirzen has taken in you.''

Jessica was too dazed to do anything but stare at me, waiting for an explanation I couldn't give. I'd seen that look before, working one of my first cases after having been discharged from the Terra-Luna Corps.

I'd been tracking a priest through the Old City slums when I came across a young girl in a dead-end alley. She was sitting beside the corpse of an older woman who looked to have been her mother. I never found who killed the woman, but from the way she'd been mutilated, the body brokers must have been close enough to save her internal organs. Probably cleaned her out while the girl looked on.

I don't remember much about the older woman, corpses are hardly a rarity in that part of town, but I can still see the girl. Too numb to feel the instinctive fear slummies always hold for strangers, she let me approach, pick her up, and take her to a U.N. house. The entire time I held her, tears ran down her cheeks in a silence; a reflex action offering no release of pain, only acknowledgment of defeat.

I looked at Jessica, her tears overly large in the meager pull of the *Far Hand,* and saw the little girl. And I knew that after all the useless prodding I finally had Vandimeer's secrets in my sights. She was too exhausted to maintain any pretenses; too overwhelmed to be anything but compliant. By tomorrow, she'd regain her strength. In the meantime, I could ask her anything, and she would tell the truth.

A month ago I would have fired away. Now I cupped her face in my hands and lifted her mouth to mine. I tried to tell myself that this too was a ploy, a trick to put her off guard. A way to get information without feeling like a slug for grilling her when she was down.

When we parted, I brushed the tears from her eyes. "It's okay. Al-Kirzen can't reach you here."

"No. It's useless. You've got to go back to Earth or he'll kill you." Having experienced Jessica's strength of will, I was startled by how quickly she collapsed. Whoever Elle was, my client never expected her to go down, even when facing someone as powerful as Al-Kirzen.

"Whitehorse can go to hell. I don't abandon my clients just because things start getting a little dicey."

She was silent for several minutes, then a tumble of words: "She was beautiful; always made me look so average. But a little strange, you know? Always so nervous. She told me once she would die before she let a man lay a finger on her. How did she end up with Al-Kirzen?"

"I'm not sure, but I know where to start looking."

25

The next day we rode the elevator up to Aesculapius. I told Jessica I wanted to thank Dr. Gahining for fixing my knee, but I had another reason for going. While speaking with the good doctor, I examined the doors. They all had low-security mechanical dead bolts. Except one. The room in which I'd seen Reinhart looking over the *Far Hand*'s hidden supply of sleeping beauties was sealed behind a ten-digit electronic keypad.

After paying our respects to Gahining, we walked around the circular hallway that separated Aesculapius from the level nine suites. By the circumference of it, Aesculapius enclosed more than just the medical section. "Where can we find blueprints for the ship? I don't mean the tourist stuff, I want the real thing."

Jessica's gave me a puzzled look. "We should be able to dig up a set on our cabin's computer. What exactly are we looking for?"

"A lot of empty space."

Back in our rooms, Jessica typed a few commands on her micro's keyboard. According to the official design, there was nothing concealed behind the security door. The door itself was drawn as a folding screen for use as a partition in case more beds were needed. I pointed it out to Jessica. "Don't you think that's odd?"

"Doesn't necessarily mean anything," she answered. "Could be a late design change or maybe it's an upgrade made after the *Stellar Knight* explosion."

"I don't think so. I need you to get the combination to the door."

"What makes you think I can do that?"

"Because you got my bank code twice. This should be easy."

She accepted that with a smile, the first I'd seen since she heard of Elle's death. "What are we after?"

"Just get me access to that room."

With a shrug, she left with a promise to get the code as soon as possible. It took her all of thirty minutes.

"Someday you're going to have to show me how you do that."

"You'd be disappointed if you knew. Besides, we agreed you'll have to find out for yourself. The code number is three sixes."

The number of the beast. Three repeating digits could hardly be coincidence. I wondered what it signified. "It's time to unpack some of my gadgets. I'm going in this evening."

Jessica shook her head. "You mean we're going in this evening."

26

We entered Aesculapius at eight-thirty P.M. Greenwich, thirty minutes before visiting hours were over. A young male intern sat at the reception desk. I had a couple of ideas about how to get past him but Jessica didn't give me the chance to try any of them. As we approached the desk, she gave me a gentle elbow in the ribs.

"Let me handle this." She kept on walking, giving me no time to argue.

"How can I help you folks this evening?" The intern addressed this solely to Jessica.

"We're here to visit Mr. Daniel Amundson."

The young man consulted his computer. "Yes, he's in room three. Pulled a thigh muscle; now under routine twenty-four-hour observation for possible low-g side effects."

I had no idea where Jessica got Amundson's name, or how she knew he was in the hospital, but I could only admire the way she handled the unseasoned intern. She delivered a petite shrug and called up a blush. "That's sort of my fault. We were in the bathroom trying to . . . to . . . well, you know."

She worked him like a professional. Her vague hints backed by her obvious embarrassment had his imagination working overtime. Whatever he was thinking was guaranteed to be far more degenerate than anything Vandimeer could have told him. The intern cleared his throat. "I see. I'll ring his room and tell you're coming. If I can have both of your names?"

"Oh no, you can't do that, it's a surprise. I brought Danny a gift."

"I'm sorry, ma'am, we have to follow procedure."

"You don't understand, you'll spoil the whole thing."

"I'm afraid—"

She cut him off, leaning over his desk and whispering into his ear. I didn't catch what she said, but the man's gaze flickered to me several times during Jessica's narrative. By the time she was done murmuring, I swear he was sweating.

"I, ah, see what you mean by, ah, surprise. I think in this case we can, ah, bend the rules a little. His room is down the hall, second door on your left. Please try and be, ah, finished before visiting hours are over."

We detoured around the reception desk and stepped down the corridor. There was a tense moment when we passed room three, but apparently the intern was too flustered to turn around and watch us. We reached the end of the hall and made a ninety-degree turn down the secluded corridor leading to the emergency room.

The door to the emergency ward was locked with a two-inch deadbolt. I kneeled in front of the keyhole and held out a hand to Jessica. "Syringe and red vial."

From her purse, Vandimeer pulled a needle and a small red bottle. After double-checking the vial's contents, I used the syringe to extract fifty cc's of the black polymer within. I injected this into the keyhole, being careful not to spill any of the molasses-like liquid on the exterior metal fitting.

"Anchor."

"What?"

"It's a small sliver of stainless steel, one centimeter wide by seven long."

"Got it."

She handed the anchor to me and I set it halfway into the lock. "Green vial and a clean syringe."

Unlike the viscous material of the first vial, the catalyst in the green bottle was highly volatile, designed to completely permeate the black polymers now filling in the lock. I injected five cc's into the keyhole.

"This will take three minutes to set. Since we have nothing better to do to pass the time, why don't you familiarize me with what you told our young doctor friend at the desk?"

"And spoil your appetite for the next week?"

"Try me."

"Well, I told him we had a Swedish jackhammer and—"

"A what?"

"It's a telescoping tube that—"

I suddenly remembered the peculiar glances the man had

given me. "You're right. I'm better off not knowing." We waited out the remaining minutes in silence.

After a full three minutes, I gingerly nudged the protruding end of the anchor. It felt secure. "Cross your fingers." I turned it clockwise and heard the gratifying sound of the dead bolt pulling back.

The intensive care unit, the chamber in which I'd first regained consciousness after Reinhart destroyed my knee, was empty. The opening through which I'd earlier seen the sleeping passengers was sealed behind a metal door fitted with an electronic lock.

"You're certain about the combination? Any mistake here will probably trip an alarm."

"Oh ye of little faith, watch and be amazed." Jessica stepped past me and typed three sixes into the door's combination panel. It opened with a whoosh that told me it doubled as an air lock. She shot me boastful grin and entered the room.

Inside was the complete picture I had only glimpsed earlier. Fifteen naked bodies lying on stainless steel gurneys; each one hooked to a full life-support system. The only sound came from the machines, breathing for their human parasites.

"What is this?" Jessica had unconsciously lowered her voice to a whisper.

I walked to the nearest table and examined the life support readouts. As far as I could tell with my limited medical knowledge, the young girl under the machines was under heavy sedation. I brushed blond hair from her eyes and was surprised to find she looked familiar. I'd seen her somewhere, she looked like one of those half-Jack celebrities on the holo. What was she doing here?

Jessica whispered from over another table. "They've all been knocked out. Why?"

She already knew, of course; she must have. But if she'd warned me, it would have blown everything wide open. Her only choice was to play the fool and hope I had enough brains not to walk into the noose. I was already sticking my neck out.

"What kind of medical training do you have?"

"Not much," she answered. "You going to try to bring one of them around?"

"Maybe they can tell us what's going on."

She pushed me aside. "Let me do it." She disconnected a secondary tube from the IV and gave the young girl an amphetamine injection. The girl's eyelids began to flutter almost immediately. Her recovery from induced sleep was swift and complete. Her eyes snapped open; sapphire blue, and I remembered where I had seen her. Little Jane Hamilton.

I tried to yell a warning; too slow by eons. I wanted to run, but my legs remained frozen in place. Jane looked at me and smiled. Her madness flowed through my head in molten waves.

"Do you want me?" I couldn't tell if I heard the question or if it arose directly in the tiny corner of my mind still self-aware. "Are you like all the rest?" She giggled and pushed to the center of my mind. *"What's Jeffie like?"*

She was scanning me. Childhood events I'd long ago forgotten bubbled up to a conscious level as she accessed large portions of my long-term memory. She moved steadily forward, progressing through my college years to the night Thomas was killed.

"I'm sorry your brother died before I got a chance to meet him. I think I would have liked him. Perhaps he could have been my boyfriend for a while." She laughed at my impotent anger and resumed shifting through my past. She scanned the day I dropped out of college and joined the military. A year of basic training, a few months on Elf Hive, then the Humboldt Station Uprising.

"A hero. You killed all those people and they made you into a hero. You can't stand that, can you? You know the truth and you can't run from it. You're a murderer, just like us."

Now seemingly bored, Jane skipped over large sections of my recent past, including my relationship with Jessica. She stopped when she came across the material I'd read on the Freak's Quartet. It amused her. *"Such misleading terms for something so simple. I can do them all. Would you like to see?"*

"Don't. Please let me go."

She ignored me, answering only her own insane yearnings. *"This is puppeteering."*

My left hand came up, middle and forefinger extended. With a jerk, the fingers moved in front of my eyes. Neon green spikes jumped across my corneas as my fingers began digging inward.

"I can preach as well."

My hand relaxed and my vision cleared. Thomas stood before me, his stomach blown open by the slugs that took his life.

"Hey, Jefferson. How you doing?"

"You aren't real."

"No, the freak is making you see me here. She's scanned your memory and warped your sensory input. Your eyes and ears, and even your skin will tell you I'm here." He reached out and I felt his hand brush my arm. "Come to think of it, don't they say the dead live on in the memories of the living? I guess by that reasoning, you could even say I'm alive."

"Why are you doing this to me?"

"Jefferson, where were you when I needed you? You let me die. Was that history test more important than your brother's life? It took a long time to die, Jefferson, I want you to know that."

The image began fading.

"Thomas? You've got to believe me, I did everything I could."

But he was gone.

"Of course you did, little man. But guilt still gnaws at you. I see the hold it has on you. I could remove it, erase every memory you have of Thomas. You would never remember having a brother. Would you like that?"

"No!"

"Yes, you're right. Remorse gives you such a wonderfully tragic slant. Shall we continue with your education? This is vulcanizing. Men don't like it when I do this. They don't like knowing how weak they really are."

Terror welled from deep inside; unfocused horror encompassing every thought. I had no way to fight it, only time for a strangled scream before it washed me under.

A surge of adrenaline pumped through my heart. It was beating out of control, every cell in my body vibrating. I was shaking apart, my heart pounding so fast now it must surely rupture.

"Stop! You're killing me!" Did I say it aloud?

The insane laughter echoed again. *"Yes, and why not? I know what you're thinking. I know what all men want. Kenny thought about it constantly. That's why I made him swallow one too many of his favorite pink-and-black pills."*

"I don't understand."

"Because you're a pathetic male. But I see what you're trying to hide, even from yourself. This is all you want from me."

She touched me again and I was vaguely aware, as if it had nothing to do with me, that I had an erection. *"You see, you're just like the rest. Perform for me, little man."*

I felt myself succumbing to uncontrollable desire for her. She played to my craving with images of herself engaged in perverse carnal acts, each holographically sharp and as real as memory . . . Jane stimulating herself on the flared barrel of the machine pistol, still warm from putting holes in Amy Austin . . . Jane underneath me, screaming for help as I raped her . . . then acquiescing . . . and finally moving to satisfy her own craving.

Each succeeding image was more depraved and each was arousing no matter how I tried to shy away, no matter how much I told myself I wasn't like that at all. An agonizing loop of feedback descending to painful orgasm.

"You see? That's what you are, you have nothing new for me. Why should I allow you to live?"

The muscles in my chest contracted, air was forced from my lungs. Still strapped to her bed, Jane began suffocating me. Her silent laughter was continuous now, flooding my skull with shrill intensity. My vision went hazy and the weak gravity dropped me to my knees.

At the edge of consciousness, one final thought passed between us. A shock of surprise and betrayal passed through the girl. Jane screamed in rage and frustration.

Jessica was leaning over me, helping me to my feet. I must have passed out a few seconds. "Come on, Jefferson, wake up." Her whisper was urgent. "There are people coming." She dragged me down the row of beds.

"What happened?" My voice was slurred.

"I locked the drug release back into her I.V. She fell asleep almost instantly."

"Instantly? You must be joking. She had me for at least ten minutes, probably—"

"We'll talk about it later. For now, just be quiet."

We crouched behind a table just as the security door was opening. I fought to keep my ragged breathing silent. Two medics wearing United Nations arm bands on their lab coats entered the room. One ran to Jane's table while the other stayed at the door, his hand hovering nervously near a large red toggle.

"What the hell happened?" The voice came over the intercom. I recognized it instantly as Reinhart's.

The one at the table was scanning Jane's EEG and using his hands to trace the tubes that ran into her body. "I don't know, sir, she seems to be completely under."

"But she was awake?"

"Seems unlikely, sir. Everything here is normal. Must have been a glitch in the system."

"Gilson, do you concur?"

The man at the door answered. "Yes, sir. I am standing three meters away from the table in question. My shield is on and operating within safety parameters. The patient looks to be fully sedated and I note no strange behavior in Swan. I do not believe he is being controlled in any manner."

What the hell did he mean by shield? The only ordnance he carried was a small belt pack. How could anything that size stop a freak?

"Very well," Reinhart's voice was cold and relaxed. "Replay doesn't show anything. You may back away from the table, Swan. Internal security will follow your movement until you are clear of the room. If you make any move toward Gilson, you will be lasered. Confirm if you understand."

"I understand, sir." The man at Jane's gurney slowly backed away from her table. A small ceiling laser mounted with an infrared pickup followed his progress to the door. When he was out, Reinhart's voice addressed the other man.

"Gilson, you are clear to step down from emergency stations."

"Yes, sir." The man took his hand from the toggle and stepped out the door.

We stayed in the room another five minutes to give the security men a chance to clear out. At any second, it seemed to me that every telepath would awake; vampires rising from their coffins to feed on weak mortals. Only the knowledge we would soon be leaving kept me from shaking.

"Okay." I jumped at Jessica's voice. "They should be clear by now."

"Good, we've got to hurry. We've to get out of here before visiting hours are over. We don't want the good doctor calling Amundson's room."

"Wait until you catch your breath. We have plenty of time."

"What?"

She pointed to her watch. Only nine minutes had passed since we entered the freak's room. Discounting the amount of time we'd spent in hiding, that left only four minutes for the exchange between Jane and me.

"That's impossible."

"Jefferson, a few seconds after the girl woke up you were talking nonsense about your brother and gouging your eyes. After about fifteen seconds, you stopped breathing. I understood what was happening and acted as fast as I could, but it took a few minutes for the anesthesia to take hold."

"But everything she did to me . . ."

"Took only a few seconds. She spoke directly to your mind. It's a much faster, much more efficient way of communicating than what you're used to."

"You seem to know a lot about it." I hadn't meant to sound accusatory but after the ordeal I didn't have the patience to be tactful.

"Not really. It just seems like the obvious explanation. Do you have a better one?" I couldn't blame Jessica for sounding a little defensive. If she hadn't been there to pull Miss Frankenstein's plug, I'd have been dead before the U.N. boys showed up. What right did I have to rake her over the coals?

"Let it drop. I'm just a bit strung out, okay? Give me a hand and let's get back to our rooms."

Had there been anything near full gravity on the *Far Hand,* I doubt we could have made it. As it was, Jessica struggled to support and guide my greater mass to the door. When we stood at the threshold, I told her to stop. The red switch so recently under the hand of Agent Gilson was labeled Emergency Atmospheric Release. The boys in the U.N. weren't taking any chances with their cargo.

We retraced our steps through the emergency ward and back past the intern at the desk. He took one look at my disheveled appearance and turned red.

"Did, ah, did the surprise go according to plan?"

"It was great," I told him. "You should have been there."

27

I spent the next several days fishing for enlightenment in the ship's library. Through Mnemosyne's mainframes, I had access to every data net in the system. Seven hundred trillion bytes of information, and no feasible explanation for why Jane Hamilton had tried to kill me.

Rationalizing that greater knowledge of telepathy might help solve the mystery of Iapetus's dying children, I pored over every bit of information I could dig up on freaks. Starting with F.W.H. Meyer's coining the word *telepathy* in the middle of the twentieth century, and working through the most recent studies in quantum field theory and electromagnetic sensory fields, I looked for the key freaks used to wind themselves up. As if the information could cure the self-loathing Jane Hamilton had left in me.

The physicists knew the mechanism, but couldn't account for its homicidal effects on the practitioner. The physicians were no better off. As near as the so-called experts could guess, telepaths were just born murderers.

Current literature on the subject was aimed at a new hormone imbalance theory. Several medics at some prestigious university in California had discovered, through a series of dissections on freaks who had been gunned down, that telepaths had slightly different estrogen and testosterone levels from humans.

Other researchers had been quick to point out that even if the Californians had their facts straight, they hadn't established any link between estrogen and the urge to kill. The debate raged on, becoming more esoteric as more shamans and charlatans aired their opinions.

Whatever sickness caused telepaths to kill, they'd found a

cure on Iapetus. Except for a recent outbreak of infanticide, which I found no mention of, the colony appeared to be holding its own. It could hardly have remained stable this long if they had been at each other's throats all these years.

Jessica didn't think much of my efforts. Each night in bed, she'd lie beside me and dispute my latest conclusions. "How do you know every telepath is a born killer? There's no physical way to tell them apart from other people. If a telepath lived a normal life, you'd never spot her."

"But can they live a normal life? If I could scan other people's thoughts and make them jump through hoops you wouldn't see me living like I do. I'd be the wealthiest man in history with a harem the envy of any sheik."

Jessica laughed. "Could it be our hypothetical telepath has less lofty goals? Maybe she just wants to be accepted as an everyday person."

"Sorry, I have less faith in human nature than you do."

I didn't mention it to Jessica, but I was after more than a dissertation on telepathy. I was just as curious to know how she had managed to stop Jane Hamilton. Jane must have realized the threat Jessica posed. Why hadn't she taken any steps to keep Vandimeer under control?

I rubbed my eyes and asked the computer for the next file.

"All work and no play makes Jefferson really boring." Jessica covered my eyes with her hands. "Are you going to brood the day away or are you going to come with me and see the ship?"

"Ship?"

"If you'd have read your morning bulletin instead of rushing down here to mope over this babble, you'd know what I was talking about. We're passing a freighter bound for the Outer Reaches."

Freighters making a run to the outer solar system are few in number. Because of the distances they travel, and the time it takes them to complete their voyages, ships bound for Uranus or Neptune are necessarily the greatest of all machines. On board the *Far Hand,* where little excuse was needed for celebration, the sighting of such a leviathan signaled another round of merrymaking.

"Must have missed it."

"Jefferson, I know what happened on Aesculapius bothers you, but you have to let it go."

"I'm trying, believe me."

The last nightmare had been the worst. Hamilton using me for . . . experiments. Jessica standing to the side offering suggestions. I'd snapped out of it covered with sweat. It was a new experience for me, living with fear.

"Come on, a change will do you good." I let her prod me down to the large-area holo display set up on Bellerophon.

Focused in the *Far Hand*'s exterior optics, our traveling companion had the inelegant and bulky shape of a vessel unconcerned with operating inside any atmosphere. Underneath her radar dishes, escape pods, and blast tubes, she resembled nothing so much as a half-inflated balloon. But her lack of beauty was more than compensated for by size. From blast tubes to bridge, she measured fourteen kilometers, bulging out to four kilometers across at the widest point of her midsection.

The *Far Hand*'s computers identified her as the United Nations barge, *Steel Towne*. Her cargo was living quarters for the U.N.'s Stellar Travel Lab on Miranda, Uranus System. Because of the huge mass involved, the ship was traveling along a Hohmann Transfer Ellipse. The computed elapsed time for the voyage out to Uranus was 190 months; more than thirty-one years for the round trip. A crew member just out of high school would be pushing fifty by the time he got back, with no chance of early retirement. I hoped they were getting paid well.

We tracked the *Steele Towne* for three days, after which the *Far Hand*'s telescopes scanned back to Saturn. We were close enough now so that on maximum magnification, the ringed planet filled the view plate. Ship's speed had slowed to slightly over thirty kilometers per second. 504 hours until we achieved orbit.

For the next week, Jessica steered me away from the library with such determination that I began to believe I'd been on to something. I was too wrung out to care, and she was too persuasive to resist. With quiet persistence she teased and coaxed me away from the celibacy I'd enforced on myself since meeting Jane Hamilton. Gradually, the nightmares began to fade.

28

Jessica placed an emerald stone on the marble table. "Atari."

Until an hour ago, I'd considered myself a moderate go player. Jessica had me looking more like a novice every minute. I placed a ruby stone to stop her capture, but once again I was on the defensive. She completed another set of eyes, leaving me that much less space to work with.

We were in Elysium, seated under a warm pool of light cast by an authentic nineteenth-century street lamp. It was midnight Greenwich Mean and we were alone amongst the tropical plants. Just as well, I didn't need any witnesses to the way Jessica was destroying me on the board. She took the third game by fifteen points.

"You cheat worse at go than I do at backgammon."

"It's not good manners to make excuses, especially absurd ones, when losing at the go table."

"That's what my great-grandfather always used to say."

"Sounds like a true gentleman." Jessica savored a spoonful of strawberry ice cream from the small glass bowl sitting on the table. "Jefferson?"

I helped myself to a somewhat larger portion. "Yeah?"

"What's going on?"

"Shouldn't I be asking you that?"

She pretended not to hear me. "None of it makes sense. Elle dying on Rhea, Al-Kirzen's people watching your office back on Earth, the empty threats made against you."

I looked at her sharply. "Empty?"

"What else can you call them? Miss Whitehorse and Hans Reinhart have both issued caveats, which you've done nothing but ignore. Their reaction to your insolence hasn't exactly been overwhelming."

"All part of the game."

"I don't understand."

"Hans and Amber have served notice that they want me to return to Earth. Even if I agreed to this, I can't start back until the *Far Hand* completes her voyage to Saturn. In the meantime, they seek to test my resolve and competence by issuing ominous-sounding ultimatums. An amateur flatfoot will often crack under this type of pressure, and even a pro who's not really interested in helping his client might take the easy way out. They must know I was coerced into taking this case in the first place."

"What happens when we reach Saturn?"

"If I stay on the *Far Hand*, they'll let me go in peace. If I follow you to Tethys, they'll try and kill me."

"Isn't that a bit melodramatic? If they wanted you dead, surely they've had plenty of chances by now."

"Corpses have the habit of raising embarrassing questions; experienced operatives always try to avoid them. But these people don't deal half-Jack ante; they play for keeps. When it becomes evident that I don't intend to bow out of the picture, they'll make their move."

"Then you have no choice but to return to Earth."

"Is that what you want me to do?"

She looked me in the eyes, her voice was a whisper. "Yes."

"If I do, you'll end up on Rhea."

"I realize you're trying to be gallant, but I can take care of myself."

"I'm sure that's what Elle thought as well."

"Don't try and frighten me, Mr. Kayoto. I'm just as capable as you are, and you know it."

"If this were simply a question of intelligence, I would agree with you. But it's not. Your I.Q. might be thirty points higher than mine, but you simply don't have the experience to deal with these people"

"All I have to do is stay out of their reach."

"Impossible to do on Tethys."

"Then what good will it do to have you along?"

In answer, I pointed to a dark clump of ferns. "Pretend Whitehorse and Reinhart are standing over in those bushes; their backs are to us. If you had my Luger and three seconds to get a clean shot at them, would you take it?"

"But they haven't done anything to me."

"Congratulations, your morals just got you a one-way ticket to Rhea. Jessica, you're a remarkable woman, but you aren't cold blooded enough to play this game. Reinhart and White-horse know that and they'll use it to their advantage."

Jessica sat in silence for several seconds, assimilating everything I'd said. It didn't take her long to see how desperate our position was. "What are we going to do?"

"We have two weeks before they'll try anything. That gives us some time to work on motives. Once we understand why you're suddenly so popular with the big boys, maybe we'll be able to see a way out."

Jessica steepled her fingers and leaned toward me, her elbows on the table. "Everything started with the children dying on Iapetus. There must be some connection."

"My thinking exactly. How good are you with accessing data bases?"

"Above average."

"That's more than I can claim. Shall we adjourn to the computer in our suite?"

Jessica wasn't kidding about knowing her way around the data nets. Her skill made my technique look prehistoric. Sitting at our computer comsole, she entered several commands, leading to the appearance of a small icon in the upper left of the screen. It looked like a rat.

"I've accessed software for a squirrel virus. All we have to do is feed it our search parameters. It will crawl through every open data base in the *Far Hand*'s library and bring the information back to us."

"Let's start with infant mortality. That's probably overly broad, but we should be able to whittle it down."

Jessica entered a few more magic spells into the computer. "We'll have the data in about thirty minutes."

"That should give us enough time for questions we should have discussed long ago. You say you intercepted the freaks' S.O.S. on your father's communication net. What exactly did it say?"

"Only that their newborn were dying, and they were unable to find the cause."

"What diagnostic equipment do they have?"

"Their message mentioned a Dresling Physio-analyzer."

"Not current technology, but fairly advanced stuff. What-ever's killing the infants would have to be small to get past a

Dresling. We'll be lucky to discover it from here. What kind of help can this computer give us in sorting through the data we've asked for?''

We were up the entire night looking for Iapetus's killer. We'd been at it less than an hour when I began to appreciate the colonists' fear that the children were being murdered. Their medical equipment was good enough to rule out 94 percent of the 3,000 viruses, chemical imbalances, and toxins that our computer listed as fatal to children.

All that remained were a few exotic bacteria and a handful of biological weapons; every one of which would have been just as lethal to the adults of the colony. Someone was targeting the children.

But how were they doing it? How could an assassin be successful in a community of telepaths? How could he possibly keep his guilty secret? We puzzled over this dilemma until morning, when Jessica finally drifted off to sleep. I poured myself another cup of coffee and stared blankly at the computer screen.

It was another hour before inspiration came. For our initial search, we'd asked the computer to omit all causes of death which could be deciphered by technology comparable to what Iapetus had. Rephrasing the question slight, I now told the machine to give me a list of people killed in the last 100 years for which the cause of death had been established by circumstantial evidence alone.

There were many such cases, of which about a hundred were particularly instructive. These were people found dead without any scientific cause ever forwarded, but whose manner of passing was nonetheless decipherable. In each case, the deceased was proven to have come in contact with a freak. The cause of death was always listed ambiguously as murder by means of telepathic invasion of the victim's neural network. To the computer, these murder cases had all been satisfactorily solved; which explained why we missed them the first time around.

I was fairly certain I'd stumbled onto what was happening to the children of Iapetus. Not that it helped much. By definition, everyone on the colony possessed the murderer's inhuman ability. And I was no closer to understanding Al-Kirzen's or the United Nations' interest in Vandimeer.

Though I felt I was on the right track, I kept my opinions to myself. Despite my feelings for Jessica, I followed my long-standing rule never to burden my clients with anything that could turn out to be groundless speculation. During our remaining hours aboard the ship, I kept my suspicions concealed behind a false smile.

The *Far Hand*'s last hurrah was Titanalia, a ten-day festival scheduled to conclude the day we reached Saturn. Most of the events were formal, a mode that didn't appeal greatly to Jessica or myself. The only function we attended was the Ringside Dinner, held on Tantalus. Every first-class passenger on the ship showed up, packing the dining hall to maximum capacity. In the shuffle to get seated, I bumped against Reinhart.

"Abdul Al-Kirzen wants you dead." He smiled as he said it.

"What he wants doesn't concern me in the slightest."

His grin vanished in an instant. "Don't be stupid. This is your last warning, so I'll make it as simple as I can. If Al-Kirzen gets his way, you'll be dead and Jessica will be left for his son Omar. You know anything about Omar? A real sadistic son of a bitch. Jessica may have thought her father was bad, but next to Omar, he's a rank beginner.

"On the other hand, if you play this my way you can return to Earth and go back to your worthless career. The United Nations will be out of your life forever. You have my word on it."

"What about Jessica?"

"She's rapidly becoming too much of—how should I put it?—an embarrassment to certain quarters. If it becomes necessary to take action in her direction, it'll be quick, I promise you. Believe me, it'll be much easier for her than living with Omar."

"I don't think that's your decision to make."

"Your sentimentality for the girl will get you killed if you're not careful."

Since I was in complete agreement with him on that, I changed the subject. "Why did you cover for us when we woke Jane Hamilton? Your camera must have caught us in the act."

"Because there are people in the United Nations who take their orders too literally. Had my two underlings found you, I'm afraid I wouldn't have been able to protect you from the consequences. It would have been a waste. Even if you continue on your current path to oblivion, you might still be of some use to me."

"Get out of my sight."

He sighed. "You're not good enough. If Al-Kirzen doesn't get you, I will. Your only choice is to return to Earth on this ship."

The lights went down and holographic projectors filled the arena with Saturn's glorious rings. The passengers hushed their voices in awe. Reinhart was gone by the time my eyes adjusted to the dim light.

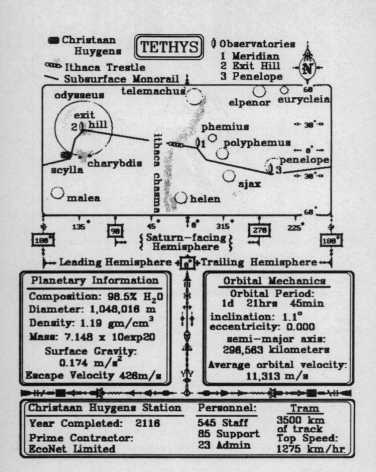

TETHYS

Christiaan Huygens
Ithaca Trestle
— **Subsurface Monorail**

Observatories
1 Meridian
2 Exit Hill
3 Penelope

N

odysseus   telemachus

elpenor   eurycleia

60°

exit hill
2   odysseus

phemius

polyphemus

30°

ithaca chasma

1

0°

penelope

scylla   charybdis

3

30°

malea

ajax

helen

60°

135°   90°   45°   0°   315°   270°   225°

180°   90°   { Saturn-facing Hemisphere }   270°   180°

← Leading Hemisphere ←|→ Trailing Hemisphere →

Planetary Information	Orbital Mechanics
Composition: 98.5% H_2O	Orbital Period: 1d 21hrs 45min
Diameter: 1,048,016 m	inclination: 1.1°
Density: 1.19 gm/cm^3	eccentricity: 0.000
Mass: 7.148 x 10exp20	semi-major axis: 296,563 kilometers
Surface Gravity: 0.174 m/s^2	Average orbital velocity:
Escape Velocity 426m/s	11,313 m/s

Christiaan Huygens Station	Personnel:	Tram
Year Completed: 2116	545 Staff	3500 km of track
	85 Support	
Prime Contractor: EcoNet Limited	23 Admin	Top Speed: 1275 km/hr.

TETHYS

29

Originally, the outer skin of the *Two Fingers* had been gloss white. Now it was pitted and scarred from micrometeors and exhaust, and only a few scabs of paint around the passenger air lock held tenaciously to the gray surface. Intra-System Shuttles had a profit margin to look after, and exterior paint was a cosmetic frill.

Resting in its hold, below the steel bulkheads of Sisyphus Arena, the smaller ship was surrounded by arm-thick cables and technicians wearing yellow Insys smocks. Jessica and I, along with about fifty others, mostly unfamiliar faces from second class, were herded aboard the *Two Fingers* and strapped down by a prim stewardess.

Engineers in the shuttle bay juiced up coils running the length of the chamber while inside the *Two Fingers,* the pilot sent a less powerful current through the shell of our ship. The duplicate electrostatic fields repelled the smaller ship out and away from the *Far Hand.*

Our trajectory was a free-fall parabola toward Saturn. If the navigational computers could be trusted, Tethys would sweep us out of the sky before we were swallowed by the gas giant. In eighteen hours we'd find out if anyone had made a mistake in their fiftieth decimal place. I crossed my fingers.

The journey was not pleasant. *Two Fingers* had little on-board entertainment and even less privacy. I spent the first several hours shamelessly eavesdropping on nearby conversations. Most of the talk was technical but a few hushed references to my companion, now dressed in a tan jumpsuit with the ringed Huygens emblem on the right breast, convinced me she was considered the resident expert on Saturn's ring systems.

"That's odd."

Jessica looked up from the fashion magazine she'd been reading. I was chagrined to find she did the eyebrow trick better than I did.

"When I searched the nets, my computer didn't come up with a single publication listing you as author. How come some of our companions here can list seven or eight ground-breaking papers by the illustrious Dr. Jessica Vandimeer?"

"I was afraid my father would come after me. I was in a unique position to give him unwanted notoriety with the press. A false name seemed like a good precaution."

"Very well done. I'll leave the obvious problems with this explanation as an exercise for the student."

She flashed a quick smile. "I thought it was pretty good. What's wrong with it?"

"You give your father alternately too much credit by saying he could have silenced you on Tethys, then too little by saying he couldn't find you through a clumsy pseudonym. You're not that naive."

She shook her head. "Not anymore, but back in college it was all I could come up with. Afterward, when I was assigned to Tethys, I kept the second name as a sign of luck and used it on all my papers."

"I liked it better without the explanation."

"How so?"

"Because I think you're telling the truth. A fake name is the sort of gimmick a college student would think of as clever. It wouldn't have stopped your father for a second."

"But it did. I never saw him again. Perhaps he failed to hire someone of your caliber to look for me."

"I appreciate the compliment but mercenaries of misfortune like myself are common fixtures in all of the large cities and domes. Someone of Jon Pierre's wealth could have certainly found a capable agent somewhere in the Mars System.

"That leaves us with only two possibilities. Either you spent your teenage and college years someplace where even your father's influence couldn't reach you, which seems very unlikely, or someone was protecting you even back then. Someone more powerful than Jon Pierre. I'd guess it was either the United Nations or Al-Kirzen.''

"You mean all of this started before the children began dying?''

"I'd lay a million-to-one odds on it. Any takers?''

"No.'' She took my left wrist in her hands, suddenly sober. "Go back, Jefferson.''

"It's too late for that.''

"No, it's not. You can stay on the *Two Fingers* when she blasts—''

"Jessica, this isn't about returning to Earth, or about Reinhart or Al-Kirzen. After what happened between us on the *Far Hand,* things have become somewhat more personal.''

"Don't you think I feel that way, too? That's why you must go back. I can no longer be responsible for your death.''

Wonderful. The one person who really understood what's going on and she's already writing me off. "I've been on thinner ledges than this. I haven't fallen off yet.''

Big words. I doubt Reinhart, sitting ten rows behind us reading Wordsworth, would be impressed. I closed my eyes and pretended to sleep.

Far from worrying about when Whitehorse would strike, or how we could elude Reinhart, all I could think about was the freaks. Since Tethys was the only landfall made by the *Far Hand,* and since the *Two Fingers* was the only vessel making the run to Tethys, the freaks had to be stored somewhere aboard. It wouldn't have been difficult to stack them in a storage hold a few hours before we embarked. How many years had the United Nations been making use of passenger liners to clandestinely ship the freaks out?

We must have been right on top of Tethys when the braking engines fired. We were pushed down in our seats as our speed was cut to zero relative to the tiny moon. Despite dire warnings of things to come, Jessica looked calm. "Home,'' she said.

30

The first thing I noticed about Tethys was its gravity. It may have been only a small fraction of Earth's but it was over a hundred times what we had on the *Far Hand*. After seven months of near weightlessness, Tethys's firmer pull was a relief.

We were unpacked from the *Two Fingers* and lined through a flexible air-lock tube to a waiting chamber. The room had a six-by-six holotank wired to a camera that panned across the moon's surface in telephoto. We were located on a plateau, planed flat by engineers and machines. In the distance a cliff—it had to be huge to be visible from here—rose on every side. Above, the pastel hurricanes of Saturn and the thin white glare of the rings, seen edge on, dominated the universe.

A diminutive woman with Oriental features and a French accent stepped through an air lock on the far side of the room. "Welcome to Tethys and the Christaan Huygens Research Station. My name is Tsuni. For those of you visiting for the first time, I'm here to show you around and answer questions."

With morbid clarity, I understood why she hadn't been waiting in the room when we landed. If something had gone wrong with the landing, this chamber would have been her tomb. Tsuni had stayed safe, further underground, until the danger was passed.

"You are on the central peak of Odysseus crater, called Exit Hill by the locals. Odysseus is four hundred kilometers in diameter, which is roughly two-fifths of the diameter of Tethys itself. It is the largest well-defined crater in the solar system." There was a chorus of appreciative sounds. I was thinking the old saying about lightning never striking twice in the same place had better damn well be right.

The screen scanned to Saturn looming over the horizon and Tsuni pushed a button, freezing the image. "Due to the great tidal force of Saturn, Tethys is locked in orbit with one hemisphere permanently facing the planet. However, because Saturn's axis is inclined over twenty-six degrees with respect to the sun, the aspect of the planet does undergo some change." She pointed to a dark swath cutting across the planet. "This line is the shadow cast by the rings across the planet. Currently, Saturn is tilting farther away from the sun. For the next three years, this shadow will continue to grow."

She kept us entertained until a green ceiling light blinked on. "Transportation to Huygens Base has arrived, if you will please exit via the far air lock." They must have kept the passenger tram away from the landing area for the same reason Tsuni had chosen to insulate herself. I wondered how many ships had splattered against the moon.

Once everyone was aboard, the tram dived under the ice and glided south toward the cliffs of Odysseus. Levitated in the magnetic mirror of Kamerlingh Onnes's newest line of organic superconducting salts, the ride was so smooth it was impossible to gauge our motion. My own estimate turned out to be off by several orders of magnitude when the tram pulled into Huygens Station, located a good two hundred kilometers from Exit Hill by rail, in under ten minutes.

Jessica spent the time chatting with Tsuni. It was clear they were old friends. At least Jessica hadn't lied about living on Tethys.

Christaan Huygens Station was built three kilometers inside the edge of the southwest crater wall of Odysseus. Some forgotten engineer must have calculated 3,000 meters was the minimum distance underground needed to assure safety for the local population. As if hiding under a shell of ice could ever be considered sanctuary against the cold touch of space.

The interior of the station was drab and cheerless. The walls were uniform gray without any pictures or plants to soften the harsh fluorescent lighting. In spirit and body it was like the primitive space stations of a century and a half ago.

Jessica led me down a series of claustrophobic corridors and elevators to her room, a small cube three meters to a side. A computer and desk filled nearly half the room; a full-sized bed took most of what was left. The only decoration was a small synth-ivory sculpture of Aphrodite rising from the foamy waters of the Ionian Sea. The goddess stood beside the computer, quietly contemplating the new power that had risen to replace her.

"I know it's cramped, but you can stay here if you want."

I couldn't see any harm in not having a room of my own. "Fine. How long are we going to be here?"

"I have to arrange a shuttle to Calypso, but we should be out of here in less than three days. The station isn't big enough to get lost in. You might as well do some exploring, it'll be better than staying cooped up in here. I've got a couple of appointments with the staff, but I should be done before supper time. How about meeting here at seventeen hundred?" I nodded and she was out the door.

Like a larger version of Jessica's room, Christaan Huygens was a cube. The station was split into thirteen levels, each crisscrossed by a series of lettered corridors running at right angles to each other. Nowhere did I see a curved hallway or a radical departure in floor plan from one level to the next. The United Nations likes things well ordered.

The lowest level of Huygens housed the environmental control machinery. Huge air scrubbers and circulating fans, smelling of hot metal and steam and chemical reagents, hummed out the heartbeat of the station. Coincidental heat produced by the machines rose through the station and kept the temperature at an even seventy degrees. So efficient was the station's insulation, a vital necessity when you're tunneled in ice, that excess heat had to be bled off by a series of copper alloy fins arrayed above us on the surface.

The next four floors were taken up with living quarters and administration offices. The upper eight levels were labs and computers, paid homage to by nearsighted Ph.D.'s. I finally found an acne-scarred junior assistant in the level three Optical Observation Lab who would consent to talk to a layperson. He wore a faded U.N. name tag with George Mahitso scrawled in orange lettering.

Mr. Mahitso sat behind a scarred plastic desk, idly running his fingers over a clear urethane globe of Tethys while he scanned an Austrian astrophysical journal. A battered optical computer and three view plates kept him company. After introductions had been made, I asked him if he could aim one of Huygens's telescopes at Rhea.

"One-hundred-centimeter short-focal is all I can get. You

know how it is, you're nobody until you've got a Ph.D. and forty papers behind you.''

''Will it be enough to see what's going on?''

''No sweat. Everyone wants to see the explosion. I'm surprised you've heard anything about it, though. Word's just now leaking back to Terra.'' His accent put his home somewhere in the Confederation of Baltic States. Considering everything that's been going on there for the last ten decades, the kid had to have a lot of guts to make it this far. He typed a few statements into the telescope's brain and the view plate zeroed in on New Mecca.

A dark smudge, looking like the flat plane of Exit Hill, panned to the center of the screen. ''This is the landing pad for Rhea. See this?'' He traced a jagged line that dived under one end of the pad and emerged from the other. ''The explosion cracked the ice under the ferro-plastic. If he doesn't pump some water in there, the next ship that lands is going to go right through.''

''Why fix it at all? He seems happy just to hole up in his palace.''

''Not possible, unless he's found a way around the second law of thermodynamics. No macro-scale recycling system, no matter how well engineered, is one hundred percent efficient.''

''What caused the explosion?''

Mahitso shrugged. ''When our spectrometers picked up a large cloud of oxygen crystals orbiting Rhea, we assumed they'd been punctured by a meteor. But look at this.'' Mahitso scanned west of the landing pad. Across the icy surface, large metallic fragments were scattered in a circular pattern covering hundreds of square meters. ''At current distance using this instrument, we can get resolution down to about ten meters. Just enough detail to catch this.'' He zoomed in to the center of the debris field. Surrounding a hole twelve meters across, jagged sheets of ferro-plastic and lead insulation arched outward.

''No way that was caused by a puncture. It was an internal explosion.''

The bits of conversation I'd heard from Amber Whitehorse's room were beginning to fall together. ''What could have caused it?''

''About three kilos of tri-nitro gel.''

''What's Al-Kirzen doing with explosives?''

"Nothing. We checked manifests for all the cargo that's been unloaded on Rhea. Except for excavating charges, all accounted for during construction, he doesn't have so much as a firecracker. The people in our engineering division went nuts trying to figure out what happened. They were stumped until Alicia Sanders over in planetary geology came up with an explanation. She's from one of those agricultural districts—Kansbraska, I think. She remembered her grandmother telling her a story about a grain elevator explosion in a neighboring town. All you need to do is get enough fine grain dust in the air and strike a spark. The carbon in the dust undergoes combustion, and boom, no more grain elevator." The young man threw his hands up in emphasis, apparently finished with his story.

"But what's the connection between a grain elevator and Rhea?"

"It turns out Al-Kirzen is using chemical air purifiers. By raising the temperature a few degrees in the catalytic chamber, you can break down carbon dioxide into elemental carbon dust and diatomic oxygen. Take a few good-sized loads of carbon dust into a room, crank up the oxygen level for good measure, light a match, and the carbon does its stuff. Just like back home in the cornfields."

"Except for one thing, Mr. Mahitso. People usually don't go around trying to blow things up."

He gave an expansive shrug. "Maybe not on Terra, but out here things get strange—mixed up. No atmosphere, no trees, no waterfalls. Sometimes people get a little crazy."

"What about Al-Kirzen? I take it he survived?"

"Yeah. Mad as hell, too. We offered to help, but he said if anyone got close, he'd blast 'em out of the sky. Said the moon was his. I guess he didn't want heathens tracking mud all over his fine Persian carpets."

Made sense. The last thing Al-Kirzen needed was any kind of investigation. No telling how much money it'd take to hush up his exploits with Elle if her kidnapping ever leaked out to Tethys. Which reminded me. "You ever meet a woman up here named Elle?"

Mahitso shook his head. "No, but I've only been here for three years. I suppose she could have come and gone before I got my assignment. Is she a friend of yours?"

"Not exactly. What can you tell me about Dr. Vandimeer?"

"She's about the smartest person here, not that anyone lets that get in the way of her looks. Every man on this ice ball, along with about half of the women, has been trying to give her a horizontal checkup since she first came here a few years back. She just returned from a sabbatical on Terra-Luna. Must have come in on the same ship you did."

"She did. We traveled together."

He gave me a look from the corners of his eyes. "Any luck?"

I let that pass. "What's over on Calypso?"

Mahitso took the change in subject as confirmation I hadn't seen any more of Jessica than anyone else. Fine with me, I didn't need the animosity of half the station.

"After you spend so much time in this hole, you need to get away from this." He spread his arms as if to encompass the whole of Tethys. "There's a small station on Calypso fit with every luxury we could think of: a swimming pool, sauna, even a fireplace, although it only burns alcohol poured over cement logs. Everyone here gets leave to the mansion at least four times a year. Since Tethys carries Calypso along in its orbit, the fuel cost isn't too high. Why do you ask?"

"Miss Vandimeer is taking me there in a couple of days."

Mahitso's eyes opened wide, and I realized I shouldn't have said anything about Jessica in the first place. "She's never gone over there with anyone." At least that seemed to fit in with what Jessica had told me.

Mahitso looked at me for a few seconds, then slapped his desk. "I knew it, I knew she would fall for someone on Terra. I told everyone, but did they listen? How did you do it?"

"Must be my stunning good looks. What about your other neighbors?" I was morbidly curious about Iapetus. What was happening down there? Mahitso lost his smile.

"The freaks?" Mahitso spoke with contempt. "Just a sec." He punched a few lines into the computer and the view-plate image swept across the sky. "Iapetus is pretty far away right now, about one hundred twenty degrees behind us."

From Tethys, the forbidden moon looked like a cratered Yin-Yang symbol. The leading hemisphere was nearly black, with the trailing side looking like Tethys ice. Mahitso was eager to talk to someone who knew less than he did, so I let him ramble on and tried to fish out useful information.

"The dark material is organic dust overlying indigenous

ices. Most of it came from Menoetius, although some of it probably came from Phoebe as well. Both satellites were captured, as evidenced by their retrograde orbits and carbonaceous character. Poynting-Robertson drag pulls dust from their surfaces inward and Iapetus scoops it up.'' He fiddled with the computer again.

''Here's the colony.'' The plate showed a thin tower of metal. Judging by the length of its dim shadow, cast in the reflected light of Saturn, the tower had to be enormous.

''Merlin's Ladder?''

''That's what the pilots who shuttle the freaks over there call it. Fancy name for an elevator, if you ask me. It lifts to a point just outside of Iapetus's gravity well. Since the shuttles don't have to fight gravity, it saves a lot of money. Out here, with no atmosphere, the electricity to run the elevator is ice cheap. Lox and hydrogen to fuel ships runs about a thousand times the cost of running the elevator.''

''Why don't you have one here on Tethys?''

''They're expensive, unstable on moons this small, and extremely dangerous. Even a minor quake would send all that mass crashing down. I expect it'd have enough momentum by the time it hit the living quarters to rip through the domes. The only reason Iapetus has one is that there's not a pilot alive who'll land on a world packed with freaks.''

''I've heard telepaths are prevented from riding up the elevator by some security measure. Do you know what it is?''

''Hydrogen fluoride combat lasers mounted on infrared scanning platforms. Anything registering a temperature above ten degrees gets zapped. A couple of years ago, pilots were reporting a lot of fried deaders on the cars. The corpses were sent back down with the new arrivals. The freaks must have gotten the message, because there haven't been any bodies for two or three years.''

As helpful as Mahitso was, he lectured incessantly the rest of the afternoon. I was glad to have an excuse to leave when evening rolled around.

Jessica took me to one of the station's cafeterias for dinner. The food looked pale, tasted bland, and had the consistency of overcooked dumplings. ''How can you eat this day after day?''

''You get used to it. After a couple of years up here, Earth food tastes like hot spice over spoiled meat.''

''Great. Is there anything else to eat?''

"No, we're on a tight budget. Everything, including the food, is affected by the need to recycle all we can. You really don't want to hear about it while you're eating."

"Got that right."

After a dessert that might have been vanilla ice cream, we went back to Jessica's room. She tossed me a set of knee and elbow pads out of her storage chest. I gave her my best lascivious stare. "This should be interesting."

She laughed. "Simmer down. I know the gravity here feels heavy after the *Far Hand,* but it's still only about a tenth that of Luna. If we don't keep up on the exercise, we'll turn to jelly." She stripped down, changing her jumpsuit for a fuchsia sports bra and a matching pair of bikini briefs. Her elbow and knee pads were chartreuse.

"Isn't that a bit bright?"

"When you're the best, you can show off." She handed me a pill and a glass of water. "Take this." I noticed she took one, too.

"What is it?"

"Dramamine."

"I have a cast-iron stomach. Whatever it is we're going to do, I don't need this."

"Yes, you do. I'm not having sex tonight with someone who's throwing up every ten seconds. Especially someone who's throwing up proteins that have already been recycled several times."

Amen to that. I swallowed the pill, put on an old pair of shorts, and followed her out the door. She led me to a corridor studded with a series of doors placed about eight meters apart. Halfway down the hall a man sat behind a desk, schedules of events and competitions wallpapering the area around him. Beside his desk, an old-style copier churned out pages of team names, brackets, and records.

"Welcome back to Tethys, Miss Vandimeer. Found another sucker to beat up on?"

"You bet, Charles. I've got a court reserved for nineteen-thirty."

He called her name up on his desk computer. "We got you down for chamber three. It's open now, go ahead and go in." He looked at me. "Good luck, buddy, you're going to need it."

The court was six by eighteen meters, halved across the

width by a net slightly more than two meters high. "What exactly are we playing?"

"Badderminton."

"What?"

"You've heard of badminton?" she asked. I nodded. "Well, this is worse. When Christaan Huygens was new, a sporting goods outlet looking for an endorsement sent us fifteen badminton sets. Great idea except for the gravity, or lack of it. A regular game of badminton here would be a choice cure for insomnia." She handed me a racket from a stack leaning against the wall. "Since you're new at this, we'll start with a flock of five." She picked up five birdies. Most of the tail had been cut off each one, apparently to cut down drag.

"The rules are the same as orthodox badminton, except we'll be playing five birdies at a time. We'll warm up for a few minutes to let you get the hang of it."

She went to the far end of the court and served all five birdies, one after the other. In the sluggish pull of Tethys's gravity they flew in a lazy arc over the net. It looked like a game for children. Pride cometh before the fall.

She got me on the first one. It came over the net, just clearing the top. Perfectly placed for me to reach over and smash it down.

I realized my mistake a fraction of a second too late. Muscles trained on Earth flexed for a ten-centimeter jump, enough to put my racket on the birdie. Of course, I was jumping in a gravitational field only slightly more than a hundredth of Terra's. I shot into the air, barely nicking the birdie. Jessica managed to return it before collapsing in laughter.

Looking down, I wasn't having any fun at all. My brain was telling me that falling from five and a half meters in this gravity was harmless, my guts were telling me I was going to break my neck. It was eight full seconds before I landed, which meant I had been in flight for over a quarter of a minute. All five birdies were sitting on my side of the court.

It took me an hour to really get the hang of badderminton. The trick was moving fast without losing contact with the floor. It involved low dives and quick changes in direction. The motion played havoc with my inner ear. The aural fluid weighed less, but still sloshed around with the same inertia. Even with the Dramamine I felt queasy.

Although Jessica's persistent limp seemed to cause her some

difficulty, I never played anywhere near her level. She had the knack of lofting one birdie, called a "sleeper" in badderminton terminology, almost to the ceiling and then timing one or more other birdies—"quickies"—to land the same time the sleeper was coming down. Invariably, I'd chase the quickies and forget about the sleeper.

I usually don't endure annihilation with a smile, but while losing against Jessica it was hard to get temperamental. Besides, I was thinking about other things. Like the copy machine. I could put it to good use against my scantily clothed but oh-so-secretive opponent. So why was I standing here playing games when I should be following leads?

Because what I had in mind was the kind of stunt a gentleman wouldn't even think about pulling on a lady he'd slept with. Still, wasn't she the same one who'd lied to me, who'd had one of my friends hospitalized? The one who'd dragged me to this dismal moon? The one who'd called me to bed last night. The one whose irresistibly sensual touch woke me this morning. When had the deceitful, manipulative client metamorphosed into the tantalizingly beautiful woman?

No longer able to objectively see Jessica as merely another customer, I fell back on one of my oldest euphemisms: Never allow propriety to get in the way of completing a job. A sound business fundamental I seemed to have trouble remembering on this case.

I waited until I was on the verge of losing another point. "Time out."

Three birdies hit my side of the floor in unison. "Oh, no, you don't. You aren't getting out of a humiliating defeat that easily. Game and set to me."

"Deal, but only if you let me catch my breath."

Jessica's reply was mockingly sincere. "Sure, if you really think it will help."

I ran a towel over my face. "Be back in a second. I want you to practice on showing respect for your elders while I'm away." I draped the towel over my shoulder and left the room, hoping Jessica would assume I was going to get a drink. I headed straight for the copy machine.

"Can I use this?"

The man behind the desk nodded. "Can't let you make more than three copies without charging you, though."

"Fine." I opened the machine's storage cabinet, and poured a third of a bottle of toner on the towel. The reek of volatiles evaporating snapped the man to attention. "What the hell are you doing? That's expensive stuff."

"Bill me for it." I took my time walking back to the room, waiting for most of the smell to dissipate.

The rest was absurdly simple. Going for an impossible save, I made a show of wrenching my knee and falling. I felt like a turncoat when Jessica rushed to my side, but I wasn't going to let that stop me. I pitched my voice to convey a moderate degree of pain. "Damn Reinhart."

"We better quit."

Jessica helped me up and I limped to my towel. I balled it tightly and let the toner run over my fingers. Walking back to our room, I took Jessica's left hand in mine. The hand she claimed to have broken. I soothingly ran my fingers across the curiously permanent purple and yellow bruise that covered the back of her hand.

Of course it was fake. The makeup smeared under the organic solvents in the toner. I caught only a brief glimpse of what lay underneath. A series of alphanumerics branded into the sensitive skin on the back of her hand.

I could understand why she'd concealed the ugly tattoo, but I had no idea as to what it meant.

31

The dormitory at the Anti-Saturn Observatory was tunneled into the central peak of Penelope crater. I decided I could handle living in its cramped quarters about three days before going cabin crazy. The five researchers manning the equipment looked like their tolerance was only slightly better than mine. They drew their hands across unshaven faces and eyed Jessica with open interest. We accepted their spartan hospitality just

long enough to be civil before boarding the tram and continuing westward.

Jessica's counterfeit bruise was back in place and I wondered if she knew I'd uncovered its mysterious message. It
seemed likely, but if she was angry with me she hadn't given
any hint of it last night. Not that I kidded myself, she could
probably play the passion game as well as I could, maybe even
better.

As for the letters and numbers someone had burned into her
hand, I could interpret them only a couple of ways. Either
someone had read *The Scarlet Letter* and decided tattoos could
still be used as a mark of some personal shame, or she'd been
numbered for the same reason a chemist labels the beakers in
his lab. I was beginning to expect it might be a little of both.

Perhaps that's why I said yes when she asked me if I'd like
to spend the day touring Tethys with her. Guilt is a wondrous
motivator. As is eros. I didn't want to think about it.

"Why did they build a complete tram circuit around the
moon? Seems like a waste."

"When you're living in a world that can kill as easily as
Tethys," Jessica answered, "it's a good idea to have more than
one exit from any living quarters. A couple of years ago, an ice
slide cut off Huygens station from Exit Hill. All our supplies
had to travel around the moon on tram before they reached us.
It was inconvenient, but not nearly as bad as it could have been.
We all would have died without a back door. As it was, we only
lost seven people."

The next terminal was Meridian Station. On Tethys, as on all
gravitationally locked satellites in the Saturn System, the Prime
Meridian was centered on the Saturn-facing hemisphere. The
majority of the Meridian Station Array was focused permanently on the cloud-covered surface of the giant planet.

Centered in the station's lecture hall, a three-meter-wide
holotank displayed a section of Saturn's equator compiled
through Meridian Station's medium baseline optical interfer-
ometer. A broiling band of white clouds arched around the gas
giant's sunlit hemisphere. According to the dimension window,
inset in the lower left of the picture, the smallest eddy in the
whipping clouds would have swallowed Earth piecemeal. Just
another breezy day in hell.

Above this display, someone had bolted an engraved plaque
to the wall.

I have bedimm'd
The noontide sun, called forth the mutinous winds,
And 'twixt the green sea and the azured vault
Set roaring war.

                              —William Shakespeare

I gave Jessica a raised eyebrow. "Isn't that a bit over-wrought?"

She pointed to the holo. "They never stop, Kayoto. Every day, on a scale so large it's almost incomprehensible, the storms encompass Saturn. After so long, they make you feel insignificant. Everything you do and every aspiration you once had begins to seem trivial. If you're not cognizant of what's happening, Saturn will warp your sense of perspective—flatten your ego. The suicide rate on Tethys is three times what it is on Earth."

"Yet another reason to get this mess taken care of and head for home."

We continued west, although by this time we had traveled more than halfway around the moon and were now approaching Odysseus from the east, until the tram slowed to a stop at another set of air locks. This time there was no station beyond the doors, only a series of observation windows. We were at least four kilometers above the ground.

Stretching to the horizon, a trench cracked the surface of Tethys. The canyon reminded me of holograms taken of Vallis Mariner on Mars but instead of water-eroded cliffs and S-curves, here there were wrinkles of uplifted ice running parallel to the canyon walls. Cutting across the relatively small world of Tethys, the dimensions of the gorge seemed absurdly out of proportion.

I thought back to the globe sitting on Mahitso's desk. "This must be Ithaca Chasma."

Jessica nodded. "Give your eyes a chance to adapt to the light, then look along the canyon walls about two meters below the rim."

At first, there was nothing, but as my eyes adjusted I saw a rainbow glow shifting along the crystalline walls. I was on the verge of asking Jessica what caused the shimmering colors when I realized it was light reflected off Saturn, then broken into a million soft spectrums by the ice.

"It's beautiful."

"Since the moons of Saturn are named for Titans, we call it Prometheus's Fire. It's visible in other areas, but never as bright as at Ithaca Chasma."

I looked out the southern windows and saw the tram tube curve into the distant side of the canyon face. Below it, tons of metal arched down to the canyon floor: support for the trestle. "Why did they run the tram out in the open like this? Wouldn't it have been safer to go around, or tunnel underneath?"

"The survey team decided it'd be marginally cheaper to span the chasm rather than run a descending grade and blast a tunnel. As for going around it, Ithaca Chasma covers a full seven percent of Tethys's surface area. Quite an obstacle."

"I hadn't realized its size. What caused it?"

"Soderblom expansion. Tethys froze from the outside in. As the core solidified and expanded, the outer surface cracked."

Irrationally, I quickly found myself hoping there wasn't some bubble of water even now freezing deep in the moon's interior; threatening to expand the gorge and send Ithaca Trestle plummeting to the frozen canyon floor. I was relieved when Jessica asked if I was ready to move on.

But as we were turning to leave, a glowing spark raced across the northern horizon. I automatically identified it as a meteor before remembering shooting stars were impossible on airless moons.

Jessica saw it as well. "That's damn odd."

"What is it?"

"Exhaust from a land hopper. Usually you don't see them this far from Exit Hill. If one crashes out here and takes its radio with it, the driver would run out of oxygen before we could trace her."

"Why would someone risk that out here?" Vandimeer had my interest now.

"I don't know. There's nothing out here worth chasing after. The land hoppers are strictly for close-in procedures and emergency repair."

I let it drop, making a mental note to check it out back at Huygens. It was probably nothing more than nerves, but the glowing exhaust seemed ominous.

We stopped at a second observation platform before reaching Exit Hill, this one carved in the cliff wall of Odysseus. Through the heavy plexiglass, I saw a natural tower, taller and rougher than Devil's Tower, sitting about three kilometers from a small impact crater. The floor of the crater had been left black by the impact that had created it.

"Scylla and Charybdis," Jessica said.

"'But she herself is an evil monster,'" I quoted Homer's description of Scylla, "'nor would anyone take pleasure to see her, not even if he should be a god.'"

"You know the story." She sounded surprised.

"I've read Homer a couple of times. Helps me to categorize the various people who walk into my office."

She laughed. "And where do I fit in with Kayoto's cosmology?"

"I'm not sure. Despite outward appearances, you're too intelligent to be Helen. You have more eyes than Polyphemus and you don't eat enough pork to be Circe. How about a Siren? Can you sing?"

Her smile was abruptly gone. "Better than you know." There was an awkward silence. After a couple of minutes, she shrugged. "It's getting late. Let's get back." It wasn't what she wanted to say. How close had I just come to learning her secrets.

After forcing down a typically tasteless meal served in Christaan Huygens's primary mess hall, we set out to find the pilot of the wayward hopper. The information was unexpectedly easy to locate. The pilot's name, listed on the hopper bay computer, was Sven Jackson, a name as unfamiliar to Jessica as it was to me.

Not knowing anyone else on the station, and not wanting to arouse suspicion by having Jessica take the name to the colony's bigwigs, I went to Mahitso. He was bending over the gutted metal of the Zeitgeist optical mainframe when we found him. He looked sore at the interruption, but covered it well in Jessica's presence. "Damn optical gates. Anything invented after the microchip is a waste of time, you know that?"

"Sorry to disturb you, but I need to locate Sven Jackson. You know him?"

"Yeah, he's the cause of all my problems."

"What do you mean?"

"He's a United Nations stooge—loves to harass people for no reason. Ever since he first showed up, money has been disappearing. I don't know what strings he's pulling, but a lot of the funding we're supposed to be getting is ending up in his pockets. See this?" He waved at the dissected computer. "Two years ago we were supposed to get rapid-reaction apertures to replace the old gallium arsenide gates. You think we've seen one since Mr. Jackson started throwing his weight around? Not a chance. Everything goes to his top-secret hush-hush United Nations project.''

"How long has he been here?''

"On and off for the last four years. He just got back from the Terra-Luna System; arrived with your ship, the *Far Hand*.''

"I don't believe I've met him.''

"Lucky you.''

"What's he look like?''

"You can't miss him. He got his throat torn out a couple of years ago when an air compressor blew next to his room. Too bad it wasn't enough to finish him. Anyway, he speaks with a microchip voice simulator.''

And his real name, at least as far as his United Nations I.D. could be trusted, was Hans Reinhart. I doubted if Mahitso could help us, but it never hurts to ask. "Any idea what he might have been doing out in the land hopper earlier today?''

"I don't know and I don't want to know. If you'll take my advice, you won't ask any questions. Sven doesn't like people who ask questions.''

We left him mumbling over his computer and headed back to our room. We were still on level three when we were intercepted by a tottering old woman. From earlier conversations with Jessica, I identified her as Sarah Denoir, the woman in charge of Huygens's administrative branch.

"You have a call, Mr. Kayoto, waiting for you in Miss Vandimeer's room.''

Since when did one of the station's executives play office girl? "Who is it?''

Miss Denoir shifted her slight weight from one bony leg to the other. "If you would just take the call as soon as possible, it would be greatly appreciated.''

According to Jessica, Denoir was well liked on the station. The way she handled the prima donnas on the science staff had earned her the respect of the entire Tethys organization. She had the reputation of being a tough old bird. What had her so jumpy?

Jessica and I started for the elevator, but Miss Denoir put a hand on Jessica's arm. "The call is for Mr. Kayoto alone. I'm sure if you'll wait here, he'll be back in a few minutes.''

I formed and discarded a hundred possibilities on the way to Jessica's room. The truth was a lot worse. Abdul Al-Kirzen waited patiently on the screen. Shit.

Al-Kirzen sat amid colored floor pillows, his florid face half-hidden under a white silk turban and a groomed beard. Behind him, two heavily robed women were sweeping the air with synthetic palm leaves. He removed a silver toothpick from between fat lips and looked me over. He spoke with a heavy Mediterranean accent.

"Mr. Kayoto, it's a pleasure to make your acquaintance at last."

"Yes, sir. What can I do for you?"

He shook his head and let out a low rumble that might have been a laugh. "Like all Westerners, you are in such a hurry to attend to business, you forget your manners. Humor this poor old man with some idle conversation before we turn to more serious matters."

I spoke with what I hoped sounded like casual indifference. "Of course." I reached under the desk and pulled out a bottle of brandy Jessica had given me during our trip on the *Far Hand*. I poured a small shot into a plastic tumbler, leaned back, and took a sip. "What would you like to talk about?"

He looked at the alcohol, taboo on Islamic Rhea, and rumbled again. "You do not disappoint, Mr. Kayoto. I was told you could not be intimidated. Did I not read a report on this very day about how your actions caused embarrassment to befall the mayor of your city? I hope you are not of the pseudo-intellectual caste who rebel against authority for the sake of juvenile ideals?"

"Not at all. The current mayor is so full of greed and larceny, he has effectively reduced other criminal organizations to petty operations. The result has greatly benefited his citizens."

"Is it not grand when two intellects see eye to eye? You must explain to me why you caused this benefactor such unwelcome publicity."

I took another pull at the brandy. "The mayor abused his power and killed several men whose job it was to see that justice is carried out."

Al-Kirzen waved this away with one meaty hand. "The people chose him. Does he then not have the right to rule as he sees fit?"

"The people chose him because his computer was able to generate sexy campaign slogans and his Watergaters had the best surveillance equipment. As for the rest, murder is not civilized behavior. Even the very powerful must have limitations placed on their ambition, don't you agree?"

There was no baritone laugh this time. "The mayor does not concern me. I only mentioned him to ascertain your beliefs on certain matters. We have more important things to discuss." He ordered the two fan-waving ornaments from the room and pulled a pistachio from a bowl outside the pickup's range. He rolled the nut between his index finger and thumb, using just enough pressure to produce an irritating crackling sound.

"One of my less able servants was unable to escape from the unfortunate position you put him in. He is being deported to Triton, where he will not live long. How will you make amends for this unfortunate occurrence?"

Diplomacy was never one of my strong points. "He was an idiot. He got in my way so I removed him."

Al-Kirzen flashed a humorless grin. "Do you presume to threaten me? You are being foolish, Mr. Kayoto."

"I don't make threats, nor do I apologize for your servant's ill manners. Besides, why should I feel remorse at his plight when you could surely reach out and save him?"

"It is true I could do this. But, Mr. Kayoto, when a tool is made from an inferior cast it is better to throw the tool away and purchase a superior one, is it not?"

A fine epitath for the man headed to Triton. He'd be dead in a few months, and all his boss cared to do was mumble Zen metaphors. Not that I didn't understand what Al-Kirzen was really saying. He did make threats; was damn good at it, too. I chose to be stubborn.

"If this servant means so little to you, then why are we wasting time talking about him?"

"Because, Mr. Kayoto, I am a man of principle. Since you have caused me some inconvenience, it is only right that you now do me a favor to balance out your previous error."

"What do you suggest?"

"I am not a vindictive man, Mr. Kayoto. It is clear to me your earlier actions were carried out in ignorance of my wishes. As such, it would be wrong for me to bear evil feelings against you. All I desire now is for us to separate and each return to his own life. I have held the *Far Hand* in her path so that you may board her and sail back to your home. Since I feel my servants have acted beyond their stations, and their actions may have caused you alarm, I will offer you the sum of three hundred million credits NorthAm in compensation.''

So far, this case had made as many promises as a virgin, and put out just about as much. If any of the parties vowing to make me rich bothered to leave me alive long enough to collect, I'd die a wealthy man. But I wasn't in the mood for daydreaming, and if I let him, Al-Kirzen would beat around the bush like this for days. Time to get to the point. ''You are truly gracious. I accept your offer. I will send my standard contract over for your signature. I'll need the appropriate fax code.''

''You are wise, my son. The code is 336699. This will place you in contact with my lawyers.''

''Then our business is concluded. If you would be kind enough to have one of your servants also purchase a ticket for Miss Jessica Vandimeer, using my funds of course, we will leave immediately.''

His jaw clinched. ''What you ask is impossible.''

''Why? Three hundred big ones ought to cover the price of a one-way pass aboard the *Far Hand*.''

''I see you have not reached full understanding. Miss Vandimeer must remain in the Saturn System. She is to be my guest at New Mecca.''

''Odd that she hasn't received an invitation yet.''

''Now you are being obstinate and unwise. I have many gifts to offer her. She will live as a queen. She will not refuse me.''

''Just like Elle.''

His eyes widened a fraction of a centimeter. ''You speak of things beyond your knowledge. I am curious as to how this name became familiar to you.''

I suddenly felt like a character in an old two-dee movie. If Al-Kirzen's stony countenance meant anything, the next scene would be the overweight Irish police sergeant standing over my remains and saying, ''Poor boy. Aye! He died because he knew too much.'' I tried to cover my tracks with confusion.

''Amber Whitehouse whispered the name in my ear last time we were screwing. She really is quite good, I appreciate the training your eunuchs gave her.'' The lie wouldn't last long, but it might be enough to get Miss Whitehouse off my back for a couple of days.

Al-Kirzen considered this for several minutes. The pistachio ground to a stop. With a quick snap, Al-Kirzen shelled the nut and ate the meat. "You are not honest with me. I will not weaken my servant's trust by questioning her loyalty. You must have received your information elsewhere." Another reach off camera, and another pistachio began its torment.

I shrugged as if it weren't important. "Believe what you will. She told me Elle was given to your son Omar."

"We are straying from important matters. You will go back to Earth and Miss Vandimeer will stay as my guest on Rhea. That is all there is to say."

"I don't think she'll agree to your terms. Even if you offer your invitation more forcefully, where will that get you? Jessica Vandimeer is a willful woman. At the very least, she'll blow up another section of your palace."

Al-Kirzen's eyes narrowed and I knew I was dead. When he spoke, it was a harsh whisper. "You have a great deal of skill at gathering information, Mr. Kayoto. It is unfortunate you have not yet learned when to keep that information to yourself." He reached up and terminated the circuit.

Good work, Kayoto. For an encore why don't you get your gun and try Russian roulette?

Knowing Al-Kirzen would move fast, I jogged back to level three, where Jessica was waiting. I wasn't sure what I could do against Al-Kirzen's servants, but right now, I was her best bet. I tried a poker face when I saw her, but she knew me too well to fall for a bluff.

"What is it? Who called you?"

"Abdul Al-Kirzen. He wants you on Rhea."

"I won't go. He can't order me around like one of his stable girls."

"You may not have a choice. From Miss Denoir's shaky appearance, I say it's a good bet he has agents on Tethys."

"What can we do?" Calm as a Sunday afternoon. Either she didn't appreciate the odds or she had steel nerves.

"Going back to the *Far Hand* is out; he's sure to expect us to try. We need room to see them coming. How soon can you get us to Calypso?"

"Forty-three hours. We can lift at three-forty Greenwich Mean, Tuesday."

"It'll have to do. Tomorrow, we'll take out a hopper. Our room is sure to be bugged, so be careful what you say. For now, it'll be safest for us to remain in the open."

We spent the afternoon mingling with the sparse crowds of Huygens's run-down bars, but when the lights dimmed in artificial evening we sought the seclusion of Jessica's room.

Yet there was no relief in our nocturnal activities. Each caress was a little more delicate, each move in the dance a little more desperate, each promising whisper a little more fragile. Perhaps we felt how fast they were closing in on us. Or maybe we knew, somehow, this was the last time.

32

Jessica hadn't gained much respect for Al-Kirzen overnight. She was gone when I awoke, having first left a note saying she was "Checking some things out." She expected to be back by eleven, which meant I had three hours of staring at the walls. I took a long shower, water being no object on Tethys, and tried to convince myself she knew what she was doing.

Toweling off, I noticed the refracted sparkle of her Urielite necklace, dangling around her twenty-centimeter statue of Aphrodite. An extra gem, a blue diamond, had been added opposite the clasp. I held it to the light and saw layers of interference patterns etched in the heart of the stone. Whatever secret it contained was none of my business. That didn't stop me from taking it up to Mahitso.

He pulled his head from the guts of his optical computer when I walked in.

"Mr. Mahitso, I need a favor."

He popped a jeweler's magnifying contact from his left eye. "I'm game. I'm not getting anything done here anyway."

"I need the primary laser from your computer."

"Come on, Kayoto, it's a bitch to realign. I just got it zeroed yesterday."

"Yeah, well then you'll have something constructive to do when we're done. Aim it against the wall."

He reached down and turned the laser's calibration ring until the beam edged over the side of the computer and struck the wall. "You owe me one."

"Remind me next time I'm out this way." I held the blue diamond in the laser and rotated it until the coherent light entered at the right angle. A hologram phased into being, glowing to life a meter in front of the wall.

Mahitso whistled. "That's one expensive rock."

At the heart of the image stood a magnificent willow tree, easily twenty meters tall. In the background, oaks and hickories clung to leaves colored by simulated autumn breezes. Only the telltale glint of plasti-steel marked the boundary between the pink Martian sky and the small Terrestrial forest of Schiaparelli Dome.

From a lower branch of the willow, a wooden two-by-six swing had been strung on braided rope. Young Jessica Vandimeer, arms wound around the ropes and wearing a navy blue boarding school dress, gazed into the holo-recorder with a Mona Lisa smile. A poem was inscribed in the upper right of the portrait.

> From childhood's hour I have not been
>   As others were—I have not seen
> As others saw—I could not bring
>   My passions from a common spring.
> From the same source I have not taken
>   My sorrow; I could not awaken
> My heart to joy at the same tone;
>   And all I lov'd, I lov'd alone.
> —E. A. Poe

Mahitso read the lines, his face reflecting growing bewilderment. "Who's Poe?"

"Nineteenth-century mystery and horror writer."

"Never got into that pre-atomic stuff, all doom and gloom. Why would a goddess like Vandimeer drag it around?"

Her tortured childhood surely had something to do with it. And yet, I couldn't escape the feeling that there was more to it than that. It was evident Jessica had left the necklace for me to find. I wondered what it was supposed to tell me.

33

The hangar on level one held ten hoppers, fueled and ready to lift. They looked like vintage Volkswagen Beatles mounted on cold-rolled carbon dioxide thrusters. The station had reinforced the Golden Age Hippie image by spray-painting psychedelic mandalas and fluorescent flowers on the exteriors. I chose one at random and gave it a thorough equipment check. Satisfied it hadn't been tampered with, I took the pilot's seat while Jessica slid into the navigator's chair.

"Where are we going?"

"I want to know what that hopper was doing north of Ithaca Trestle. Can you get me close to where he was?"

"Shouldn't be too hard. What are we looking for?"

"I'll tell you when we see it."

She entered a string of commands into the nav board and a red guidance vector glowed to life on my heads-up display, pointing us in the general direction of Phemius Crater. The hopper's computer read off information to my earphones in a husky whisper. "Destination is 1,411,045 meters away, E.T.A. is one hour forty-five minutes." It sounded just like the hopper I used to reach Humboldt Station on Luna.

The area was disappointingly barren when we got there. Only fractured ice and, off to the south, the distant gleaming of Ithaca Trestle in the dim sunlight. Above, flashes of lightning illuminated the dark hemisphere of Saturn.

"Looks like I've been on a wild goose chase."

"Hold on a second," Jessica said. "We have several kiloliters of reserve fuel. A simple drunkard's walk will give us three hours of juice to investigate."

Two hours later she called out, "Slow and descend. There's something resting by the crevasse at two o'clock."

I looked to my right and barely made out a bundle of white hospital sheets. We dropped until we were hovering two meters away, and I juiced the hopper's spotlight. It was impossible to see what the sheets were covering, but guessing from the size it could only be one thing. I maneuvered until the hopper's forward steering nozzles were a few centimeters away, and gave the bundle a blast of carbon dioxide. It bounced over the ice, the sheets flapping away.

The distorted features of a young man stared back up at us, the lifeless face frozen in a grimace of pain and rage. I heard Jessica inhale sharply.

"Do you recognize him?"

She shook her head, unable to speak.

"I do. He was one of the telepaths aboard the *Far Hand*."

"I don't understand. He was headed for a life sentence on Iapetus. Why kill him?"

"I'm more interested in knowing how it was done. Look at his face. He was aware that he was being attacked. How come he didn't stop it? Either he was killed by another telepath or—"

"Jefferson! Someone's coming."

I frantically scanned the sky. "Where?"

"From Huygens Station, behind us."

I couldn't see anything, but experience has taught me that lone corpses tend to harvest a good number of converts from the ranks of the living. Hanging around this one definitely wasn't a good idea. I gunned the aft thrusters and pointed us north. "Call and find out who it is."

Jessica spoke to her throat mike, running her fingers over the communication controls when she received only a blast of static.

"He doesn't answer."

"Call Huygens."

She worked at the controls for another minute.

"The radio's dead."

"Impossible, I checked it carefully before we left."

She typed a few commands into the computer. The screen above the console cleared and displayed an oscillating wave. Information on frequency and amplitude scrolled across a data window.

"What radio check did you use?"

"Standard military. Three squirts of high-density information bounced off the station's communications net. Except for one or two minor blips, the reflection matched the original signal. Good enough for me.''

"But with one important flaw."

"What do you mean? The test is—"

"The test was performed in the hangar, at short distance. From what I can tell, our radio has a range of slightly under thirty meters."

"Power drain?"

"All energy readouts are nominal."

"How can that be?"

"Someone has removed the radio and replaced it with not much more than a toy. It works well enough to fool the standard checks, but it's useless out here."

I'd picked the hopper at random, which meant Al-Kirzen had replaced all the radios in all the hoppers. Each one would have taken at least three hours to replace. He must have had a crew of ten or twelve people working through the night.

More unnerving was how well his people knew me. Had I used any number of unconventional checks, I'd have quickly spotted the switch. Instead, I'd stuck to the procedure taught to all cadets in the Terra-Luna Corps. Just as they predicted I would.

"How far behind is he?"

"Three hundred meters."

"You want me to believe you saw someone following us at that distance?"

"Trust me. He must have us on a homer beacon. He's closing steadily, about ninety meters a minute."

"Impossible, I have the throttle wide open." All hoppers I'd checked had the same maximum speed.

"Then he's in something else. 215 meters. He's showing up on radar." I glanced over and saw a yellow blip closing in on the screen. "How did he get this close without us picking him up sooner?"

"He's hugging the terrain."

185 meters. "He must be damn good at it."

Jessica's voice was tense. "He is."

"How far away are we from the nearest entrance?"

"82,203 meters to Meridian Station. E.T.A. six minutes, fifteen seconds."

103 meters and closing. We weren't going to make it. "Give me a heading."

He came from behind, gaining altitude now that secrecy was no longer possible. His voice crackled in my earphones.

"Set it down, Kayoto. You don't have a chance." The voice was deep, the same one I had overheard talking to Amber Whitehorse back on the *Far Hand*.

"Not until I know what the great Al-Kirzen wants."

"He wants you to be reasonable. Hand the woman over to me and you'll be left alone."

"What's the problem? Omar finally tired of sodomizing himself with salad spoons?"

"Don't be stupid, Kayoto."

"I don't plan to be. You have no intention of letting me off this ice ball."

"Of course not, but it would have been so much more easy to do it the other way. Amber will be disappointed when she finds I had to take care of you out here. She felt she owed you something after the imaginative story you told Kirzen."

"My heart bleeds for her."

"A most appropriate remark. Good-bye, Kayoto."

He gained altitude, opening his throttle until he was above us. "What the hell is he doing?"

In answer, the hopper's metal hull reverberated like a sheet metal gong. A few centimeters from my left ear, air whistled out onto frozen Tethys. Integrity sensors sounded their alarm and the hopper squirted the breach with a urethane polymer. The pungent odor of vinegar filled the hopper as acetic acid boiled off the gel and the polymer hardened.

"Better suit up."

I heard another whoosh of escaping air as I locked my helmet into place. Jessica's voice came over the radio.

"He's using sounding balls."

"What?"

Mr. Baritone, eavesdropping over the open circuit, answered my question. "They're used to test seismographs, Mr. Kayoto. A small electromagnetic gun fires ball bearings in the vicinity of detectors planted around Tethys. Since the velocity of the ball bearing is known to several decimals, the resulting impact can be used for instrument calibration. For such a small weapon it really packs quite a punch, wouldn't you agree?"

Another hole appeared a half meter in front of me. Did it take a little longer to close? The hopper had only a small reservoir of polymer sealant. Not that it mattered, we had more than enough air in our suits to get us to Meridian Station. I was beginning to think the gun was an impotent weapon when our attacker demonstrated otherwise.

The next ball bearing tore through the top of the hopper and right into my helmet. It had just enough momentum to crack the face plate. Air whistled from my suit into the hopper, a bad sign since it meant the little ship could no longer maintain air pressure at one atmosphere.

Jessica reached behind her seat, an awkward maneuver in a full suit, and pulled a clear plastic tube from the wall. She snapped off the end and worked a stream of polymers over the cracked faceplate. The overpowering smell of vinegar made my head swim.

She turned off her radio and touched her helmet to mine. "That's the last of the sealant."

I slammed the hopper's fore thrusters on max and watched the other craft shoot over our heads as we came to an abrupt stop. It was a desperation maneuver that would only work once. With all our momentum gone, he'd have us holed before we could work up the speed to make the trick work again.

Although my visibility had been cut in half by the sealant, which was clear but too irregular to be transparent, I could see the modifications added to the other hopper. Her thrusters were smaller, but looked thick enough to handle about triple the pressure ours could.

Jessica was studying the other craft as well. Her voice once again came over my helmet radio. "Except for the seismic gun, it looks like it's been modified as an ambulance."

Mr. Baritone's voice crackled in my ears. "Correct, Miss Vandimeer. The designers wanted a craft that could move quickly in case of an emergency. I have used it for just such an occasion." He turned his machine around and brought it to a stop five meters in front of us. "A desperate move, Mr. Kayoto, but considering the circumstances, it was the only hand you had to play. I can't see you clearly at this distance, but your face plate looks smudged. Did I score a hit?"

"Yes." I kept my voice conversational. If nothing else, I'd keep this man from getting any enjoyment out of my death.

"Wonderful. And your supply of sealant?"

"Out. Cabin pressure stabilized at point nine three atmospheres."

"Then one or two shots ought to finish it."

"I don't think so."

"Really, Mr. Kayoto. What hope to you see?"

I turned off the radio and duplicated Jessica's trick of touching helmets to carry my voice through the metal. "Take off your helmet."

"What?"

"Do it now!"

She popped it off, a puzzled frown on her face. I took it from her and held it to the hopper's fore view port. I flipped the radio back on. "You see this?"

"What are you doing, Mr. Kayoto?"

"This."

I smashed the helmet down on the edge of my seat. It took me four tries to shatter the reinforced plastic visor. Jessica's face went pale, but I didn't have any time to explain. She must have thought I just signed her death warrant. I held up the broken helmet so the other could see it.

"Look at it. You next shot might miss me, but it'll kill her. You understand? What will Al-Kirzen do to you when he finds out you killed her? How long you going to live?"

"That's a dumb move, Kayoto. Your luck's going to run out sooner than you think. If you do anything to harm Miss Vandimeer, it'll just be a lot slower and painful when the time comes. Think about it."

The other ship fired her aft thrusters and shot over our heads, back toward Christaan Huygens.

I set us on a course for Meridian Station and removed my helmet. My ears popped in the lower air pressure, but a quick look at the oxygen readout showed we were in no danger.

"Jessica, I know that seemed like a gutless trick to—"

"He was going to take me to Rhea, wasn't he?"

"Yes."

"Jefferson, after what happened to Elle, I'm not going. I'll suicide first."

"Then let's make sure it doesn't come to that."

The hangar deck at Meridian Station was much smaller than the one we'd left at Huygens. We cycled through a freight air lock and landed our hopper next to the only other two on the deck. Underneath the nearest one, a teen wearing grease-stained overalls was banging a carbon dioxide line. He scooted out from under the machine when we made our bumpy landing.

"Oh wow!" He spoke in a slow Pacific drawl. "Dude, what

happened to the sheen? Looks like you've been off-roading.''

''Who's in charge of security here?''

''That'd be Miz Doralius, but you don't want to peep her with this. She's brand spanking from Terra on the *Far Hand*, and she goes ballistic amply faster than her predi. But don't go bleary eyed, I'll do a cosmetic and have it looking showroom in no time. What's the storyline, anyway? Flash her through a stone storm?''

Once every three years or so, Tethys swirled through a cloud of chondrite debris. The astrophysicists were still arguing about where the meteor cloud came from. About the only thing they knew for certain was that you didn't want to be caught outside when it happened.

''No, we were shot.''

''Oh, wow. Real double-oh-seven stuff.'' He turned and skated for the door. ''I'll get Doralius stat.''

The kid's willingness to help reinforced my feeling of being a stranger in a strange land. Back home, people were always shooting at one another. It was one of the more popular means of social communication. Out here, where an errant shot could puncture some vital bit of machinery and kill everyone, it was a different matter. The ruling council on Tethys, as well as most of the outer moons, had the authority to enforce the death sentence for anyone caught shooting a firearm under or around the domes.

Jessica stripped off her full pressure suit and began relacing the lower legs of her maroon jumpsuit. ''You don't think security is going to do any good, do you?''

I began wiggling out of my suit. ''No, but if it causes problems for Al-Kirzen, it'll be worth it.''

The last thing I expected was to see the kid march through the door with Amber Whitehorse. She had a full security detail backing her up.

''These are they, Miz Doralius.''

She turned to the mech. ''Thank you, Billy, we'll handle it from here. You are excused.''

''Sure.'' He walked past us and crawled back under the hopper he had been working on when we'd landed. Miss Whitehorse threw an acid look in his direction. She had certainly meant for him to leave the room. Witnesses can be so messy.

Amber nodded in our direction. ''Mr. Kayoto, Miss Vandimeer, if you want to report the shooting, you'll be required to enter your statement at the security mainframe in Huygens. If you'll please follow me?"

I held my ground. "Hold on, we were the targets, not the hunter. What's the goon squad for?"

"To protect you in case of another attack."

The whole thing was so ludicrous I had to laugh. "You mean to keep us from escaping."

"Hardly, Mr. Kayoto. Tethys is impossible to escape from."

Good point—so why had she called in the cavalry? I'd seen her fight, she was more than a match for anything Jessica and I might try. All she had to do was knock me out and lift to Rhea with Jessica. Damned if I could figure out what was going on.

"Actually, Miss . . . Doralius? Is that what you go by here? I would have expected something with more of a new world swing to it. Miss Vandimeer and I have decided not to file charges. I'm sorry about the inconvenience. Had I known you were going to call in all your friends and make a party of it, I wouldn't have bothered."

Amber kept up with the humorless routine. "I'm afraid that won't be possible, Mr. Kayoto. A homicidal man is a threat to us all. You are required by Tethys law to file a report. Failure to do so will lead to imprisonment and deportation back to Earth."

"You mean deportation for me, and imprisonment for Jessica."

"Mr. Kayoto, I don't have time for games." She pulled an ugly, squat gun from a holster at the small of her back. The barrel looked too large for any reasonable caliber of ammunition.

"It appears we don't have a choice." I turned slightly and raised my voice. "Billy?" The speed with which the young man extracted himself from under the hopper proved he'd been listening all along.

"Yeah?"

"We're going to file a report with these people, in the meantime, do me a favor, will you?"

"Sure thing."

"Do you know Mr. Mahitso? He works as an assistant in the optics lab."

"Definitely. Pimples and dimples."

"Good. Give him a call and tell him to meet us at the monorail port at Huygens Station."

"You got it, Mr. K." He wiped his greasy hands off on a towel and was out of the room.

I turned back to Amber. She was smiling, thin lips covering her perfect teeth. "Clever, but not nearly good enough. You were safer with him in the room."

She leveled the gun's chrome barrel at Jessica's chest.

"There are two ways we can do this, Jessica. You can either try your luck against all of us, and probably get your boyfriend here killed, or you can cooperate."

"Jessica? What the hell is going—"

Amber cut me off with an order to her goon squad. "If he says one more word, kill him."

Jessica considered the odds for a few seconds. "You'll let Jefferson go?"

"Of course, we were never interested in him."

"Jess—"

"Shut up, Jefferson! There's no point in both of us going down." She wiped sweaty palms on her jumpsuit, she was almost hyperventilating with fear. "Deal."

Whitehorse brought up her right hand to steady the gun, and fired. Jessica was jerked off her feet as she was hit. Whitehorse calmly adjusted her aim and fired again. And again.

"When dealing with dangerous individuals, it is always best to be safe. Don't you agree, Mr. Kayoto?"

Three darts protruded from Jessica's chest. I ran to her side, but she was already out cold. Her breathing was shallow and irregular.

"What the fuck have you done? What do you want?"

"That doesn't concern you, Mr. Kayoto." She reloaded her dart gun. "You should have stayed on the *Far Hand*."

At least twenty weapons were pointed at me. My chances of getting away were exactly zero. I'd long ago promised myself that when the time came to check out, I'd try for a little class. I sat beside Jessica's prone form, and took her limp hand in mine. Whitehorse shook her head and centered the gun on my chest. "Good-bye, Mr. Kayoto."

With deliberate slowness she pulled the trigger. I felt a sharp pain over my heart. "Pathetic," she said. And the world melted away.

34

The cell was modern compared to others I'd been in. I rested on its sole bunk, trying to think through the haze and pain that had pooled in my brain. The subsonic hum of the containment field felt like molten iron flowing through my synapses. With all the tranks available on the black market, you figure Miss White-horse could have at least picked one without side effects.

I should have been working on a way out, but I couldn't see any reason to. Jessica was probably halfway to Rhea by now. Even if Al-Kirzen let me live, I'd never see her again. For whatever he wanted from her, I hoped she made him pay more dearly than Elle had been able to. What I wouldn't do for a drink.

I must have been conscious for one or two hours before I heard anyone approaching. I struggled to sit up but the best I could do was prop myself up against the cold wall. Getting to my feet was out of the question. I didn't think my mind was up to making my legs work. If anything, my grip on matters seemed to be loosening by the minute.

When the cell's bright yellow sodium lights came on, they felt like darts stuck in my temples. Through squinted eyelids, I saw Mahitso walking toward the cell. Mr. Baritone was right at his heels.

The young assistant stopped about a meter outside the containment field. Random currents spilling off the field made his closely cropped hair stand on end. He looked nervously over his shoulder at his hulking companion.

"Mahitso." I had to stop and catch my breath. "Glad you could make it." I tried a smile, but it must have looked ghastly under the yellow light.

Mahitso licked his lips. "They say you killed Jessica Vandimeer."

So she was gone and I was going to swing for it. The man behind Mahitso gave me a smirk. I ignored him.

"Yeah? I'm not surprised. Look, Mahitso, find Mr. . . ." What name was he using here? I tried to come up with it through the sludge in my mind. I rubbed my forehead and my hand came away damp with sweat. That shouldn't happen, I must be sick. What was I doing here? Where was Jamie?

"Mr. Kayoto? Are you all right?"

"What?"

"Who do you want me to find?"

The man with the metal voice. What name did he use here? "The guy that's causing you all your troubles. Tell him everything. You hear me, Jamie? Tell him what happened."

The figure at the door left. Funny, he didn't look like Jamie. The other one, the tall one with the deep voice stayed behind. I wondered who he was.

"You don't look so well, Mr. Kayoto. I told you Miss Whitehorse was mad. Don't worry, it's only a hydromorphone analogue. Don't know what she added to it, though. Must be bad if you're feeling any pain past the 'morphone. I'm sure it'll wear off before the trial." For some reason, he was laughing.

The day faded in and out. Periods of lucid thought interspaced with complete loss of reasoning. During the times I could think, I realized the drug Miss Whitehorse had nailed me with had some sort of time release. I'd get over one hit just in time to realize another was coming. I hoped I had enough sense when I was juiced not to walk into the containment field. Hours slipped away without any sign of Reinhart. I wondered if Mahitso had been able to reach him.

Five-thirty-two Greenwich Mean. The previous period of drug-induced fog had only lasted fifteen minutes. I could only hope that whatever narcotic was playing fantasyland with my brain was finally wearing off. Whitehorse's male goon was still at the door.

"Back in reality, eh? All things considered, you'd probably be happier if you stayed unconscious."

"Considering the dismal quality of the company I presently find myself in, you're probably right. What are you doing here, anyway? Think I'm going to walk through the containment field if you turn your back?"

"Amber wanted me to discourage visitors. I couldn't stop the first one, but I doubt Mahitso will be of any help. According to the station's personnel files, he's a third-rate technician. He has just enough clout to clean test tubes without permission. I would have expected something more intelligent from you. Why didn't you try for Miss Denoir?"

Exactly for the reason he mentioned. With any luck, Mahitso was small enough fry to slip through their nets. They would have sidetracked someone as important as Denoir.

"Where's Jessica?"

The man laughed. "It's true, then. When Amber told me, I couldn't believe it. You're actually in love with her. Hell, I don't know why we had to cook up this murder rap. All I'd have to do is report you to the United Nations and you'd be on the next shuttle to Triton."

"Really? Last I heard, sleeping with a beautiful woman isn't a capital offense. But I guess you wouldn't know anything about it."

"You're as dumb as they come, you know that? Or hadn't you figured out yet she's—"

It happened just as Whitehorse's chemical sedation was making a return engagement with my cortex. The man's left eye dissolved in a drizzle of fluid and tissue. Amber's drug bled into my awareness; time slowed down. His body jerked forward, face first into the containment field. There was a gathering of energy and the field flowed to life. Like a CAT scan, it peeled away layers of flesh and bone until there was nothing left above his neck. Heat from the field cauterized the stump. Standing above the corpse, Reinhart was smiling. The Uzi in his right hand still smoking . . .

My watch read 6:05 A.M. Reinhart was kneeling beside me with a pressure injector. He was shining a bright light in my left eye.

"That should do it. Al-Kirzen's assassin hit you with a layered dosage of Short Circuit. I've given you some adrenaline to wash it out of your system."

I'd heard of Short Circuit before. A boutique drug for teens who wanted the thrill of having their short-term memory scrambled. It had the advantage of leaving no traces in the body after the effect wore off. I tried to keep still while the adrenaline rush ran through my veins.

Reinhart waited until I stopped shaking, then helped me to

my feet. I kept my eyes averted from the headless body stretched out on the floor behind him.

Reinhart glanced back at it. "One of my better jobs, actually. Not only did the containment field destroy the head wound, it disintegrated the bullet as well. For all the investigators will know, he simply fell asleep and slumped into the field."

"Congratulations. I'm sure your mother would be proud."

"Sarcasm? Not much of a thank-you, considering I just saved you life."

"I'd be happier if you'd tell me why. I expected you to go after Miss Vandimeer. Her last wish was to die rather than be shipped to Rhea for Omar's pleasure. Knowing your skills in the body bag business, I figured I could count on you to make a quick job of it. What are you doing here?"

"Although Vandimeer is of some importance to the U.N., we are not officially involved with Al-Kirzen's gambit to obtain her. It would be unacceptable if anything were to happen to me while I made the attempt to free her from Amber Whitehorse. However, if you should die in the attempt, you'll be just another poor sod who got in Al-Kirzen's way. It won't even rate a page three headline."

"Wonderful. How do you expect me to reach her? She must be halfway to Rhea by now."

"Nothing of the sort. Amber Whitehorse's craft developed a leak in its port lox chamber a few minutes after I got your message. Even if she's had crews working on it round the clock, she won't be ready to go for another six hours."

Liquid oxygen leaks are about as common as tsunamis on Luna. About the only thing that might cause one was skillful sabotage. Since Amber was certain to have placed guards in the hangars, Reinhart must have had some help in disabling her ship. "Is there anyone on Tethys not working for either you or Al-Kirzen?"

With a tight grip behind my elbow, he steered me away from the cell. "Not many. Lucky you chose Mahitso to deliver your message. He's one of the few naive persons left on the whole moon."

Reinhart led me through a series of little-used corridors, slowly working upward to the top level. From a hallway on the very periphery of the station, we entered a room through an unmarked door. Unlike the tarnished passageway, the room was brightly lit and meticulously clean. Twenty or so United

Nations personnel, each wearing sky blue security armbands, were busy at computer consoles and communication ports.

A young man with first lieutenant's bars saluted and escorted us over to a view screen. "Welcome to United Nations Outworld Security, Mr. Kayoto."

I walked beside him, rather than ahead, and used my greater height to glance at the papers on his clipboard. There wasn't time to read anything, except for a red "Operation Proselyte" stamped in the upper right corner of the top sheet. Right above a picture of Jessica Vandimeer.

The view screen showed a small planetary craft surrounded by technicians. Amber Whitehorse stood to the side, giving terse orders to her underlings. Everyone was armed.

"You expect me to get in there? You're dreaming."

He ignored my objections. "When you have retrieved Miss Vandimeer, you will proceed by steamer to Calypso. From there, I imagine Miss Vandimeer has plans of her own."

"Assuming you don't blow us both away."

"Mr. Kayoto, the time for radical solutions is past. After your guard's demise, two more dead bodies on Tethys would be impossible to cover up. You must understand that present circumstances are such that both Al-Kirzen and the United Nations would find publicity troublesome. You may rest assured that I will not try to stop you. I suspect, though, that once you leave Calypso, you will wish I had."

I doubted that. "You still haven't told me how I'm supposed to rescue the damsel in distress."

"Like this." Reinhart entered three lines of code into a small computer beside the screen. The station's symbol for air circulation systems flashed brilliant red in response, but with another command, Reinhart erased it from the screen.

"Sometimes, Mr. Kayoto, the simplest solutions are the best. In an age when everyone depends on machines, he who controls the machines has ultimate power, don't you agree?" He pointed to the screen. "Considering the volume of the chamber, it will be about two hours before carbon dioxide poisoning sets in. Would you like a cup of tea while we wait?"

It was a nightmare experienced secondhand. The people working on Whitehorse's craft knew something was wrong, but the automatic alarm system that should have saved them wasn't talking. Reaction times slowed down and the workers in poor physical condition were dropped to their knees within ninety minutes.

Amber was the first to figure it out. Unfortunately, her gut reaction was to head for the air lock leading back into the station. The U.N. crew gave a cheer when the door held tight against all her efforts, both electronical and physical, to open it. Had she not been suffering from oxygen depletion, she might have turned back to her ship, sealed herself in, and pressurized the cabin. Now it was too late. Over several minutes, her movements became more confused and finally ceased altogether.

"I'll give you a two-minute head start before turning the oxygen on again. The hangar number is Twelve A, on the outer ring and furthest south, so you better run. I suggest you take a supply of air."

I grabbed a medical respirator and oxygen tube from a wall locker and sprinted down the hallway. Our boys in the U.N. didn't seem to care if oxygen deprivation turned Jessica into a vegetable before I got there. Compassionless are the mighty; that's how they got there. I wondered if they enjoyed watching their weaker cousin run through the station.

The hangars attached directly to Huygens were arranged in two concentric horseshoe arcs; thirteen in the outer band, four in the inner. They held a variety of ships, from hoppers to short-range intra-satellite vessels only slightly less massive than the relatively large ships that required the blast pads on Exit Hill.

By evil coincidence, Whitehorse's ship was housed almost as far away from Reinhart's playroom as possible. I arrived at the outer lock hyperventilating. Reinhart, enjoying his omnipotence, opened the air seal by remote, just I was reaching for it.

The gas in hangar 12, most of it exhaled carbon dioxide, smelled hot and wet. I covered my mouth with the breathing mask and inhaled cool oxygen. Knowing Amber Whitehorse would soon regain consciousness, I quickly boarded the ship, cursing the slow-moving pneumatic doors as I checked each cabin.

Jessica was tucked away in the modest medical hold, lying unconscious on a Stokes litter. She had been stripped naked and wired to a life-support system. An auxiliary tube injected a thick green gel into a saline drip running to her arm.

Despite the urgency of the situation, an alarm in my

subconscious yelled for attention and I found myself pausing over Jessica's prone form. With her hair tumbling over her breasts, she looked, as Mahitso had said, like a realist holo of a Greek goddess. But as I more closely examined her flawless form, an ugly suspicion came over me.

Feeling like a cad, I brushed her hair away and studied her chest under the harsh lighting. Her breasts were perfectly matched, the pink areolae and nipples exact duplicates. Exactly the kind of rigorous symmetry never found in nature. How could I have missed it before? Still, now was not the time to worry about it.

I pulled the I.V. needle out of her forearm, and gave her several hits of oxygen from my mask. She came to, eerily reminding me of pretty Jane Hamilton coming awake.

"What . . . ?" Her voice was thick and slurred.

"Jessica, come on. We're in a bit of a rush here."

Her glazed eyes tried to track to my voice. Someone in the hangar was coughing. I picked Jessica up and carried her through the ship. Her head rolled from side to side as I bumped around corners. Down the ramp and across the hangar. Someone struggled to her feet as I went out the air lock. Reinhart must have pushed some buttons because the door sealed behind me.

I stopped long enough to take off my shirt and pull it over Jessica's head. It took fifteen long minutes to carry Jessica back to her quarters. Faces registered surprise as I rushed through the hallways and down elevators. Wondering what I was doing loose with the woman I'd been accused of murdering.

Guessing Whitehorse had used the same drug on Jessica as she had on me, I gave Jessica an injection of epinephrine from the emergency medical kit in her room. It helped, but she remained drowsy and distracted.

Three minutes to pack my duffel and another five to get Jessica dressed; but not before I ran some quick tests. While Jessica stared blankly through a passive haze, I encircled each of her wrists in turn with my right hand. As far as I could tell by this crude method, they were exactly the same size. As were her ankles. Just like her breasts.

I'd never been able to find any evidence of surgical enhancements on Jessica's faultless body because you don't need them if someone's tinkered with your genetic makeup.

Nature doesn't create perfect animals, but bio-engineers employ symmetry as a necessary shortcut.

As much as I wanted to know why Jessica had been fabricated and who had paid to have the work done, it'd have to wait until I got us away from Al-Kirzen's goons. I threw some of Jessica's clothes in her smallest suitcase, tossing in the diamond necklace before zipping it shut. The Stoeger went into my shoulder holster. Jessica's leather flight jacket fit me well, and was bulky enough to cover the machine pistol.

My hands full, Jessica had to walk back to the upper decks. The stimulants must have helped because she became more coherent with each step back toward the hangar. By the time we got there, I'd told her enough to give her a reasonable picture of what was happening.

The Calypso shuttles were stored in the third hangar of the inner band. It did nothing for my nerves to think Whitehorse was across the corridor only a few chambers away. I didn't kid myself into thinking I could gun her down with the machine pistol if she found us.

In the dim light of the shuttle bay, three short-range Stanley Steamers slumbered, one suckling fuel from an umbilical connected to a water pump. Back on Terra, Steamers were used to shuttle the elite to one of the seven low-earth-orbit satellites. They ran a little cheaper out here, water not being such a scarce commodity.

Larger and less streamlined than their sisters back on Terra, these Steamers were thirty meters long, most of which was accounted for by a large water fuel cell. The cell was connected to the cockpit by a webwork of nickel alloy struts. Eight smaller canisters of carbon dioxide were placed around the ship, for use in landing and steering. A polished titanium plate had been bolted to the back of the capsule, just in case the ground laser misfired and hit it instead of the thrust chamber. I helped Jessica into the nearest steamer, dropping our bags to support her while she climbed the ladder to the two-man cockpit.

"Jefferson, don't do this. Go back."

"It's a little late for that. How long to complete the preflight check?"

She was already working with the shuttle's computer. "Five minutes. The sequence is automated, I've already keyed the start-up routine."

I waited outside, feeling hours pass for each minute. Someone began pounding on the air lock. Finally, Jessica waved me over. "We're green."

"You feeling good enough to pilot?"

"I think so." Jessica's skin was waxy under the ship's lights. Whatever Al-Kirzen's assassin had shot into her veins, it was a lot worse than what I lived through.

"Sorry, but that's hardly reassuring. Take the nav board; call the tower and have them start depressurization."

I ran to the other two shuttles, shooting several rounds into the innards of each cockpit. The deafening sound of the air pumps kicked to life, muffling the sound of the Wildcats tearing through delicate machinery. My ears were popping from decreasing pressure by the time I climbed into the pilot's seat of the steamer.

Jessica, eyes glazed over, stared blankly ahead. When the all-clear alarm sounded and the hangar doors opened, I reached for her shoulder and gave her a rude shake.

"Wake up, Jessica. I need your help."

In a slow voice, sometimes trailing off so low I had to ask her to repeat herself, she went through the launch sequence. On the second try, I correctly aligned us with Tethys's laser canon and gave the go-ahead. The laser was dead on target, hitting us in the center of the thrust chamber. The open throttle fed water into the already white-hot rhenium chamber, where it flashed to vapor. The steam boiled back toward Tethys, pushing us from the icy moon.

35

Saturn's malevolent glow, shining through the craft's tiny canopy, colored the instruments in pastel shadows. Jessica had slipped out of consciousness again, her face pasty in the yellow light of the gas giant. Contrary to everything I'd expected, the ship continued running smoothly.

Traveling on a beam of light might be romantic, but it has the obvious drawback of being dependent on ground lasers for thrust. If Amber Whitehorse and her gang reached Tethys's lasing installation, they'd be able to pull our plug. No way the carbon dioxide thrusters would have enough juice to get back to Tethys. We'd be left out here with nothing to do but wait for Amber to arrive. Hardly an ideal situation.

For five hours and twelve minutes I stared at the energy readouts, waiting for the telltale fluctuations that would signal imminent shutdown of the laser. By the time Calypso came into range, I was too exhausted at our safe arrival. I told Tethys to cut the laser, and jockeyed the steamer down to the landing pad on her carbon dioxide thrusters.

I gently massaged Jessica's neck and cheeks until she came awake.

''Where are we?''

''Calypso. We made it.''

Instead of the relief I expected, she covered her eyes with her hands. ''I'm sorry, Jefferson. This isn't what I wanted.''

''It can't be what Al-Kirzen wanted, either. For the moment, we're still one step ahead of him.'' Chances of things staying that way weren't all that great, but after Whitehorse's drugs, Jessica looked liked she needed all the reassurance she could get.

She gave me a wan smile and brushed her hand through my tangled, sweaty hair. ''I wasn't thinking of Al-Kirzen.'' Was that pity in her voice?

From the pressurized blast pad, we took an elevator down to the living quarters. It didn't take long to see why the inhabitants of Tethys called it the Mansion.

Commuting from the stark corridors of Christaan Huygens to Calypso station was like moving from black-and-white film to full-color holography. Tropical ferns sprouted from huge floor planters, and flowered vines covered the walls. Each plant seemed to have been chosen for the deep color or sweet smell of its blossom. By comparison, the botanical gardens on the *Far Hand* were mundane.

Each of the Mansion's twenty rooms was furnished with overstuffed chairs, dyed with bright pigments. Every fixture was finished in polished chrome and brass. Back on Earth, it would have been considered garish. Out here it was a relief.

A short hallway connected the main room, called the

Arboretum, to the Red Room. It housed several orchids, each blooming in a different shade of carmine. On the far wall, a print depicted a bowl of ripe strawberries done in high-gloss paint and framed in gold. The sheets on the king-size water bed were transparent, as was the bed itself, allowing us to see the clear liquid inside. I figured it was water until I saw the end of the bed had a spigot tapped into it. I gave Jessica my raised-eyebrow demonstration.

"White wine from Nix Olympica Ag Station, Mars System. They can't get water rights to grow anything but wheat, so we cut them a deal. We give them water, which they put to use on their three acres of non-sanctioned vineyard, and every year they ship us a couple of kiloliters of their finest. It's not bad, considering what they have to do to grapes to get them to grow on Mars."

"But why put it in the bed? Either we're going to be chilled, or it's going to get warm. Right now, I'm more concerned about me."

She took my hand and led me to the foot of the bed. A tray had been built under a spigot. Jessica took a glass from the tray and filled it with fluid drained from the bed. It was cool but left a chemical aftertaste. I could see why she thought the vintages on the *Far Hand* were good.

"The bed is made from a polymer with low thermal conductivity. The wine stays cold, and we don't catch pneumonia."

"Thank the gods for the wonders of modern science."

Between the recent influx of pharmaceuticals and exhaustion, I fell asleep without crawling out of my clothes. There would be time enough tomorrow to see the corpses of the children shipped up from Iapetus. Time enough to radio the freaks and tell them what I knew about the murderer.

Rapidly descending into monochrome dreamscape, I copulated with a man-made construct of metal and gears that looked like Jessica Vandimeer. Every time I spoke to it, the machine convulsed with Jane Hamilton's mad laughter.

36

Jessica had completely recovered by the time we awoke; so much so that she tried to sneak off without me hearing her. I waited until she was out of the room, then followed her.

Stalking someone in low-g isn't easy. Calypso's gravity well is so weak, the builders of the Mansion had installed hand rails along the walls to help people move without flying off the floor. Unfortunately, the rails were cloned hickory. They creaked every time any type of pressure was put on them.

I managed to stay out of sight as Jessica worked her way through the Arboretum and further into the back halls of the Mansion. She stopped along a section of bare wall, suspicious in itself due to the lack of clinging plants, and put her palm on a slight indentation. The wall must have recognized her because it slid back. She stepped into the recess and I edged forward.

"Identity request." The voice was metal, probably some kind of low-grade artificial intelligence.

"General Molly Kulerin, United Nations Security number fifteen ninety A: transport pilot Operation Mind-Set."

What do you know? Jessica had yet another name. I was beginning to see why Reinhart had called her an embarrassment. If she'd broken into U.N. security, a lot of world leaders must be scrambling to cover their tracks. I wondered if it had anything to do with the current rash of assassinations plaguing the United Nations General Assembly.

"Vocal scan complete. Identity of agent General Molly Kulerin confirmed."

"Request craft for client transportation be sent to Calypso pad three for immediate transfer."

"Hard copy verification required for changing standard procedure. You have three seconds to comply."

Damn her. She should have known there'd be safeguards for gaining access to the United Nations' supply of fleet ships. U.N. identification cards, like the one Reinhart had shown me, have a series of alpha numerics inscribed on the back. The code is written by using a tunneling scanning microscope to punch Xenon atoms into microthin foil. Impossible to see, except with state-controlled technology, it's impossible to counterfeit. The reward for being caught in the attempt is a short burst from a molecular laser.

I rushed around to the recess, knowing I'd be far too late to yank Jessica out before the computer opened fire. I got there in time to see her slide a blue card into the machine's scanning slot. Jessica turned to me and held out a hand of warning. She didn't seem surprised to see me.

"Confirmation complete. Shuttle transfer request approved, United Nations' Outer Planetary Command, Operation Mind-Set, May third, 2186. Pilot John Stevens will fly the craft via telemetry uplink from Tethys. Origin: Exit Hill, pad two. Shuttle ETA on Calypso pad three: twenty-three hours fourteen minutes twenty-nine seconds. Acknowledge."

"General Molly Kulerin, O.P.C. acknowledged. Transaction complete."

She stepped out of the small room and shut the door. And slapped me hard across the face.

"You idiot! The defense system was active. If you'd stepped in, you'd have been fried."

I absentmindedly rubbed the stinging skin along my jaw. First she pulls my bank access code, and now this. The feeling of uneasiness Jessica had occasionally left me with on the *Far Hand* came back tenfold. "How'd you get the U.N. card?"

"It's not important."

"What? You crash the government's most sophisticated security system like it was programmed by a child, and you want me to believe it's not important? How did you alter the card to match your voice pattern?"

She turned without answering and walked hurriedly down the corridor.

"What is Operation Mind-Set?" She ignored me and kept marching. I raced after her, grabbed her arm, and forced her around. "What's going on?"

Her eyes narrowed in anger, then relaxed. "I'm trying to get us out of here in one piece."

"Reinhart said you could arrange a ride off this snowball. He knew you'd broken into U.N. security. Why didn't he arrange to have the computer kill you back there?"

"Because I'm smart enough to rank myself in the upper echelons. Officers don't murder their superiors, even in the U.N."

"A perfectly reasonable explanation that I don't happen to buy for a second. I know Reinhart. He'd kill the U.N. General Secretary if he thought it was necessary."

Jessica gave a long, tired sigh. She seemed to cave in on herself. "Jefferson, if there were any other way, I'd use it. But if I sent you back to Tethys now, you'd be dead within a few minutes. I didn't believe that before, but I know it now. You can't outrun Al-Kirzen and the United Nations both. And you know too much to be left alive."

"Like hell." The time for calm discussion was past. "I don't know shit. I don't know anything because you haven't told me anything."

In contrast to my growing anger, her reply was subdued, almost lost in the cool, still air of the Mansion. "If there were any way I could undo the last seven months, to spare you all of this, I would do it."

"I'm not asking you to undo anything! All I want is the truth."

"You will know it soon enough."

"Now there's a cheering thought. I bet it'll make a great epitaph." I left her standing alone in the hall.

Of the next twenty-three hours, I used half of it to search the Mansion for any signs of dead freaks. If any of Iapetus's deceased children had ever been shipped here, they were long since gone. Just another one of Jessica's lies.

I spent the remainder of the time locked in Callirrhoe, a room named for its modest swimming pool. A greasy polymer additive, used to keep the water from splashing in the low gravity, coated my fingers as I dangled them in the pool. Probably the one place in the solar system where the water was less pure than home. And I was supposed to swim in it.

No one to blame but myself. I'd let Vandimeer lead me around on a velvet leash when I should have been thinking about saving my skin. She was right about my chances, I'd never make it against the people who were out to get us.

37

Fifteen minutes before her shanghaied United Nations transport ship was due, Jessica's voice came over the Mansion's intercom.

"Jefferson? The computer has identified two ships vectored for Calypso. From their current position, they must have lifted from Rhea. I scanned them with a low-power scope. Both of them carry Al-Kirzen's circles and triangles on their sides. ETA two hours, fifteen minutes. In addition, there is a fleet of seven United Nations corvettes coming in from Tethys. Spectroscopy shows they're burning hydrogen in lox. They're moving over five times as fast as the shuttles from Rhea, and will be here within the hour. Our ship is on schedule and I think we can outrun both groups of pursuers. Will you come with me?"

What choice did I have? "I'll be at the pad in five minutes."

Waiting in the pad's pressurized observation booth, Jessica seemed a ghost of her former self. Her natural vibrancy and humor were gone. Her eyes were puffy from either lack of sleep or crying. I steeled myself not to feel anything.

"Where are we headed?"

"The ship is short range only. Our best bet is to try and lose them in the rings."

Further conversation was cut short by the landing U.N. ship. We waited in stony silence while the hangar closed and repressurized. We got a green light, and Jessica boarded the ship to radio a landing confirmation to the pilot back on Tethys.

The United Nations' *Raptor* had sacrificed aesthetics for speed. No messing around with lasers or reflective solar sails here. A collection of bulky hydrogen and liquid oxygen tanks surrounded the living quarters. On each side, stubby delta wings protruded from between fuel cells. Useless in space, they must have originally been for emergency landings on either Earth or Mars. Too bad we didn't have a tenth the amount of fuel to get us to either place.

From the outside, I'd have guessed the ship could carry up to thirty people. This was belied by the cramped conditions of the interior. The cockpit was built for one, while a small chamber, roomy enough for three people if they crowded, was just inside the air lock. An internal air lock, now opened, separated the two chambers.

Jessica waved to one of the acceleration couches in the passenger cabin. "Take a seat. There are a couple of external checks to complete before we lift."

"Need any help?"

"No, I can do it more quickly alone."

Muffled thuds, heard through the electronically sealed door in the aft bulkhead of my cabin, hinted that whatever she was up to, Jessica was struggling with a good deal of mass. She reappeared at the airlock just as I was considering going out to check on her.

"You better strap in. Lift acceleration will only be point nine g's, but after months in low gravity, it's going to feel like a Tipler compacting vise."

"How far away are the other ships?"

"The steamers from Rhea are still over an hour out. The corvettes are closer but I doubt they can catch us. Considering the fuel they must have burned to reach their present velocities, they'll likely have to stop and refuel here."

After making sure I was strapped in, Jessica exited to the pilot's pod, sealing the air lock behind her. I was prepared for a ten-minute wait while the hangar cycled air out, but a loud *whoof* told me Vandimeer had used the emergency override to blow the outer door.

"Not a bad move," I said aloud. Anyone landing would have to suit up to enter the station, then reset the door before they could service their ships without wearing full suits.

"Thank you," Jessica's voice sounded from a speaker. "Brace yourself, this is going to be uncomfortable."

Understatement of the year. With only nine-tenths of a g pressing down on me, I felt like a beached whale. The burn lasted three minutes before Jessica cut power and the pseudo-gravitational force dropped to more comfortable level.

"There's a small view plate on the table to your right. If you turn it on, I have the port cameras focused on the United Nations' corvettes."

At this distance, the ships were only visible by their exhaust. Seven plumes of flame stabbing the dark sky. What the hell were they doing out here chasing us? Their Colonel Reinhart could have sent us to the morgue on Tethys with considerably less trouble. Perhaps not everyone in the U.N. agreed with his decision to let us go.

As I puzzled over the implications of this, the ships' fiery signatures elongated to pencils of light. "They're not vectored for us."

"No," Jessica answered. "As I suspected, they'll have to stop at Calypso to refuel. Even then, the Mansion has limited supplies of hydrogen on hand. They'll have to fire up the electrolysis machine and sit on their hands while it fills their tanks."

"That should give us some time. What's the plan?"

"There's an emergency station on Mimas. We should be able to refuel there. After that, we'll head to the periphery of the Saturn System. If the *Far Hand* is still around, maybe we can get close enough to flag them down with an S.O.S. Al-Kirzen ship or not, they'd have to pick us up."

"Good an idea as any. How do we stay alive long enough to get back to Earth?"

"I'll worry about that after I'm sure Al-Kirzen doesn't have any other surprises waiting for us."

The next two hours passed without incident, and I was beginning to think we were going to make it. On the view plate, the rings of Saturn spread out below us, their intricate structure hypnotic in complexity. Marveling at their splendor, I suddenly recalled something I had read, way back on Earth. Like the rings, all of Saturn's major moons had orbits lying roughly inside the gas giant's equatorial plane. All except one.

What had Reinhart said: *You may rest assured I will not try to stop you. I suspect, though, that once you leave Calypso, you will wish I had.*

Below us, more rings were coming into view. We were shooting out of the equatorial plane. Far too much if we were going to dive back into the rings to lose our pursuers. I quietly unstrapped myself from the seat, suspicious now of Jessica's ability to hear me.

The electronic security in the aft bulkhead looked like a duplicate of the one on the *Far Hand* medical section. That didn't mean anything, there could be a hundred things behind it, or nothing at all. But I knew, as clear as if I'd watched her, what Jessica had been doing during her so-called external preflight check. Arranging bodies for a high-velocity takeoff.

So obvious now. Jamie somehow had figured it out after his trip to the hospital. Whitehorse and Reinhart had certainly known all along. The distance everyone kept, her knowing my bank card number, Amber bringing a gang along with her on Tethys when she nailed us. How could I have missed all of the signs?

I stood in front of the door for what seemed like hours, paralyzed by the revelation. There was no place to run to, and even if I'd been on Earth, there'd have been no place to hide from Jessica Vandimeer. Any hope of escape here was surely illusory.

The machine pistol was worse than useless and nothing in the cabin looked any more promising. I had to get to the room behind the security door. There had to be something there to stop Vandimeer's kind.

Chances were slim that all phases of the operation used the same combination code, but the United Nations might be overconfident in their security. I could only try, hoping Jessica wouldn't be alerted to my actions by the cockpit's security panel.

There was a whisper of motion when I typed triple sixes into the door's security keypad. On fifteen gurneys, fifteen bodies were strapped down and hooked to life-support machines. Three tables away, Jane Hamilton slept on the way to her final destination. I had just enough time to realize something didn't quite fit when I heard Jessica step behind me.

I pulled the Stoeger and backed away.

"So now you know what I am." The sadness in her voice was unmistakable. Ironic that now of all times she seemed so frail. Or was she only making me see her that way?

I fired a shot to her left, careful to hit an internal bulkhead rather than the hull. "Don't come any closer. I don't want to kill you, but I will."

"No, you won't. If you wanted me dead, you wouldn't have missed your first shot. Fire now, if you can. I'll do nothing to stop you. I owe you that much." She started forward again.

The machine pistol shook in my hand as I backed away. When I felt a solid wall at my back, I aimed the gun directly at her head. She came slowly and brushed it aside, her hand rising to cup my head. Her kiss was soft, and I felt her passion flow through me.

Pleasure and desire washed over me; rapture so pure that for a moment I could think of nothing else—wanted to think of nothing else. For a brief instant two became one, transcending the physical world that separated us. I knew the perfect coupling of male and female; a bond of sexual intensity without clumsy physical movement. I knew paradise: a place where I need never to be alone again.

But there was the memory of Jane Hamilton. Leering at me. Overpowering me. Seeking to control me as surely as Jessica did now. With a shock the mood was broken.

"Jefferson?" Her voice was soft, crystal tears gathered at her eyes, forming spheres in the low gravity. "Don't fight me, you can't win."

"You going to kill me? Stop me from breathing like Jane did?"

"No."

"Going to turn me into a zombie? Make me do tricks? You really had me going for it back on the *Far Hand*. How often did you manipulate me then?"

"No! I never made you do anything. What passed between us was real. You must know I'm telling the truth."

"Why am I here?"

"Our children are dying. We don't know why. We need help."

"Too bad. It's not my problem." I lunged at her. Hoping to knock her out before she gained control.

Too slow by ages. She was inside. My muscles froze in midleap. I hit the floor hard.

"Jefferson! Stop it. Don't make me do this!"

From the floor, I fought until I was facing her. "You can't stay awake forever."

"I know." She reached out to one of the tables, removed an I.V., and approached me. There was no pain as she slipped the feed into my arm.

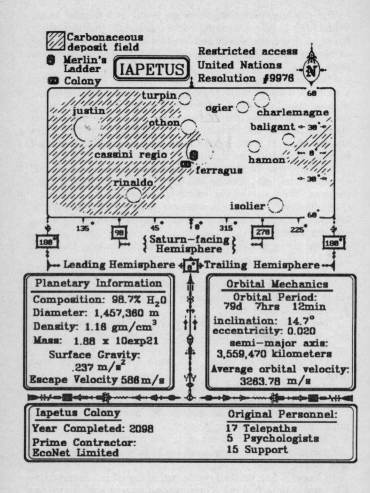

Carbonaceous deposit field
▨ Merlin's Ladder
⬤⬤ Colony

IAPETUS

Restricted access
United Nations
Resolution #9976

N

turpin
justin
ogier
charlemagne
othon
baligant ◄ 30°
cassini regio
hamon
ferragus
rinaldo
isolier
68°
8°
30°
68°

135   90   45   8°   315   278   225

{Saturn-facing}
Hemisphere

◄► Leading Hemisphere ◄■► Trailing Hemisphere ◄►

180°   90   278   180°

Planetary Information
Composition: 98.7% H_2O
Diameter: 1,457,360 m
Density: 1.16 gm/cm^3
Mass: 1.88 x 10exp21
Surface Gravity:
.237 m/s^2
Escape Velocity 586 m/s

Orbital Mechanics
Orbital Period:
79d 7hrs 12min
inclination: 14.7°
eccentricity: 0.020
semi-major axis:
3,559,470 kilometers
Average orbital velocity:
3263.78 m/s

Iapetus Colony
Year Completed: 2098
Prime Contractor:
EcoNet Limited

Original Personnel:
17 Telepaths
5 Psychologists
15 Support

IAPETUS

38

There are no blast pads on Iapetus. The last United Nations crew on the moon placed heating coils under the three pads used during construction. The foundation beneath each pad had turned to water, which quickly boiled away in the nonexistent atmosphere of the moon. Robbed of support, the pads collapsed inward. The only way to reach the surface now was by descending Merlin's Ladder.

Sometime during my drug-induced slumber, Jessica docked at the top of the largest construct in the solar system and unloaded her sleeping charges. She muscled the freaks, still imprisoned by their medical machines, from the *Raptor*'s hold onto waiting elevator cars just large enough to hold three riders at a time. Jessica loaded five cars and followed them down. She traveled in the sixth, me sleeping at her side.

A second telepath, somehow eluding Merlin's defense systems, took an elevator car up from the surface of Iapetus. She piloted the United Nations' ship back to its clandestine pad on Calypso. Her voice was close enough to Jessica's to pass the daily radio checks from Tethys. The first thing she did was pull some strings, easy enough to do when you have the ability to make other people's minds up for them, and get Calypso reserved for the next three weeks. In the meantime, with the exceptions of Reinhart and Whitehorse, no one knew I'd been kidnapped. I wasn't exactly counting on them to save the day.

The room I awoke in was small, less than three meters to a side. The plastic form-walls were painted hospital white, as were the ceiling and floor. This being hell, there were no windows. A narrow doorway just beyond the foot of my bed was the only break in the otherwise featureless room.

My arms and legs were strapped to a metal gurney that was doing nothing good for my bare shoulder blades. Had I been in a better mood, I'm sure I would have appreciated the black irony of the situation. As it was, the only thing I could think to be thankful for was that Jessica's tranks didn't have the same deleterious side effects as others I'd recently consumed.

Speaking of Lady Iscariot, she must have been watching me. I had been awake for less than three minutes when she came into the room. I didn't see any cameras, so she'd been using other means. Probably crawling through my thoughts while I slept. Seeing if there were any other tricks I could do, other than the more elaborate suicide schemes I'd currently taken to practicing.

"Planned it all out, didn't you?"

She looked down at me, her eyes dull and expressionless. "No."

"Can you at least untie me? I promise to behave—not that it matters much now anyway."

She stepped over and undid the restraining straps. I sat up and unconsciously flinched away from her. She noticed the movement and backed away to the far side of the room, in front of the door. Damn me if she still wasn't a beautiful woman.

"Jamie knew, didn't he?" I eyed her closely, irrationally looking for some hint of her true nature. Of course there was nothing.

"Your associate found out when the black market surgeon started working on him."

"You made him scream so the medic wouldn't get suspicious, but you kept him from feeling any pain."

"I didn't want to hurt him. It was you we were after."

"But it was more complex than that. You had to watch him afterward. Make sure he wasn't able to tell me anything."

"Rather than permanently erase the experience from his consciousness. I removed his ability to access long-term memory of the event. He knew something had happened, he just couldn't move the information to an accessible level. The process is a bit disconcerting, like having a name on the tip of your tongue, but the effects are temporary. As soon as I was a certain distance away, I could no longer manage him. At that point, he remembered everything.''

''And he knew it was you who stood watching while a medic broke his bones and wrote the message with his blood.''

''But he never felt anything. Even now he can't remember ever being in pain. The neural pathways that should have delivered the message to his brain were not in operation.''

''Why couldn't he talk to me on Elf Hive?''

''Once I know a mind I can identify it over long distances. Just as you can recognize Jamie by the way he walks or by his clothes, even if you're too far away to see his face, I can now pinpoint his thoughts in a crowd. But control—or puppeteering, if you prefer—drops off with an inverse cube to distance. The best I could do from Elf Hive was make his mind foggy. Even then, he nearly got his message through. I had to resort to stimulating the neural input of his brain's pain center.''

Was it remorse that hushed her voice? Fine with me. Guilty people talk and I needed answer. ''But it cost you something. You ended up in the hospital.''

''Reaching over great distances produces a mild neurotoxin that after a short time builds up and reduces brain function. The only cure is sleep. I had just enough energy to use my bank card to transfer your funds to my account.''

''You got my new withdraw code when I gave it to Jamie.''

She nodded. ''I lost consciousness soon after. Had Jamie kept talking for another three minutes, he'd have been able to tell you everything. You'd be home right now, and I'd have slept to Saturn with the rest of the freaks.'' She said the word with caustic bitterness.

''And Holly?''

''I had nothing to do with that, Jefferson. I don't know who got to her.''

Was she telling the truth? Vandimeer's mental tricks could certainly be duplicated with drugs; 3-quinuclidinyl benzilate for disorientation, sodium pentothal and a syringe for the bloodletting. That meant Al-Kirzen or the United Nations had also taken an interest in pressuring me off Earth. Why? Because Jessica wasn't leaving Earth until some sap agreed to help her. And whoever worked on Holly figured Vandimeer would be an easier target on the *Far Hand*.

That meant Al-Kirzen. He owned the ship, and he wanted

Jessica Vandimeer back in the Saturn System. Putting screws into me, both with Amber Whitehorse skulking outside my office and the attack on Holly, accomplished that nicely.

Everything was falling into place. Vandimeer turning out to be a freak was the last piece I needed to figure Al-Kirzen's game. One more question would bring confirmation.

"Elle was one of you, wasn't she?"

"Yes."

The symptoms were there for anyone to see: tabloid rumors of Al-Kirzen's eugenics program, his unmistakable signs of megalomania, his desire to keep Jessica in perfect health after Elle had died—a telepathic mate for his son. Abdul's disease was as old as mankind. Aspirations of founding a progeny of supermen.

That left the United Nations. Their moves didn't make any sense at all. Or maybe they did to Reinhart, and maybe he was high enough in the company to be the deciding factor. Keep looking for answers.

"On the *Far Hand*, you were surprised when your room was bugged. Why?"

"Because most surveillance wavelengths modulate in frequencies that feed back in a telepathic field. I could no more ignore it than you could an electric guitar played too close to an amplifier."

Physics had never been a favorite subject. If Thomas were here, he'd tell me right away what I needed to know. All I could make of it was that the United Nations had developed a box, like the one I'd found in Jessica's room, that flooded an area with the right frequency of electromagnetic waves to obstruct a telepathic field. A necessary invention if you want to keep track of a freak, but why keep such a close eye on someone who must be exiled the moment his or her secret is out? Only Reinhart knew the answer. Every question I had seemed to lead back to him.

"Why were you so certain Reinhart wasn't the one who broke my knee?"

"After you told me about him, I tracked him down among a group of people dining on Tantalus. I scanned them all without finding any memory of the incident."

"Why did you bother checking everyone instead of just him?"

"I wasn't familiar with him. Among all the people there, I had no way to target on his mind."

"So what you're saying is, that of all the thoughts you were able to scan, none of them revealed any connection with my busted knee."

"Yes . . . what are you getting at?"

Reinhart must have had another jumming device on hand. Jessica never caught wind of his assault against me because she never really scanned his mind. Sheltered in a crowd, where Jessica would naturally assume she'd caught his thoughts along with everyone else's, he'd defeated her abilities.

And yet, to be entirely safe he'd have had to carry it with him at all times. But where? There'd been no sign of it when he won the Adonis contest and he hadn't been wearing a stitch of clothing while parading on the winner's stand. Time to worry about it later. For now, keep her talking.

"Who designed you?"

"What?"

"Come off it, Miss Vandimeer. It's a little late in the game for any more of your deceptions."

"I don't know what you're talking about. Nobody designed me. My father was Jon Pierre Vandimeer, my mother was Sylvia Andreeson."

"Yeah? Look in a mirror and see if you still believe that."

"Jefferson—"

"Skip it." Just because someone broke every rule in the book and designed a telepath didn't mean the subject had to know anything about it. Especially if access to that knowledge tainted carefully planned research. Vandimeer was beginning to look like someone's sick idea of an experiment.

"You kept me from discovering the truth, didn't you?"

"I had to. We need your help."

"What did you do?" If a man could snarl, I was doing it.

"Your brother's death left you with a mind-set against telepaths. The first time we met, I altered your emotional character in order to strengthen this perspective. Afterward, when I failed to comply with your conception of a telepath— that is to say a bloodthirsty maniac—it became almost impossible for you to see the truth."

I still had a few hundred questions left when Miss Vandimeer moved from in front of the door a second before it opened. Back home it would have been called an act of presentiment. Here it was only a token of a society that could communicate without cumbersome vocalization.

The reception committee consisted of an old man, eyes covered by bottle-thick glasses, a woman who must have been born in a low-g environment, and a heavily muscled middle-aged man. The woman towered above her comrades, her ropy body the result of Earth genetics coping in a null-g environment. There was no way to tell, but she probably had internal differences as well: a large inner ear and a natural resistance to the carcinogenic effects of solar radiation ten times what mine was.

To her left, the old man looked like a librarian. He had high cheekbones that hinted at Asian or AmerIndian ancestors. If he ever had any hair, it had long since given up. His beard must have at one time been coal black, but now it was sparse silver wire.

The younger male I recognized immediately. Benjamin Wheeler, who'd left an estimated 300 people dead before the U.N. caught up with him. The exact number was uncertain because Butcher Ben didn't leave a whole lot behind when he did someone in. Half of his victims had been identified solely through D.N.A. scans.

He looked at me and smiled. "So this is our savior. How pleasant to meet you, Mr. Kayoto."

I flashed a grin back. "Ben Wheeler, if the composite sketches the police made are correct. You must be slipping. Four other people in the same room with you and you haven't killed even one of us yet. Going soft in your old age?"

The woman cut in before he could say anything, but he gave me a dark look. "There's no need for that, Mr. Kayoto, the past is but water under the bridge."

"Yeah? Tell that to the people he killed."

To my amazement, the old man broke into wheezy laughter. The others stared tolerantly at him until he found his voice. "He's right, you know. You can't blame him for hating us."

Ben's voice ground out between clinched teeth. "I've paid my dues, a hundred times over. I'm not going to stand here and let this evolutionary throwback insult me."

"Then don't," the old man shot back. "Lisa, why don't you and Ben go back to the chambers. You don't look too good, either, Jessica. Go with them." It was more of an order than a request. The others obeyed with surprising meekness. Jessica kissed the old man's cheek softly as she passed.

"Let me guess," he said when the others were gone. "On the whole, you'd rather be on Terra."

"You got that right, pops."

"My name is Avry, Mr. Kayoto, and you look like a man in need of a drink."

The police call this routine hard and soft. Expose the suspect to someone ruthless, then use a harmless codger to coax the needed information out. I was working under the added handicap of still not knowing what they needed out of me.

"You're wrong, Jefferson. Your thinking is based on a faulty presumption. If we wanted information from you, we'd just reach in and take it. You are right about Benjamin Wheeler, though, he is a vicious son of a bitch."

I felt like twisting the old man's arm off. "I don't need you digging through my head."

"Then you best not be calling me a codger. You want a drink or not?"

"Might as well." What else could I do?

39

He led me down a series of corridors that originally had been as stark as the hallways of Tethys. But here the walls were covered with drawings and paintings made by the children of the colony. Crayon mountains and pastel beaches, sketched replicas of places none of the children would ever see.

Avry took me to his personal chamber. A spacious five meters to a side, the room was lined with shelves of old books. Tucked in the lone corner not taken up by shelving was a cot, its sheets in disarray. A library terminal and microfiche reader took up most of the space on the only table. Beside the reader, a five-by-eight picture of a beautiful Oriental woman dressed in a traditional kimono was the only thing in the room not covered with paper dust. His wife? Daughter?

He motioned me to a battered old chair and punched a few commands into an ancient ethane synthesizer. After a few seconds he handed me a tumbler of bourbon. Of course he knew what I liked without asking.

He settled into a chair across from mine. "We need to have a long talk. You have a lot of questions which others in the colony will not answer. After all these years, I find that I no longer feel the need to protect our secrets. Feel free to ask anything."

"Why don't you just grab the questions out of my head?"

"Touché. I scanned you in the lobby because I had to know if after everything you've been through, you would still help us. A necessary indiscretion on my part. However, the codger here knows how to be a gentleman. I doubt you will ever trust us, but for the sake of civility, please pretend that you believe me when I say that I will not presume to invade your privacy again, nor will I allow others of the colony to do so."

I didn't see I had any choice. Not that I was going to start pitching slow ball. "Fine. You can start by telling me why telepaths get such a kick out of murdering people."

He took a long pull at his drink; the same cinnamon concoction Jamie favored. Coincidence, or was he doing it for effect? The spicy smell of the esters brought back memories of better times.

"No one back home has figured it out yet?"

"Not that I know of. Telepaths from every continent, out of every gene pool in the solar system, from wildly different social backgrounds, all end up being on the homicidal side. Other than telepathy, there's no common factor among them."

He pointed to a series of books covered with gaudy dust jackets. "My science fiction collection. Telepathy was a favorite subject of twentieth- and twenty-first-century writers, you know. They droned on and on about the powers and abilities a mature telepath would have. They saw only the obvious advantage of being able to know other people's thoughts."

The man's bitter tone caught me off guard. I must have been treading on sacred ground but I wasn't about to back off. "I can't say I see where they were all that wrong. If I had the ability, I would be rich, oversexed, and happy."

"Wrong! You'd be just like us. You'd be a killer who started with someone close, most likely your parents, and you wouldn't stop until the U.N. terror squads had you strapped down, or until they split your skull with a bullet."

"I don't think—"

"Shut up and listen. Telepathy isn't like knowledge or abstract thought, it's not something you learn, it's something you're born with. You have it the second the doctor slaps your butt and you start bawling, maybe even before."

The last thing I wanted to do was sit here and listen to this geezer justify the death of my brother with psychological double-talk. "So you're an Einstein at two because you can scan everyone within several hundred meters. What's the problem?"

Avry tried to remain calm, but was obviously getting as worked up as I was. "The human brain isn't developed enough in infancy to encompass the complexities of the adult world. At best, it can comprehend only the simplest of stimuli, most of which are on an emotional rather than intellectual level."

"I can't say you're making any sense."

"A baby in mama's arms pisses his pants. Happens with every baby, right? Mama changes his diapers and he forgets about it and does the same thing six hours later. But what about the telepath? What about the baby who senses the aversion and disgust behind the kind words? She isn't smart enough to understand what's happening is only natural, she understands only that her parents, who oftentimes feel warmth and love toward her, also often feel repulsion. You have any idea what that does to a two-month-old baby's perception of the world?"

The endless cases of patricide and matricide. What had seemed so macabre now began to make sense. "I never looked at it that way."

Avry nodded and pressed his point. "The older she gets, the worse it becomes. She discovers her peers do not have her ability and they despise those who do. So she learns to hide it. But that doesn't mean it's gone. Her father comes home from a hard day in the bread lines and finds his daughter has broken the holovision. The anger, frustration, and rage of the entire day are focused on the girl. Even if the father doesn't do anything to the kid physically, the damage has already been done.

"And when she reaches puberty? She gets a crush on a

handsome upperclassman. She causes him to fall in love with her. And while they're in the sack, he starts fantasizing that he's making it with the leader of the cheerleading squad.''

"What's the big deal? Everyone fantasizes. I'm not naive enough to think my partners don't. You don't see me out there slitting throats.''

"Good for you.'' He slammed his empty glass down. "You don't know shit, you know that? You sit here talking as if you know what it's like. Well, you don't. It's not some logic problem you can rationalize away. It hits you in the ego.'' Avry thumped his bony chest in emphasis. "You can't run, you can't hide. Every minute fault your partner sees in you is yours for examination. I don't think an adult could handle it without help; a teenager doesn't stand a chance. So don't try that psychoanalysis crap on us. You haven't earned the right.''

He topped off his glass and took a small sip. "Think about what's inherent in growing up in the modern world. The malicious lies of people you considered your friends, the carefully pent-up emotions of your parents as they struggle to understand their strange child, the violence and terrorism on the holo every night.

"That barely scratches the surface of what the real experience is like. Is it any wonder our minds fracture? Can you even begin to understand the hell we're born to?'' The anger was gone, his eyes unfocused—looking at his own childhood. How had it fallen apart for him?

"How many people did you finish off?''

He glared at me. "None of your damn business.''

"How about Jessica Vandimeer? How much blood does she have on her hands?''

His face went red with anger but when he spoke his voice sounded more tired than hostile. "I must remember the circumstances you're in. This must be extremely hard on you.'' He slowly got to his feet and took another pull at his drink.

"When a new colonist arrives at Iapetus, he is put through an intensive period of therapy. Part of the process is to make the person let go of his past. For some it takes months, or even years. Questions about life before arriving here are strictly taboo. You must henceforth keep your curiosity in check.

"I will answer you question about Jessica Vandimeer, though. Her father was Jon Pierre Vandimeer, a powerful corporate head, one of the first zero-g moguls. You've probably heard of him, he's the one with the industrial solar polymers.''

"I looked into him. There were rumors he abused her. Vandimeer wasn't too eager to talk about it.''

"His extravagances were not mere rumor, Mr. Kayoto. His tastes ran toward young girls. He started in on Jessica when she was two. If you've seen pictures of him, you know he was somewhat overweight. You want to hear about the reconstructive surgery we had to do on her pelvis and legs?''

I swallowed hard. "No.'' How many times had I wondered about her limp?

"So she does mean something to you. Are you sure you want to hear the rest of it?''

Not trusting myself to speak, I nodded.

"Like any other kid faced with the same home life, Jessica ran away as soon as she could. Ended up in a boarding school in the Schiaparelli Dome. Her father's arm, however, was very long. He hounded the local U.N. marshal until he hunted her down. Although Jessica remained in school, her father visited her quite frequently.

"She was in her second year of college, a pathetically broken girl, when she walked into a U.N. detention center. They didn't want to believe she was a telepath; after all, she had no record. She cranked out three perfect Rhine scores in succession and they shipped her out here. The only place her father couldn't reach her.''

"There was nothing about that in the data nets.''

"Her father didn't want made public the embarrassment of having sired a freak. He cut a deal with the United Nations to keep her deportation a secret.''

There was the United Nations again. They had been a shadowy presence all of Vandimeer's life. Their appearances might seem like coincidence to her but it was surely more than that. "What about the numbers tattooed on the back of her hand?''

"Another of her father's sick jokes. Wanted her always to know she belonged to him.'' That didn't sound quite right to me, but Avry believed it and I figured Vandimeer did, too. My guess was Jon's buddies in the U.N. had more to do with it.

"Why didn't she kill Jon Pierre?''

"Her reaction to her father's treatment was to withdraw into herself. Because of her childhood she harbored no illusions about the nature of the human race. Ironic that her father's inclinations toward rape spared Jessica the need to pick up a gun and start blasting. She's the closest thing Iapetus has to a true innocent.''

''She never told me any of this.''

''She went through the same program the rest of us have. She doesn't like thinking about the past.''

I put my drink down, half-finished. I hadn't bargained for any of this.

''I appreciate the information, Avry, but I've had one of those days. There are several questions I'll need answers to and I'm still not completely sure why I'm here. Would you show me to my quarters?''

''Your chamber is directly across hall from this one. I'll leave orders that you're not to be disturbed. We can talk more in the morning.'' He paused to make sure he had my attention. ''You might as well know that I'm being held responsible for your conduct. Try to remember that I am also one of the few people here who will protect you against my overzealous comrades.''

''Yeah? I've got news for you, old man. I don't trust you any more than anyone else here, so trying to blackmail me into behaving isn't going to work.''

He shrugged. ''Be that as it may, there's something else you should know. There are few secrets in our society, our abilities make them hard to keep. Jessica will not be able to hide her feelings about you, they are too strong.''

''That's between her and me.''

''Not on Iapetus it isn't. Benjamin Wheeler is in love with Jessica; he has been ever since he got here. He will not be pleased when he finds he has been replaced. Be careful, he's a dangerous man.''

''So I've heard.'' I was halfway out the door when I caught sight of several thick volumes in Avry's collection. ''You mind if I borrow a couple of these Bibles?''

He gave me a questioning look. ''I can't believe you're out to find God at this late hour.''

''Wouldn't want to wake him up. Just trying to remember a message someone left me at Elf Hive.''

It was three in the morning before I found the source of Reinhart's warning, the one he'd pinned to my table at the Hotel Saint Matthew, in the book of Deuteronomy. Reading it

over, the United Nations' involvement with Vandimeer began
to make sense. The official document I'd glimpsed on Tethys,
with its designation Operation Proselyte written above a photo
of Jessica, strengthened my convictions. The U.N. was after the
same thing Al-Kirzen was, only for different reasons.

I slept poorly that night; Jessica's absence from my side a
dull ache.

40

I had breakfast with Avry in his chamber. The food was as
bland and pale as the rations on Tethys but that didn't stop me
from eating two portions. I tried to convince myself it was
because I was really hungry rather than the possibility I might
be building a tolerance for the tasteless paste. In contrast to my
gluttony, Avry's quarter-portion allowed him plenty of time to
lecture.

"The colony is ruled by a triumvirate, the members being
elected by popular vote. I'm a member because I'm the oldest
of the colonists. Lisa got her post by being level-headed. Her
knowledge of low-gravity environments has also been helpful.
Ben has moved up through old-fashioned brute force and
intimidation. Not that he'd have made it this far with making
some contributions. He was the one who figured out how to
beat the security on Merlin's Ladder. More luck than skill I'd
say, but for many people here it lifted him to hero status."

"I don't think he'll ever be called a hero back home,
although he did make a few body brokers happy. From what I
can tell, conditioning or no, he doesn't seem too upset about
carcasses he left behind."

"Ben's a special case. He's convinced telepathy represents
the next step forward in human evolution. He thinks no more of
killing non-telepathic humans than you would a chimpanzee
who was attacking you."

"And you wonder why we ship you out? I think one of our

greatest fears is that sooner or later there'll be enough telepaths born to kill the rest of us off. Survival of the fittest gives you the edge.''

''Bullshit.''

I laughed in spite of myself. ''Would you mind being more clear?''

''Sorry, it's a subject of great debate around here. As the spokesperson for the minority opinion, I tend to get carried away. Let me see if I can explain my ideas to you better than I've so far been able to do with my comrades.'' He took a minute to organize his thoughts before continuing. ''The problem lies in a fundamental misconception most of us have with the theory of evolution. We tend to look at the process as being a linear succession, with each generation somehow being a little better than the last.''

''Like humans emerging from apelike creatures.''

''Exactly. But are we really an improvement over apes?''

''Can there be any doubt? Look at all we've accomplished. You don't see monkeys building spaceships.''

''But biologically speaking, swinging from trees is just as successful a way of scattering genes as building skyscrapers, and spreading your genes around is the only yardstick by which evolution measures success. Considering what humans have done to their own environment, apes might be more successful, evolutionarily, than we are. Your garden-variety cockroach certainly is.

''The point is, evolution isn't marching toward some apex of creation. To say that telepaths are more advanced than our ancestors is like saying a cheetah is more advanced than an earthworm. If you really believe that, then ask yourself why cheetahs are extinct and earthworms aren't.''

I'm not much for long discourses in science but I hung tough. ''Then why are there telepaths at all?''

''Because somewhere in the dance of genetic drift, telepathy is possible. Evolution makes no a priori judgment as to whether telepathy is harmful or not. If it turns out to be unsuccessful at increasing the human gene pool, the environment will naturally kill it off.''

''Shipping people off to Iapetus hardly seems something the environment would be doing naturally.''

''I'm not so sure of that. If you accept sociobiological

arguments, then it's possible there's a genetic reason for our exile.''

I thought back to my days at the university. From what I remembered, the sociobiologists tried to explain every facet of human behavior as a function of biological necessity. I'd always considered the theory the result of too many armchair philosophers and not enough common sense. ''I thought sociobiology had been pretty much discounted.''

''The usual end to less glamorous theories. No one wants to believe they don't have free will. But what if even part of it is true? What if our removal from the gene pool is a biological necessity?''

''That's a little farfetched.''

''I don't think so. Did Jessica say anything about why we brought you here?''

''The colony's recent upward trend in infant mortality.''

''Exactly. Of the last forty pregnancies on Iapetus, thirty-seven have ended in stillbirth. Our doctors, meaning those people who have learned as much medicine as is possible with the colony's limited resources, assure us there is no medical reason for these deaths. The children appear to just give up the ghost.''

''What do you make of it?''

''I believe humanity is rejecting us because along with telepathy, our unique genetic makeup also inevitably leads to this reproductive dead end we are experiencing. We can't find a disease or toxin to account for the children's death because there isn't any. I believe the children are dying because death is hard-wired into their genetic makeup.''

I had to admit it made as much sense as the explanation I arrived at on the *Far Hand*. ''Great. What am I supposed to do about it?''

He adjusted his glasses with a nervous twitch. ''As I said, my views on the matter are not widely accepted. The majority of the colonists tend toward more mundane, if not provoking, interpretations. They whisper about a United Nations program of genocide. They prefer conspiracy no matter how illogical. Still, their theories are not completely without justification. It's well known the base on Tethys exists as much to keep an eye on us as to observe Saturn.''

''Any evidence they're doing anything but looking?''

''So far, my companions' investigations have proven fruitless. Having struck out miserably, they felt a different batter might see something we've missed. That's why you're here.''

"And if you're right? If there's nothing I can do, what are my chances of getting home again?''

He sighed. ''I'm sorry, Jefferson, you know we can escape from Iapetus and you must have figured out that we control Jon Pierre's assets. Without those Andy Jacks, and a few vagabonds who leave us supplies on the top of the ladder, we'd all be dead inside a Terran year. I, and others who feel as I do, will try to make your life here comfortable, but you might as well get used to it.''

Avry's life sentence evoked memories of the documentary I'd seen on Elf Hive. The *Queen of Night* and her doomed voyage. With absolute lucidity, I understand the endlessly spooling tape of the Amazon rain forest found in Captain Cantral's cabin. A dying lemming with memories of home.

41

After breakfast, Avry assumed the job of tour guide and showed me around the colony. My new home.

The three floors of living quarters were arranged, much like the levels of the *Far Hand,* in concentric circles. However, rather than large public arenas, the bull's-eye of each of these floors housed one of the ruling triumvirate. Avry on the top level, Lisa on the second, and Benjamin Wheeler below.

As we worked our way downward it became apparent that the successive levels were increasing in size. The bottom floor was three kilometers in diameter, large enough so the outer chambers had been excavated downward to keep them a constant distance beneath the moon's spherical surface. And they were still building outward.

In addition to living chambers there were several other facilities on this lower level. Halfway out from the central hub, a school had been set up for the colony's children. I watched as lessons were given and recited in complete silence. A young girl caught sight of me outside the door and the whole classroom erupted in laughter at some joke she'd sent through the ether.

A quarter-turn clockwise was the hospital. Doctors inside the only operating room stitched a minor arm injury with instruments a hundred years out of date. The young man on the receiving end of the needle looked at me with unconcealed contempt.

"It's going to be centuries before I win any popularity contests here. Perhaps Ben Wheeler has made more converts to his telepaths-are-superior cause than you think."

"I think you're overlooking a more obvious possibility."

I gave him the eyebrow trick.

"Surely you haven't forgotten all that history they crammed into your skull at the university."

"Must have missed the lectures on telepathy."

"I wasn't referring to telepathy, Mr. Kayoto, but ancient leper colonies."

"Leper . . . ?" I shut up and considered it. Before a cure had been found for leprosy, anyone found with the bacillus had been exiled to a colony, a remote area that offered only the most miserable living conditions. People forced to live in these areas, even those who recognized the need for their own exile, more often than not came to despise the populace who had abandoned them there. Several cases of murder had been recorded, even against the few Good Samaritans who braved the disease to bring the lepers food.

Seeing that I understood this point, Avry made a gesture to include all of Iapetus. "None of this is new. Because of your educational background, you recognize it for what it really is. You must give the colonists time to overcome their natural enmity toward outsiders."

"But the freaks—the telepaths—are murdering us wholesale. Other than killing them, which happens often enough, what choice do we have but exile?"

He gave a weary sigh. "If my theory concerning the deaths of our children is correct, then perhaps there are no other options."

Another quarter-turn around the colony brought us to a park; a pathetic construction of artificial plants and painted walls. A sign over the entrance gave the park's name as Arden. Sitting on a molded plastic bench, two women in their late teens held hands. We left them to their peace, continuing clockwise.

"How many inhabitants are there?"

"I'm not sure of the exact count," the old man answered. "Last I heard, it was over ten thousand."

About triple the amount the United Nations said was here. No wonder they'd had to resort to shipping the telepaths out on passenger liners. Looked like business was booming.

Considering the level of panic one telepath brought to Earth, it wasn't surprising the U.N. had lied about the number of freaks exiled. And what would the people back on Terra think if they knew every one of them could leave their prison moon? Fear has always led to war, and this one would be very tough for either side to win.

Below the lowest living chambers, more protected from outside hazards than the people themselves, was the colony's life-support system. Five chemical/biological carbon dioxide scrubbers towered fifteen meters above the floor. Heavy machinery drove the fans that kept Iapetus breathing. On the far side of the vast chamber, iron doors to the colony's fusion reactor stood like the gateway to a temple. The smell of oil and electricity pervaded the dimly lit arena.

I raised my voice over the din. "If the United Nations really had a campaign against you, all they'd have to do is poison your air cleaners here. It wouldn't take more than a mild organic acid and you'd be trying to learn how to breathe carbon dioxide."

"That's true, but in order to reach this point they'd have to go through several thousand telepaths. No way they'd make it."

Reinhart and his black box could, but I wasn't about to tell Avry. One of those mind jammers could be my ticket out of here.

"So why not just H-bomb the colony? If they're out to get you, they're being damned inefficient about it."

"The few legitimate scientists on Tethys would surely take note if we were vaporized. While telepaths are fair game singly, it wouldn't be politic to massacre us en masse out here. Sooner or later word would leak out, and the last thing the United Nations wants is to be accused of cold-blooded murder, even if the victims are telepaths and their children."

The level above the living chambers held, or maybe imprisoned is a better word, new members of the colony. They were kept in confinement while undergoing therapy enabling them to live in peace with the other telepaths. The average time it took to ''stabilize'' a new colonist was seven months of intense work.

Jessica, dressed in a medical smock and white slippers, stepped into the corridor from the sealed passageway detaining the new colonists. Her long black hair was in a tight ponytail, her large green eyes washed out under the artificial light of the colony. I didn't believe for a second her appearance here was accidental, Avry had almost certainly alerted her to our presence. She said little and kept her distance from me.

If the old man was uncomfortable caught between us, he didn't give any sign. ''How're our new colonists doing?''

''I think they'll be okay. We had some trouble with Jane Hamilton.''

''No surprise there.''

Jessica glared at me. ''We finally have the hemorrhaging under control. She was bleeding the entire time she was on the *Far Hand*.''

''Odd, I didn't see any blood when she took time out of her busy schedule to try and kill me.''

''The bleeding wasn't external. Those U.N. bastards—''

''What Jessica's trying to say,'' Avry cut in, ''is that U.N. security teams sometimes take advantage of their status. About one in thirty people we get up here has been molested in some way.''

I thought of pretty little Jane Hamilton strapped down, spread-eagled in some dark room while the brave men and women of the United Nations took turns. Just when you think humanity has graduated from Neanderthal 101, some old pastime goes through a revival.

''The infection had been festering too long to save much from her ovaries on down.'' Jessica struggled unsuccessfully to control her outrage. ''Another freak brought to justice.''

I wasn't doing any better with my temper. Forgetting everything Avry had told me the night before, I cut loose on Jessica. ''Fortunately, telepaths hold a higher standard. I'd tell my friends on Earth about it if I wasn't too occupied with being held prisoner.''

She looked ready to reply, but the old man interrupted.

"Cut it out, both of you. You've both been used by the other side. You can either accept it or carry on like children."

The slow burn I'd been doing since I awoke on Iapetus erupted. "I don't need your condescending platitudes, old man. I need a way home."

He looked hurt, but let it drop.

42

"How did it start?"

Avry didn't look surprised by the question, but then after he'd looked inside my skull, he'd known the decision I'd eventually reach. The three of us sat over an early dinner of flavorless white pudding served with skim milk substitute. I'd made the choice to ante up and play the cards I'd been dealt. As long as I was here, I might as well find some way to pass the time.

"Forty-seven standard months ago, one of our younger colonists had a stillbirth. Our medics were unable to find the cause."

"Hold it. How good are your people? Miss Vandimeer here mentioned some of your equipment, but I wasn't aware there were any formally trained medical personnel on Iapetus."

"Technically true, but when the colony was initiated there were seven non-telepaths who volunteered to join us. Two were medical doctors. They instructed us as best they could. No doubt doctors on Earth are superior, but we get along. Certainly we have the ability to perform simple autopsies."

"And?"

"We found nothing. The fetus was perfectly healthy when she passed away. The best guess, as crazy as it sounds, was that the child lost the desire to live. The incident would have eventually been forgotten had not the next child died, born two and a half weeks later, in the same manner. The third child went through a natural birth, only to pass away within two hours. Since then, thirty-four children have died during birth, or shortly after.''

''Any chance at all of some environmental poison?''

Jessica answered. ''Impossible. We did complete scans.''

''Maybe you missed it.''

''Our equipment is outdated, but not that ineffectual. We have a medical A.I. interfaced with the diagnostic scanner. Even if we missed something, it didn't. All scans fell within the norm.''

Which brought me right back to my original hypothesis. It wasn't much, but it was all I had. ''When did you gain access to the top of Merlin's Ladder?''

Avry was confused by the quick change of topic, but Jessica was used to my questioning.

''Just over four years and two months ago.''

''So it predated the first death by several months.''

''I don't know what you're driving at,'' Avry said, ''but there's no way anyone could have—''

''Probably not. Why did you start sending people up? From what I understand, quite a few of you died in the attempt. There must have been some compelling reason to continue with the endeavor.''

''A number of ships independent of the government land necessary supplies on the top of the ladder. Charities and sympathizers mostly, many of whom have relatives down here. We learned by radio they were being hunted down and destroyed. Without their cargo, this colony does not have the ability to expand with our growing population.''

''So you decided to break out and see what was going on. What conclusions did you reach?''

''It has to be either the United Nations or our neighbors on Rhea,'' Avry said. ''Who else would it be?''

I chose to disregard his open question. ''Tell me how Ben Wheeler made it to the top of the ladder. Was anyone with him?''

''No, he went alone,'' Jessica answered.

''Then how do you know he was the one who beat the security system?''

Avry was more confused than ever. ''What other answer is possible?''

Old habits die hard. I held my cards close, even though Avry could take a peek at them any time he chose to. At least I'd find out if he was serious about allowing me my privacy.

"Two people were sent to Earth to get help. One was Jessica Vandimeer, the other was a young woman named Elle. There are no records of a telepath by that name. Where did she come from?"

"She was Ben Wheeler's daughter by Melissa Renoir," Jessica said.

Melissa Renoir, the *enfant terrible*. Coming back from Reunified France a couple of years ago, Holly had told me some of the quarantine walls, topped with rustling laser mounts, were still standing around Rouen.

When it had become clear, forty years ago, that a telepath was roaming the streets of Rouen, the French Socialist Assembly panicked. Unfortunately for her citizens, Rouen boasted not a single Central Assembly member. The military was called in and a wall of laceration aluminum topped with reflex pulse lasers was thrown around the city overnight.

Temperatures that summer had reached record highs, but the wall was not taken down. Rouen baked in its aluminum oven for seventy-three days. Between Melissa roving the streets slaughtering everyone in her path, heat exposure, and the automated defenses on the wall, 300 people died. It'd be a long time before the locals forgot Miss Renoir. At least they'd been able to catch her before she got to Paris.

"I thought she had been lasered down."

"That rumor was spread to suppress civil unrest after the press was allowed into Rouen. Melissa was exiled here. She had been rendered unconscious after a laser took her in the abdomen."

"I haven't met Miss Renoir yet."

"She took her own life several years ago."

Avry's tone made it clear I was verging on a taboo subject. "Is suicide common on Iapetus?"

"No. Melissa was only the second case."

There was more to it than that, but Avry wasn't going out of his way to enlighten me. I went back to more relevant matters. "How were the selections made?"

As usual, Miss Vandimeer followed my train of thought despite the ambiguity of the question. "Elle and I were chosen because we had no police records and because we passed a battery of social adaptation tests administered by the ruling three.''

Of which Benjamin Wheeler was a member. Half the mystery solved. Wheeler hadn't conquered Merlin's Ladder, Al-Kirzen had. Someone—Amber Whitehorse?—had been waiting at the top to turn the system off. She'd juiced everyone but Ben Wheeler. Why? Because he would have been psychotic even without the telepathic gene. Al-Kirzen must have studied his past closely.

''Tell me about your next door neighbor. How many children does Abdul have?''

Again Vandimeer answered without seeming surprised at the change in topic. ''Omar is the only one. His daughter Miriam died shortly after birth.''

If I had had any doubts about being on the right track, that settled it. Al-Kirzen had only male offspring. It was no coincidence that two females were selected to leave the relative safety of Iapetus. Despite all the advances in genetics, it still takes two, or at least the contributions thereof, to tango.

What had Amber said to Benjamin the day he reached the top of Merlin's Ladder? How had she survived being alone with one of the greatest single mass murderers in history?

Perhaps she told him of Al-Kirzen's well-laid plans, plans that must eventually necessitate the destruction of Iapetus. Al-Kirzen was nothing if not thorough, and he would certainly take steps toward protecting his monopoly on the telepathic gene pool. Had Whitehorse promised Wheeler genetic survival through his daughter? Did he know the bargain had already been broken—that Elle had suicided on Rhea?

''When is the next birth due?''

Avry answered. ''Four days.''

''And how are you going to stop her from dying, Mr. Detective?''

Benjamin Wheeler was standing behind me, arms folded over his chest, clenched fists pushing out his biceps. I wondered why he felt he had to put on the muscle-man routine. If he was trying to be intimidating, he would've had more success with his bag of mental tricks. If he scanned me now, everything was lost.

When treading on uncertain ground, it's usually best to take the offensive. ''Al-Kirzen has killed your daughter.''

"So I've heard." No reaction. Wheeler pulled a chair up to our table and sat beside me.

"Answer my question, Mr. Detective, how are you going to save our children?"

I gave him a tight smile. "With a little addition. If I go too fast for you say something, and we can get you a calculator. Jessica, how many new colonists did you load on the U.N. *Raptor* at Calypso?"

"Fifteen. I checked against the manifest."

"And how many telepaths were there aboard the *Far Hand*?"

"I didn't notice."

"I did. Three rows of five."

Wheeler's loathing was palpable. "What do you know, he can count. Why are we wasting time—"

"Shut up, Ben." Jessica looked at me. "That's impossible. One was killed on Tethys."

"Exactly. I noticed the discrepancy before we had our little encounter on the *Raptor*. How did you transport new colonists from the top of Merlin's Ladder?"

"I put them on a car, then followed them down."

"But you weren't on the same car as they were."

"So what? What are you getting at, Mr. Detective?"

I ignored Wheeler. "Avry, call whoever's in charge of receiving new members. How many people came down the lift?"

The old man walked over to an intercom and spoke. He nodded at the answer and rejoined us. "Fifteen people were rolled off at the bottom, the number they'd been told to expect."

"Except one of them was me, and I wasn't along for the ride until the end. Jessica counted fifteen bodies when the *Raptor* landed the colonists on Calypso, but only fourteen reached the surface of Iapetus."

"Speculation, you're playing hotshot with a bookkeeping error."

"No, he's right, something strange is going on. We saw a dead man on Tethys. There should have been an empty gurney when I checked them over at Calypso."

Avry leaned over the table. "What does it mean?"

"Jessica wheeled someone on at the top, someone who

wasn't there at the bottom. Someone who's hiding on the ladder."

"Not likely, Mr. Detective, there isn't any place to get off."

Avry surprised me by coming to my defense. "We don't know that, Ben. The lift was built by the United Nations. Just because we haven't found any secret rooms doesn't mean there aren't any there."

I pressed the story. "And the only people who'd know about it would be high-ranking United Nations personnel. I think a gentleman named Reinhart is the newest addition to their assassination crew. A minor cosmetic job so Jessica doesn't recognize him, and he's got a ticket to Iapetus." I'd just opened the escape hatch. Now if only the killer would use it.

"You might be on to something," Wheeler conceded. If the other two were surprised at this abrupt change in attitude, they didn't say anything. "Most of us believe the United Nations is behind it somehow. It's possible this kickback has found part of the answer. I'll round up some people and check into it."

He excused himself from the table, thinking I was on the wrong track. Fine by me. As long as he thought I was sniffing up the wrong tree, he had no reason to kill me.

43

I spent the evening, that is to say from five to seven Greenwich Mean, walking the station in solitude. Actual sunset on Iapetus would not take place for another 430 hours, at the end of Iapetus's year. Without the anchor of Greenwich time to keep us running on the same track, life here would have dissolved into chaos. If God had meant for us to travel to the planets, he'd have given us variable metabolisms.

At first the walk seemed like a good idea, but within the first fifteen minutes I was having second thoughts. After every kilometer of sealed corridor, my subconscious would send a message to step outside for some fresh air. Every time conscious thought answered with, ''There is no fresh air outside,'' the walls closed in a little more.

''Mr. Kayoto?''

Lisa topped me by seven centimeters but must have massed less than fifty kilos. Her blond hair was cropped short and her brown eyes were large and sad. She wore a pair of faded cotton overalls and pale green tank top with a menorah airbrushed over her heart. Seeing her now, I realized she was a striking woman, perhaps even beautiful. I also recognized her.

Elizabeth Anstein had been raised in one of Earth's high-orbit ecologies. During her ninth Hanukkah, she'd gained control of one of the orbital's engineers and puppeteered him to a chemical vapor deposition lab. The man opened seals from the lab, flooding the station with nickel tetracarbonyl. The unstable compound quickly broke down, mostly inside the lungs of the stations' personnel, and 230 people died of carbon dioxide poisoning. Seventy of them had been children under the age of ten. Just about the same number of children I had put in the bag on Humboldt.

''What can I do for you, Lisa?''

''I need to talk to you in private. Shall we go to the park?''

Arden was not my idea of a secluded site, but when we reached the large chamber it was suspiciously vacant. Looking at the pathetic plastic trees and painted sky, I suddenly realized the true purpose of the park went beyond recalling memories of home. In a society where walls could not build privacy but distance could, the park was as close as the telepaths could come to a soundproof room.

Lisa waved me over to a bench. Her frame was mismatched to the low seat; her long legs curled in a lotus underneath her.

''I have been talking to Jessica.''

''And?''

''She was telling me about the *Far Hand*.''

''She used me and I fell for it. Nobody's fault but mine. I don't hold it against her. What happened is past.''

''No, it's not.''

''What do you mean?''

''She replaced your LHRH-A analogue with a sugar capsule.''

''Jesus Christ.''

''She's fourteen weeks pregnant. The embryo is female and perfectly healthy.''

White-hot anger. The telepathic gene was recessive in simple pairs, but distant relatives in my family had been born freaks. There was no guarantee the girl would not be one. "She had no right."

"No, she didn't."

"Why? What reason did she have? Did she think she could hold on to me through a child?"

"Don't be melodramatic. Logically, you'd be more likely to help us if you had something at stake. Don't bother to tell me that's immoral, or that you had started to help us anyway. We're fighting for survival and frankly your well-being is of secondary importance."

A sarcastic laugh escaped. "Nothing like honesty."

"Those were the reasons we encouraged Jessica to choose the path she did. They're most definitely not hers. She did it because she loves you. And don't accuse her of trying to use the child against you in any way. She's stronger than that, and you know it."

I backpedaled with what style I could muster. "Yes, she is."

"What will you do?"

"I don't know yet." Shit. Why me? Thomas always wanted to be a family man. Kids made me tense. "Why couldn't she have told me the truth from the beginning?"

"You know the answer as well as I do."

"I suppose so. I never would have helped her had I realized what she was."

Lisa shook her head. "You're wrong, Mr. Kayoto. We on Iapetus needed your help. From the second she walked into your office, Jessica herself wanted much more."

"What do you mean, 'the second she walked in my office'?"

"That is for her to explain, but remember this: Jessica Vandimeer is very special to this colony. If you are no longer capable of loving her, then that's your own loss. Don't take it out on her. She deserves better."

The colony's grapevine was in perfect running order. Half an hour after Lisa left me sitting in the park, Benjamin Wheeler stormed in. His face was livid in outrage.

"What gives you the right, ape man? We don't want monkey genes in our children."

"Yeah? Too bad no one told your parents." Jamie had always said that sooner or later one of my flip remarks would get me killed. One of these days, I'm going to start listening to him.

Wheeler grabbed the front of my shirt. I looked him in the eyes, daring him to take the next step. He outmassed me by a good ten kilos, but he was too slow to give me much trouble.

"Wrong again, Mr. Detective. I'm as fast as they come." I felt his dark thoughts rush in my skull, and every muscle in my body turned to concrete. My eardrums pounded like I was under twenty meters of water. *I'm going to tear you apart, Mr. Detective, but not before I know what you did to Jessica.*

"Ben. Stop it. Now."

Avry was there, Jessica walking beside him. A flash of pain streaked across my temples, then Ben's presence was gone.

Avry stepped in front of Wheeler, the older man's eyes level with Ben's chin. "You are supposed to be examining Merlin's Ladder for United Nations trickery. What are you doing here?"

"I don't have to answer to you. I am one of the Ruling Three."

Avry's leathery hands shook at his side. "You must answer to the wishes of the colony. What you think about me is irrelevant. Answer the question."

Ben remained silent long enough to convey his complete disrespect for Avry before answering. "Mr. Detective was lucky. We found a concealed door in the level fifteen power station. Because the elevator cars must slow and change tracks directly above the power station, there is plenty of time to force the doors and jump to the floor below. This would allow someone to exit the elevator without stopping the car and thereby tripping several alarms.

"The room we discovered was well stocked with supplies, and had obviously been in recent use. It also had a transmitter powerful enough to reach Tethys anywhere in its orbit. The place was empty when we got there."

"Excellent, progress is already being made. It's only a matter of time before we track the intruder down. Were you able to scan him?"

"No."

"Then reassemble your team and go over it again. We should have people based around the ladder's axis around the clock."

"I'm not doing anything until I settle with this sniveling Earthman. He took privileges that were not his."

"What are you talking about?"

Wheeler nodded toward Jessica. "He took advantage of her."

Avry's laugh was too loud to be natural; loud enough to tell me he feared Benjamin Wheeler. "I doubt Mr. Kayoto would agree with that. I imagine he sees it the other way around. However, if Mr. Kayoto solves our problems, then Jessica's little girl will be a welcome addition to our colony."

Wheeler turned to Jessica and appealed directly to her. "What do you have to say, Jessica? I know you were forced by certain members of the colony into accepting whatever this barbarian did, but there's no reason now to keep up the facade. You don't have to keep the half-breed child."

Jessica's voice was steely calm. "The choice is mine and I will keep my daughter whatever you or Mr. Kayoto say."

"No! You will not. The child would carry undesirable genes from this biological anachronism. I want the fetus aborted now."

I read the pain in Jessica's eyes and reacted before considering the likely folly of my actions. I pivoted toward Wheeler and caught him square on the chin with a right jab. After that, it was a toss-up which was more astounding; the fact that I connected before he could shut me down, or the pain lancing through my hand. Wheeler careened through Iapetus's weak gravity and bounced into a wall. He was out cold before he hit. I cradled my hand, my breath hissing out between clenched teeth.

Jessica used a wall intercom to call for medical help, then kneeled to examine the prone man. When she rejoined us, I irrationally found myself looking for signs of her pregnancy. With a gentle touch she opened my injured hand.

"Third and fourth fingers are broken. The ring finger looks bad. You need to have them examined. The doctors will be here—"

Avry cut her off. "No time for that now. Mr. Kayoto, you better come with me. Jessica, you stay with Ben until help arrives. Don't tell anyone what happened. With any luck I can get our pugilist out of here before the crowd arrives."

He hurried me down a series of corridors, always moving up and away from Arden. "I hope you realize what a stupid move that was."

''What are you going to do? Put me on trial for breaking his jaw?''

He turned and faced me, his eyes narrowed. ''You still don't get it, do you? There won't be any trial. Ben will never admit to being injured by a non-telepath, but he will never forget it. What's going to happen the first time he finds you without Lisa or Jessica or me around to save your hide?''

''I don't need your help.''

''That's a comforting fantasy, isn't it? If you're lucky, you'll be dead before he can get his temper under control. If he starts thinking about, he'll probably make you feel a little pain first.''

''What do you care? It's not your problem.''

''The hell it isn't!'' He was outraged now, his wiry frame shaking in harmony with his anger. ''Jessica spent two years tracking down someone to help us. Elle lost her life. Our children are dying. We need you to find out why. A lot of good you'll do us dead.''

He led me to a vacant room close to the new colonists' wards. We waited in silence for five minutes, until a sandy-haired doctor came in. He nodded at Avry; greetings passed back and forth beyond my ability to hear.

''So this is the hired help. Welcome to Iapetus, Mr. Kayoto, my name is Toulane. I'm second generation, so you don't have to worry about trying to match me with 'most wanted' posters. Let's have a look at your hand.''

He used a pocket X-ray plate to examine my fingers. ''Middle finger looks okay. You'll be flipping us all off in no time. But the ring finger . . .'' He let out a soft whistle and pulled out an injector. ''Just a local.''

It took only a few seconds for the anesthetic to take hold. Toulane took my fourth finger, and bent it until it was flat against the back of my hand. I heard the soft scrape of bone on bone. ''Feel anything?''

I shook my head. He worked on my hand for half an hour, humming and whistling all the while. When he was finished, my hand was wrapped in white medical tape reaching down to my wrist. Just as Jessica's had been when she first came into my office.

''That should do it. My only regret is I wasn't there to see it.'' With a silent farewell to Avry, he was gone.

''You'd better return to your room. I'll be across the hall in case Ben decides to take things into his own hands. The official story on your hand is you injured it in an accident climbing around the carbon dioxide scrubbers. I've already spread it through the colony and Ben is sure to accept it to save face. Just make sure you stick to it.''

So now I was the one hiding a secret behind a bandaged hand.

44

It was well past dinnertime when Jessica brought two supper trays into my chamber. Odd that after all of this, she now looked so fragile. Fifty-five kilos of ephemeral flesh and blood, nothing more. Nothing like the Medusa I wanted to believe her to be. She stayed as far away from me as the chamber would allow.

''May I join you for supper?''

Was her waist a little rounded? Portents of a little girl, doomed to live her life on this godforsaken ball of ice. If she lived at all.

''Yes.'' I unfolded a table from the wall, and sat on the bed. She pulled the room's lone chair from the computer console and sat opposite me. The foam trays opened into a three-course dinner of bleached dough. She slipped them into the microwave, vainly hoping for some miracle to make them edible in fifteen seconds.

Watching her now, it seemed the fluorescent lights of Iapetus had sapped the vitality from her. Hard to believe this was the woman whose energy had been boundless on the *Far Hand*. Even her voice sounded flat. ''Thank you.''

I gave her the eyebrow routine.

''For stopping Ben.''

''That's why you hired me, remember? I'm the one who's too stupid to know when he's outgunned.'' The attempt at humor fell flat in the tension between us. We ate in silence, the sound of plastic forks scraping against Styrofoam embarrassingly loud.

Long minutes passed before, unable to stand the painful quiet any longer, I broke the stillness. "Was it just me, or was Avry upset with the topic of Melissa's suicide?"

"Elle was only a child when it happened. Benjamin claimed she was the one who killed Melissa."

"Any basis ever found for Ben's allegation?"

"None whatsoever, but Avry has always suspected Wheeler. You notice Wheeler wasn't too upset when you told him Elle was dead. His relationship with her was always tinged with paranoia."

Interesting; one might almost be tempted to say conclusive. One of Wheeler's children, Melissa, dies with her father being the odds-on favorite as the killer. It was the last piece in the puzzle. After all, when hiring an assassin, it's best to get someone with previous experience.

I had the case of the dying children solved, right down to the differing motives of the killer and his employer, but nailing the murderer wasn't going to be that easy. Even if Donaldson miraculously appeared with cuffs and a warrant, the only thing he could do here was get himself killed. Until I figured out some way to avoid the same fate, I would keep my mouth shut and use the time to fill in details.

"Tell me about Tethys." As always, she knew exactly what I was talking about. I had the feeling this had nothing to do with her telepathic ability and everything to do with the affinity we shared for one another.

"After Ben solved the security arrangements on Merlin's Ladder, I was elected first to leave the colony. I stowed away on a United Nations transport. The ship was returning to Tethys after making a delivery of new colonists to the top of the ladder. Once on Huygens research station, telepathic control of a high-ranking administrator got my name on the roster of new researchers arriving on the next ship from the Terra-Luna System. I remained unobtrusive until the ship arrived, at which time I assumed my new identity."

"And anyone on the station who recalled seeing you before the ship docked was conveniently made to forget the experience."

"Yes. And once I became accepted I published several

papers, using ambiguous initials so as not to arouse suspicion in the ranks of professional astronomers back on Earth.''

I nodded. ''A whiz kid with absolutely no background in the field would have certainly stimulated curiosity in the established circles back home. Yet to the researches on Tethys, you were just a new face from Earth.''

''Correct once again. The entire operation was absurdly simple. After scanning the experts, all I had to do was repeat their pet theories in different words. I published a new paper once every three months, attended the odd colloquium, and was soon wholeheartedly accepted as one of the crowd. I stayed on until we had thoroughly penetrated United Nations security.''

''How was that done?''

She tried a smile. ''I was right about you.''

''What's that mean?''

''After everything that has happened, you're still willing to help us.''

''You didn't exactly leave me any options.''

Her smile turned to gentle laughter. A trace of animation returned to her green eyes. ''You're lying to the wrong person. You're the most pighead-stubborn man I know. If you really didn't want to help us, you wouldn't, no matter what we did.''

''Really? If I didn't offer my assistance voluntarily, can you promise me a member of your colony wouldn't force me to go through my paces anyway?''

''Jefferson, you don't understand. We could scan every bit of your memory, we could alter your perception of reality, we could make you love us, we could make you do back flips through a ring of fire if we wanted to. But we cannot access your intuitive capabilities, the very trait we're banking on to save our children. Your skills are yours alone, permanently beyond our reach.''

''That's some comfort. I won't become a second-class citizen until after I've helped you out.'' Her smile vanished. I let out a long sigh. She wasn't making any of this easy. Why couldn't they have sent a man? ''Jessica, look, I'm sorry. I don't mean to take it all out on you. Let's get back to the original subject. How did you infiltrate United Nations security?''

''The program to rid the entire Sol System of telepaths is coded Operation Mind-Set by the United Nations. Operations for the program are based on Tethys. I targeted a female operative roughly my age and over a period of several weeks scanned her memories. During one of my solo trips to Calypso's Mansion, I was met by members of Iapetus's medical crew. They tailored my vocal cords to fit her voice pattern. She was later abducted while unloading telepaths on the ladder. I confiscated her I.D. card; the same one you saw me use to obtain the *Raptor*.''

''And no one noticed she was gone?''

''The rigid compartmentalization of the U.N. helped us greatly. Only about seven people were familiar enough with her to know she was missing. I was able to alter their perceptions to the point where they accepted me as her replacement.''

''Where is she now? I haven't met her yet.''

Jessica looked away. ''Ben took care of her. I don't know where the body is.''

''Wonderful. My future's looking brighter all the time.''

We lapsed into another long period of silence. When Jessica finally spoke, she whispered as if she were talking to herself as much as to me. ''I was going to leave you on Tethys.''

''What?''

''That's why I fiddled with your birth control. I wanted to take a part of you back to Iapetus. I was going to tell you everything and give you enough AJs to return on the *Far Hand*.''

''Jessica, why? In nine months, the child would have died with the rest of them.''

''I hoped we'd have figured it out by then. I thought it was the United Nations and we could pin them down somehow. Now it seems hopeless.'' Her voice was dulled by sorrow.

''I don't know about that. We're making some progress.''

''Don't lie to me. You and I both know the United Nations isn't behind the deaths. Maybe Avry's right about it being genetic.''

''No, he's not.''

She gave me a sharp look. ''What?''

I shook my head. ''Not yet. There're some things I have to do first. Like flush Reinhart out of Merlin's Ladder. He's got something I need.''

Knowing I wasn't going to say anything else, she changed tracks.

"I'm going top-side tomorrow; a short voyage away from the colony. I would like it very much if you joined me."

"Never said no to a beautiful woman yet."

"Yes, actually you have. Would you like me to refresh your memory on when and where?"

I exhaled through a self-conscious smile. "That really bothered me back on Earth. You seemed to know everything about me. How long did it take you to scan it all?"

"I started when I stepped into your office. I was finished before we even spoke. I . . . duplicated your memory and transferred the copy into my own thoughts. We use so little of our brains, there's plenty of room for a second set of memories. Of course I haven't assimilated it all yet. That will take years."

It was worse than I thought. "You know everything I've been through? Even down to what I was feeling?"

"For those events that I've studied, yes."

"Wonderful. I'm feeling better about this all the time."

"I'm sorry, such things are commonplace on Iapetus. I understand why it might shock you."

I tried to shrug it off. "I didn't exactly put on kid gloves when I went digging around your past. I guess neither of us is in line for sainthood. Still, if you have any other surprises for me this would be a good time to spring them."

The quiet intensity of her answer laid bare the strength of her feelings. "I never used you . . . never made you do anything. I slept with you because I wanted to."

"I know." I leaned across the table, bringing myself closer to her than I'd been since I awoke on Iapetus. "If it makes you feel any better about all the rotten things you've done to me, you should know the only reason I slept with you was to get information."

Her face registered anger, then, amazingly, her smile returned. "I can see through that even without scanning."

I didn't doubt it for a second. "Jessica? Just give me a little more time. To make peace with Thomas."

"Believe me, on Iapetus, time is never in short supply."

45

"Where are we going?" Jessica and I were zipping across Iapetus in a military hopper. I sat in front of the controls for the hopper's external arms while she drove.

"A collection area on the near side of Justin crater."

"Collection area?"

"You'll see when we get there."

I was jittery. Ever since last night, my mind had been drudging up the most sordid episodes of my past; begging, it seemed to me, for Jessica to scan them. So far, every attempt to think about things other than the dead children of Humboldt Station or the painful list of women who came and went after my military discharge was in vain.

"There it is." I followed her pointing finger to a large-sized crater, covered with the same dark stain that blanketed most of Iapetus's leading hemisphere.

"Justin is the best crater in the area for collecting soil. And don't bother giving me the third degree with your high-altitude eyebrow. You'll understand what I mean soon enough."

She guided us over the lee side of the crater wall, where I used the waldo jacks to scrape and collect several jars of the black material. It was the same kind of setup I'd used on Luna.

"Haven't lost your edge."

I turned to her, feeling the adrenaline rush color my face.

"I was right, you have been thinking about it. It's not an uncommon phenomenon, you know. New arrivals on Iapetus call it the MemoRage; the subconscious recalling of shameful events."

"Is that supposed to make me feel better?"

"No, it never does. Just keep in mind that you'll get over it."

I filled the last jar, and she pointed us back to the colony.

"Whatever you think of your superiors in the Terra-Luna Corps, what you did to the terrorists on Humboldt Station was necessary. They would have carried out their threats. Ninety percent of the people on Luna would have died from the blast alone. The corps had to take action, and you were the best man for the job."

"Ironic that you also think I'm the best man for saving your children."

"Jefferson, you blew Humboldt's overpressure vents with a mechanical arm, but it was the station's leaders who made the decisions that led to the death of their population."

So I'd told myself a million times since then. Odd that when Jessica said it, I almost believed it.

"You really do know everything about me. Every milestone in my life, every night spent wide awake, performing my penance with a plastic half-liter of synthahol."

"I had to scan you, Jefferson. Every doctor we tried to send to the Saturn System had been killed. Too much time had already been lost."

I wasn't going to let her off the hook that easily. "What's it like, living a step above us mortals? Sorting through our dirty laundry?"

"That tone of voice isn't doing anything positive for the revival of your sex life. I know the real cause of your anger, even if you don't."

"Yeah? Why don't you tell me?" Dumb question. Unlike the people I was used to dealing with, Jessica could answer that sort of bluff.

"It's your blasted male ego. Look, if it's any comfort, I fell in love with you after I scanned you. How many men do you think are secure with the knowledge that a woman might know everything about them and still share their bed?"

"You might have something there."

"Damn right I do. Look at that deserted-island fantasy of yours. Is it any wonder you don't want a woman snooping around your mental playground? I couldn't compete with that even if I were a virgin."

"Maybe not, but you could always try."

She flashed her smile and shook her head. "You're incorrigible."

"Yeah, but—"

"Your other sterling qualities make up for it. I know that line, too."

"Score one for the opposition. Do you think you could get around to answering my question?"

"About being a step above mere groveling humans? It's not all it's cracked up to be. When you first see everyone else's sordid thoughts, you think you're pretty superior. After a while, you discover telepaths don't have the monopoly on high moral standards. You realize you're no different from anyone else as far as guilty secrets go. It's not a particularly enjoyable moment of truth."

I mulled over that until the small ports of the Iapetus hangar came into view. I was relieved to be getting back inside. Although barely discernible, the massive orb of Saturn's night side teased my unconscious mind. The product of a thousand generations born under Earth's friendly moon, my psyche wasn't prepared to handle Saturn's oppressive dimensions. I began to understand the high rate of suicide on her moons.

Jessica passed our velocity and position to the computer in the shuttle bay. It must have decided Jessica knew what she was doing because it gave us permission to land. We gratefully exited the cramped pod of the hopper and unloaded the jars of black dust onto a nearby cart.

"I assume all of this has some meaning?"

"We are going to the rose garden."

I went over the details of the tour Avry had given me, not able to come up with anything resembling a patch of flowers. "We must have missed that one."

"It's a special place. Avry's too much of a romantic to spoil it by including it with the more mundane things he took you to see."

She led me down to the lowest level of the colony, through an unmarked door off to the side of the air scrubbers. The dank room, filled with stale air, didn't seem romantic to me. A circular ceramic tub three meters in diameter squatted in the middle of the floor.

"Dump the jars, but be careful not to touch the liquid, it's a brew of several inorganic acids, mostly concentrated hydrochloric."

"Acid and sterile soil. I can't say I think much of your rose garden's chance of thriving." We dumped the rest of the samples into the tub, filling the room with acrid fumes. I was about ready to suggest some other, less noxious, pastime when we finally finished. Jessica pointed to a second door in the back of the room.

The rose garden of Iapetus was in a room painted baby blue. A fine mist, falling lazily from overhead sprinklers, drenched the black soil. The flowers were translucent crystal, emerald leaves below blossoms of every hue in the rainbow. Light refracted through glassy petals streaked the walls with deep prisms of color.

"I have the feeling we're not in Kansas anymore."

"Do you like it?"

"It's beautiful. How many hours did it take to sculpt?"

"None."

"I'm supposed to believe you found crystal structures that just looked like this?"

"No," she laughed. "It's a computer program."

"You mean like a hologram?"

"No, they're real enough. The program is an algorithm of the DNA instructions of *Rosa carolina*, a wild species of rose that used to be found about one hundred miles south of the city."

"Let's try that again, this time in English."

"I don't pretend to understand all of it myself, the best I can explain it is by analogy. Think of the sample jars we brought in from Justin as soil and detritus. It's mostly carbon, but contains a measurable amount of silicon along with trace amounts of other elements, including several light metals. The acid bath serves the function of breaking soil down into usable humus. In this case, simple inorganic compounds are broken down to their constituent elements. Okay so far?"

"Sounds like freshman-level chemistry."

"Mostly acid-base reactions forming ionic bond salts, if you're interested. From there, the plant food is fed into this room, where these roses use it just like a natural rose would incorporate nutrients into its structure. Growth of the crystal, which is based on either a silicon or carbon matrix—"

"You mean diamond?"

She smiled. "Yes, most people do call it that. Various impurities; nitrogen, boron, aluminum, beryllium, and the like are added for color. The whole show is governed by software that mimics rose DNA, with the differences between crystal growth and organic growth programmed in."

"Software that duplicates genetic text? Unbelievable. That's years beyond anything they have back on Terra."

"The result of two heads being better than one. Our telepathic scientists have much better methods of data dissemination and synthesis than Terran researchers. Written language really is an unwieldy medium for the transfer of information."

"But how does this computer of yours physically carry out its instructions?"

"Touch one of the flowers."

I ran my hand over the hexagonal petals of the nearest flower. Intermitten shocks of low current tingled my fingertips. I looked closer and saw that each petal had a tiny internal skeleton of barely visible copper wire. Whenever the wires broke the surface of the petals, a small current juiced my hand.

"Just as a plant uses osmotic pressure and capillary lifting to move nutrients around, these roses use electricity to move ionized elements to the correct place. This process can only be accomplished in a mildly acidic solution."

"Hence the constant rainfall. I assume it won't start burning holes in our skin?"

"No need to worry. The pH of this rain is closer to neutral than what you're used to in the city."

"That's hardly reassuring. What happens after the ion is in place?"

"A shock from the copper wire, helped by a catalyst in the rain, causes an oxidation-reduction reaction with an electronegative compound carried in the water. This replaces the missing electrons in the ion, which then precipitates into the crystal matrix. When a leaf or petal is complete, the copper withdraws by the same process. It takes about three years to complete a single flower."

She picked up a small geologist's hammer hanging from the wall. A light tap at the base of one of the flowers produced a pure harmonic, echoing clear in the small room. Jessica hit the stem with more authority, and the plant split just above the dark soil. Tiny emeralds, broken from the stem along their fracture lines, fell to the ground.

"For you." She held the amethyst flower out to me.

"It must be worth a fortune."

"It probably is, but you of all people know how easy it is for us freaks to get Andy Jacks. Besides, it was meant as a peace offering, not as nourishment for your greed."

"In which case, I accept it as down payment. As for the balance of the misery you've caused me, I have a couple of ideas . . ."

"Yes, I know you do."

I took the brittle flower, finding out too late that even these roses had thorns, and that a razor-sharp diamond did a credible job of slicing through skin.

46

Jessica rang at my door late the following morning. After pressing me most of the previous evening, she had gotten me to agree to visiting the new colonists' wards. She felt it was an important step in my acclimatization process.

I was ready to go but, almost as an afterthought, I strapped on my Stoeger machine pistol. I hadn't worn it on the colony yet, figuring it worse than useless against people who could control my thoughts. But today, some tiny inner voice told me it might come in handy.

After the usual drab breakfast, we headed outward and counterclockwise to the new arrivals' ward. Inside the sealed access door, a dimly lit hall stretched for forty meters. On both sides of this corridor, high-voltage containment fields sparkled across entryways to several occupied rooms. Most of the new colonists were still heavily sedated; only a couple were fully awake, talking softly to counselors.

Jane Hamilton was in the medical bay, located at the end of the hall. She was lying on a medical table, her head propped up by pillows. Her face was devoid of expression. Avry was sitting in a chair next to her, reading *The Lord of the Rings* in a gentle and soothing voice. Jessica took Jane's hand and Avry paused in his recitation.

"How are you feeling today, Jane?"

She gave a lopsided smile, looking for the first time like a sixteen-year-old girl rather than a seasoned killer. "Better."

"I have a friend who wants to see you." Jessica motioned to me. "This is Mr. Jefferson Kayoto. He's here to help the colony."

Her eyes widened when she saw me. "I met Mr. Kayoto aboard the *Far Hand*." She tried the smile again. "I'm sorry for what I did."

It happened in liquid-crystal slow motion. From a distant point, I watched my hand move to the shoulder holster . . . and my right arm came up with the machine pistol . . . and the first shot caught Jane in the left temple . . . and she must have died instantly . . . the recoil pushed me off balance in the weak gravity and then I was turning toward Jessica Vandimeer . . . and, too shocked to stop me with her ability, she watched while I fired at her point blank . . . and the bullet took her in the throat . . . and her body tumbled from the impact . . . and the gun was moving to my own head and . . . a thick haze covered my mind.

The machine pistol shook in my hand, the warm silencer dancing a tatoo on my temple. My finger strained to pull the trigger.

Stop.

The word appeared in my mind without vocalization. I knew it was Jessica. She was dying.

It was Reinhart. Save our child.

"Jessica." She moved through my thoughts and the gun fell from my hand. I stumbled to where she lay, her blood spilling across the floor from a great rip in her throat. What to do? Her spinal cord must be shattered; don't move her. Don't let her die! Blood all over my hands; bubbling from her lips. Do something!

Jefferson.

All urgency left me, erased by soothing tranquility.

"Jessica I love—"

I know. I've known since the moment I met you. I looked. Are you angry with me?

"No." For a second we were together again. Euphoria filled my mind, Jessica's emotions flowing through me, her passion a tangible power closing my eyes to the blood-spattered body lying before me.

There's something I want to give you.

"What?"

On Iapetus, there's a special way to say good-bye.

I can't explain what happened; I have no adjectives for the encompassing force of telepathy. It was not touch or sight or hearing; it enveloped all my senses and yet remained beyond their grasp. I felt her presence move inside me. I felt her alter an infinitesimal part of my consciousness, embedding a spark deep within the folds of my mind.

Take my offering, and for us there will be no end.

I summoned it like an old memory.

And I heard the sturdy rhythm of her breathing; smelled the muskiness of bed. I felt her caress and tasted her soft kiss. I saw her beside me, our legs and arms intertwined. And we joined. Vibrant ecstasy. Quiet joy.

You will find that there is more. For now, it is enough that we are together.

I don't know how long it lasted, but suddenly she was gone. Like a man waking from a dream I slowly became aware of my surroundings. The bloody body in my hands. Avry walking up behind me. And then a fist exploded in my cortex.

47

Avry was asleep on a chair in the corner of his chamber. I remembered everything the instant I awoke. The shots, Jessica falling backward. I struggled to sit up, my head feeling like hot molasses.

Avry's head snapped up at the sound of my movement. "Where do you think you're going?"

"Jessica. Where is she?"

He looked away. A sick boiling hit my stomach. I grabbed the old man by the shoulders. His eyes were bloodshot and swollen.

"Where is she!"

"Our medical facilities aren't as good as Earth's. We tried everything. She regained consciousness for a few seconds at the end, but resuscitation failed. I'm sorry."

The gun in my hand, my finger squeezing the trigger . . . I turned my head and vomited. Avry's hands held me steady until it was over. I wanted to scream.

"Our child?" It was Jessica's question as much as mine.

"We're doing everything we can. A volunteer has already stepped forward to attempt a fetal transplant. We're breaking down her immune system to avoid rejection. Despite the relatively advanced stage of the pregnancy, our technology should be up to it. It'll be another day before we know if we've been successful."

"Who."

"Only the surrogate, Dr. Toulane, and I know. There are people—followers of Wheeler—who would like to see the child killed. They wouldn't hesitate to scan you if they thought you knew."

He ran a damp sponge over my chin. "Drink this." He gave me a glass of cool water. "Can you walk?"

The smell of vomit was thick in the air. "Yeah."

He helped me up and steered me to the door. A nurse with a mop and pail entered as we left, summoned by Avry's silent call. The old man started across the hall to my chamber.

"No. Take me to the park."

"That might not be safe right now. Several members of the colony blame you for Jessica's death."

"Do it."

Arden was empty. Avry helped me to sit down on one of the benches.

"Someone knocked me out after I spoke to Jessica."

"Ben Wheeler. I was able to stop him from killing you."

"How long was I out?"

"About forty minutes."

"How long for Jessica?"

"She passed away about a minute after Wheeler knocked you out. During her last moment of consciousness, she left a message for you: 'Tell Jefferson that the Siren was enchanted by her prey.'"

I squeezed my eyes shut and fought back consuming anguish. "What happened?"

"As near as we can piece together, you'd been programmed by a member of the U.N. security force. It happened on the *Far Hand*. What do you recall about your stay in the medical section?"

"I was in for a broken knee given to me by Hans Reinhart. He showed up the first night and injected something into my arm."

"How many other times did he come in?"

"None. The doctor on board took steps to keep him out."

"Think, Jefferson, are you sure that's the way it happened?"

"Of course. I would have . . ." A sudden image came to mind. Reinhart's oily machine voice, telling me things. Over and over again. "Wait a minute. He did come back. Every night he was there. Why didn't I remember it until now?"

"The old-fashioned term would be brainwashing."

I looked at him suspiciously. "How do you know all of this?"

"After she was shot, Jessica scanned you and uncovered the truth. From her exclamation about Reinhart, it was clear she thought you innocent."

"I heard her."

"We all heard her. You might as well know it's the only reason you're still alive. Without her testimony, so to speak, you'd have been found guilty of first-degree murder regardless of what we scanned in your skull."

"What programming had I been given?"

"The trigger was Jane Hamilton's voice. Your response was to kill her, then Jessica, then yourself."

"Why did you stop me?"

"I didn't, Jessica did."

The memory of our last seconds of shared rapture came back as a dazzling spark, quickly smothered by guilt. I struggled to put it aside. "Gahining must have been a United Nations agent."

"The doctor on board the *Far Hand*? The only other explanation is Mr. Reinhart's threats were effective. Not that it matters now. It's unfortunate Jessica let her emotions get in the way."

"What do you mean?"

"It's clear that after a certain point, she no longer felt it right to scan you. She certainly would have seen Mr. Reinhart's meddling if she had been looking. What I can't understand is why she didn't catch Reinhart."

I knew why, but given the mood on Iapetus, I wasn't about to tell the colonists that non-telepaths had a weapon effective against telepathic control. "How is it I remember all of Reinhart's visits now?"

I half expected him to lie but he didn't even hesitate.

"After you passed out, I was pressured to find the truth of the matter. Knowing what to look for, thanks to Jessica, it wasn't hard to do. Reinhart trampled across your consciousness like a tank division crossing a snowfield. I figured as long as I was in there, I might as well free your memory from the fused spiral he'd put it in."

"How much snooping around did you do?"

Avry shook his head. "As little as possible. I did catch Jessica's parting gift, though. It's a wonderful invention. On the surface it appears little more than a feedback loop of elation and contentment accessed whenever you think of her. But it is so much more. If you live to be a hundred, it will never lose its power. Why do you refuse to accept it?"

"Because I killed her."

He looked ready to argue but I didn't want to talk about it. "Avry, it's not over yet. People are going to keep dying unless we move. If you want to try and convince me it wasn't my fault, I promise I'll give you a chance later. Right now, I need answers."

He ran a hand through his steel wool beard, shooting me a calculating look. "I'll hold you to that." I had the uncomfortable feeling I'd said something I'd regret later. "As for your question, I did nothing beyond unraveling the conditioning you were under. Mr. Reinhart used barbiturates to help the hypnotic state, fed you a set of behavior traits, and then locked it behind a three-word access code. I removed the compulsion behind the words and eliminated the memory insulators."

"There had to be more to it. You can't hypnotize people into carrying out acts they'd never consider in the first place. I threatened Jessica a few times, but after what happened between us on the *Far Hand,* I'd never have killed her."

"If you want to be more truthful with yourself, you should admit you wouldn't have killed her after her first five-minute visit. Your cynicism has a remarkable blind spot for women in over their heads. I'd have thought someone in your line of work would be less sympathetic."

I shrugged. There was no point in denying anything he'd scanned.

"At any rate, after what happened to Thomas, you would kill

a telepath. Reinhart shifted your perspective until that's all you saw Jessica as; another freak like the one who gunned down your brother. After the act was done, a second trigger had been placed to reinforce your strong feelings toward her. Now you saw her only as your lover. Reinhart pushed your emotions to the point where you felt a greater dependency on her than you naturally would have. After killing her, getting you to suicide was possible. It was really a very capable job of conditioning. Are you going to tell me why he went to all that trouble?''

If he'd gone any deeper than Reinhart's mental playground, he already knew the answer. Was he just asking the question to gain my confidence? If he knew what was going on, he'd blow everything. He didn't have the instinct to survive.

''Not yet. What's important is that Reinhart will be back for me.''

''You're not even sure he's here.''

''He is. He knew Jessica was taking me to the new arrivals' ward, otherwise his programming wouldn't have worked. I might have heard Jane's voice while Jessica was on the other side of the station. I never would have reached her before being stopped.''

''But how could this be?''

I didn't like having to trade away secrets to Avry, but I needed his cooperation. ''My room must be bugged.''

''Impossible—''

''It's the only explanation. He heard Jessica and me talking, then gave me instructions, probably through a two-way transmitter built into the bug.''

''Even if you're right, what makes you think he'll come after you?''

''Because I know his game. I know why Jessica was killed.''

''What—''

I found myself echoing Jessica's favorite evasion. ''Trust me. Reinhart doesn't realize you're planning to keep me here; we had that conversation in your room—a chamber he had no reason to wire for sound. If word of what has happened here ever reached the fax machines, the United Nations would blow apart. He has to come after me.''

''What will you do?''

''Nothing. He still thinks he can turn me on and off with his access words. I'll sleep in my room tonight. Tell everyone I haven't recovered from Wheeler's blast. Have the hallways and elevators between Merlin's Ladder and my quarters cleared. I don't want anyone else hurt.''

"Why not just let us wait for him? We could get far more out of him than you."

"No, it won't work. He can stop you."

He looked dubious. "I'm willing to go along with this for one night. After that, we go after him in force. Just because he fooled Jessica doesn't mean he can prevail against all of us. We can't sit around and let him continue killing our children."

"Fair enough. One more thing. No one, and I mean not you or anyone else, can come to my room tonight. I plan to shoot first and ask questions later."

48

Even had I not been waiting for Reinhart, sleep would have been impossible. The last moment of passion shared between Jessica and me was awake in my thoughts. I rolled it over in my mind, marveling at its peaceful jubilation; the euphoria it brought on each time I touched it. Other moments were fading, but this—what had Jessica called it? A gift?—remained somehow bright and clear. Magnifying my inability to save her.

Around midnight, Reinhart's voice, made soprano by the size of the hidden speaker, squeaked from behind my bed's headboard. "Biosphere. Athena. Galileo."

A nauseating pull in my head answered the three access words, but there was no compulsion behind them. Score one for Avry.

"You will listen to me, Kayoto. You shot Jessica, killed her in cold blood. You loved her, Jefferson. She was everything to you. What's the point of going on now? She's dead despite everything you did. Worse, she's dead because of you. You butchered her. Do you understand? Answer me."

I remained quiet.

"Kayoto, answer me."

Although useless against Reinhart, I wished for Jessica's telepathic ability: *The transmitter's busted. You're going to have to come down here and do the job yourself.*

A soft burst of static signaled that Reinhart's device had been shut off. The minutes ticked away in painful silence. Reinhart's conditioning might have lost its power, but his accusations were dead on target.

The sound of my door sliding open cut through my morbid thoughts. I remained still until he shut the door behind him. Even with the silencer, there was a chance the shots would be heard and people would come running. I needed some time alone with Reinhart.

He was two meters away when I pulled the machine pistol from under the covers and sighted through the infrared scope. The hollow-point Wildcat caught him square in the left knee. There was the wet, muffled sound of his patella shattering.

I flipped on the light above my bed. Reinhart was on the floor, hands clasped above his destroyed knee. He wasn't making a sound. I centered the gun on his head.

"Keep your hands away from your body. You make a move for the pocket Uzi and I'll end it right now."

His breathing was shallow and ragged. "Biosphere. Athena. Galileo."

"Try again, Reinhart. Maybe you got the order wrong."

For the first time he looked me in the face. "What do you want?"

"Information."

"Why?"

"Because I have a deal to offer. The locals aren't too hot on letting me live after the brainwashing stunt you pulled. You must have a ship waiting somewhere on standby, and I know you have some sort of telepathy jammer lodged in your throat. You can get me out of here. Under other circumstances, I'm sure you'd have killed me by now and gone on your merry way. Too bad about your knee. Without my help you're not going anywhere."

"I don't believe you. The halls were empty when I came down. You've got some deal going with the freaks."

"Of course. I told them I'd sucker you in and kill you. I also told them about your electromagnetic scrambler. They were only too anxious to clear the decks. They must have thought with any luck we'd kill each other and their problems would be over.''

"I'm not the one they want and you know it."

"Oh yes, the infanticide epidemic. They wanted to believe it was the United Nations, and I helped the delusion along. It doesn't matter that they're wrong. Right now they'll butcher you with their bare hands. If you kill me now you'll still be here in the morning. You can't possibly reload your Uzi fast enough to stay alive." I gave him a minute to consider the odds before continuing. "On the other hand, if we help each other, we can both get out of here. The decision is yours." I put my Stoeger-Luger down beside me.

"You've made your point. Help me to my ship and I'll take you off Iapetus."

"So you can shoot me at the first opportunity? Not a chance." I held up a microdisk recorder. "First you're going to tell me all about Operation Proselyte, then I'm going to put this recording someplace where you can't find it. Then I'm going to leave instructions for it to be released if I should suffer some unfortunately fatal accident."

I turned the recorder on. "You can begin anytime you want. I have all night."

He eyed the recorder, calculating his chances of destroying it before I could blackmail him. He must have liked the odds.

"How much do you know already?"

"I know certain branches of the United Nations are working to breed telepaths. Jessica was designed from the ground up; her telepathy could hardly have been a mistake. Jon Pierre Vandimeer must have been part of it."

"No, he didn't know anything. Neither did his wife. We implanted the embryo in Sylvia during a midnight raid on their Mars orbital station. We chose Jon Pierre because we knew of his sickness. Part of Jessica's training entailed removal of her ability to resist commands given by authority figures. Jon was admirably fitted to the task."

"But Jessica got away."

"Yes. Jon got careless and Jessica reached the police. From that point on, she was in the hands of United Nations factions who were not aware of our project. For security reasons we had to remain silent while she was deported to Iapetus."

"Why did United Nations ships try to follow us from Calypso?"

"Not all members of U.N. Security agree with our techniques. A few mice want the program canceled. The colorful manner of your departure from Tethys made it rather impossible to keep them out of the picture."

So, I had been right about a split in the United Nations. "I saw the inventory number you tattooed on Vandimeer: 175-03-14-73-D. I assume it indicates she was the hundred seventy-fifth specimen born in 2173, with the other numbers indicating the month and day of birth."

"Correct."

"What happened to the hundred seventy-four before her, and the hundreds who followed?"

"She was the last one. My superiors felt the risks were becoming too great. Several reporters were close to uncovering the operation and had to be eliminated. We could not trust the general public to deal rationally with such sensitive information."

"And Jessica's predecessors?"

"All proved to be unstable, and were terminated."

"So Jessica was the last link to a potentially embarrassing research project. Why didn't you kill her the second she stepped off Iapetus? You must have spotted her when she started working under false U.N. records."

Reinhart's breathing was becoming labored but he gave no other indication of pain. "There was always a chance she could yet be employed for the original purposes of the operation. We kept Al-Kirzen's people off of her until we determined she was no longer pliable enough to be of use."

And then they killed her. A pretty lab animal running an impossible maze. "What was so special about Jessica's genetic makeup?"

"She was tailored from gene samples taken from freaks during their stopovers on Tethys. We engineered Jessica to carry a dominant telepathic gene."

And incidentally constructed the perfect mate for Omar Al-Kirzen. A woman who could guarantee Al-Kirzen's grandchild would be a "superior" human. Elle must have carried the same dominant gene naturally. "Why?"

"Don't be stupid. What happens when telepaths outnumber humans? It's our duty to protect our citizens. Docile telepaths bred to be friendly to our cause are the best answer."

Hence Jessica's flawless beauty. If she'd have turned out as

planned the press would have ogled her; carved a marble
pedestal for her pretty little feet. Another P.R. scoop for the
boys in the United Nations, with only one pathetically broken
woman to show on the debit side. Every politician would jump
on the bandwagon. Before you knew it, we'd have whole
divisions of government-sanctioned telepaths.

Toy soldiers. But for whom to command? I realized the
implications were far broader than I earlier imagined. "It won't
wash, Reinhart. You don't need an army of telepathic slaves to
stop the freaks' killing binges. A troop of U.N. soldiers
equipped with your jamming devices could accomplish the
same task with half the risk."

"No. Our jammers, as you call them, are too limited in
range. We needed something more."

The history books are full of military commanders who
made the same rationalization. *What we have isn't good
enough, we have to have something bigger or the enemy will
overwhelm us!* That's how we got the A-bomb. And the
hydrogen bomb. And the dumps full of biological weapons.
Just think how much more secure they've made the world.

"How long, Reinhart? How long before these telepaths
would have been used against ordinary people? How long
before some U.N. general decided to use your freaks to put
down some uprising, or to keep some government in line with
United Nations' wishes?"

"Never. The telepaths were going to be used to protect the
people."

"So who protects the people from you?"

"What?"

I had the whole story now; everything behind the aptly
named Operation Proselyte. There was no reason to go any
further.

"You left a Biblical passage for me on Elf Hive. I believe
your intention was to warn me away. I wish to return the favor
with a verse from the same book. 'You travel over land and sea
to make a single convert, but once he is converted you make a
devil of him.'"

I tossed him the microdisk recorder. He had just enough time
to register surprise before I picked up the machine pistol and
fired. I aimed for his left temple, the same place I'd shot Jane
Hamilton. His left hand was reaching for the Uzi when he died.

The only knife I'd been able to locate was an aluminum

dinner blade with a serrated edge for cutting the chalky synthetic steak the colonists served on special occasions. My hands were covered with blood and tissue before I got Reinhart's electromagnetic jammer out of his throat. It might have been easier to tear the room apart and find the box he'd used to screen the bug in my room, but it had probably been built it into the walls during construction and I didn't have the time to find it. At least that's the way I justified desecrating Reinhart's body.

I carefully cleaned the small black box and inspected it for breaks. Finding nothing, I had to assume it was working. I'd know tomorrow.

I took a shower and changed clothes before crossing the hall and ringing Avry's door. The speed with which he answered showed his night had been as sleepless as mine. I led him across the hall to Reinhart's body.

"Then it's over."

"Yes," I lied.

"We're in your debt. I am sorry there's nothing we can do to repay you."

"Not as sorry as I am." Jessica would have made spending my life here bearable. Now I was consigned to hell with people I barely understood. And that was if things went well. Unless certain steps were taken soon, the babies would go right on dying. If that were to happen, no doubt the colony would be more than happy if I joined them. "Get me Dr. Toulane."

"Can't it wait? It's three-thirty in the morning."

"No. Wake him up and have him meet me in my chamber. Be quick about it. We have things to discuss not for public consumption."

"What are you talking about?"

"I'm sorry, Avry. it's not that I don't trust you, but there's one more thing I have to do and Dr. Toulane is the only one who can help me. If he doesn't agree with my reasoning, we'll come and tell you everything."

"You're not making it easy for me to keep my promise not to scan you."

"I know. But I got Reinhart, didn't I? Play along for another twelve hours, at least until the next child is born."

"I don't like it. Ben's already furious with me for taking orders from you."

"Then don't tell him about it. And, Avry? Get someone in here to clean up this mess, will you?"

It took me only a few minutes to explain my plan to Toulane. He took Reinhart's device and was gone before anyone saw him.

49

They fed Jessica's body into the maw of the colony's fusion reactor at seven A.M. July 18, 2196. Back home, the few trees and bushes struggling in the city were dressed in green leaves already wilting in the concrete desert. Most of the pedestrians would be wearing breathing masks and praying for wind. On Iapetus, there was no wind. The temperature outside the entombed domes was seventy-one degrees absolute. The long-term forecast was for more of the same.

Standing by the colony's fusion powerhouse on the lower level, it was twenty-three degrees centigrade. The only breeze was an occasional metallic whisper from the colony's circulating fans. Beside me, Avry was decked out in traditional black, the clothes draping over his shrunken frame. I wore my hammered-silver hair ring, a black jacket, and my best jeans. I held Jessica's diamond rose. On the other side of the conveyer Lisa and Benjamin Wheeler, both in formal black, stood in silence. Wheeler's jaw clinched tight as Jessica's body, inside a translucent block of urethane, was transported to the outer door of the reactor.

I had insisted Jessica's remains be destroyed as soon as possible. Even dead, her genes could be stolen if Al-Kirzen got hold of her fast enough. At least cremation would leave her some dignity.

My emotions were chaos and confusion. Every time I looked at her resting form, Jessica's euphoria loop kicked in. But it was not enough to clean her blood from my hands. Each ray of elation was refracted into dirty shades of guilt.

Vocal speech was used for all formal occasions on Iapetus. Being the senior-most present, Avry delivered the eulogy. I heard very little of it, the words flowing through me leaving no trace. As Jessica's body moved past me, I placed the crystal flower on her coffin. When the titanium-nickel baffle door closed behind her, I whispered my own good-bye. "I'm sorry."

The service over, Wheeler looked me in the eye. "You think you got your man last night, Mr. Detective. Maybe so, maybe not. We'll know when the child is born today. All I know is that you murdered Jessica. If the child dies, then I promise you, I'll destroy you no matter what the consequences."

I ran my hands over my eyes. "I believe you, but the killing is over."

50

The delivery room was hospital white and smelled of antiseptic reagents. A cylindrical delivery pool, three meters in diameter and 125 centimeters deep, took up half the floor space. Dr. Toulane stood in the blood-warm water with a nervous-looking middle-aged woman and a man I took to be her husband.

She asked Toulane again and again if her baby was going to live. He whispered reassuring phrases and positioned her in the stainless steel stirrups.

The ruling triumvirate watched through a plexiglass window. I stood a few meters to the side, playing out my fears in cold sweat. What if Reinhart's black box wasn't working? What if its range was too narrow? What if the child died from natural causes?

Movement in the pool. Waves, large in the weak gravity, lapped at the sides. A wash of red fluid, and Dr. Toulane pulled the infant above the water. Forced from her warm, safe home, the child cried loudly. Her mother's and father's eyes showed relief and amazement.

I looked quickly at Wheeler. His disbelief was obvious.

"It's over, Wheeler."

"What are you talking about, Mr. Detective?"

"I've taken action to protect the child. Tell your boss the colonists are onto him. But be careful, Al-Kirzen isn't kind to people who fail him."

Wheeler's look of outrage undid him. Avry acted faster than I ever would have given him credit for. Just as on the *Far Hand,* when Jessica had been able to control Jane Hamilton by acting first, Avry now had mastery over Wheeler. Benjamin struggled to move, his muscles betrayed by a brain no longer under his command.

"Let me go, Avry. Can't you see he's babbling? I admit he was right about the United Nations killing our children. I'm sorry I tried to discredit him. You can't hold me like this."

Something passed between Avry and Lisa, and Wheeler's next words were frantic, climbing an octave as some internal vise screwed tighter.

"Avry! Lisa! Stop! You have no right to scan me."

There was a curious heaviness in the air. I felt the gathering of the station's collective consciousness. Ben's head was back at an impossible angle, his hands over his temples. A trickle of blood streamed from a shattered eardrum. He fell to his knees, then to the floor.

Muscles straining for freedom finally relaxed in death. Without ceremony, four young men walked in the observation room and carried the body away. Wheeler's head rolled toward me, his face a rictus of pain and horror, gummy fluid dripping from his tear ducts.

"He always wanted to be with Jessica. Now he'll get his wish." The old man looked accusingly at me. "Come with me."

We double-timed it to his chamber. He slammed the door behind us and turned on me. "You knew all the time."

"No, but I suspected it."

"How did you protect the child?"

I told him everything I knew about the electromagnetic jamming boxes. "My guess is they have several planted around the colony. You ought to be able to wire together some kind of detector to snoop them out. I understand your ability should be able to take care of any unprotected surveillance devices?"

"Yes."

"Good. In the meantime, I take it you scanned Wheeler's side of the story before you pulled the plug?"

"There was a woman at the top of Merlin's Ladder the first time he went up. She talked about genetic experimentation; about the powers of our children being greater than our own. Benjamin listened, and began to fear for his own safety. He murdered our children out of fear."

"Sounds vaguely familiar."

"Spare me your attempts at humor. Why did you lie to me?"

I ordered his synthesizer to build two cinnamon bananas on the rocks. Handing one to Avry, I motioned for him to sit down. "I wasn't sure Wheeler was behind it. If I'd told you he was guilty, you would have marched into his room and scanned him. But what if he'd been innocent? After being so humiliated, how long do you think he would have let me live?"

The old man pulled at his drink. "Humph. Your paranoia makes you a difficult man, Mr. Kayoto."

"Keeps me alive. What did you learn from Wheeler?"

"Abdul Al-Kirzen was behind it. At least that's who the woman at the top of Merlin's Ladder said she worked for. She told Mr. Wheeler she would keep the most dangerous telepaths away from Iapetus."

"I figured it had been be something like that."

"But you don't believe it any more than I do. What's the real reason he was after us?"

"Al-Kirzen wanted Iapetus destroyed. He wanted sole control of the telepathic gene pool. He wanted his son to give birth to the ultimate human."

"Someone with the telepathic gene."

"Correct. Al-Kirzen shot down your supply ships until you were forced to try and contact outsiders for help. His agent waited at the top of the stair, zapping people until you decided to send up a psychopath for him to play with."

"But how did he know he could make use of Ben?"

"Money, Al-Kirzen's type of money, can buy a lot of information. He probably has a complete dossier on each of you. He handed the information over to his psych boys and waited for you to send up the right man. It's a safe bet that by the time Ben came down from the top of Merlin's Ladder, he was taking orders from Al-Kirzen. That's when your children started dying. After that, you played right into Al-Kirzen's hands."

Avry nodded. "We decided to send two agents to Earth, in search of help."

"But first, Benjamin suggested giving prospective agents a test to assess their fitness for the journey. It was a sham, he selected two women chosen by Al-Kirzen's genetic research team. Women who would guarantee telepathic offspring."

"But why didn't he grab the two women as soon as they were away from Iapetus?"

I hedged on the truth. "Soon after Wheeler solved Merlin's security system, the United Nations was alerted to your activities. They wanted to put a lid on the whole thing. Just think of the bad press that would have resulted if the public ever caught wind of a couple of freaks who'd escaped from Iapetus. The U.N. solution was to insulate Jessica and Elle until they could be dealt with quietly. As powerful as Al-Kirzen is, he couldn't go rampaging through the curtain the U.N. had put up around your two agents."

"So between the United Nations' desire to hush things up and Al-Kirzen's wish to keep the two alive, they were able to operate freely for a period of time."

I sighed. It was more complex than that, but there was no reason to worry the old man. "Yes."

Avry was silent, staring into the bottom of his drink. Considering decisions he'd made. After several minutes, he looked up again. "After Jessica left Iapetus, there's no way we could have saved her, was there? Even if you would've stopped Reinhart, they'd have kept sending people until she was dead."

I downed the rest of my drink. "Yes, they would have."

51

The corridors were dimmed in artificial night when I knocked on Avry's chamber door. Despite the lateness of the hour he was fully dressed, hunched over a thick tome. Two days since Wheeler was killed. Saving the colony had done nothing to alleviate the pain of Jessica's death.

"You haven't told me everything, Avry."

The old man looked up from the book. "What do you mean?"

I sat opposite him. "The United Nations, or at least one fraction of it, has a device that thwarts telepathic ability. Al-Kirzen has almost limitless resources. Yet neither was able to catch Jessica during her six-month stay on Earth."

"What are you getting at?"

"She had some help."

"Conjecture, Mr. Kayoto. You underestimate Jessica's talents. Don't forget she had Jon Pierre's considerable wealth backing her."

"It won't do, Avry. Every year, telepaths kill hundreds, yet not a single one has ever been tried."

"Of course not, we would surely affect the outcome of our own trials."

"Don't play the fool. The hearings could be held with the telepaths in absentia. After the Skirmish War Trials, there is a precedent. I doubt any of you would have escaped the death sentence."

Avry took off his thick glasses and rubbed the bridge of his nose. "Which leads you to conclude?"

"Someone's shielding the telepaths; the same someone who tried to protect Jessica and Elle. Since I can't believe a non-telepath would go to all the trouble, he must be one of you. Considering the influence this person has, he'd have to be well placed in the U.N."

"Who do you suspect?"

I named a member of the U.N. Secretary's Cabinet of Interior Welfare. Avry was silent for a moment. "You're right. He is one of us. Somehow he was able to deal with the homicidal urges the rest of us succumbed to. He uses his abilities to persuade key people to ensure our survival."

"And the charity organization he sponsors? The one for the 'Systems' Neediest People'?"

"A front, of course. But not a lie. The money, along with Jon Pierre Vandimeer's wealth, keeps us alive."

"I don't see how he will be able to shelter you now. After what's happened, the United Nations will certainly take steps to restructure the security system on Merlin's Ladder. Your escape hatch is about to be closed."

Avry laughed. "They will try, and we will allow them to

think they've succeeded. However, we already have several agents on Tethys, one of whom should be able to scan the information necessary to shut the system down again.''

''Then you're set.'' My voice was bitter.

''Thanks in no small part to you, yes. In return, it may surprise you to find that I have spent considerable time considering your predicament.''

''To what end?''

''I might be in the position to repay you for your services. Can you pilot intermediate lox/hydrogen ships?''

''I'm certified from my days in the Terra-Luna Corps, but it's been a long time. What do you have in mind?''

''You are guilty, at least in body if not mind, of shooting three people. Two of them were telepaths, an act not considered a crime back home. As for the other, no one outside Iapetus knows how Reinhart died.''

''What are you getting at?''

''Jessica used a United Nations cruiser to get you here. We happen to have the surplus body of a high-ranking United Nations official. I'm suggesting you use the cruiser and the body as your tickets back to Tethys.''

And then home. ''I notice you're making this offer solo. What does the rest of the colony think?''

''They don't know and they wouldn't agree with me if I told them. But the fact is, we'll be better off if we can rid ourselves of the United Nations corpse. The less hoopla about all this, the better.''

''Why the change of heart? What makes you think you can trust me to keep my mouth shut?''

''Jessica trusted you. That is enough for me.''

I considered it. ''Sounds good except for one thing. What happens when the United Nations investigates my story under a direct-feed polygraph and finds I'm lying?''

''I can help you there.''

I didn't like the sound of his voice. ''How?''

''I can make you believe things happened differently. The only obstacle is to come up with a story that makes Reinhart a hero and Jessica a monster—''

''And then you get inside my head and turn the switches that make it real.''

''If you want to put it that way, yes. All we need is some tale to account for Jessica's missing body after she's shot Reinhart.

Of course we'll need to keep his jamming box here for further study, but we should be able to come up with a reason for its absence as well.''

I thought of her, of the gift she had left me. ''I won't do it.''

''You can't be serious. This is a chance for you to go home.''

''I do not wish my memories of her altered.''

He assumed a look of concentration. ''It can still be done.''

''How?''

''If they decide to use direct-access equipment, they'll have to do certain things, right? Shave parts of your skull, use certain drugs; that sort of thing.''

''So?''

''We can use their preparations as a flag. Whenever those actions occur, the false memories will kick in. They'll last two or three days, and then you'll remember the truth again.''

I paced around the small chamber. ''I don't want any other parts of my memory affected.''

''Of course not.''

''Do it.''

52

Lisa was waiting for us on top of Merlin's Ladder. She had gone up earlier, escorting Reinhart's corpse. Her rail-thin stomach had a noticeable bulge. Avry had told me to expect it.

''Have you thought of a name yet?''

''Persephone.''

The beautiful maiden doomed to live her life in hell. Did Lisa know the story? Looking at her, I was sure she did. ''It's a fine name. Take care of her.''

''I will.''

I shook hands with Avry.

''Good luck, Mr. Kayoto, and thank you.'' I nodded and stepped aboard the *Raptor*.

The inside of the ship was barely recognizable. Scars of small-gun fire pitted the walls. The air purifiers fought a losing battle with the stench rising from Reinhart's bloated body. I didn't bother going through a preflight check. A couple of buttons pushed, and I was rising from the ladder.

53

The back of my head itched where they'd removed the hair. I tried to ignore it, although there was little else to keep me occupied. The medical section of Christiaan Huygens Station was as drab as the rest of Tethys. A sandy-haired doctor came in and hummed and whistled over a display of my blood pressure. Why did he seem so familiar?

"How do you feel?"

"Washed out. Tired."

"You're one lucky son of a bitch, you know that? How many people you figure going to live through abduction by a telepath? Not that the Vandimeer girl was bad looking, for a freak."

He flipped through several pages on a computer screen. "The most amazing thing I've ever seen. Surviving was miracle enough, but to walk away without a scratch . . ."

The false memories Avry had implanted came back in a rush. Reinhart getting it in the throat while Jessica was laughing. Me in the escape boat, using a remote to open the cruiser's air locks. Jessica's body spiraling out to space.

"How much do you remember?"

"Everything." Now that they were finished with the tests, Avry's fictionalized account was deteriorating rapidly. I remembered almost all of the truth now. Reinhart entering the hospital ward shooting, getting Jane Hamilton first, then gunning down Jessica. I perforated him with my machine pistol, but too late to save her.

Then our final moment together, the bright feedback of

ecstasy she'd placed in my mind. I caressed the memory and found it as pure as the moment she'd put it there. In the somber surroundings of the hospital, I found myself smiling.

"How long before I can leave?"

"Well, physically there's nothing wrong with you. What's going on inside your head is another matter. You have to free yourself from Vandimeer's influence. God only knows what she did to you."

"Look, right now all I want to do is get back home. Get back to work."

He sighed. "That'd probably be best after all." He disconnected me from the machines. "Go ahead and get dressed, you have a visitor. As soon as you're ready I'll send her in."

Amber Whitehorse had a fresh scar on her face, the duplicate of the one I'd noticed when I first encountered her outside my office. Two scars. Twice she had failed Al-Kirzen. She didn't speak until the doctor had excused himself.

"You have a cabin on the *Starry Messenger*. She leaves the Saturn System in four days. Her shuttle, the *Runner*, lifts from Exit Hill in thirty-four hours. I've already made arrangements."

"Who do I have to thank? Abdul Al-Kirzen?"

"Does it really matter?"

"Yes."

"Mr. Al-Kirzen feels this . . . project is no longer feasible. It is his desire to see that its unfortunate failure remains in the family. To that extent, he thought it prudent to return you home rather than take other avenues of action."

"You mean have me killed."

"That was one of the possibilities, yes. However, at this time, that option was considered too likely to lead to unnecessary publicity."

"Such a wonderful way to put it. Will you try for Iapetus's gene pool again?"

"The attempt is now unfeasible, as they are alert to our methods. In addition, Benjamin Wheeler was the perfect subject for our operations. His natural psychosis coupled with his fear of power in others made him highly susceptible to our techniques. His demise broke a crucial link in our program."

"And the unofficial landings on Merlin's Ladder? They'll be allowed to continue?"

"Yes."

I looked at Amber's cold features. "You get what you came for?"

"No. Miss Vandimeer's remains were destroyed before Ben—"

"Is that all you have to say?" I was too tired to be angry. "Doesn't it mean anything to you that people died down there? That children died down there? Whatever the great Al-Kirzen thinks, they were more than a collection of genetic material for your breeding program."

"I was just doing my job."

"Yeah? It's a good excuse, isn't it? Make sleeping any easier?"

"I can't change what happened." She handed me a plastic I.D. card for the *Starry Messenger*. "Your boarding pass. The original amount Jessica promised for the job has been deposited into your account. This is to ensure your cooperation with Al-Kirzen's wish to keep this matter private." She walked to the door, turned as if to say something, then walked out.

George Mahitso accompanied me to Exit Hill. We said very little as the tram glided north. At the terminal, he handed me my duffel bag.

"They told me she was a freak. Is that true?"

"Yes."

EPILOGUE

EARTH

The *Starry Messenger* was a clone of the *Far Hand*. The same gothic interior, the same empty people. Whether by a trick of fate or some last reminder from Avry about my promise of silence, my cabin was 7-A3, the same number Jessica and I had on our voyage out. I flipped the Do Not Disturb logo on the computer and told the synthesizer to work up a bottle of Jack Daniel's.

A glass in one hand, I pulled Jessica's Urielite necklace from my duffel and sat in front of the holo stand. Using the keyboard, I kept the viewplate centered on the white-black orb of Iapetus. Even with the strongest magnification, no detail was visible. A mirage, dwindling further behind each second.

Running my hands through her diamonds, I remembered her smile. Her silent thrill of elation answered, whispering through my thoughts.

We were going home.

ABOUT THE AUTHOR

William Kirby was born exactly eighty-five years after Albert Einstein. So far, the only resemblance is unruly hair and a dislike of mathematics. Mr. Kirby attended a midwestern university, more noted for its prowess on the gridiron than its excellence in the classroom, where he studied chemical engineering. Through processes not yet fully understood, he graduated with a B.S. in education and ended up with a teaching certificate in high school chemistry and physics.

In the past, Mr. Kirby has done everything from tutoring athletes at an exorbitant rate, to hanging sheet rock, to setting new standards for clumsiness on downhill skis. He now lives in Denver with Kathryn, a physicist whose only fault is an inordinate fondness for calculus. *Iapetus* is Mr. Kirby's first novel.